Bridges

DEBORAH RANEY

Enjoy!
Deb Raney

RANEY DAY
PRESS

Published by Raney Day Press.
Cover and interior design by Ken Raney.

Printed in the United States of America.

Created with Vellum

For my brother, Brad, and his precious bride, Sharon,
who know all about love the second time around.

"Men build too many walls and not enough bridges."
— Joseph Fort Newton

CHAPTER ONE

J.W. McRae braked at the stop sign where St. Charles dead-ended at Clark Tower Road. He shifted his pickup into Park and rested his forearms atop the steering wheel, his chest constricting. If he didn't know better he'd think he was having a heart attack.

But he did know better. His body was simply reacting to the memories this town always dredged up. He would never admit––to anyone but himself––the fear he felt at returning to Winterset. It was a good thing he was alone in the truck because his white knuckles on the steering wheel would have given him away.

He rolled down the passenger-side window of the dusty Dodge Ram and looked out at the billowing clouds that floated in a clear blue sky above the county road. He could turn left onto Clark Tower Road and wind his way back to the Interstate...pretend he'd never been here. And never return.

If it wasn't for Rina, the daughter-in-law he'd met only once, he would be back in Kansas City, oblivious. *Oblivious.* He could hear Char's shrill voice even now. *You don't have a clue, do you, J.W.? You're oblivious!*

And he had to admit, the woman had been right. For too many of their nine years together, he'd lived in a self-centered fog.

But Rina had reached out and offered him a chance to redeem himself. She'd wanted him here for Father's Day, but he just hadn't been able to gather the courage for a day that was fraught with such guilt and regret for him. But Rina had opened the door, and he intended to walk through it, even if it killed him.

And it just might.

He sucked in a deep breath, turned the steering wheel to the right, and hit the gas.

Since the day Char sent him packing, he'd set foot in Winterset exactly twice—that disastrous summer twelve years ago when he'd come back for Wynn's high school graduation, and then two years later for Char's funeral. Cornfields rose up on either side of the road and stood at attention in the June sun, reminding him of his roots. He wasn't sure he wanted to be reminded.

His cell phone rang. Grateful for the interruption, he dug the phone out of his pocket and checked the ID. Work. Correction: *former* work. What did they want? Reluctant, he clicked Talk. "McRae."

"Mr. McRae, this is Britney...Linscome. At Hartner & Hartner?"

"Yes, I know." *Be kind, McRae. It's not her fault.*

"Oh. Well, anyway, Mr. Hartner--Matt--is working on the Citizens Bank project, and he wondered if you could answer a few questions to get him up to speed on the project? Would you have a few minutes for me to go over a list of questions he sent?"

J.W. stared straight ahead, his jaw gaping. Were they serious? Matt Hartner had some nerve—and apparently no guts if he couldn't even make the call himself. Thanks to that weasel, J.W.

had all the time in the world…the rest of his lousy retired life. But it would be a cold day in Tucson before he'd talk to Matt Hartner through his assistant. If the man needed help, he could ask for it himself.

J.W. bit his tongue and shot up a prayer that he wouldn't say something he'd regret. "I'm sorry, this isn't a good time."

He punched End and tossed the phone onto the passenger seat beside his camera bag, feeling his blood pressure ramp up. His boss's nephew had dismissed him—called it early retirement —and a week later, from what J.W. heard through the office grapevine, moved into his corner office at the Kansas City firm. They'd thrown him a bone with the offer of consulting for them, and he hoped he hadn't just put the kibosh on that. Though he doubted it. Matt Hartner didn't know the first thing about being an ad exec. The kid would be calling him twice a week trying to figure out how to read a spreadsheet.

"Early retirement, my eye," he muttered into the truck's cab. He'd made decent money as an account executive at the advertising agency, and he'd been frugal and invested well. But he was at least five years from the comfortable retirement he'd planned toward. And at his age, he'd be lucky to get an interview, let alone a new job. Of course, Hartner & Hartner had waited until the stock market was at an all-time low and 401Ks had shriveled to half of what they'd been the previous year before they started laying people off. Sure, he'd survive, especially if his house sold as quickly as his Realtor thought it would. But it would not be the early retirement he'd dreamed about. Not by a long shot. And he'd go stark raving mad sitting around watching TV. Or even playing golf every day. Not his thing. He liked working.

He took his foot off the brake, cranked the wheel to the right, and navigated the curvy roads into Winterset's city limits. Glancing at a street sign as he passed, he chuckled. Clark Tower Road had turned into John Wayne Drive. His mother would have approved of him coming back to the birthplace of The Duke.

Third Street appeared on his right and he veered onto the tree-canopied road. In the decade since he'd last been here, everything about the town seemed to have changed, but he was pretty sure they hadn't moved the cemetery. It should be just ahead on the right.

He turned onto East Summit Street and slowed the truck. There it was, the twin entrances still intact. The cemetery was bigger than he remembered. Seemed death had been busy in his absence. He wondered if he'd be able to find the gravesite.

Guilt gripped him. Was he only here so he could tell Wynn and Rina that he'd paid his respects? Did it matter? Knowing Wynn, he'd probably quiz him on what the gravestone looked like or what kind of flowers were planted there. Better be prepared to pass the test.

The gates were open and J.W. eased the truck through them. The graves were still littered with leftover flowers and flags from Memorial Day weekend, which was a big deal in Winterset, thanks to the combined birthday celebration of the town's most famous son, John Wayne. Turning down a narrow lane at a good clip, he perused the rows of granite stones in vain. Rina had given him vague directions, but he'd been picturing the much-smaller cemetery of his childhood, not this sprawling—

A figure crouched at the edge of the path. Too close—

He slammed on the brakes, his heart banging in his chest.

The woman—maybe in her late forties, if he was any judge of a woman's age—wore a bright red shirt, and tendrils of pale hair escaped beneath the wide brim of her straw hat. What on earth was she doing? She was lucky he hadn't mowed her down!

He tapped the horn and veered to the opposite side of the lane.

Heart still racing, J.W. pulled onto the grassy shoulder. He squinted into the rearview mirror, but all it reflected was the cloud of dust his hasty stop had kicked up.

He cut the engine, pushed open his door, and jumped down from the pickup's cab. A film of Iowa dust coated his throat, and he coughed as he strode around the back of the vehicle. He approached the woman who was hunched over a child's red wagon loaded with flowers.

"You okay?" he shouted, jogging toward her.

She didn't look up. He hadn't actually hit her. He was sure of that... Maybe she was sick. "Hey, are you all right?"

No response. His chest constricted further. He covered the distance between them in two strides and touched her shoulder.

She gave a little gasp and reeled back, eyes wide.

She wore earbuds attached to a cell phone with a bright pink case that stuck halfway out of her hip pocket. Her music was turned up so loud that even over the breeze rustling the poplars overhead he could hear the tinny strains of jazz coming from the earbuds.

The woman straightened and tugged at the thin white wire, popping out one earbud. "You scared me to death!" But she was smiling. A very becoming smile.

"I nearly ran over you. You should be careful."

She shrugged and threw him a grin that was closer to a smirk. "This isn't usually a high traffic zone."

He was not amused. "I'm serious. I could have killed you." He motioned at her left ear that still wore an earbud. "You ought to at least turn down your music so you can hear if a truck is about to flatten you."

She laughed at that. "Don't worry, I heard you." She brushed off her palms on faded blue jeans, and yanked out the other earbud.

He extended his right hand. "I'm J.W. McRae."

"Oh! You're Wynn's dad." The open friendliness turned wary. "I'm Tess Everett." She said it like he should know who she was.

"I forget how small Winterset is." He rubbed the back of his neck, still irked that she didn't seem one bit remorseful for nearly causing him to commit involuntary manslaughter. He squinted against a ray of sun that breached the poplars. "Yes, Wynn is my son."

She suddenly looked stricken, and put a palm up to shield her eyes. "Everything's okay with the baby, I hope?" She panned the cemetery as if she expected to see a funeral in progress. "I heard they had to take her back to the hospital, but I thought it was just for some routine––"

"Baby's fine as far as I know. Haven't seen her yet. They're supposed to be home with her tomorrow."

She gave a nervous laugh. "I don't know why, but for a minute...well, I was afraid something had happened...with the baby."

"No. Baby's fine," he said again.

She hesitated. "Can I help you find something then? Here in the cemetery, I mean..."

He couldn't exactly say he was just browsing. "I'm trying to find a––certain grave. It's been a while since I was here." She didn't need to know that he hadn't been here since the funeral. And he'd hung back in the shadows that day, not sure he was welcome, but wanting to be able to say he'd been there. For Wynn's sake.

She slipped her phone from her hip pocket and glanced at the screen. "City Hall closes at five on weekdays, or I'd call them for you, but I know the cemetery pretty well. I might be able to help." She waited, curiosity clear on her pretty face.

"I'm looking for a...family member's grave. McRae." The last thing he wanted was her sympathy. "It's a rather tall memorial. With an angel statue." What had his son been thinking? Char was about as far from an angel as––

He clipped the thought short. He'd vowed to give up vilifying Charlotte now that she couldn't defend herself.

Shading his eyes, he let his gaze sweep the sprawling cemetery. "The funeral--burial--would have been about ten years ago. The place has filled up quite a bit since then."

She gave him an odd look. "Yes, I know which one you mean."

"Really?"

Her eyes—the same blue as the sky—held a question, and something akin to sorrow crept in, then dissipated as she pointed down the main lane he'd driven in on. "See that copse of pines to the north?"

He nodded.

"Hang a left just past there and go about fifty yards. You'll see some newer graves in that section. Behind that, you'll see the tall one with the angel. I'd show you myself but I need to get these geraniums in before it gets dark." She tilted her head toward the little red wagon where her pots of flowers waited, looking as perky as their caretaker.

"Need some help with those? I can put the wagon in the back of my truck."

"Thanks, but"--she angled her slender neck in the opposite direction she'd just sent him--"I'm almost there."

He wondered whose grave her flowers were for, but decided it was none of his business.

Besides, he didn't want her asking *him* any more questions.

CHAPTER TWO

Tess stood and watched Wynn's father climb back into his pickup and head the direction she'd pointed him in, his Dodge kicking up dust on the unpaved cemetery lane. She'd seen Wynn in the man's gait. Lanky and self-confident. And handsome as all get-out. Not at all what she'd always imagined. Certainly not the picture Char had painted.

She brushed the thought away, picked up the handle of the wagon, and tugged it in the direction of Dan's grave. A bump in the road caused a pot to tilt precariously, and she stopped the wagon and righted it. She wasn't in the habit of noticing handsome men. Still, Wynn's father was nothing like she'd pictured. Char had painted J.W. McRae as an unfeeling ogre, and Wynn––when he talked about his father at all––seemed to have an even lower opinion of the man.

She'd often wondered how her friend had ever been wooed by the man she'd died hating so deeply. Now Tess thought she understood. Char had failed to mention that her ex was so ruggedly attractive and...well, almost charming in a devil-may-care way. She made a mental note to keep her distance. Those green eyes of his kind of did a number on her and––

She shook off the ridiculous thought and parked the wagon between Dan's humble gravestone and the monument adjacent to it.

She lugged the heavy flowerpots onto the marble slab that bore her husband's name and dates. Daniel James Everett. Forty-nine years old. *The age she was now.* Far too young for a heart attack. How gossamer thin the veil between this world and heaven. It still broke her heart--and, if she was honest, angered her a little--that Dan hadn't lived to see their girls graduate from high school. She'd been left alone to get the twins through the toughest years. And she'd done a bang-up job, if she did say so herself. But it hadn't been easy.

She arranged the geraniums on the ledge and pruned the spent blooms and brown leaves. They were pedestrian flowers in cheap terra cotta pots, but at least they wouldn't tempt thieves the way the miniature roses she'd placed on Dan's grave two weeks ago had. She had a hard time imagining a person so heartless he--or she?--would steal flowers from a grave on Memorial Day. But apparently there were people like that in the world.

It struck her that Char had portrayed J.W. McRae as just that heartless. And who knew, maybe McRae was here to decorate Char's grave with stolen flowers. *McRae.* Char had always referred to him by his surname--a name she'd apparently shed after their divorce, though Wynn had always gone by McRae.

Wynn hadn't mentioned anything about his father coming to visit. Of course, things had been crazy for the young couple, getting the nursery ready for a baby they hadn't expected until July, then driving back and forth from the hospital's NICU in Des Moines until last week when they'd brought the baby home. But now, little Amelia was back in the hospital with jaundice--though, from what she'd heard downtown, only for a day or two.

She wondered how Rina would feel about Wynn's father

being here. Especially if they didn't know he was coming. Maybe McRae planned to surprise them. Or maybe he knew Wynn wasn't likely to welcome him, so he just showed up so they couldn't send him packing. All her speculation made her realize she hadn't done a very good job of keeping in touch with Wynn McRae. She felt a twinge of guilt that she hadn't even been to see the baby yet. But Rina's mother had been in Winterset since the baby girl was born and Tess wanted to respect their privacy. She might feel like Wynn's second mother, but Rina wasn't her daughter-in-law.

Wynn. He was a sweet boy—a man now, with a wife and child. But he'd struggled deeply before Rina came into his life. Char, his mother, had died the summer after Wynn's first year of college. Colon cancer that took its sweet time. Tess met Char when she was assigned as her hospice volunteer. But Char beat the odds and had lived almost a year after that. And during that time, they'd become fast friends. For some reason, Tess had quickly cut through Char's bitterness—about her ex-husband, about the cancer—and they'd connected on a deep level.

When Char died, all the hospice training about staying professional and maintaining emotional distance had gone out the window. Tess had ached at the loss of her new friend. But she'd found great comfort in seeing the transformation from bitterness to acceptance. From a walking death to new life.

And for Tess and Dan, it had been a privilege to take Char's son under their wings. That Thanksgiving, the poor kid had come home to an empty house—one that would eventually have to be rented out to make payments on Char's hospital bills. Tess and Dan had taken Wynn in and given him a place to be for the holidays, and later, a place to come home to when the dorms were closed for spring break. Dan had often said Wynn was like the son he never had.

Jodi and Jaci, her precious twin daughters, had turned nine the first Thanksgiving Wynn was with them, and even though they were now grown and in their second year of college, they still adored Wynn McRae. Jaci had already dubbed herself Auntie to Wynn and Rina's baby. Speaking of which... Tess slipped her phone from her pocket. She'd felt it vibrate earlier and hadn't checked the message yet. She read Jaci's cryptic text and giggled. *Baby wants to see Auntie J bad! Pls send $$. Pay you back NEXT week! Promise!*

You will see her in 5 weeks, Tess typed. Jaci would ignore her and mope, no doubt hoping Tess would change her mind. But she wouldn't. Despite her promise, Jaci *wouldn't* have the money "NEXT week" or the week after that. The girl, darling though she was, still owed her two hundred dollars from Christmas. Somehow her firstborn––by three minutes––still didn't seem to get that she didn't have a bottomless bank account. Dan's insurance had left her reasonably comfortable, but she still had to be careful with her budget. Tess had finally put her foot down and declared "no more loans" and she was determined to stick to it this time.

The anemic *toot-toot* of a car horn jolted her from her thoughts.

Still on her knees in front of Dan's grave, she looked up to see J.W. McRae with an elbow hanging over the rolled down window of his pickup. His grin turned her insides a little soft–– and reminded her of her resolve to keep her distance.

"You want a ride yet?"

With the pruning shears still in one hand, she pointed aimlessly at the little red wagon. "Thanks, but I'm fine. Did you find the grave?" Odd that he would visit his ex-wife's grave.

"I did. Thanks." He hooked his thumb toward the back of his pickup. "There's room in the truck for the wagon."

"No thank you."

Still smiling, he gave a nod. "Suit yourself." With a little wave, he put the truck in gear and rolled toward the main gate.

She shook her head and gave the flowerpot in the middle of the gravestone a two-degree turn before struggling to her feet.

Well... She was making progress. For almost six months now, she'd forced herself to keep her visits to the cemetery to once a month. Her friend Merrie would have said it was still too often. But Merrie didn't need to know everything.

Dan had been gone for almost three years now. Some days it seemed like thirty. Others, the pain was still so raw, it seemed like only yesterday she'd lost the one who made her heart beat.

TESS PULLED the wagon home and parked it in the detached garage behind the house. She lowered the door quickly, before she could get depressed by all that needed doing in the two-car garage. Probably ought to call it a zero-car garage since that's how many cars she could fit inside it right now. Dan's tool bench overflowed with half-finished woodworking projects and the dust-blanketed boxes of his clothes that Merrie had helped her pack up a month after the funeral. The idea had been to haul Dan's things off to Goodwill, but she simply hadn't had the heart to do that yet.

She ought to at least move enough things into Pop's shed so she could get her SUV in the garage before the birds completely ruined it, or before the next hailstorm. But somehow it seemed fitting that Dan's things had found a home out here in his shop where he'd spent so much time. And besides, she didn't want to junk up the shed.

A few years ago they'd fixed up the shed attached to the garage as a guest house, and Dan's father had lived there for almost two years until his death––just a year before Dan died. The roof needed repairs and the bathroom shower leaked. But the building was insulated and had a cute little kitchenette and a side porch railing perfect for putting your feet up on, and she had once dreamed of turning the place into her own little hideaway complete with coffee pot and CD player so she could leave her phone behind. Now that the girls were grown and she had the whole house to herself, that seemed a little redundant.

She checked the time and looked at the sky, trying to gauge how much daylight she had left. Enough to get in a couple hours of work at the park, she decided. She checked the back of her Mariner to be sure her gardening tools were still there and climbed behind the wheel.

The Winterset City Park was mostly empty on this warm late spring afternoon and Tess got right to work, cleaning up stray debris and trash that had collected since her last visit. Tess had been pleasantly surprised by how much she enjoyed her volunteer work here planting and weeding flowerbeds, policing the grounds for litter and graffiti, and generally helping out where she was needed. The volunteer gig was an unofficial "job" that she did as much in secret as one could keep a secret in a small town.

She'd taken the tasks upon herself the last time the girls were home, after she and Jaci jogged the mile and a half up to Clark Tower, the park's castle-like monument, and Jaci had commented on their way back to the car that the park looked a little "sad" from the way she remembered it.

Tess hadn't noticed the park's decline, but her daughter's observation bothered her. She'd brought a garbage bag and her garden gloves with her the next time she came to hike up to the tower, and by the time she came back down, she'd filled it with beer cans, fast food wrappers, and weeds. She'd been coming here twice a week ever since to walk and "police," and earlier this spring, to help with the plantings.

A few of the city employees had told her, only half-joking, that she ought to write up a job description and apply for the job so she could get paid. "But then I'd have to clean the toilets," she told them. Besides, she wasn't doing it for the money. This was more a way to fill the hours. And get a little exercise.

She heard the sound of tires on the gravel and looked up to see J.W. McRae's midnight blue Dodge Ram pull into the park's entrance. He pulled into a parking space and climbed down from the truck's cab, slamming the door behind him. He strode across the parking lot toward the Cutler-Donahoe bridge. The famous covered bridge, a landmark of the city park, was dressed in a fresh coat of red paint.

J.W. walked with purpose, and she felt strangely disappointed that he hadn't come to see her. Ridiculous, since he couldn't have even known she would be here. Feeling awkward working with him so close by, she watched him walk onto the wide covered bridge, looking up at the rafters. The thud of his boots on the bridge floor faded, then crescendoed, and he reappeared a minute later and left the gravel path to sidestep down the gentle slope. He inspected the bridge struts, then squatted down, studying the underside of the structure like an engineer might.

If he'd seen her when he drove in, he gave no indication. What if he noticed her and thought she was stalking him? She was here first, but he didn't know that. *Don't be ridiculous, Everett.*

She *was* being ridiculous, but nevertheless, she started packing up her gardening gear and loaded it into the back of her vehicle. She was almost finished anyway, and there was plenty she could be doing at home.

"Hey there...again."

Too late. *Caught.* She closed the hatch and brushed off her hands. "Touring the old hometown, huh?"

"Actually, I was looking for a place to stay."

"Under the bridge?" She pointed to the slope he'd just climbed.

"Oh…" He grinned. "No, that was for…something else. What do you know about camping around here?"

She looked back at his pickup. His truck bed was empty save for a large suitcase. "What kind of camping?" Maybe he had a tent stowed in the back seat.

"I'd just be sleeping in my vehicle."

"In the park? You know there's a campground just across the way." She pointed. "You're not staying with Wynn and Rina?"

"Her mom's there now. But it wouldn't matter either way." He nudged a pebble with the toe of his boot. "Let's just say I'm not exactly welcome there."

"What? Said who?"

"There's never been any love lost between me and my son."

That much was true, but he didn't need to know she knew it. "Wynn wouldn't turn his own father away."

"Wanna bet?" His grin challenged her. And looked pained.

She honestly couldn't see Wynn McRae being that way. He didn't have a relationship with his father, but he wasn't vindictive. "Rina must not have been home. I know she would have invited you to stay with them." But maybe it was uncomfortable to have both sides of the family together.

He nodded. "Rina's the one who talked me into coming to town. But apparently she forgot to inform Wynn. When I got hold of him, they were back at the hospital with the baby. Amelia…I guess that's what they named her."

"Yes… Amelia." Tess felt funny confirming his own granddaughter's name for him.

"Anyway, I guess I spoiled the surprise. Wynn had no idea I was coming. Let's just say it wasn't going to be a pleasant surprise. He told me it'd be late when they got back from the hospital––if they even came back tonight." He looked at the ground. "I can take a hint."

She ignored that. "Everything's still okay with the baby, right?"

J.W. shrugged. "Wynn didn't say it wasn't."

And you didn't ask? For a minute she was afraid she'd said it out loud. But she was beginning to think Wynn had legitimate reasons for being estranged from his father.

Feeling awkward, she bent to pull a healthy stand of henbit from between the brick border, tossing the weed into a nearby trash can.

"Well, there's no reason to sleep in your truck. There's a hotel out on the highway, you know. Maybe it wasn't here last time you were in town."

"I'm not going to spend a hundred dollars just so I can have a bed."

"And a shower."

As if by the power of suggestion, he lifted the neckline of his shirt to his nose and sniffed.

She laughed. "That wasn't a hint. You smell fine." She wondered if he was struggling financially, or if he was really as frugal as Wynn claimed. "And honestly, it's not a hundred dollars. It's a Super 8, nothing fancy, but more like seventy dollars, I'd say. Maybe eighty by now."

"Yeah, and then there's a room tax, and sales tax and a state tax and they probably charge you for every phone call and every chip of ice you use. Thanks, but I think I'll just use the showers here." He pointed toward the campground on the other side of the park.

"Oh... Sorry, but you have to have a permit for the camp-ground. The park is very strict about that. The showers are only for registered campers. Unless you've made prior arrangements with the staff?" Good grief, she sounded like a tour guide. Or the *Gestapo*.

He cocked his head as if he didn't believe her. "How much is a permit?"

"Not much. Under twenty dollars a night. If you get a permit, you can park in the campground."

"Shoot, I may as well get a hotel."

"And then you could have a *free* shower." She smiled, hoping he'd see her humor.

He made a face that could have been a grin. "Maybe I'll just find a corner in the maze over there." He pointed to the well-trimmed hedge maze on the opposite side of the pavement.

"I assume you're kidding, but in case not, I'd recommend against it. It's supposed to be cold tonight."

"I guess the hotel it is." He gave a little wave and started for the pickup. Halfway there, he turned back. "Thanks."

He didn't wait for her to acknowledge his belated thank-you.

A spray of gravel stippled the pavement as he drove off. She could have sworn he was watching her in the truck's rearview mirror, and she had the strange feeling that he only turned in the direction of the hotel for her benefit.

CHAPTER THREE

A jean jacket was a poor substitute for a blanket. J.W. shifted on the narrow back seat and tried in vain to burrow deeper into the warmth of the denim. Outside his pickup, the endless *chirrup* of crickets made him want to clap his hands over his ears. He'd always heard that crickets didn't chirp until the temperature hit the fifties, but it felt more like forty and they were going at it. He'd gone camping with his dad as a kid many times, but he didn't remember ever being this miserable.

After what seemed like an hour of tossing and turning, he checked the time on his phone. *Ten-fourteen.* Great. Another eight hours before it would be light and he could call Rina. He had half a notion to drive back to Kansas City, but by the time he got there, it'd be time to turn around and head back. Besides, he could pay for a night in the hotel for the price of a tank of gas.

It wasn't that he was cheap. But it made no sense to shell out a hundred dollars or more for eight hours in a hotel when he had a perfectly good place to sleep in his truck. *Yeah, right, McRae. Tell yourself that all you want.*

His stomach growled, reminding him he hadn't eaten since the Burger King drive-through on the way out of Kansas City this afternoon.

The crunch of gravel and a flash of lights made him sit up, then duck quickly below the back windshield. His presence had already discouraged two carloads of teenagers from staying. But it was late now. The sound of tires on gravel came closer. That woman--Tess--had said he needed a permit to stay overnight in the park's campground. But this parking lot near the Cutler-Donahoe bridge was public property. And it wasn't like he needed electric or water hookups. He sure wasn't going to pay for a parking place on public land that his taxes had paid for. Well, a few years ago anyway.

It sounded like someone was pulling up beside his truck. *Great.* Well, if they kicked him out he'd go park in front of Wynn and Rina's house. They couldn't keep him from sleeping in a legally parked car, could they?

He heard the slam of a car door. He slid up far enough to peek out the side window--and found himself looking directly into the eyes of Tess Everett. The flush of heat that came over him would have been welcome a minute ago, but he pushed his embarrassment aside when he realized Tess hadn't seen him yet. Apparently the tinted glass afforded him a curtain of darkness.

She lifted a fist tentatively to the glass, as if she intended to knock, but then she hesitated and dropped her hand to her side.

What was she doing here anyway? He slunk down in the seat. He would just play possum and wait for her to go away. Her car door slammed again and he breathed a little easier, but a moment later a knock at the window made him jump.

He threw off his makeshift blanket and sat up on the seat. He could see her smiling in the dark showing even, white teeth. He unlocked the back door and opened it.

"I had a feeling I'd find you here. I hope I didn't wake you up." She thrust something soft and bulky at him. A quilt. "It got a little colder than they predicted."

This was no time to be proud. He took the quilt from her, revealing the large grocery bag in her arms.

She held out the bag. "Nothing fancy, but I brought you granola bars––for breakfast––and some water. And in case you're hungry now…" She produced a pouch of microwaved popcorn. It was still warm––and smelled a little like heaven.

He eyed her suspiciously. "Not to seem ungrateful, but you're not going to make me get a permit are you?"

"It'll be our little secret. But the park officially closes at 10:30, so if the city police chase you off, don't say I didn't warn you." She actually winked. "Oh, and if you're not hungry now, that popcorn should still taste okay in the morning."

"I am hungry. Thank you." He sure hadn't counted on this. He opened the bag, scooped up a handful and popped it in his mouth, then held the bag out to her. "Want some?"

"Oh, no thanks." She waved him off.

"This was very nice of you," he said over another mouthful of warm popcorn. "But how'd you know I'd be here?"

"Just had a hunch." She shivered and rubbed her hands together. "Well, I'll let you get back to sleep…"

"No," he said a little too quickly. He scooted over on the seat and motioned for her to climb in beside him. "You bring me all these goodies, and I've completely forgotten my manners. Come in out of the cold."

She took a step backward. "No… Thanks, but I really should get back."

"At least stay long enough to help me eat this popcorn."

She eyed the popcorn, but took another step back, looking conflicted. "It does smell awfully good."

"Have some. Please." He patted the folded quilt on the seat beside him and offered his hand.

Looking like someone who was about to dive into deep

water, she took it and climbed in beside him. The dim glow of the overhead dome cast harsh shadows, but after a few seconds the light flicked off and her features softened. "Just so you know, I don't make a habit of meeting strange men in public parks after dark."

"I'll make a note of that."

"It's just that--I feel bad about Wynn turning you away. And I was watching the ten o'clock news, and they said it was supposed to get down in the forties tonight. This might sound weird to you, but I...I just felt like God...like I was supposed to bring you a blanket and something to eat."

"Now that I think about it, I may have mentioned to God that I was freezing my tail off."

She laughed and the sound made him feel something he hadn't felt in a very long time. He pushed the thought away. *Don't get crazy now, McRae.* "I still don't get how you knew I'd be here."

Her eyes narrowed. "Let's just say I know the ways of a stubborn man."

"Your ex?"

"No!" She looked at him askance. "My husband. Why would you think *ex*?"

For a moment he was speechless. "What does your husband think about your--premonition?"

"Premonition?"

"About me being out here. What does he think about you bringing a strange man a bedtime snack?"

Now she was the speechless one.

"Ohhh... He doesn't know you're here."

"Wait a minute." She scooted away to hug the door. "I came because you're Wynn's father, okay? And I'm sorry, I should have been more clear. My husband... I'm a widow." She said the word as if it had turned sour and she couldn't wait to get it out of her mouth.

Now her presence in the cemetery made sense. He tried to remember if he'd said anything heartless earlier. He sometimes had a knack for that. "I'm sorry. I didn't know."

"Of course you didn't. I just didn't want you to think--"

"Right. I get it." They sat there in silence a moment, as he struggled to figure out how to steer their conversation on to...*anything* else.

"So, how do you know Wynn?"

She looked taken aback. "You don't know? I was a hospice volunteer when Char was..." She let the word trail off. "Wynn stayed with us that first summer after she died. My family and me. Our girls were just ten then. They're in college now--in Missouri--but they still think Wynn hung the moon."

He racked his brain to remember if Wynn ever mentioned staying with anyone that summer after Char passed away. He came up empty. Wynn had been grown, in college by the time Char got sick. J.W. had left the house in Winterset to Char, and he made sure ownership would go to Wynn after she died. He assumed that's where Wynn had lived whenever he was home from college. Apparently not.

But Char had succeeded in poisoning Wynn toward dear old dad long before that, and Wynn made it clear he wanted nothing to do with him. J.W. had made an effort at first, but too soon, it was just easier to convince himself to give the boy what he said he wanted: to be left alone. And dear old dad had been supremely good at that. It bothered him now to know that other people had stepped in and done what a father should have done. What *he* should have done. And it bothered him more that he hadn't considered this until now.

He closed his eyes, and the faces of his boys in Kansas City played on the screen of his eyelids. Michael, Patrick, and DeShawn Creve were brothers—half-brothers anyway—that he'd sponsored through a Big Brothers-type mentor program that Hartner & Hartner had started a few years ago. It was supposed to have been a one-summer commitment, but one summer had turned into five of them now. Michael and Patrick were out of high school and working now. DeShawn would be a senior in the fall. He called the three his "bros," but the truth was, he felt more like a dad to them. *More than he'd ever felt like a dad to his own flesh and blood.*

J.W. wondered what the bros would make of him selling the house—being essentially homeless soon. Having lived in their mom's car for more than a few weeks of their short lives, they'd no doubt have some words of wisdom for him—after they razzed him good about it. But it was too late for wisdom now. He'd let them down just like their own fathers—at least two different so-called fathers. But then that title fit him too. *So-called father...* He'd let his own son down every bit as hard as those faceless men had shirked their duties. The Creve boys just didn't know about *his* betrayal yet.

Tess cleared her throat, and J.W. realized he'd drifted too deep into troubling thoughts.

He shook himself back to the present. "I didn't know about any of that. You taking Wynn in, I mean. Then you probably heard all about what a terrible father I was. *Am.*"

She didn't flinch. "I'm sure my own daughters would have some criticism of my parenting. I just considered the source and tried to give you the benefit of the doubt."

"I appreciate that." He meant it more than she would imagine.

"So, Wynn says you're in advertising...an account executive, is it?"

He hesitated. "That's right." Well, he *was*. Once an AE, always an AE, right?

"I would imagine that's a pretty stressful job."

"It can be." He scrambled for something to divert the topic. "How about you? Do you work full-time here at the park?"

"Oh, no. The park is just...volunteer work." She said it like she was afraid she was bragging. "I did transcription work for a while to help save some money for the girls' college. But the work kind of dried up."

"What about hospice? You still volunteer with them?"

She shook her head. "Not for many years. Once the girls got into high school, it seemed like they kept me busy around the clock." She shrugged and took another handful of popcorn from the bag he held between them. "Thanks for sharing. I'd better get going, but I hope I'll see you around. You will stay long enough to meet your granddaughter, won't you?"

"If he'll let me. Wynn."

"He will. Give him time. If I know Wynn, he'll warm up." She opened the car door and the lights flicked on. "Don't give up on him."

Like you did before. She was too gracious to say it, but he read between her lines. "Thanks again for the care package."

"Any time. You can just give the quilt to Rina before you leave." She slid from the back seat and shut the door behind her.

Around two a.m. a light rain began to fall. The crickets quit chirping so he knew the temperature had dropped, but he was warm as toast beneath her quilt.

So why wouldn't sleep come?

CHAPTER FOUR

"I'm so glad the baby's doing better." Tess cradled the phone between her ear and her shoulder while she poured her first cup of coffee. She allowed herself two cups on Saturday mornings. The rich aroma sharpened her senses even before she took the first sip. "Listen, Rina, I know you have a lot on your plate right now, but I wasn't sure you knew Wynn's dad was here?"

"What? In Winterset?" Rina McRae's voice went up an octave. "Oh, my goodness. I didn't think he'd come. When did he get here?"

"Yesterday. He slept in his truck in the park last night."

"You have got to be kidding me."

Tess laughed, then felt bad, since she knew Rina would feel responsible. "I take it you didn't know he was coming?"

"I invited him. For Father's Day. But I didn't think he'd actually come. He never said. Why didn't he let us know he was here?"

So Wynn hadn't told her. She scrambled for a way to answer the question without getting Wynn in hot water. "I think he... assumed your mother would be here. He didn't want to interfere. I reminded him Winterset does have a hotel, but he wouldn't hear of it."

"No, he wouldn't waste the money." Rina didn't sound surprised. "But he could have stayed here. I gave him both of our cell phone numbers."

"Isn't your mom there still?"

"No, she went home after we had to come back to Des Moines. She made up the guest room before she left and everything. In case J.W. came. And even if Mom had been there, he could have slept on the daybed in the nursery. The baby will be in our room for now. There was *no* reason for J.W. to sleep in the park."

"He said something about there being no love lost between him and Wynn."

"Well, that's true." Rina sighed. "I didn't dare tell Wynn that I'd called his dad. They're both stubborn as goats. It's just ridiculous."

"I took him a quilt and something to eat last night. To the park. Just so you know…"

"Oh, you're so sweet. I'm sorry you had to do that."

"I didn't have to. And really, he could have gone to the hotel. It's not like he's destitute or anything. Is he?" By the looks of the pickup he drove, McRae was doing all right.

"Of course not. Wynn says he probably makes six figures." Rina sounded disgusted. "He's just stubborn. They both are."

"When will you guys be home? I'm heading to the park in a little bit. I could deliver a message if you want or––"

"We're heading home as soon as the doctor sees Amelia. Wynn just went down to get the car, in fact. We should be home before noon. Maybe sooner. And I don't care if Wynn freaks, J.W. is staying at our house tonight. The whole point of getting the man here was so this ridiculous rift between them can end. I want Amelia to know her grandpa. And after all, tomorrow is Father's Day."

Tess winced. She loved Rina's heart, but sometimes Wynn's wife ramrodded things that would be better gently prodded. "Not to tell you what to do, honey, but I know men––especially stubborn men––enough to know that it'd be best if they thought it was their own idea."

"How am I supposed to make that happen when J.W. doesn't even let us know he's here?"

"I don't know the answer to that, but I trust Wynn will do what's right by you and the baby. And a baby should know her grandpa. Maybe that's the angle you should take." She'd already bitten off more than she intended, and she had no desire to get in the middle of this family situation, but neither did she want Rina to derail a chance for reconciliation.

"Could you maybe talk to Wynn?"

"Rina, I––"

"He'll listen to you, Tess. You don't have to tell him I put you up to it."

"I don't want to be dishonest." She'd called Rina on going behind Wynn's back before. That was never a good idea—something she'd learned the hard way when she and Dan were newlyweds.

"No… I didn't mean that…" Rina backtracked. "Just…well, you don't have to tell him unless he asks."

Tess laughed. She wasn't proud of it, but she'd used that loophole many a time in her own marriage. "We'll see. If the opportunity comes up…"

"You know I'll be praying hard that it does."

"Hey! Not fair."

Rina's giggles were drowned out by the sound of a baby crying.

"Oh, I hear her!" A lump came to Tess's throat. "I can't wait to hold her again. She's doing okay, huh?"

"She's doing great. They just wanted to get her bilirubin

levels regulated. A couple of days under the lights and she's good to go."

"Wonderful. And listen, I'm bringing some food over. I did a roast in the Crockpot last night and I have tons of leftovers. You can put it in the freezer and warm it up whenever you like. I'll drop it off later today if that's okay."

"Thanks, Tess. That'd be wonderful. Gosh, I haven't had to cook for two weeks. I won't remember how when I finally have to get back in the kitchen."

"Oh, yes you will. It's like riding a bicycle."

"Oh! The doctor's here. I've got to go. But thanks, Tess. I'll see you soon."

"You guys drive safe, okay?" Tess hung up the phone, remembering what it had been like when she and Dan had brought the twins home from the hospital. Her mom had been at their house waiting to help with the girls, and Mom's help had been a godsend. But she wasn't sure she would have wanted her father-in-law as a guest so soon after having the babies. And she'd known and loved Dan's father. J.W. was virtually a stranger to Rina––and to Wynn for that matter. Of course, Rina was far more adventurous than Tess had ever been. If anyone could handle J.W. McRae, his daughter-in-law was a good prospect.

THE RUSTIC LIMESTONE edifice of Clark Tower had just come into sight through a dense cover of leaves when J.W.'s cell phone jangled in his pocket. He slowed to a fast walk and took a couple of deep breaths before sliding the phone from his pocket. It was Wynn's wife. "Hello?"

"Hi, it's Rina. I heard you were in town."

"Yeah? From who?" He had his suspicions.

"And I heard you slept in the park last night. In your truck!"

That confirmed it. Tess. Or the Winterset grapevine was alive and well. "And you're calling to tell me what I already know because...?"

"Because I want to make sure you stay here tonight...at our house."

"And what does your husband think about that idea?" Rina was a sweet girl, but she sorely underestimated the depth of Wynn's feelings toward him.

"We want Amelia to meet her grandpa."

"I want to meet her too." He didn't have the first idea what to do with a baby, but it did give him kind of a warm, fuzzy feeling to think about the fact that he had a grandkid. He supposed he should bring a gift. He didn't have a clue what to buy a baby girl. "How about if I take you kids out to eat tonight?"

He heard Rina's hesitation on the other end. "Would you maybe want to pick up a pizza instead? I don't really want to take the baby out in public yet...since we just got home from the hospital. We're still trying to get the hang of all this. Having a baby in the house, you know?"

He *didn't* know. Or didn't remember anyway. A few flitting images of Wynn as a baby flashed through his mind, but they were quickly overtaken by other images. Char screaming at him while toddler Wynn sat on the floor squalling like a little girl. He pushed the memories aside. "I'll bring pizza. What time do you want me?"

"Come right now if you want. You can go pick up pizza later. Where have you been hanging out anyway? You surely haven't been sitting in your truck all morning."

"I'm hiking. Just got up to the tower."

"Oh. That's nice. Wynn likes to jog on that road, too."

"Then don't tell him I'm here." J.W. turned a three-sixty, eyeing the narrow road as if his son might come jogging around the curve at any moment.

"Stop, J.W. Just stop. Why do you do that?"

"Do what?"

"Act like Wynn hates you?"

"Hate might be too strong a word."

"Okay... Why do you act like he despises you so much?"

He laughed. "I'm not sure that word's any weaker." He turned serious then. "Listen, Rina, I don't blame my son for not wanting anything to do with me. I essentially...abandoned him. I was wrong, and I've told Wynn that. I'm sorry. I really am, but it's too late now to try to make excuses for why everything happened the way it did. I get that I'm not his favorite person on the planet."

"You can't be his least favorite person when he doesn't even know you. That's my point. Maybe he needs to hear some of those excuses. Maybe they were *reasons*. I trust you had your reasons."

He was liking this girl better by the second. He looked up at the sun, which had quickly grown warm, then glanced at his watch. "Why don't I just bring pizza around five? I don't want to wake the baby or anything."

"You won't. Newborns could sleep through a war."

"That's good, because there just might be one when Wynn finds out I'm staying there."

"Cut it out. Let me worry about Wynn, okay? Just come. The guest room is all ready for you. If you want to come early... shower here, or take a nap, you can. The doctor says I'm supposed to nap when the baby naps. Wynn usually gets home from work around five-fifteen."

"Okay. I'll be there with pizza around five. Anything special you guys like? Or don't?"

"No anchovies. We'll eat anything else. Thanks, J.W."

He clicked off the phone and tucked it back in his pocket, but an idea struck and he dug the phone out again and opened Google. He had to try three different spellings of Everett––and she was listed under Daniel--but he finally found a number for Tess.

She had two girls. She'd know where to go in this little town to find a gift for a baby. And what to buy once he got there. Maybe she could steer him right on where to order pizza too.

CHAPTER FIVE

*J*ess lugged the second bushel basket of twigs and debris to the trash can and went back for another load, scanning the parking lot as she walked. The overnight shower had washed leaves and mulch from the flower beds into the shelter in the city park and it made a good excuse to stop and see if Wynn's father was still here. The truck was parked where it had been last night, but she hadn't seen the man himself. Probably walked downtown for some breakfast.

She crossed the parking lot, pretending––even for her own sake––that she wasn't hoping to see J.W. McRae. With the glare on the pickup's windows, she couldn't tell if he was inside it or not.

She swept another pile of debris toward the center of the shelter, then knelt and scooped the soggy mess into the basket.

"Hey! I thought that was you."

She turned at the gravelly voice. J.W. jogged toward her across the stone bridge.

"Oh… Hi." Did her sheepish expression give away the fact that she'd been thinking about him all morning?

"I was just about to call you."

"You were? What about?"

"Well, to return your quilt for one." He pointed toward his truck. "I'll go get it for you."

"No problem. You could have just left it with Wynn and Rina."

He knelt to hold the bushel basket steady while she gathered the last of the twigs and deposited them inside.

"Actually," he said, "I have another favor to ask of you."

"Oh?"

"I need to get a gift. For the baby--Amelia. You don't know of a place in town that carries that type of stuff do you? The truth is..." A sheepish look colored his complexion. "I don't know enough about that kind of stuff to pick something out if I was surrounded by it. Pink. I know pink. And that's about the extent of it."

She feigned a wince. "Actually pink isn't even a given any more."

"What? They changed the rules on me again? That's really not fair at all."

She laughed. "It's not, is it? But I can give you some ideas. There's not a huge selection in town, but you'll be able to find something special. Have you thought about jewelry?"

His eyebrows lifted. "For a baby?"

"Sure. A little silver necklace or engraved bracelet... It's more for a keepsake, really. But it's something she can wear when she's dedicated, and it would be really special to her when she gets older to have something from her grandpa. And Rina will like it now."

"Wow. Who knew? I was thinking booties or a rattle or something."

Tess curbed a smile. "Booties are nice too."

He cocked his head. "You say there's someplace here in town that sells stuff like that?" He hesitated, and kneaded the grass with the toe of his boot. "You wouldn't want to go with me would you?"

"Well…sure. I'd be glad to." She looked down at her frayed jeans and chambray shirt. "I'd need to run home and change clothes first. Could I just meet you downtown in half an hour or so? Most of the shops don't open until ten anyway."

"Sure. That'd be great. You're sure you don't mind?"

"Not at all. Do you know where the jewelry store is?"

"I have no clue. Until yesterday I hadn't been to Winterset since––since Char's funeral."

She chose to ignore that. "You remember where the Rexall is, on the west side of the square?"

He scratched his head. "I remember where the square is."

She laughed again. "West side of the square, south of the pharmacy. Just across the alley. You can't miss it."

He still looked dazed.

"I'll watch for you wandering aimlessly on the sidewalk."

"I think I can probably find it." He straightened and took the bushel basket from her. "Let me get that."

She followed him to the trash can, then took the empty basket from him and tossed it in the back of her Mariner. "See you in a few."

He stood there while she backed out, and she watched him waving in her rearview mirror.

It was only a few blocks to her house, but far enough that by the time she pulled into her drive she'd had time to second-guess herself. Why on earth had she just agreed to help a man she'd only met yesterday pick out jewelry for his infant grand-daughter? Had she abandoned every ounce of common sense she'd ever possessed?

But it was too late to back out now. She'd already agreed, and J.W. wanted the gift to take today when he went to meet little Amelia for the first time. She would do it for Wynn and Rina. That was all.

She parked on the drive and went in through the front door. If she hurried, she'd have time to run a curling iron through her hair.

~

THE JEWELRY STORE was right where Tess had said it would be. And somehow seeing the Rexall sign above the drugstore––no doubt the same sign that had hung there back when he'd lived in Winterset––made it feel like it hadn't been so long after all since he'd called Winterset, Iowa home. He'd forgotten how quaint and quintessentially Midwestern the little town was, with red brick downtown storefronts surrounding the gray stone courthouse with its distinctive cupola and clocks.

As he climbed out of his pickup, an elderly man strolling by waved at him. "Mornin'!"

"Good morning." The man didn't look familiar, but he sure acted like he knew J.W. He returned the congenial smile in kind, reminded that small-town friendliness didn't require actually knowing someone. Still, he hadn't thought about the fact that while he was in town he might run into people he'd known before.

Not a comforting thought. As he recalled, small towns had long memories and short fuses. He hadn't been gone so long that he didn't remember what small town-gossip and small-town loyalties were like, so if Char had poisoned Wynn against him, the whole town might very well hate his guts.

He looked up and down the street. No sign of Tess yet. Unless she was already inside the jewelry store. As he stepped up the curb, he recognized her silver Mariner pulling into the parking space three down from his. She slid from her vehicle and he had to make an effort not to gawk. She wore white pants––the kind that stopped just below the knee––and a turquoise shirt that played up her blue eyes and her tan. Her blond hair was clipped on top of her head in an intriguing style, and long turquoise earrings bobbed from her earlobes.

He walked to meet her. "You clean up nice." *Real* nice.

She laughed and touched the clip in her hair. "This is my can't-do-a-thing-with-it hairstyle. You ready?" She stepped up from the curb.

Her smile made his stomach do flips—in a good way. "Ready as I'll ever be." He motioned for her to precede him into the store.

The shop looked like it hadn't been updated since the sixties. The woman behind the counter greeted Tess like an old friend, then eyed J.W. suspiciously. "What can I do for you today?"

Tess touched his arm briefly. "This is J.W. McRae, Wynn's father."

"Ah..." A look he couldn't interpret came to the clerk's eyes. "Came to meet the new little granddaughter, I bet."

"That's right."

"That's why we're here," Tess said. "For a baby gift. Could you show us something that might be appropriate for a first baby gift?"

"Certainly." The woman led them to a case at the back of the store that held an array of tiny necklaces, bracelets, even a pair of diamond earring studs so tiny they looked like they'd be lost before you got them gift-wrapped.

"I'm in foreign territory here," he said, "but aren't those pierced earrings? Do people really pierce baby's ears?"

"Sometimes," the clerk said. "Of course you'd want to wait and see about the parents' preferences before you purchased something like this. You could always give a gift certificate if you're not sure."

He turned to Tess to see what she thought about that idea.

She frowned. "I think you want something more personal, don't you?"

"Sure. If you say so."

The clerk gave him another indecipherable look. "What about a little silver cup. We could engrave it with the baby's name and birthdate."

"I like that idea," he said. Something about the idea of jewelry for babies didn't sit well with him. Again, he looked to Tess hoping she liked the idea.

"I think that would be perfect. If they don't want to actually use it for a drinking cup, they can display it on a shelf in her room, or put cotton balls or swabs or whatever in it."

"Okay. Let's go with that." His relief at having this decision made was incongruous with its importance. "Can you engrave it today…while we wait?"

The clerk frowned. "The owner stepped out to lunch, and I'm the only one in the store right now, but we could probably have it ready within the hour."

He looked at his watch. "Sure. That works."

"I'll need you to fill this form out with what you want engraved." She slid a slip of paper across the counter.

"We might have a problem here." He looked at Tess. "I'm not even sure how they spell her name."

"It's A-M-E-L-I-A," Tess said. "But I don't remember her middle name."

"Would they want that on there?"

"I think it would be nice," Tess said.

"Maybe I should give Rina a call," he said.

"Just a minute…" The clerk held up a finger. "I think I still have the *Madisonian* with the birth announcement in it. I bet we can find what we need there."

"Do you think we can trust that they got it right? I'd sure hate to get it engraved and find out we fell for fake news."

Tess laughed. "I think we can count on the *Madisonian* to get it right."

"Well, if for some reason it's not," the clerk said, "you can return the cup and we'll burnish it and make a correction. Or if you'd rather find out for sure and come back later——"

"No, I'd like to have something to take now."

"Well, you could just buy the cup now and bring it back in later to be engraved..."

Again, he turned to Tess for advice. Thank goodness she'd agreed to come with him.

"If you can find the newspaper, I think it would be more personal to have it engraved now."

"Certainly." The clerk went to the back where they heard her rustling newspapers. She returned, shaking out a section of the *Madisonian*. "Found it! She was born June 8, and this says 'Amelia Charlotte'... Does that sound right?"

Charlotte. It didn't sound right at all, but he managed to nod, wondering if Tess noticed his hesitation.

The clerk filled in the boxes on the form and had him approve them. "Do you want this gift-wrapped?"

"Sure. That'd be good."

"Okay. If you have other shopping to do downtown, you can stop back in about an hour, or I can give you a call when it's ready to pick up."

"Is there someplace nearby to get a cup of coffee?" he asked the clerk, then turned to Tess, wishing he'd checked with her first. "Does that sound okay?"

"I'd love it." She motioned toward the front door. "There's a coffee shop just up the street. Or there's always the cafe, if you'd prefer."

"Either one sounds good to me."

The clerk rang up his purchase and he paid for it, managing not to cringe when he saw the total. He was going to have to start being more careful with his money. But he *would* buy Tess Everett a cup of coffee. It was the least he could do after she came with him this morning, not to mention her care package from last night.

Feeling relieved to have the gift out of the way--and confident in his choice, since Tess had approved it--he followed her to the front of the store and held the door open for her.

Before they headed for the coffee shop, he got the quilt out of his truck and took it to her car.

"You sure you won't need this again tonight?" she teased.

"I'm good." He returned her wry smile, but didn't tell her he'd considered investing in a sleeping bag.

THE COFFEE SHOP was bustling with Winterset residents apparently fueling themselves for Saturday chores, or shopping, or whatever people did in this town on Saturday.

They waited in line to place their orders and after he paid for their coffees and two slices of pound cake, he let Tess lead the way to a table for two by the window. As he pulled his chair out, he felt a tug on his sleeve and turned to see a woman looking at him as though he should know her.

Though she looked vaguely familiar, he drew a complete blank. He looked to Tess, hoping she knew the woman, but she was checking something on her phone and didn't seem to notice.

"J.W. McRae? I thought that was you."

He gave a weak smile. "I'm sorry... You're going to have to tell me who you are."

"Sheralane Jenkins. I was Sheralane Pinehurst." She leaned around him and gave Tess a little wave.

"Hi, Sheralane." Tess waved back. "You know J.W.?"

"I should think so. We were on the PTA together for three years when Wynn and Rick were in elementary."

"That's right, we were." He sent up a prayer of thanks for the clue. "It's been a while. What is Rick up to these days?"

"He's in Iraq. The Marines."

J.W. shook his head. "You must be very proud of him." How's…Bob doing?"

"Um… Bill, you mean?"

He closed his eyes. "Of course. I'm sorry. Bill."

She looked stricken, and pressed her lips into a firm line.

What had he said now? He glanced at Tess, who looked rather stricken herself. *Uh-oh.* Was the guy dead or something?

"Bill left me twelve years ago." Sheralane's eyes narrowed. "Not unlike the way you ditched Char, actually."

Whoa. He'd walked right into that one. Never mind he had *not* "ditched" Char. But he resisted the urge to correct her. "I--"

"Yes…must have been something in the water back then." She glared at him, as if daring him to offer a good excuse why her husband had left her.

"I'm sorry. I…didn't know."

Tess rose and came to stand beside him. "I think I see our coffees up there. You want to go get them? I'll save our table."

"Sure, I'll get them." God bless that sweet woman. He practically lurched for the front counter, waving at Sheralane as he swept past her. "Tell Rick hello for me."

He didn't wait around to hear if she had a reply for that. He took his time gathering napkins and sugar packets. When he turned away from the condiment counter he was relieved to see that the woman had disappeared.

But now he had to face Tess.

CHAPTER SIX

$\mathcal{J}$ess felt sorry for J.W., even if she was curious to see how--or whether--he'd defend himself against Sheralane Jenkins's attack. She'd never been a fan of the woman, and Sheralane's antics just now hadn't improved that opinion any.

She watched J.W. pan the room, obviously trying to stay under Sheralane's radar. When he arrived at the table, she decided to be forthright. "I'm sorry about that. Sheralane can be--well, rather blunt."

He winced. "You got that right. Well... It's not like she wasn't saying anything my own son wouldn't say to me."

"Don't put words in Wynn's mouth, J.W."

"Oh, believe me, I don't have to. He has plenty of words on his own."

She hesitated, then plunged in. "What did happen between you and Char? If you don't mind me asking..."

His eyes narrowed. "Maybe first I should ask you what she *said* happened?"

"That was a long time ago. I honestly don't remember details. She wasn't exactly your biggest fan. I do remember that."

She gave a wry grin, hoping the comment wasn't hurtful, but it seemed like a little levity was needed.

Thankfully, he laughed.

Tess blew out a breath of relief. "To be honest, I always made an effort to forget the things patients told me when I was doing hospice. Obviously those conversations are confidential. But Char became a friend. And J.W., she softened a lot at the end. It's too bad she wasn't able to communicate that to Wynn. I tried, but––I think he thought I was just making excuses for her. And you."

"Me?" He studied her. "Do you mean she softened...toward me specifically, or just in general?"

It seemed important to him, and she framed her answer carefully. "A little of both. I probably don't have to tell you that Char was rather––" She groped for the right word. "Brash, maybe? She was bitter, and it made her a little harsh."

"Well"—he looked briefly at his lap—"that made two of us. In the marriage. Sheralane got some details wrong, but...she wasn't just making things up either. Just so you know."

Tess weighed her words carefully, not wanting to dismiss his acknowledgment too casually. "I'm sorry you had to run into Sheralane, of all people, J.W., but she's not all of Winterset. Most of the people in this town are warm and caring. And forgiving. If you'll let them be. Please give them a chance. Don't paint the whole town with one brush because of people like her."

He held up a hand. "I apologize. I'm sorry."

He hung his head and when he looked up again she actually felt sorry for him––and regretted opening her big mouth.

"She...embarrassed me," he said. "My pride was wounded and I got defensive. I'm sorry. But neither am I foolish enough to think there aren't others in this town who won't exactly welcome me with open arms. Wynn is proof of that. Not saying I blame any of them either. I––"

"Wynn will come around. I promise you that."

"I wish I could believe you. But he hasn't come around in twenty years. Why should it be any different now?"

"Because of Amelia, of course."

"Oh."

"That baby changes everything." She tilted her head and regarded him, deciding she had nothing to lose by telling him exactly what she thought. But Wynn had everything to lose if this man walked out of his life—and Amelia's.

Dan had always said she meddled too much in other people's business. She shut out the memory of her husband's voice. And maybe her good sense with it. But she was in Wynn's corner now. "Whether Wynn is ready to admit it or not, he's scared to death of being a father. He's scared of failing. You have a chance to show him he doesn't have to make the same mistakes you and Char did. Not that he won't make mistakes. Goodness knows, Dan and I made our share with our girls. But Wynn needs to have hope. And you can give him that, J.W. If you'll stick around long enough to give it a chance."

He shook his head. "I'm not sure there's that much time in the world."

"Baby steps. You guys will have to earn each other's trust again."

"You're being generous to say 'each other.' I'm the one who lost Wynn's trust." He took a sip of his coffee, and Tess had a sense that he'd been about to say something else but caught himself.

She reached to touch his arm. "I'm sorry. In case you haven't noticed, I tend to be a busybody. My husband always accused me of trying to practice psychology without a license. 'If you want to be a psychologist, go back to school, babe,' he always said."

That earned her a grin. "I do see your point. I'm just not sure my son is open to any attempts at reconciliation. It's Rina that's pushing it."

"Well, God bless her, then. I hope she'll keep pushing."

He shrugged, and Tess decided it was time to change the subject. They made easy conversation, talking about the changes J.W. saw in the town of Winterset since he'd last visited, and discovering they had some friends in common.

Her cell phone rang. She glanced at it, planning to ignore the call, but when she saw the name on the screen, she held up a hand, grinning. "Speak of the devil… It's Rina. Let me take this real quick."

He nodded and drained his coffee cup.

"Hi, Rina. Is everything okay?"

"Fine. It's good to be home. The baby's sleeping and I'm trying to get all the stuff from the hospital put away. Listen, Wynn's dad is bringing pizza over for supper and I wondered if you'd want to come. Maybe you could be a buffer between him and Wynn."

She tried not to let her expression give anything away. "Actually J.W. and I are having coffee."

"Right now?" She didn't miss the surprise in Rina's voice.

"Uh-huh."

"Oh." Rina hesitated. "Well, would you still want to come for pizza?"

"I'd love to. I was going to bring some meals for your freezer anyway." She looked at J.W., who'd turned to glance out the front window onto Main Street. "Hang on a second," she told Rina.

J.W. turned back to her, his brows knit in a question.

She muted her phone. "You okay with me coming to Wynn and Rina's for pizza tonight?"

He shrugged. "Sure. Why not?"

She couldn't tell whether he was really okay with her coming––or if he was merely indifferent about it––but it beat her usual salad so she chose to take him at his word. "I'd love to, Rina. What time?"

"J.W.'s bringing the pizza around five, but we probably won't eat until closer to six."

"Sounds perfect. I'll be there. Can I bring dessert?"

"I know you won't hear any argument from Wynn on that."

"Okay, it's a deal then. See you tonight. Thanks for the invitation." She hung up and looked at J.W., suddenly wondering if she'd overstepped her bounds. Again. "You're sure you don't mind? Would you have said anything if you did?"

"Why should I mind? It's not my party." An ornery spark came to his eyes. "I'll probably go broke buying pizza now that there's another mouth to feed, but hey…"

She laughed, relieved that he was taking it with good humor, whatever he thought about the idea of her coming.

He held up his cup. "Do you need a refill?"

"No, I'm fine."

He looked at his watch. "I could probably go pick up the gift now." He pushed back his chair.

"Wow, is it eleven o'clock already?" She gathered her jacket and purse and followed him out the door.

They walked back down the street, and when they neared the jewelry store, Tess veered toward her car. "Thanks for the coffee."

"It was the least I could do for your shopper assistant services. Never mind your popcorn and blanket rental."

"Rental? I guess I need to send out an invoice." She grinned and stepped off the curb. "See you tonight."

CHAPTER SEVEN

ess was surprised to see that J.W.'s truck wasn't in front of Wynn and Rina's house when she pulled up to the curb around five-thirty. She hoped he'd just gone to pick up the pizza. She didn't want to hold his new granddaughter before he did. She considered waiting in the car, but just then, Wynn appeared on the front porch holding the door open for her.

She went around to the passenger side and checked to make sure the cake was secure before lifting the box of frozen casseroles from the floor of the back seat. She'd gotten out the recipe to make her grandmother's German chocolate cake from scratch, but then remembered that, as a nursing mother, Rina might be avoiding too much chocolate, so she'd ended up making a pineapple upside-down cake instead—also from a recipe that had been a specialty of her grandmother's.

Feeling more nervous than she should have for a simple pizza supper invitation, she headed up the sidewalk to the house where she'd first met Char. For a long time after Wynn and Rina moved back to the house, Tess couldn't enter the living room without picturing the hospital bed set up in one end of the room. Thankfully, Rina, who'd never known Char, had put her creative touches on the house, and a colorful coffee bar and bookshelves filled the wall at that end of the living room now.

"Hey Tess." Wynn held the door open, wearing his trademark smile, which Tess now recognized as his father's smile.

She climbed the porch steps and greeted him with a hug. "Hi, Daddy. How's it going?"

He looked a little bleary-eyed. Who wouldn't be with a new baby in the house and the recent scare that sent them back to the hospital? She only hoped exhaustion didn't cloud his judgment when it came to dealing with his own father.

Wynn took the box from her. "Does any of this need to go in the fridge?"

"The casseroles go in the freezer, but the cake will be fine on the counter." She looked over his shoulder. "Now where is that little girl?"

Just then, Rina appeared at the end of the hallway, a pink blanketed bundle in her arms. Tess hurried over and touched the tiny pink stocking cap peeking out above a pink-striped blanket. So much for what she'd told J.W. about pink not being a given. Apparently for this little girl, it was.

"Hello, Amelia," she cooed, carefully pushing the blanket aside so she could see the baby's face. She was a dainty, olive-skinned beauty with dark hair like her mother's. Unexpectedly, Tess's throat constricted and she felt herself tearing up. Now she was grateful J.W. wasn't here yet. "She's perfect...just perfect," she said when she trusted her voice again.

Wynn came to stand beside Rina and peered down at his daughter—a perfect little family portrait. Wynn looked so proud, and Tess wished she'd remembered to bring her good camera.

A sound from the open front door made them all look up.

"Oh, there's our supper," Rina said.

"Our church has been bringing meals ever since this little spud was born," Wynn explained to Tess before turning back to Rina. "Who'd you say was bringing it tonight?"

"I *didn't* say." Rina looked pointedly past him. "But it's your dad. He offered to bring pizza. And I invited him to stay the night, too. The guest room is all—"

"No." Wynn took a step back, his eyes narrowing. "I told you I didn't want him here."

"Wynn…" Rina glanced at Tess as if hoping she'd take up for her. But Tess knew better than to get in the middle of a marital spat. But oh, her heart went out to J.W. He didn't know what he was walking into. Or maybe he did.

"Wynn, honey, please." Rina's voice went all whispery. "Please don't make a big deal of this. Please, babe. He's your dad."

"You could have fooled me." He shook his head as if he were a horse tossing off a bridle, then headed down the hallway to where the bedrooms were.

Tess gave Rina a look meant to convey sympathy. The poor girl looked near tears. She'd already been through enough with the early birth, and the baby having to go back into the hospital. Tess remembered how her hormones had raged in those first days after the twins were born. Dan only had to look at her cross-eyed and she'd fall apart. Why couldn't Wynn just grow up and act like an adult?

She felt somehow responsible for his behavior, as if she could have warded off this whole scene if only she'd been a better "mother" to him those few months he'd stayed at their house after Char's death. Tess just hoped he would snap out of it and be civil to J.W.

The doorbell rang, and Rina took a deep breath. "Pray!" she mouthed to Tess.

Tess patted her back and followed her to the door. She opened it to J.W. and reached for the stack of pizza boxes with his baby gift balanced on top. "Here, let me take those so you can get to that baby."

J.W. looked like he wasn't so sure it was a good trade, but he let her take the boxes from his arms.

She set the gift bag on the coffee table and carried the pizza boxes in to the kitchen, grateful for the line of sight the open floor plan afforded her. She tried to look busy rinsing dirty dishes in the sink, all the while feeling guilty for eavesdropping on the exchange between J.W. and Rina. And suspecting Wynn was down the hall doing the same.

Rina offered the pink bundle to J.W. and he took it, looking reluctant. "She's a featherweight," he said, jiggling her a bit. The baby made mewling noises, and J.W. glanced at Rina as if hoping she might rescue him.

Rina laughed. "She's okay. She's just stretching a little."

"She's an awfully cute little thing." He brought the bundle closer to his face and baby-talked to Amelia as if no one was watching. "Hey, little pilgrim. You're a pretty cute one. Yes you are…"

Tess couldn't see the baby, but by the expression on J.W.'s face, little Amelia must have responded to his cooing. He seemed instantly comfortable with the baby, in spite of his hesitance earlier.

Rina grinned. "She must like you. Look at that smile."

"I thought they said it was just gas when babies this new smile."

Rina didn't answer that, but J.W. looked pleased. "I think she looks like her daddy."

Rina gave a little laugh. "Then she looks like *you* because Wynn is the spitting image of you."

"Really? You think so?"

Tess could have sworn his chest puffed out a little. It reminded her of the way Dan had been with their girls. With any baby, really. Dan had adored babies, and she'd spent too many hours regretting that their girls hadn't come along until she was almost thirty. And then, the twins had been such a handful that they'd decided their family was complete with the girls. But she knew Dan had always secretly wished they'd tried for a boy. Of course, if God had granted her and Dan other children, she would be raising them alone now. The thought sobered her.

J.W. went on cooing at the baby, then looked up at Rina. "Is Wynn home?"

"He just got off work a little while ago. He's in––freshening up." Rina avoided Tess's eyes.

Wynn worked at the city offices. He'd started on a maintenance crew there right out of college. Tess wasn't sure exactly what his title was now, but something in payroll, she thought. He made enough that Rina had quit her teaching job at semester and planned to stay home with Amelia.

"Shall I put ice in glasses?" Tess headed for the kitchen, hoping to divert the conversation away from Wynn and prayed he was listening from the back of the house and would make his appearance soon.

"That would be great," Rina said. "Let's use paper cups and plates, if you don't mind. Here, I'll show you where they are."

"Absolutely. The last thing you need is a sink full of dirty dishes."

"Well, I feel like a slug. Everybody has been so good to bring us food and gifts. Shoot, I'd have a baby every year if I thought––"

"Whoa, whoa! I heard that." Wynn appeared in the hallway, and with only the slightest hesitation, he strode, hand outstretched, to where his father stood. "Hey, man..."

Laughing—and looking relieved—J.W. tucked the baby into the crook of his left elbow and shook Wynn's hand. "Congratulations, son. She looks like a keeper."

"She is, but that doesn't mean I'm looking to have another one just yet."

Rina rolled her eyes. "Well, now I know how to get your attention. Just mention multiple babies."

"I'm not saying the multiple part is a bad idea," Wynn said. "Just so they come one at a time, and preferably with a few years in between." He shot Tess a look. "I remember your two little rug rats ganging up on me all too well."

Tess laughed. "Sorry, Rina. I take full blame."

Rina leveled her gaze at her husband and affected a pretty pout. "You're no fun at all."

"Do I smell pizza?" Wynn inhaled, pointedly changing the subject.

"It's ready when you are," Tess said, opening a pizza box and sliding it forward on the island counter. The savory aroma of pepperoni met her nose, and remembering that she hadn't eaten since the coffee and pound cake with J.W. this morning, she suddenly felt ravenous.

Rina turned to Wynn. "Would you say the blessing, honey?"

Tess thought she detected resistance in the set of his jaw, but he nodded and bowed his head. "Thank you, Father, for this food and bless it for our good health. Amen."

Amens chorused around the table. Tess had heard Wynn pray far more heartfelt prayers, and it would have been nice to acknowledge his dad's presence, but at least he was making an effort to be civil.

Rina eyed the pizza with longing, but she reached instead to take the baby from J.W.

"Here..." Tess stepped in. "Let me take her while you eat. I haven't gotten my fill of this little sweetie yet."

Rina flashed a relieved smile. "Thanks, Tess. I'll fix you a plate."

Tess settled into a chair at the table in the roomy kitchen-dining room combination and adjusted Amelia on her left arm, much the way J.W. had. The baby scrunched up her eyes and stretched, then relaxed and settled back into the cocoon of the blanket.

"You've got the touch," J.W. said. He took the seat adjacent to hers.

"Oh, I don't know about that. It's been a long time since I held a baby."

Rina set a plate and a glass of fizzing soda in front of her. Tess leaned over the baby and took a bite from a slice of pizza.

"*Now* I'm really impressed," J.W. said. "That takes talent."

She laughed. "Eating pizza?"

"Eating pizza while holding a baby. Major multi-tasking."

"Tess probably invented multi-tasking," Wynn said over a mouthful of pizza. "Had to with twins, right? Man, I don't know how you did it. One baby is about to do us in."

"Well, I had lots of help. Dan was great about helping out and––" She stopped short, realizing her comment might sound to J.W. like an indictment. She felt herself flush and finished lamely. "And our friends and family, of course... I rarely had to wrangle two at a time." She feigned a laugh, wishing someone would change the subject she'd thoughtlessly stumbled into.

Whether he'd noticed, she couldn't tell, but J.W. bailed her out anyway. "How old did you say the twins are now?"

"They turned nineteen in April."

He asked where they lived and discovered they had mutual acquaintances in Springfield.

The dinner conversation was civil, if a little stilted, thanks to Wynn. There was definitely tension in the air. When the baby drifted to sleep in her arms, Tess decided to make her exit. Maybe it hadn't been such a good idea to come. "Well, I need to be getting home," she said, pushing her chair back and handing the baby to Rina. "Thanks for the pizza, J.W."

"But what about your dessert? Won't you stay?" Rina gave her a pleading look.

"Thank you, but I really should go." She grabbed her purse from the floor near the kitchen door.

J.W. rose and stood at his place at the table.

Wynn did likewise. "Thanks for coming, Tess. And thanks for the food you brought."

"I'll walk you to your car," J.W. said.

"Oh, you don't need to do that, but thank you."

"The guest room is ready if you want to bring your stuff in, J.W.," Rina said.

"Rina..." Wynn looked stricken. "You're seriously going to do this," he said through clenched jaws, though he didn't make any effort to keep his father from hearing his protest.

Tess looked from one to the other, then at J.W. She did not want to wind up in the middle of this.

"It's okay, Rina. I won't be staying." J.W. scraped his chair back. He touched the baby's head in Rina's arms.

"Where will you stay then?" Rina looked near tears.

"I probably ought to head back to Kansas City."

"No... Wait, J.W." She turned to Wynn, a pleading look in her eyes. "Please, Wynn?"

No response except for the furrow in his forehead deepening.

"Don't do this, Wynn," Rina said quietly. "Why do you have to be so stubborn?"

A muscle twitched in Wynn's jaw. "I am not going to have this conversation right now."

"Thanks for everything, Rina." J.W. took a step toward the door. "You two have a beautiful baby. You're very blessed."

It put a lump in Tess's throat to hear him saying what sounded like a final goodbye—an attempt at a blessing even. In that moment, she wanted to throttle Wynn McRae. Why couldn't he just put the past behind him and at least offer his father a chance?

"I'm going to go," Tess mouthed to Rina, slipping past J.W. She should have left five minutes ago.

But J.W. noticed and put a hand on her arm. "Didn't mean to chase you off," he said, an apology in his doleful eyes.

"Oh, no. It's okay. I...need to get going anyway."

"It was very nice to meet you," he said quietly.

"You too. Maybe we..." But she let her words trail off. There was no maybe anymore. The pang of sorrow that came at the thought surprised her. After all, she'd only known the man for a few short hours.

CHAPTER EIGHT

Wynn looked at the worn carpet in front of the front door. "I'm sorry... I mean, I appreciate you coming and everything, I really do."

"No. I should have waited till––" *Till what?* J.W. didn't even know how to finish the sentence. It was apparently too late to make amends for the years of apathy and neglect he'd inflicted on his son––his only son.

For the hundredth time, he regretted all the times he'd felt that prompting to call Wynn, to send a gift, to write a note. Now it was too late. And he didn't blame his son for being reluctant to share more than a casual dinner with him.

He stood with one hand on the doorknob, knowing he needed to just walk out the door, but knowing, too, that if he walked away now, he would likely never come back. He already felt the heaviness of yet another failure on his shoulders.

"Wynn, let me just say again, I'm sorry. I know it's too late... I can't go back and change the way things were, but I want you to know I recognize what I did and––I'm sorry. I was wrong."

"Yeah, well––" Wynn's Adam's apple bobbed in his throat. "I'm just trying to figure out how to do this dad thing. And I hope you understand, but I don't need a constant reminder of everything I *don't* want to be."

Rina gasped. "Wynn!"

J.W. couldn't keep from cringing. *Ouch.* Wynn may as well have punched him in the gut. But sadly, he couldn't say he didn't deserve it. He cleared his throat and willed his voice to stay steady. "I understand. Whether you believe it or not, I do. And... again, I'm sorry. For not being there for you. For not being a better example."

Wynn looked at the floor. "I'm sorry, too." His tone made it clear his words were not intended as an apology.

"I'll head on back then. To Kansas City. But...I'd like to see Amelia from time to time if that's okay."

Rina took a step toward him. "Of course you can see your granddaughter. Any time." She gave Wynn a withering look from beneath lowered brows.

Wynn took a deep breath. He shoved one hand in his pocket and lifted the other to rub the back of his neck. "Look, I'm not kicking you out of town. It's a free country. I just think this was enough, you know? Tonight. We broke the ice and all that. But maybe... I don't know...maybe you could come by again in a day or two. If you can stick around..."

He heard Wynn's unspoken "stick around, *unlike* when I was a kid." It wasn't fair putting words in his son's mouth, but J.W. heard them all the same. He turned the doorknob. "Thanks, but I probably should just go."

Rina shot Wynn a pleading look, which he ignored. She reached up and hugged J.W. The baby squirmed in her arms between them. "I'm sorry, J.W. Please come back soon. And I'll send pictures, of course. Do you have an e-mail address?"

"I––I need to get a new one." He'd never used anything but his office e-mail. "But I've got yours. I'll shoot you a message when I get home." He pulled the door open. "Well, I'm going to hit the road."

Wynn lifted a hand in a halfhearted wave.

J.W. walked out, refusing to glance back at Wynn and his little family, standing in the very doorway that he'd passed through so often as a young father.

Rina followed him out the door, and J.W. thanked her again, even as he felt a little irked that she'd set him up for this grand, final rejection. But there was nothing else to be said. Rina meant well. And if he hadn't come today, he might never have met his granddaughter, nor had the chance to give his son one more apology.

Still, walking down the sidewalk to his truck, he felt disgraced. The feeling was too recently familiar, the sting too much like what he'd felt as he walked out of his office at Hartner & Hartner for the last time. Sent away, with the implication that they didn't care to ever see him again.

As he pulled away from the curb and headed south out of town, he was grateful that at least Wynn had waited until Tess Everett left before delivering this humiliating blow. But the thought brought little comfort. Instead it brought a new sting of shame. His son had only meted out the rejection J.W. deserved.

He was a pathetic piece of humanity.

He flipped on the radio and messed with the tuner until he found some mindless talk show. But nothing would distract him from the rejection of his own son.

AN HOUR SOUTH OF WINTERSET, his cell phone rang. J.W. had the audacity to hope it might be Wynn, apologizing for blowing him off. But one glance at the name on his phone told him otherwise. It was his Realtor.

He tapped Accept. "This is J.W."

"Hello, Mr. McRae. This is Bethanne calling from Coldwell

Banker." The young agent was the definition of perky. "I have some *very* good news for you."

"Oh?"

"We have an offer on your home. It's not full price, but very close. I think you'll be pleased. And the buyers are a newlywed couple. They've been in an apartment, so no house to sell first. It really couldn't be more ideal. Their lease is up in August, so they're eager to make this happen sooner rather than later."

The young woman effused about how perfect this whole deal was, but J.W. tuned her out at "they may even want to buy some of your furniture if you're wanting to sell." If he took this deal––and he had no reason not to––he would not only be jobless, but he'd be homeless as well.

What kind of idiot put his house on the market before he had a clue where he would go next? The answer was sobering: an idiot who couldn't afford his house without the job that bankrolled it. His was a nice house and he had a decent amount of equity in it, but it wouldn't go far if he was throwing away ten grand a year on a cheap apartment. And where? It made no sense to sign a lease or buy another house in Kansas City when he had no clue where––or if––he'd find his next job.

His mind swam with all that needed doing before he could close on the house. Maybe this was God's way of taking the sting out of Wynn's rejection. He'd be busy enough that he wouldn't have time to think about everything that had happened with Wynn.

Something about that thought brought him up short. That kind of attitude was exactly why he'd been estranged from his son for all these years. Char had put a wedge between him and Wynn even before the day he left them. But he hadn't fought it. He'd let it happen. Even when he knew it was wrong.

And the truth was, he'd ignored God's gentle––and some-times not so gentle––promptings for far too long. It was time to man up and do the right thing.

But Wynn didn't want him there. Was it right to force himself on his son and their family?

Wynn wants a father. It's what he's always wanted. He just needs to learn that it's not too late for you to be that father.

J.W. was startled by the--*voice.* He couldn't call it anything else. Was this that still, small voice his grandmother had always talked about? The world called it a conscience. But he knew better. Yet he'd ignored God's voice for so long it was a wonder he recognized it any more.

He pulled the truck off the road and sat hunched over the steering wheel, feeling as if he were in a wrestling match between the man he was and the man he knew God was calling him to become. He knew himself well enough to know that if he kept driving, returned to Kansas City, he would never come back to Winterset. At least not before it was too late.

He gripped the steering wheel, contemplating the huge decision that lay before him--perhaps the second most important decision he'd ever made.

"Help me, God," he whispered. "For once in my life, I want to do the right thing."

TESS PARKED the car and went in the back door, praying Mrs. Bayman next door didn't stop her for her usual over-the-fence chat. The woman was sweet, but she'd taken to magically appearing every time Tess came outside--particularly if there was something on the grill.

She knew--oh, how she knew--how very lonely the elderly widow was for someone to talk to. Once in a while Tess put an extra piece of chicken or another burger on the grill to share, and enjoyed the company herself. But it had gotten to where she felt a little like a prisoner in her own backyard. She was starting to suspect her neighbor was taking advantage of her generosity.

The phone was ringing when she came inside and she put her things away before answering. Except for telemarketers ignoring her no-call-list status, hardly anyone used her landline phone anymore.

"Mom? Where were you?"

"Jaci! Hi! What do you mean where was I?"

"I've been trying to call you for two hours."

"Why didn't you try my cell phone? What's wrong?"

"Nothing's wrong. And I did try your cell phone! About eighty-two times."

Tess reached for her purse and unsnapped the compartment where her phone was––or should have been. It was gone. "Hang on, honey." She rummaged in her bag in vain. Her cell was gone. "I can't find my phone."

"I thought maybe you were at church or something."

"At church on Saturday night?"

"Well, that's the only time you turn off your phone."

"No. I was at Wynn and Rina's actually."

"Ohhh… How's the baby?"

"Every bit as cute as you'd expect Wynn and Rina's baby to be. I got to hold her for most of the evening."

"No fair! I'm dying to see her!"

Tess laughed at her drama queen. "Well, you're the one who chose to go out of state to college. Don't blame me."

"Oh! That reminds me of the second thing I called about."

Tess waited, steeling herself to say no to yet another plea for money or a ticket home.

"What would you think if I came home for the summer?"

"Home? You mean, like, to live?"

Jaci giggled, sounding like the giddy teenage version of Jaci Everett that Tess remembered best. She still had trouble thinking of her girls as grown young women.

"Yes, to live. Like, for the whole summer."

Tess could tell from the way the line was delivered that Jaci thought she'd be thrilled with the news. And in a way she was. But in another way, the thought brought apprehension. The girls had lived at home the first summer after college and there'd been all the tension one might expect of three women living in the same house, sharing the same kitchen––added to the fact that the girls were testing their wings.

And of course they were all still grieving Dan deeply. In truth, she'd been a little relieved when they left for college last fall. And they'd both been firm about their plans to stay in Missouri over the summer. They'd already arranged for the three of them to meet in Kansas City next month for a mother-daughter vacation.

"Where would you work if you came home to live?"

"I don't know yet," Jaci said. "But I hate my job. I'm talking hate, hate, *hate*, Mom. It stinks."

"Honey... I don't know very many people who love their jobs. Especially at the place you are in life. Until you get your degree you sort of have to take what comes, you know?"

"I know, but my boss is the devil incarnate. I'm serious, Mom. I don't think I can take another day there."

"Jace... You'd need to give two weeks' notice and by the time you work two more weeks and then move, there'd only be six weeks before it was time to move back for next semester. Who's going to hire you for only a few weeks? And what about your apartment? You don't want to break your lease..."

"First, there are, like, at least three people who would take over the lease for me, so that's not even an issue. And I wouldn't have to give two week's notice. Even if that jerk Thornton deserved it, I wouldn't have to give notice because they're already trying to cut back our hours. And I could get babysitting jobs and––"

"Jaci, nobody is going to pay you fifteen dollars an hour to babysit. Isn't that what you're making at the agency?" Jaci had landed a good job at an ad agency. It was a job that paid the bills and would look good on her resumé. Quitting after a month would not. "Besides, I thought they wanted you to stay on even after school started. Honey, have you prayed about this?"

Tess recognized the sigh on the other end all too well. Reminiscent of the not-that-long-ago teenage years.

"So, are you saying I can't move back?" Defiance had inched into her daughter's tone now.

"No. I'm not saying that. But this isn't something you do without thinking it through first. What does Jodi think about you moving?"

"She wouldn't care."

"In other words, you haven't talked to her about it?"

"Not yet. What does it have to do with her anyway? It's not her business."

A red flag went up. "Are you two getting along okay?" The girls had gotten separate apartments for the first time when they moved out of the dorms last month. Tess hated to see them drifting apart, and yet she knew it was a good thing that they both wanted to assert their individuality.

"We get along fine. But she doesn't need to be in on every decision I make about my own life. We're not joined at the hip, you know."

Tess bit her tongue. She was a pushover when it came to her girls. Especially since Dan's death, she hadn't wanted her daughters to suffer any more pain than they already had. "Well, listen, if you do decide to do this, you'd have to have a job lined up before you came back. I can't afford to––"

"I would, Mom. I already know who I'll call first. In fact, I'll call them as soon as we hang up."

"And you'd have a curfew and chores…everything you had when you were living under this roof before."

"I know."

"I might even need you to pay a little rent––toward groceries and utilities."

That caused a pregnant pause. But Jaci recovered quickly. "That's fine. I'm prepared to hate you by the time the summer is over."

Tess laughed, knowing her daughter's wry comment was meant in jest. But she did worry a little that they might truly be enemies by the end of the summer. Her firstborn was an independent young woman, and last summer hadn't exactly been a picnic with the girls living at home. It was why she hadn't been too disappointed when the twins both announced they would be staying in Springfield over the summer.

An idea began to formulate, and she debated voicing it before she'd thought it through. She decided to risk thinking out loud. "What if we fixed up Pop's shed for you. I've been thinking about renting it out for a little extra income. If we fix a little apartment out there for you, maybe we won't get on each other's nerves like we did last summer, and then when you go back to school I could find a renter."

"Are you...having money problems, Mom?" It sounded like Jaci had never considered the possibility.

"No. Not really. Not yet anyway." Her daughter's concern touched her and made her feel a little guilty that she'd made things so hard, but her daughter needed to learn some responsibility. "But I do need to watch what I spend. At least until I get you two through school. So, what would you think about that? Living in Pop's shed? If you come home?"

"I haven't been in there in forever. What all has to be done to make it livable?" Jaci sounded skeptical.

"Well, it was livable for Pop, so if that's not good enough for you maybe you don't—"

"Mom! You know what I mean."

"The roof does need some work, and I think the shower might have developed a leak, but I need to get those things fixed anyway. It could probably use a fresh coat of paint..."

"Actually, that'd be kind of cool. Can you have the roof and the shower fixed right away though? I wouldn't mind painting it myself, but the other stuff—"

"It can't be lime green and magenta, you know." Jaci's bedroom still sported the garish color scheme from her high school days.

"I know, I know. I think I'll go with jailhouse orange and purple."

"Ha ha, very funny." But already Tess was warming to the idea of having Jaci home. "I'll make a few calls. But Jace... I do hope you'll pray about this and not rush into anything."

"I will, Mom. Pray, I mean. Not rush into anything. I promise."

"Okay. Call me tomorrow after church and we'll talk some more."

Tess hung up the phone and sat at the bar counter contemplating the conversation. The idea of having at least one of the girls home for the summer after all did appeal to her. But not at the expense of her girl missing an important life lesson. Jaci had a tendency to be a quitter and this might only encourage making that a habit.

Sighing, she grabbed a memo pad and jotted a note to call the plumber Monday. First things first. The roof could probably wait, but the shower was a necessity. She would arrange for someone to come and look at it, but unfortunately, the plumber couldn't even get to the shower if somebody didn't clear a pathway through the shed first.

And unfortunately, last time she checked, she was the only somebody around here.

CHAPTER NINE

"I'm sorry, Mr. McRae, but those are the only rentals we're aware of." The woman behind the front desk at the Chamber of Commerce office on the north side of the square rummaged in a drawer. "I'd be happy to introduce you to some of the Realtors here in town. It's a buyer's market, and there are some nice properties for sale here in Winterset."

"I appreciate that, but I'm…not ready to make that kind of a commitment. I'm only interested in rentals." J.W. took the pile of brochures and maps she offered, and on his way to the door, he made a show of browsing the trinkets, souvenirs, and post-cards that were on display in the old building. With his hand on the door, he turned back to the clerk. "There aren't any other hotels in town, are there? Or lodges? Bed and breakfasts?"

She clicked her tongue. "Not any more. You might try Airbnb, though those aren't usually affordable for the long term. They can charge a lot…because of the covered bridges, you know." The woman had already given him some information about a couple of inns in surrounding towns, but the prices were even higher than the Super 8 where he'd bit the bullet and spent the last two nights.

The woman launched into a detailed history of the hotels, motels, and inns that had tried and failed in Winterset. When she finally stopped long enough to take a breath, he jumped in and thanked her, then ducked out the door. He turned right and headed to the Northside Cafe. At this rate, between the hotel and eating every meal out, he'd drain his 401K quicker than he could say John Wayne. The stock market wasn't looking very promising right now either.

He'd laid low since leaving Wynn and Rina's Saturday night. Mostly he'd watched TV at the hotel and jogged up to Clark Tower a couple of times. He knew he'd never forgive himself if he left Winterset before he'd at least tried to build another bridge with his son.

He hadn't told Wynn or Rina he was still in town, but he'd showed his face in the café enough times that it probably wasn't any secret. He hadn't told a soul about losing his job, and he didn't want Wynn taking him in out of pity. No, he had to have a game plan before he approached Wynn or Rina again. If God really wanted him to stay in Winterset and work on a relationship with his son, then He'd better start showing him how he was supposed to live on a fixed income without a job, a house, or a pot to cook in.

WIPING her brow on the sleeve of her shirt, Tess aimed a stream of breath at a wisp of hair that clung stubbornly to her forehead. She'd been working all morning trying to get Pop's shed cleaned out enough that the plumber could get to the shower this afternoon. It had turned into a much bigger project than she'd anticipated.

Worse, she'd forgotten that the window air conditioner unit had quit working at the end of Pop's last summer on earth. With the tiny apartment empty, they'd never replaced the AC unit and now the old-fashioned thermometer Pop had nailed above the kitchen sink declared it to be eighty-seven degrees, despite Tess having every window open and the door propped ajar. She'd have to get the unit fixed––or buy a new one––or Jaci would suffocate out here.

The longer she worked, the more Tess regretted offering Jaci Pop's apartment. It might have been a good plan if her daughter wasn't leaving a good job at a bad time to move back. But that girl needed to learn to stick to what she'd started, and she feared this plan would accomplish the opposite.

Tess sighed. She could've kicked herself for giving in so easily. Especially when all the work of getting the shed ready for occupancy was falling on her. Ah well… It was something that needed doing eventually. May as well be now.

She lugged another box off of the sturdy metal-framed bed and opened it up. Going through Pop's things had brought back too many memories. Dan's father hadn't owned much by the time he moved in with them, but the beloved collections of books and photo albums, and Pop's old Brownie camera that he'd used until he couldn't afford—let alone find—film for it anymore, not only brought back memories of Pop, but of Dan, who'd been so much like his father it was uncanny.

She could just picture the two of them fishing the streams of heaven. Well, maybe not fishing. She smiled to herself. That sport probably wasn't a fish's idea of paradise. But if heaven was anything like she hoped, the two Everett men would be exploring and hiking and having a wonderful reunion. If she was honest, she felt a little bit jealous of them.

It comforted her to think of Dan and Pop together, but it also made her feel weary being left behind to handle all the woes earthly life held. She shook her head, mentally chiding herself. *First World problems, Mom,* Jodi would have said. And Tess's problems *were* small compared to most of the world's. She should be grateful.

She closed the box and put it in the giveaway pile. She'd need to make a trip to Goodwill next time she was in Des Moines— or have a garage sale. Maybe she could put Jaci in charge of that project. That would be a good way for her to earn her keep. She ought to call the Fareway and see if they had any openings for Jaci. No. She stopped herself. If she let Jaci come home, she was not going to coddle her. She would have to figure out her own job and live her own life.

Tess ran a hand through her hair and gave a little growl. It just might kill her to stay out of her daughter's business. Not for the first time, she remembered how she'd hated her own mother's meddling when she'd gone off to college. She sympathized now, deeply, and regretted the revelation had come too late to share it with her mother. Mom would have gotten a kick out of it—and probably had some words of wisdom for her regarding Jaci.

She heard something and stilled to listen. She'd left the back door open in the house and now the faint ringing of the phone grabbed her attention. She clambered over boxes and hurried across the backyard to answer it.

It was the plumber. He was on his way, ready or not. She went back to the shed and finished clearing a path, hauling the boxes to the garage with Dan's things. With the boxes out of the shed, it appeared larger than she remembered. There was a tiny kitchenette at one end, bedroom and bath at the other, and the large living-dining room in between—perfect for Jaci. And already, Tess was decorating the little space in her mind for after Jaci went back to college. This would be a perfect place to spend autumn evenings reading. But she quickly dismissed the idea. Once Jaci moved out, she'd need to see if she could rent the apartment out. Probably couldn't get more than four or five hundred dollars a month for it, but that would pay her utility bills and then some. Of course, she'd be picky about who she rented to. The last thing she needed was a renter like Kressie Bayman who wanted to share her life—and her pantry.

The plumber arrived and she showed him to the shed, then left him to work while she headed for the grocery store.

The Fareway parking lot was crowded when she got there, and Tess almost decided against going in. She was hot and sweaty and not in the mood to see anybody, but she was out of milk and bread and almost out of coffee. It was desperation time. She parked as close as she could and jogged across the parking lot, praying she didn't run into anyone she knew. She reached for the door, but it swung open before her. She went through and turned to thank the kind soul who'd held the door for her.

"Tess?"

Even before her eyes adjusted to the dimmer lights in the store, she recognized J.W. McRae's gravelly voice. "You're still here. Good!" She hadn't meant to blurt that out, but he seemed--or pretended?--not to notice.

"More like I'm back." He looked at the floor before meeting her eyes again.

"Oh? I didn't know you'd left."

"It's a long story." He didn't elaborate.

"Are you staying at Wynn and Rina's?" Oh, how she hoped Wynn had reconsidered.

"No." J.W. paused, as if weighing his words carefully. "I-- It's--complicated."

"I didn't mean to pry." She reached for a grocery cart, wishing she'd kept her mouth shut.

"No... You're not prying. I didn't mean that. It's just that I'm not even sure yet what I'm doing here. Hoping, I guess."

She tilted her head. "About Wynn?"

He nodded.

"And your granddaughter. She's precious."

"She is. But it's more about Wynn right now. I--I want to make things right with him."

For a minute Tess wondered if J.W. might be dying or something. He seemed so...*urgent* to reconcile with his son. She took her hand off the cart, not wanting him to think she was in a rush. "He'll come around," she said softly. "I really think he will. He's a good guy."

"I hope you're right. And I want to thank you for"--he shrugged--"being there after Char passed away. That's when I should have come back." His shoulders slumped. "Maybe it's too late now."

She reached out and touched his arm, catching her reflection in the plate glass as she did so. She blew her bangs out of her eyes. She'd forgotten how awful she looked. But suddenly she didn't care so much. J.W. was obviously hurting, and it pained her to think what it must feel like to have your own child reject you. Even if you did deserve it. "It's never too late. Wynn will do the right thing."

"Well, we'll see."

A couple Tess recognized from church came in through the door where they were standing. She gave a little wave, and they waved back, casting curious glances at J.W.

He stepped out of the way so the couple could get to an empty cart, apologizing to them before turning back to Tess. "You looked like you were in a hurry. I'm sorry... I didn't mean to interrupt."

"Not at all. Just needed a couple of things." She looked down at her rumpled clothes. "I don't usually go out in public looking so raggedy."

"You look like you've been hard at work. No shame in that. Is it weeding or planting today?"

"Neither. Cleaning out a shed. At home."

"Ah. Well, I won't keep you."

She maneuvered the cart in front of her, hesitating, then

going for broke. "I don't know how you feel about this sort of thing, but I just want you to know that I'm praying for you—— and for Wynn."

"I appreciate that." He cocked his head. "It's funny you should even say that..."

"What do you mean?"

He started to speak, then closed his eyes and shook his head, seeming to change his mind. Finally he said, "It's just interesting, your timing."

Her expression must have said *I don't get it* because he laughed. "I'm being cryptic. Sorry." He looked around like he was about to share a state secret with her. "I do believe in... I put a lot of stock in prayer. Or at least I used to. I kind of got away from that and... You might think I'm crazy, but I was halfway home to Kansas City when I felt like God was telling me to turn around and come back here. To do whatever it takes to make things right with my son."

"Then I'm glad you listened." She couldn't have told anyone why his simple confession made her heart soar, but it did. And not just for Wynn's sake. "I don't want to interfere, but if there's anything I can do to help, please let me know. In the meantime, I'll be praying extra hard."

His smile reached his eyes this time. "I appreciate that."

She'd lied to J.W. on one count: she *did* want to interfere. She was so tempted to go have a talk with Wynn, to ask him to go easy on his father. To give him a chance. But her relationship with Wynn had changed since he and Rina married——as it should. In truth, the change had started when Dan died. It seemed Dan had filled a spot in Wynn's life that only a man could fill——only a *father* could fill.

She knew Wynn had to feel his father's rejection even more deeply than J.W. felt Wynn's. But Wynn was a grown-up now. He ought to give his dad a chance. Couldn't he understand what an effort J.W. had made even in coming here to see the baby? And now that he'd come back…

Still, it wouldn't be right to interfere, even though she thought Rina would support her. This had to be between J.W. and Wynn. But oh, she would be praying. How could God not want father and son to reconcile at last?

"So, how's that baby?" she asked, wanting to move to a brighter subject.

"You've seen her as recently as I have. Haven't seen her since Saturday. Haven't told them I'm back in town, actually."

"Really?" He'd been in town for two days—supposedly with the express purpose to reconcile with Wynn—and he hadn't seen them yet? "What have you been doing?"

His amused expression confirmed that she'd been too blunt. Again. But he answered as if it was a legitimate question. "I've been doing some hiking, working a little bit, shooting some photos."

"For National Geographic?" She grinned.

"Huh?" His wrinkled brow clearly said he didn't get her joke.

"You know, *The Bridges of Madison County*."

"Yep. Those bridges."

She laughed, feeling awkward. "I was trying to make a joke. About the novel… *The Bridges of Madison County*? You've surely heard of it."

"Ohhh." His brow smoothed. "I've heard of it. Haven't read it."

"Sorry. The hero—the main character—was a photographer for National Geographic." She would hardly call the character from the novel a hero.

"Ah."

"He came to Winterset to--" She waved a hand. "Never mind. You sort of had to have been there. Or read the book anyway. Not that I'm recommending it. I didn't really appreciate its message."

He shrugged. "I don't read much."

"You said you were doing some work? You have a project here?" Maybe his reasons for coming to Winterset weren't entirely altruistic. She wasn't trying to call him on it. But she did wonder.

His lips formed a straight line and he raked a hand through his hair. "My only project here is Wynn. By work, I just meant the photography. It's more of a hobby really. I play at it. But we sometimes used––*use* photos in our campaigns." His color heightened as if he'd said something inappropriate.

"Did *I* miss a joke now?"

"No. Not you. I just––" He waved her away the way she'd done with him a minute ago. "I'm just...getting used to some new terminology."

She'd pushed the boundaries with her questions, and she felt bad about it. He looked like he desperately wanted to change the subject. She looked up at him, attempting a mischievous grin. "If you're not staying at Wynn and Rina's, does that mean you're camping?"

He matched her grin, looking relieved. "Do I smell like someone who's been camping?"

She giggled, loving that he remembered their conversation in the park––and apparently found it humorous. "If you do, I hadn't noticed."

"I'll have you know tonight will be my third night at the infamous Winterset hotel."

"Wow, I'm impressed."

"Yeah, well, if I don't find a place pretty quick I may yet be camping under a bridge somewhere."

"A place? Besides the hotel, you mean?"

"I'm looking for an apartment, actually. Apparently they're hard to come by around here."

She couldn't hide her surprise. "You mean you're moving here? To Winterset?"

"Depends...on a lot of things. First of which is how supper goes tomorrow night."

"Supper?"

"Rina texted early this morning and invited me for supper tomorrow. Apparently the Winterset grapevine is alive and well." He cocked his head and tossed her a suspicious look.

She held up her hands, palms out. "I didn't say a word. I swear."

"Okay." He didn't sound convinced. "Anyway, Rina promised that Wynn knows I'm coming this time. In fact, it sounds like he's cooking."

"Oh, I'm so glad. That's a good sign."

He shrugged. "I hope. Anyway, if you hear of anything for rent around here, let me know."

"Did you ask at the Chamber of Commerce? They usually know if something's available." Was he really moving to Winterset? A lot of people worked from home, but he surely couldn't be an AE for a firm in Kansas City if he lived in Iowa. Maybe he was just looking for a weekend home.

She was relieved that Rina had reached out to J.W., but she wondered if he'd consulted Wynn about this move––not that he should have to. But coming for supper and moving back to Winterset would be two very different things in Wynn's eyes.

What she'd admired as determination a few minutes ago now seemed closer to desperation.

CHAPTER TEN

ess clicked the calculator app on her phone and balanced the columns in her checkbook register. The plumber hadn't been able to finish yesterday and had come back this morning and spent almost two more hours fixing the shower in Pop's shed. Tess could almost feel her bank account draining as he explained the bill to her.

She knew the repairs needed to be done anyway, but at this rate it would take the whole summer of what little she would charge Jaci for rent to pay the plumbing bill. And the roof was next. She loved this house where she and Dan had raised the girls, but lately it seemed every week something else broke down or needed painting or repair. How much did she spend before it made more sense to sell this house and move into something smaller?

Her friend Merrie often reminded her that once grandkids started coming along people needed a *bigger* house, not a smaller one. But that would be a lot of years yet for her. At least she hoped so. She wasn't ready to be a grandma, not in her forties.

Despite being alone in the house, she actually blushed at her self-deceit. *Forties? Ha!* She was so close to fifty she could feel it breathing down her neck. Still, she intended to cling to her youth for all she was worth. She reminded herself that she'd felt the same way about turning forty. And her forties had been the best years of her life––until Dan's death anyway.

She pushed away the gloomy thoughts that came, popped her cell phone in her pocket, and went out to dive into the shed project again. Last she'd talked to Jaci she still hadn't told her boss she was quitting, but she'd informed Tess to expect her sometime next week, so there was a lot to do and not much time to do it in. At least she could work in the comfort of air conditioning now. Merrie had insisted she take an old unit that was just sitting in their garage, and Merrie's husband, Mark, had even offered to help her get it installed and running.

Her throat clogged with unshed tears thinking about all the dear people who had stepped in to help her since Dan's death. She griped too often about the quirks of small-town life, but the truth was, she didn't know what she would have done if she'd lived in a city where no one knew their neighbors, and even if they did, they stayed out of your business to everyone's detriment.

A twinge of guilt came as she thought of Kressie Bayman. She hadn't been a very good neighbor to the older woman lately. She needed to remedy that.

"Please remind me, Lord," she whispered. *And thank you for taking care of me.*

And He *had* provided for her beyond anything she could have imagined. The day of Dan's funeral, her pastor had reminded Tess of God's promise to take care of His children. It hadn't been easy to believe, looking at the tear-stained cheeks of her sixteen-year-old daughters that day. But she'd clung to the promise––clung to it still––and not once had God ever let her down.

She finished paying bills and went out to work in the shed

for a couple of hours, scrubbing every inch of the little apartment, washing curtains, and exchanging Pop's masculine striped bedsheets for pretty floral bedding and some lavender curtains that had once hung in the twins' room. She touched up some of the paint on the woodwork, but the walls really needed repainting. Still, that could wait until Jaci could help.

As she worked, she remembered her dream of turning this space into her own hideaway, only now, her excitement grew for Jaci to be here and to live just a short walk away through the backyard. She imagined the yard full of the girls' friends in the evenings. It would be wonderful to have laughter and music filling the yard once again.

Tess hoped whatever job Jaci found here would still allow her to take time off on the weekend they'd planned to meet Jodi in Kansas City next month. But they'd cross that bridge when they came to it. Maybe Jodi could just come home that weekend if Jaci couldn't get away.

Tess scavenged the house and outfitted the shed's kitchen with a coffeemaker and a few essential dishes. She brought a floral painting she knew the girls liked from the guest room and hung it on the far wall of the shed, and placed a couple of trendy lamps on either side of the daybed. She tried a lacy tablecloth on the little table near the window, but decided it was too frilly for her daughter's taste and not really practical either.

The sun was low in the sky when she finished her spruce-up, and she stood in the doorway admiring her handiwork, imagining Jaci's reaction when she saw how cute it had all turned out. She would pick up some flowering plants to hang under the porch eaves and a new welcome mat for the front door, and Jaci would be right at home.

She locked up Pop's shed--she'd have to remember to start calling it *Jaci's* shed now--and headed across the backyard to the house.

"Yoo-hoo!" Kressie Bayman came tottering across the lawn.

She smiled inwardly. *Wow, Lord. That was fast.*

Kressie waved some colorful papers that flapped in the breeze and almost got away from her. Clutching them to her bosom, she met Tess at the edge of the lawn. "I brought you some coupons. They delivered a free Sunday paper last week and I thought maybe you could use them."

"Thanks, Kressie." She'd gotten the same free copy of the *Register*. Now that the girls were away, she rarely even looked at newspaper ads, let alone clipped the coupons.

Her neighbor thrust the wad of coupon pages into her hands. "You haven't been cooking on the grill much lately, I noticed."

"No, I guess not."

"Well, you let me know next time you do. I'll fix something to go with it."

Mrs. Bayman's contributions to Tess's meals usually consisted of a sleeve of soda crackers or a can of green beans. "I'll do that. We need to catch up. It's just that I've been keeping pretty busy trying to get ready for Jaci to come home."

"Jaci? Now remind me...is she your oldest?"

"Well, the girls are twins, remember? But yes, Jaci came first."

"She coming home for the summer?"

"Yes. She thinks she needs a break from her job in the city."

"I wondered what was going on with all the vehicles in your drive. Thought maybe you were moving or something."

"Oh, you probably saw the plumber's truck." There'd only been one truck, but Kressie had a tendency to get confused. "I'm having some work done on the shed."

"The shed? Where your father used to live?"

"Father-in-law. But yes, Jaci's going to use the shed for the summer."

"Use it?"

"For an apartment," she explained.

Kressie wrinkled her nose. "While you're living in the house?"

"Yes." She edged her way to the back door, eager to extricate herself from this conversation.

"You two not getting along or something?"

Tess forced a laugh. "We get along fine. I just thought, since the apartment was available, that she'd enjoy having her own space."

Kressie shook her head and muttered something under her breath. Tess heard "if I had a daughter…" She couldn't make out the rest, but she could guess. Would the whole town think it was odd that Jaci wasn't staying in the house with her? And since when did she care so much what other people thought?

Even as she made a mental note to invite Kressie for a little picnic soon, she made excuses to the woman and stole into the house to freshen up a little so she could run by the garden center and pick up the flowers for the porch before the nursery closed. She'd go out to the park, too, and get in a walk before she came home. She could pick up trash along the way and get her exercise at the same time.

TESS HADN'T GONE a quarter of a mile when she saw a jogger coming down from the Clark Tower lane looking winded. Feeling guilty that she was merely walking, she lifted a hand in a wave. The jogger did the same, but as he drew closer, she realized it was J.W.

"Hey," he said, stopping a few feet from her. He removed the baseball cap he wore and wiped his face on the tail of his T-shirt. "No fair. You're not even breaking a sweat."

"You'll notice I'm not running either," she said with a wry smile.

"Well, it didn't take me long to figure out if a fellow is smart, he walks up, runs down." It sounded like he'd made the trek numerous times.

She shook her head. "Not me. Walk up. Walk down. No running, period." She held up the grocery sack she was using as a litter bag. "But I'm working. That's my excuse anyway."

Hands on hips, he smiled as if she'd said something genuinely funny. He motioned up the trail. "I planned on going another round. Would you mind if I walk up with you from here? I can help you pick up some trash."

"Sure. But…back up to the tower? That's a few miles."

"I usually run five or six. But I'm also usually on flatter ground than this. Back in Kansas City, I mean."

"I'm impressed." She wasn't just saying that either. He had the trim physique and muscular legs of a runner and only the slightest pooch of a belly, which, she suspected he was holding in on her account.

He pointed down to the parking lot. "You go on ahead… I'm going to run back to my truck and get my camera. I'll catch up with you. Thought I might get some nice shots once the sun gets a little lower."

"You don't have much confidence in my speed, do you?" she teased.

"If you don't walk too fast," he said quickly, looking sheepish.

She laughed. "I'm just kidding. But you won't have to work too hard to catch up. In fact"--she bent down to tie a shoelace that was coming loose--"I'll give you a head start."

That won her a grin. "Fine, but don't let me slow you down. If I don't catch up with you, well…it was good to see you again."

He went past her at a good clip and she watched him over her shoulder as she finished tying her shoe. She'd gotten the distinct impression he was showing off a little. *And* that he'd picked up his pace.

When he'd disappeared around a curve, she walked on but half as fast as she usually walked. She had nothing to prove to him, she justified to herself, and it would be nice to have the company up to the tower and back.

Not ten minutes after they'd parted, she heard the crunch of gravel behind her and turned to see him jogging her way. He steadied the camera around his neck with one hand and swung the other in a somewhat awkward gait as he ran to catch up.

"That was quick." She was genuinely impressed.

Again that sheepish look. "I may or may not have been showing off a little. And I may or may not be about to pass out right now."

She laughed. "I had a feeling. Men. Everything's a contest with you."

"Well, of course." He matched her slower gait and they walked for a minute, neither speaking, a cacophony of birdsong in the woods providing a delightful surround-sound experience.

They kept to the far side of the narrow lane in the shade of the thickening branches and were rewarded with puffs of an evening breeze at each turn in the trail. Every so often, Tess stopped to pick up a pop can or a gum wrapper someone had carelessly tossed out and put it in her garbage bag.

J.W. bent and scooped up a brown beer bottle half-buried in the leaves and added it to her bag.

"You don't have to do that."

He shrugged. "No biggie. I can get in my lunges this way." As if to demonstrate, he bent a knee and scooped up a fast-food wrapper and a beer can in one smooth motion.

She laughed and held the bag open for him. "There you go again, turning it into a competition. Just so you know, I'm not playing."

That earned her a laugh, but he continued to help her pick up trash as they walked.

When they rounded the last curve and Clark Tower came into view, J.W. stopped. Shading his eyes with one hand, he looked up toward the crenellated tower of the limestone landmark that stood twenty-five feet tall. "That view never gets old. Kind of startles me every time I see it."

He lifted his camera and removed the lens cap, then snapped shot after shot, moving from one side of the lane to the other.

Tess watched, loving the clicking sound the shutter made. "I guess I sort of take it for granted by now. I shouldn't though. It's pretty amazing."

"Not something you see every day in Iowa, that's for sure."

"Are your photos for work or just for fun?"

He hesitated as if it was a trick question. "For fun, I guess you'd say. I'd actually like to do some painting. The photos are just for reference."

"You paint? That's so cool."

He chuckled. "Well, you might want to wait until you've seen my work before you gush."

She flushed, embarrassed that he'd deemed her comment *gushing*. "What's your medium?"

"Usually watercolor. I've been wanting to try some plein aire painting." He cringed. "Until the weather goes south anyway."

"Better hurry." She looked up at the bright sun overhead, shielding her eyes with one hand. "This has been a perfect spring, but it'll be beastly hot before we know it."

"Yep, I remember. Not much different than Kansas City." They walked closer to the tower and he framed a couple of shots, then squatted on his haunches to shoot from a lower angle. "I remember we used to bring Wynn up here every spring, as soon as the weather was warm enough. We didn't dare come to the park without being prepared to hike up to the tower with him."

"I bet you see a lot of changes in Winterset since you lived here. We've always--" She cleared her throat, not sure where that plural *we* had come from, except that J.W. had used it referring to Char. She decided to follow suit. "We moved here just before the twins were born. And they're in college now. You don't really notice it when you're always here, but I suppose things have changed quite a bit in two decades."

"Maybe that's why the tower speaks to me. It hasn't changed since the day I first saw it. Unlike just about everything else. It feels strange to be back. A little unsettling to realize that all my memories here are wrapped around my childhood—or my marriage. And they're all gone now. Char, my parents. All but Wynn."

It startled Tess a little to hear him reminisce so fondly reminiscing about Char. Especially to hear him talk about them as a family––and a seemingly happy one. Char had always made it sound like the marriage to J.W. McRae was doomed from their wedding day––if not before.

Silence hung between them as she tried to remember if Wynn had ever mentioned an outing to Clark Tower with his father. She came up blank. But then, Wynn rarely spoke of his father. "Have you climbed to the lookout since you've been back?"

He shook his head. "I've been half afraid I'd find pay-per-view binoculars up there. Or, God forbid, an audio headset with step-by-step viewing instructions. I guess I'd rather remember it the way it was. Sorry. I don't mean to be such a party pooper."

She deposited her garbage bag into the receptacle near the small parking lot, then took his elbow and steered him toward the spiral stairway that wrapped around the outside of the round tower. "You can rest easy. Except for some regrettable graffiti, I don't think one stone has changed in this place since it was built. And unless something happened since last Tuesday, it's one hundred percent technology-free up there"—smiling, she held up her cell phone—"although I will say you can get great reception at the top." She let her arm drop when they reached the stone stairway and stepped aside to let him lead the way to the top.

J.W. stopped to look out from one of the arched windows on

the tower's first level, then climbed the short iron ladder to the lookout tower at the top of the monument.

Tess waited until he'd disappeared through the opening before she reached for a rung and pulled herself up. She'd just navigated the awkward top ladder rung when her cell phone jangled in her hip pocket. She checked the screen. "Sorry... Hang on. It's my daughter," she explained. "I'd better take this."

"Of course. No problem." He gave a little wave and turned his back, offering her the illusion of privacy.

She tapped Talk. "Hey sweetie. What's up?"

"Mom?" Jaci was crying. Sobbing.

CHAPTER ELEVEN

"Jaci? Baby, what's wrong?" Tess's heart constricted in her chest and she splayed her fingers against the rough, cool stone wall of the castle tower, bracing herself for whatever news was to come. "Honey, what's happened?" She looked up at J.W. who wore an expression of concern that no doubt echoed her own.

But he looked away as if he'd been caught eavesdropping.

Tess turned back to her phone, strolling a dozen paces to the opposite side of the tower landing from where J.W. stood. Trying to keep her hands from shaking, she spoke quietly into the phone. "Jaci, please. Calm down and tell me what's wrong. You're scaring me."

"I don't know... I just–– I think maybe it would be stupid to quit my job."

Tess deflated with relief. "So... You haven't quit yet?"

"No. How could I when––" A sob morphed into a giggle. "Mr. Thornton gave me a raise yesterday?"

"A raise? You have got to be kidding!" Tess didn't know whether to chew Jaci out for giving her such a scare, or laugh with relief. She opted for laughter.

"Not kidding. And now I don't know if I should quit after all because, I mean—"

"Listen, sweetie…" Tess cut in on what she knew could turn into a ten-minute monologue. She glanced over her shoulder at J.W., who was leaning out of one of the crenels in the tower, surveying the woodland vista below, obviously trying not to appear overly interested in her conversation. "Let me call you back later this evening, okay? I'm at the park right now. With a friend," she added, since she often talked on the phone to the girls while she worked at the park.

At that, J.W. turned and shot her a disconcerting smile. He leaned against the curve of the castle's stone wall and watched her.

His gaze unnerved her even as it stirred her. Her face heated and she turned her back to him again, trying to concentrate on her phone conversation––without much success.

"Yeah, I guess you can call tonight," Jaci said. "When do you think you'll be home?"

"Oh, in a couple hours. Before dark for sure."

An overlong pause, then, "Okay. Don't forget."

"Don't worry. And listen, you scare me like that again, I'll give *you* something you won't forget."

"Oooh, I'm real scared, Mom."

Tess laughed. "Talk to you later, honey. Love you." She clicked off the phone, still smiling and dying of curiosity about what had happened between Jaci and her boss…and what that meant for the summer. But she hadn't wanted to have the conversation with J.W. clearly listening in.

It struck her that Jaci's news probably meant she wouldn't be moving home after all. That disappointed her—and worried her, too—given how much she'd already committed to, financially, getting the place ready for Jaci. But she wouldn't let herself get too worked up about it until she had the details.

Knowing Jaci, everything could change again before she had

a chance to call back. She replaced her phone in her pocket and looked up to see J.W. still watching her.

"That makes me totally jealous, you know?"

"What's that?"

"The relationship you have with your daughter."

She frowned. "I'm sorry, J.W. I didn't think about––"

"No, no…" He held up a hand. "Don't apologize. It's a wonderful thing you have. It gives me hope."

"Yes!" she said with a little too much enthusiasm. "There is hope… I really do think Wynn will warm up to you, given a chance."

Ignoring that, he pointed in the direction of the pocket where she'd tucked her phone. "I couldn't help but overhear… except I couldn't tell if it was good news or bad."

She made a face. "A little of both, I think. My daughter got a raise––from 'the devil incarnate'." She chalked quote marks in the air, laughing. "According to Jaci anyway. That's the good news. The bad news is that it looks like she won't be coming home for the summer after all."

"Oh, I'm sorry."

"No… Don't be. It's actually a good thing for *her*. She's better off staying at this job. I should have encouraged her to see it through from the beginning." She paused. "It's just––a little lonely without the girls."

He grinned, a spark igniting in his green eyes. "I can't even imagine how much quieter it is *without* two teenage girls in the house."

She giggled. "That is just the reminder I needed to cheer me up."

"Any time," he said, obviously pleased he'd made her laugh. "So, the empty nest hasn't been all you were hoping for so far?"

"I'm…adjusting. I guess I never have been one of those moms who couldn't wait for the kids to leave home. Not after Dan died, for sure."

He nudged a loose stone with the toe of his shoe. "How long has it been?"

She looked away, frustrated that even after all this time, tears still threatened at that question. "Three years…in April. Heart attack. Totally unexpected."

"I'm sorry, Tess."

She was grateful he didn't try to offer platitudes like so many did when they discovered she was widowed. Still, she tried to redirect the subject. "I should be happy Jaci decided to stay at this job. She needs the money. I do wish she would have made this decision before I spent four hundred dollars fixing the plumbing."

He shot her an amused look. "You wouldn't have fixed it if she wasn't coming home?"

"Oh, no… We have a little shed in the backyard," she explained. "My father-in-law lived there. Before his death." *Well, of course before his death. He wouldn't have lived there after his death.* "Before Pop's death, I mean. He passed a year before Dan did." She was stuttering and rambling like an idiot.

"I got what you meant." His expression held wry humor—and made her grateful for his grace.

"Anyway, I'm fixing the place up for Jaci. Or I was. I guess I should look at the bright side. Maybe I'll get that 'she shed' I've always talked about now. I can probably get by with just patching the roof. But"—she quirked a brow, and turned to meet his gaze—"see the dollar signs scrolling in my eyes?"

Laughing, he raised an eyebrow. "I actually can! Seriously though, I don't think kids have a clue what life costs. Even a frugal life."

"True," she agreed but wondered how he knew anything about kids, given that he hadn't been around Wynn since he was in elementary school. "Still, I was excited about having Jaci home. Being twins, the girls were always kind of a package deal.

I was looking forward to getting some time with Jaci one-on-one."

"I always heard people talk about sibling rivalry, but with Wynn being an only, like me, that wasn't an issue." He winced. "Not that I was there for much of his childhood. I suppose he's the spoiled 'only' though. Like me."

"Wynn? Not in the least!" *Though he's been acting like a spoiled brat ever since you showed up.* She refrained from voicing that thought. The man seemed remorseful enough about the rift between him and Wynn without her adding salt to the wound. And Wynn *had* agreed for Rina to invite J.W. for supper. Maybe he was coming around after all.

"Good to hear." He gave a low huff. "I guess I'd know that if I'd spent any time with him."

"It'll be a pleasant surprise then. When you *do* get to know him."

"I guess so. Seems like a big *if* right now."

"I hope not, J.W. I'll be praying that tonight goes really well."

He gave a noncommittal nod, and an awkward silence rose between them.

Finally, Tess slid her phone from her pocket and checked the time. "I'd probably better start back down if I'm going to call Jaci back in an hour."

"Sure." He waved toward the ladder. "After you."

She motioned toward the camera hanging around his neck. "Didn't you want to get some photos from up here?"

He shrugged and squinted at the sun, which hovered atop the tree canopy. "I can come back sometime. The light isn't that great right now anyway. I'll walk down with you."

"You sure?"

He nodded, and she tucked her phone safely back into her jeans pocket before backing down the ladder.

She waited for him before starting down the winding stone stairs to ground level. Despite the sun that filtered through the trees, the limestone felt cool on her palms as she steadied herself for the final steps that fed onto the small parking lot.

They trudged in silence across the empty lot to the narrow road they'd climbed just a few minutes ago. Hearing a county truck coming up the lane, they stayed in single file, with Tess leading the way, until it passed. She recognized Bryan Avisen in the driver's seat and waved. "I hope he's up here to spray for mosquitoes," she said, more to herself than to make conversation.

"Were you getting bit?" J.W. asked, coming alongside her.

"Not yet, but I will be by the time we get back to the park. I left my bug spray in the car. Are they getting you?"

He shook his head. "Never do. Must not be sweet enough."

"Not fair! They never bothered Dan either. I read somewhere that it has to do with your blood type. I'm O negative."

"That explains it then. I'm A. I don't remember if it's negative or positive. Haven't given blood in a while."

"Dan had Type A blood too. Negative." Why did she keep making comparisons? When Dan was alive it had been somewhat of a defense mechanism to start talking about her husband anytime she felt another man was edging toward flirtation. But J.W. wasn't flirting, and even if he had been, it wouldn't have been inappropriate given that they were both single. So why did she feel so guilty?

She checked her phone. It was almost six. "Wait… I thought you were having dinner with Wynn and Rina tonight?"

"Yes. Wynn's making spaghetti. But they're not eating until later. I'm good. I'll still have time to run back to the hotel for a quick shower."

"Tell them hello for me."

"I will."

"And give that baby a squeeze."

"That's guaranteed."

She grinned, loving his enthusiasm for his little granddaughter. She shot up a silent prayer that Wynn would be kind to his father. And vice versa.

The rest of the way down to the park, they talked about the wildflowers and other flora that grew in the woods beyond. J.W. regaled her with stories from his childhood spent on the outskirts of Winterset. His late mother sounded like a character and J.W.'s obvious affection for the woman made her miss her own mother.

"So, have you always been J.W.? What do your initials stand for?"

A spark came to his eyes. "I could tell you, but then I'd have to...well, you know." He grinned smugly.

"I'll just ask Wynn then," she teased.

He chortled. "You can ask all you want. Wynn doesn't know."

"What? Your own son doesn't know your real name?"

"Let's just say J.W. *is* my real name. Haven't gone by anything else since I was knee-high to a June bug, as my mom used to say. Char only knew because the county clerk told us we had to put our full names on our marriage certificate. When Wynn came along, I made sure his birth certificate gave nothing away. And vengeful though she could be, I'm pretty sure Char took it to her grave." His tone was playful, but it seemed like he was telling the truth.

"Is it *that* bad?" she risked. "Your real name, I mean?"

"Doesn't matter. No one will ever know."

"Jedediah Wigginbotham."

"What?" He looked at her like she was speaking Greek.

"I bet that's what J.W. stands for."

"Huh-uh..." He rolled his eyes. "I'm not falling for that."

"Falling for what?" She attempted wide-eyed innocence.

"You know very well what. You just go ahead and make up a name that's worse than the real one. But don't think you'll coerce me into telling you the real one."

She shook her head. "It must *really* be awful."

"Save it," he deadpanned. "I'm not falling for your little tricks."

She snapped her fingers, laughing. "Well, you can't blame a girl for trying."

"Oh, you bet I can." He threw her a stern look, but she didn't miss the twinkle in his eyes.

They rounded a curve and the park came into sight. "Well, enjoy your time with Wynn."

"Wish me luck. And pray I can keep my mouth shut when I should."

She laughed, but stopped abruptly when she recognized in his countenance that he was dead serious. "Sorry. I *will* pray for that. You'll be fine. Wynn really is a great guy. He just needs to get to know you better."

J.W. looked doubtful. "That usually has the opposite effect in my experience."

"I must not know you well enough then." She felt bold saying the words, and yet, she wanted to leave him with some encouragement.

He lifted his chin and a slow smile came. But all he said was, "Thanks for the company." He waved and started toward his truck.

She waved back and headed for her own vehicle. She'd said enough, and she needed to rein in the emotions this man stirred in her.

CHAPTER TWELVE

*H*e hadn't been this nervous since the day Matt Hartner had called him into his office to inform him that he no longer had a job.

J.W. turned off the ignition and wiped damp palms on his jeans. There wasn't much that scared him, and there was something seriously wrong when a man was afraid of his own son.

It didn't help that Tess Everett kept hammering home what a great guy Wynn was.

Looking through the windshield he studied the house. To be honest, his memories of living here with Char and Wynn were indistinct. But he was pretty sure the house had been white then. Now it wore a coat of buttery yellow paint and crisp white trim.

He'd been too nervous the other night to notice any of it. But now he took in the neatly landscaped yard and the giant blue flowerpots with something pink spilling over the sides. They flanked the steps to the front door, which was painted the color of a robin's egg. He wondered if the landscaping was Wynn's handiwork. With a new baby, and a stay in the hospital, Rina surely wouldn't have had time to keep the yard looking so immaculate.

He grabbed the roses he'd picked up at the grocery store for Rina and climbed out of the truck. He wasn't sure what Wynn expected of this night, but he was determined to keep it low-key and unemotional. He'd already apologized to his son as much as he knew how without shifting some of the blame to Char. Lord knew she deserved at least some of it. But he wouldn't do that—tempting as it was.

Rina met him at the door with a sleeping Amelia in the crook of her arm. "You came!"

"Did you think I wouldn't?"

"I wasn't sure...what with the reception you got last time. But where are my manners? Come in! Are those for me?" She eyed the bouquet he gripped tighter than necessary.

He granted her a grin. "No, they're for Wynn... Of course, they're for you, silly." He hugged her briefly around the bundle in her arms.

"Here..." She thrust the baby at him. "Take her while I find a vase for these."

A door closed somewhere in the house and Wynn appeared from around the corner of the kitchen. "Hi... I thought I heard your truck. Here..." He motioned to a chair at the kitchen table. "Have a seat."

It was a good start. "You just getting home from work?"

"No, I'm on errand duty." He held up a six-pack of Diet Coke. "Hope diet is okay with you."

"I'm not picky." He *was*, actually, but he wasn't about to say so. Not tonight.

"I have iced tea if you'd rather," Rina hollered from behind the island that divided the living area from the kitchen.

"Tea would be great. Thanks."

"I see you already got put on baby duty." Wynn put a hand on his daughter's head.

"She's a pretty thing." J.W. rocked from side to side, willing the baby not to cry. "I don't want to hog her, if you want her."

He shook his head. "Don't worry. I'll get my turn around two a.m."

"She still not sleeping?"

"She's sleeping. Just not for very long stretches." Rina carried the flowers—which looked much more substantial in Rina's vase than they had in the grocery store wrappings—into the living area. "Look what your dad brought me." She cleared off a stack of magazines and set them on the coffee table.

"Nice." He gave J.W. a thoughtful look, as if the gesture surprised him.

"That expression, 'slept like a baby,' doesn't mean what everybody thinks it does," Rina said wryly.

"I'll have to remember that." J.W. scouted out a rocker in the living room, which looked nothing like what he remembered when he and Char had lived here. "Okay if I sit here with her?"

"Help yourself." Wynn kissed his wife. "You need a hand with dinner?"

"You already did the hard part, babe. But you can ice the glasses and pour drinks, if you don't mind. I hope you like spaghetti, J.W."

"I like anything I don't have to cook myself."

"Is everything okay at the hotel? They have a breakfast, right?" A fragrant steam rose from the pot Rina stirred.

"Yes, a pretty decent breakfast. Continental."

Wynn reached over Rina's shoulder to get drinking glasses out of the cupboard. "That taste okay?" He eyed the bubbling sauce.

"It's perfect. You make it better than I do."

"That's what you always say when I cook. Don't think I'm not onto your angle." He smiled and planted a kiss on top of her head before carrying the glasses over to the fridge.

J.W. felt a pang of jealousy at their easy, sweet way with each other. Had he and Char ever had that, even in their newlywed days? Surely they had, but he couldn't remember. Thankfully, the racket of the ice dispenser kept them all quiet for a minute.

After Wynn poured drinks and placed a glass at each place, Rina surveyed the table. "Well, I think we can eat. Let's put Amelia in the swing, J.W."

He looked down at the now sleeping baby in his lap. "I'll let you come and get her from me, if you don't mind. I don't want to get the blame for waking this child up." Too late, he realized that Wynn might think he was making a passive aggressive reference to the blame Wynn had placed on him.

But his son's face gave away nothing. While Wynn dished up plates of spaghetti with marinara sauce, and green beans and carrots, Rina propped the baby in a swing contraption that took up half the kitchen alcove.

J.W. sat where the iced tea glass was, and when Rina was seated across from J.W., Wynn sat beside her. He took her hand and cleared his throat. "Okay… Let's pray."

J.W. bowed his head, clasping his hands in his lap under the table.

"Thank you, Lord, for this food and for the hands that prepared it." Wynn cleared his throat again. "We ask that you'd bless…our guest…and guide our conversation this evening. In Jesus's name, amen."

J.W. mouthed an *amen*, half tickled at Wynn's label for him —*our guest*—and half surprised that his son had prayed with such…familiarity. Char had never been much for religion. At least not while he'd lived with her. Not that he had been a paragon of faith himself in those days. He suspected he had Rina to thank for any spiritual leanings his son had. Or maybe Tess Everett and her husband? Guilt mingled with relief. It should have been him, but he was glad someone had stepped up to the plate.

"Care for bread?"

"Oh. Yes, please." He took the basket of steaming French bread Wynn handed him and placed two buttered slices on his plate. "Everything looks delicious, you guys."

"It's nothing fancy." Rina dished some vegetables onto her plate and passed the bowl to J.W. "I thought about making lasagna, but a certain somebody didn't cooperate, so Wynn volunteered to cook."

"It's good," J.W. said over a bite. "Real good."

"Yeah…" Wynn shot Rina a sidewise smile. "I'm getting plenty of practice since the baby fusses every time Rina tries to set her down."

J.W. nodded toward the swing and smiled. "She looks pretty cooperative right now."

They followed his gaze to the baby now scrunched up in the well-padded contraption, her downy head tilted to one side, rosebud mouth slack in sleep.

"Oh, and I almost forgot, J.W." Rina bestowed a sweet smile on him. "Thank you for the gift for Amelia. I didn't find it until after you'd left the other night. That was so sweet of you. It'll be perfect in her nursery with Q-tips in it."

"That's what Tess said. She helped me pick it out. I wasn't sure what you needed." He wiped his mouth and took another slice of bread from the basket. "By the way, Tess sends her love. And a squeeze for Amelia."

"Oh, you saw Tess? Today?" Rina wore an expression he couldn't quite read.

"She was at the park when I went to run there this afternoon."

"Probably volunteering," Wynn said. "She's up there a lot. Doubt she will be as much once Jaci's back though."

"Oh…" J.W. hesitated, not sure he should say anything. But he felt sure Tess would tell Wynn and Rina anything before she'd tell him. "She actually got a call from her daughter while I was with her. Sounds like she's decided to stay...wherever she's working. I forget."

"Springfield? Oh dear." Rina's brow furrowed. "I hope Tess isn't too upset."

"Disappointed, I think. And maybe a little ticked—since she just spent four hundred dollars getting the apartment ready for the girl and everything."

"Oh, that's right. She said she had a guy coming to look at the roof, too."

J.W. nodded. "That wouldn't be cheap."

"No. But—" Rina's eyes lit up. "That means there's an apartment for rent, right?"

"Whoa..." He held up a hand and scooted his chair back a few inches. "She never said anything about renting the place out. The daughter could just as easily change her mind. Or the other one —I forget her name...the twin—might decide to come home."

"But if they don't, Tess's place would be perfect." Rina's brow knit. "I don't remember what it looked like inside, but Dan's dad lived there for a couple years, I think. He was pretty self-sufficient. I think it even has a little kitchen, and there's a place to park behind her garage so you'd have your own—"

"Rina." Wynn gave an almost imperceptible shake of his head.

J.W. cleared his throat. "I wouldn't want to impose like that. Tess has enough to worry about."

"But for all you know, it would really help her out." Rina scooted her chair back. "You have to at least ask!"

"Hey..." Wynn reached over to pat his wife's knee. "It's not your problem."

"What? I'm just trying to help. Tess needs some income and your dad needs a place to stay. It sounds like—"

"Rina... Give it a rest." His words were harsh, but his tone was gentler.

J.W.'s phone trilled from his pocket. He shot a sheepish grin at the two of them. "Saved by the bell."

But when he looked at the text message, his mouth went dry. *DeShawn.* Usually the Creve brothers waited for him to reach out to them. Especially DeShawn, who would call his older brothers before bothering J.W. Something must be up.

He pushed his chair back. "Sorry guys, but I need to respond to this."

Wynn waved him away. Rina started clearing the table, her mouth set in a firm line. Whether aimed at him or Wynn, J.W. wasn't sure.

He moved to the living room and opened DeShawn's text again.

Where are you? I need to talk to you.

J.W. didn't like the sound of this. He probably should call, but sometimes his phone calls with the kid ended up lasting for an hour. He texted back: *Is everything okay? I'm out of state visiting family.*

The message pinged that it had been delivered and almost immediately a reply came back. *This is pretty important. Can I call you?*

He tapped clumsily on the phone's glass. *Give me a minute and I'll call you.* The first guy to invent a keyboard for fat fingers would be his hero.

Stepping back into the kitchen, he could hear Rina on the phone in the little office off the kitchen. Wynn was trying to quiet a now awake and fussing Amelia.

"I apologize, but I need to make a phone call. Okay if I go out on the porch?"

"Sure."

"I'll try to make it quick, but this might take a while." He hated being so cryptic, but neither did he want to explain the whole thing with the Creve brothers to his son.

Wynn shot him a comical grimace. "No problem. Everything's kind of falling apart in here anyway."

J.W. picked up his mostly empty plate. He noticed Wynn's and Rina's plates were already cleared. "Let me at least clear the table."

"I've got it." Wynn took the dishes from him. "Don't worry about it."

J.W. nodded, but carried his water glass to the other side of the island, taking a couple of gulps before he set the glass in the sink. He nodded toward the office Rina's voice emanated from. "Tell your wife the spaghetti was great. In case I don't get to talk to her again."

"I'll tell her." Wynn lifted Amelia from the swing and propped her over one shoulder. The baby immediately gave a man-sized burp. Wynn and J.W. burst out laughing.

J.W. stepped toward Wynn and patted the baby's back. "I bet you feel better after that, huh, little pilgrim?"

Wynn looked at him with curiosity in his eyes.

"What?" J.W. patted the baby's back harder.

But his son just shook his head. "Nothing. I'll tell Rina for you."

"I do appreciate the meal. Maybe I can take you guys out sometime?"

"Yeah. Maybe."

It wasn't the worst response he could have gotten to his invitation. And thanks to the baby, they'd actually laughed together. Maybe the evening wasn't a complete bust.

"I'll try to make it quick," he said again. He stepped onto the back porch, dialing DeShawn as he went. The phone rang three times, then four. If DeShawn didn't pick up, he was not going to be happy.

He'd just about given up when he heard DeShawn's voice on the other end.

"Hey, J.W. Thanks for callin' back, man."

"What's up?"

"Where have you been?"

"What do you mean?"

He had let the bros into his life more than he should have, but he'd never made a habit of giving them his schedule or being at their beck and call. And he'd encouraged them not to use his phone number unless it was really important.

"I called you about a million times."

A bolt of alarm went through him. "What's going on, DeShawn?"

"I screwed up."

Uh-oh. "What'd you do?"

The boy let out a sigh that sounded as if it held the weight of the world. "I cut summer school and now they're saying I can't graduate with my class next spring. I'd have to take another semester of summer school to get my diploma."

"DeShawn! What did you go and do that for? You knew you were on thin ice already. When did you cut?"

"Um...which time?"

"Oh, man. What are you *doing*, bud? Come on." He paced the length of the porch before stopping to lean against the wooden railing, more frustrated than he likely should be over a kid who wasn't his own. But even though he'd let DeShawn hear the frustration in his voice, his foremost emotion right now was relief. In the scheme of things, this was small potatoes. "So, have you told your mom?"

"Yeah, but she's...not doing so hot."

"Is she using again?"

"I don't know. Probably. But either way she's not going to do anything about it. She'll just say I had it coming."

"Well, what do you *want* her to do?"

"Tell them to let me graduate. Tell them it's stupid to punish me for cutting one day. They can't really do that, can they?"

"Keep you from graduating? Of course they can." J.W.

thought for a minute. "So, why are you calling me? What do you expect *me* to do about it?"

"I don't know. Talk to 'em or something. Make them see reason. Or make my mom talk to them."

"You're the one that needed to see reason, son. And now it's too late. What was so important that you thought it was worth cutting?"

Silence.

"Listen, buddy, I'm out of town for a while. You're going to have to figure this one out on your own."

"What? You're just gonna let me lose a year of my life?" He blew out a curse word.

"Hey, you watch your mouth." It came out louder than he intended. He turned back toward the house and was chagrined to notice that a window was open to the kitchen. He lowered his voice and walked to the far end of the porch. "And quit exaggerating, DeShawn. You might have to take a couple of night classes or something to make it up but—"

"Yeah, well then I can't work. You know I've got to work."

"And again, son, you should have thought about that before you made such a boneheaded decision. We've talked about this, you know. Little decisions make a—"

"Yeah, yeah, I know…a big difference." His tone said he was not taking this seriously.

"Well, now you see it's true. Tough life lesson, but do you get it now?"

"I get that you just don't care."

J.W. clenched his fist. He was not going down this road with the kid. "You know better than that, DeShawn."

"Yeah, whatever." The phone went dead.

J.W. ground his teeth and gripped the porch railing. He took a couple of deep breaths, wishing he didn't have to go back inside. DeShawn seemed about as happy with him as his own son was. Great. He was two for two.

He waited until his heart quit beating a mile a minute then went inside.

Wynn was at the sink loading the dishwasher.

"Sorry about that. Need some help there?"

Wynn eyed him with what looked like suspicion. "Everything okay?"

"Yeah. Or at least it will be."

Wynn watched him, waiting.

"It's nothing. Just some issues back home. In Kansas City."

"You called him...*son?*" Wynn's voice rose on the word and he scrubbed at the spotless counter with a dishrag, not meeting J.W.'s gaze.

So he'd heard the conversation. "It's just...an expression."

"It sounded like more than that. Is there something you want to tell me?"

"Excuse me?" He wasn't sure what his son was getting at.

"Sorry." He waved a hand. "Not that it's any of my business, but I couldn't help but overhear. Do you have...another kid?"

"No, of course not." He pulled a chair out a ways from the table and leaned on the back for support. "You would have known about that, Wynn."

"Like I knew about all the other stuff in your life, you mean?"

He bit his bottom lip. "Okay. I had that coming."

Wynn waited without comment.

J.W. blew out a breath. "Who you heard me talking to was a kid I mentor. Kind of like Big Brothers. They match kids with—"

"I know what Big Brothers is. So...you have a Little?"

"In a manner of speaking."

"What's that supposed to mean?"

"Well, DeShawn isn't exactly little. He's seventeen. Almost eighteen"

Wynn looked like he'd been punched in the gut. "You're mentoring a teenager?"

J.W. nodded. He didn't dare say *three of them*. This wasn't the time.

"Well, that's rich."

"Rich?"

"Just funny you could find time for that. Given how busy you are and all."

That hurt. And wasn't wholly deserved. But he'd promised himself he would never cast the blame on Char, and he wasn't about to start now. "Yes, I am busy. And I'll be going now. I'll let myself out."

Rina appeared from around the corner, her phone still at her ear. "I'm just about done," she mouthed. "There's dessert." She disappeared again.

J.W. shook his head and took a step toward the front door. "I won't stay. Please tell Rina thank you again."

Wynn sputtered something unintelligible behind him.

But he kept walking. He wasn't going to hang around and take the abuse. This whole thing had been a bad idea.

CHAPTER THIRTEEN

.W. tossed his cell phone into the passenger seat and immediately it began to ring. That had to be a record for apologies.

But when he picked up the phone to answer, Rina was on the other end. Not sure what Wynn might have told her, he aimed for levity. "Don't tell me: I forgot my leftovers."

She laughed. "Well, I would have loved to send some spaghetti home with you, but that's not why I'm calling. Is everything okay?" She was fishing.

"Why wouldn't it be?" It was a disingenuous reply, but too late now.

"Wynn said you had...words."

He sighed, weighing his words. "I'm not going to get in the middle of things with you two, Rina. I'll let him tell you what he wants to."

"Was he rude to you?"

"I... I wouldn't say that." He thought for a minute, wanting to be honest. But ultimately, he opted to change the subject. "Dinner was delicious. Thank you. Sorry I had to eat and run."

"No problem. And hey, I may have some good news for you."

"Oh?"

"I just talked to Tess, and she might be interested in renting her place to you."

"Might be?"

"No, she is. She's pretty sure neither of the girls will be using the shed, and she's considering renting it out for the summer."

"Did she know it was me you were asking for?"

"Of course. I called her just a little bit ago. Why? You don't think she'd want to rent to you?"

"I have no idea. But I'm guessing she had someone of the female persuasion in mind, given that she lives alone. I don't want to impose."

"You wouldn't be. It's not like you'd be *in* her house. And it sounds like you'd be helping her out. She, um…she did say something about the roof needing work. Maybe you could offer to help with that. In exchange for rent, of course."

He huffed. What had Rina told Tess about him? Did they think he needed charity? He wished his daughter-in-law had listened to Wynn and given it a rest. "I'll think about it. Tell her not to hold it for me or anything. I…I don't know what I'm going to be doing yet." This issue with DeShawn had definitely put a wrench in his plans. Not that he had any real plans to begin with, but now he felt torn between DeShawn and Wynn. And they both felt a little like lost causes.

"J.W., please don't give up. On Wynn. You guys are just getting to know each other. It'd be a shame if you left now."

"I'm not so sure Wynn would agree." As much as he liked Rina, he didn't like feeling manipulated. "So, what did you tell Tess?"

"That I'd have you call her about the apartment. Either way. I'll text you her number." The line went dead.

Thanks a lot, Rina. Way to leave the ball in my court. Not that he didn't look forward to seeing Tess Everett again. But surely it would be awkward for her to have him living in her backyard.

And if she felt awkward about that, how awkward would it be when she found out he really wanted to ask her out?

∼

"No, honey, I'm not upset. I promise." Tess plopped down on the sofa, settling in for what would, no doubt, be a long, rather one-sided conversation. Not exactly how she wanted to start her weekend.

Jaci was second-guessing her decision to stay at the job. When would this daughter of hers ever learn to make a decision and stick with it?

"But you said you were glad I was coming home and—"

"And I *was* glad, honey. But this isn't about me. I think you made the right decision. To stay in Springfield. In fact, I think God was probably confirming your answer when you found out you were getting a raise."

"Probably. But that doesn't mean my boss is going to suddenly start being a nice guy."

"No, but it might make it a little easier to tolerate him."

Jaci giggled. "That's funny since he's about the least tolerant guy I've ever met."

Tess smiled into the phone.

"So, what are you going to do about the shed?"

"I don't have to do anything, do I?"

"But you said you already paid to fix the plumbing."

"I did."

"I'm sorry, Mom. I know that couldn't have been cheap."

"It was pretty steep. But I'll be okay. We were going to have to fix it up at some point anyway. Don't you worry about that. I think you're doing the right thing. And maybe I'll just embrace that she-shed I've always wanted."

"Mom. That doesn't even make sense. You've got the whole house to your—"

"I'm kidding! But I might actually rent it out. Rina mentioned...someone she knows that might be looking for a place." She hadn't yet told the girls about meeting Wynn's father. And she certainly hadn't decided whether or not she'd rent to him...if he even asked. Rina had called her about the possibility of J.W. renting her place Tuesday night. That was three days ago, and she hadn't seen or heard from him since. Even though she'd volunteered at the park every day she could, mostly hoping he'd show up for a run.

She felt her cheeks heat at the thought. If she didn't cool it, people were going to get suspicious of her sudden fit of volunteerism.

"You don't, do you?" Jaci's strident voice pulled her back to the present.

"Sorry, honey. What was that? I...lost you there for a minute." Not exactly a lie.

Her daughter gave a frustrated huff. "Never mind. I need to go anyway. A bunch of us are going out for pizza after work."

"Oh, that's nice. I'm glad you have friends there."

"Yeah. They're all right. Okay...I'll talk to you later, Mom."

"Okay, honey. Love you."

"Love you, too."

She hung up, feeling bad that she hadn't given Jaci her full attention. When had she become such a self-absorbed bore? If she didn't snap out of it, she was going to push away the people she cared about most in the world.

Stretching, she eased off the couch and went into the kitchen to finish the potato salad she'd been making when Jaci called. Maybe she'd take a bowl of it over to Kressie. She hadn't yet found an opportunity to reach out to her neighbor, and besides, she couldn't eat a whole recipe of the salad herself before it went bad.

She turned on the TV in the living room and turned up the volume, listening to the five o'clock news while she chopped celery and onions in the kitchen. The onion brought tears to her eyes and she hurried to finish so she could find a tissue before her mascara was a total loss. The doorbell rang while she was still washing her hands. She swiped at her cheeks with the back of her hand and hurried to answer.

J.W. McRae stood on her front porch.

"Hi there," she said through the screen door. She opened the door and started to let him in, then thought better of it, and stepped out onto the porch.

He studied her and his eyes widened. "Is everything okay?"

"Yes. Fine."

He pointed, his expression holding deep concern. "You look like you've been...crying."

"Oh!" She covered her eyes with her hands, laughing. "Just chopping onions. I'm surprised you don't smell them."

"Smells good, actually."

"Potato salad."

"Ah. Picnic or potluck?"

"Excuse me?"

"The only time my mom made potato salad was if we were having a picnic or if there was a potluck dinner at church."

"Well, I'm embarrassed to admit it, but I've just been hungry for it."

"No shame in that." He leaned against the pillar with one foot on the step below him. A pose that made him look all the more ruggedly handsome. "Rina said you might be thinking about renting out your apartment."

"Oh... Yes, she did talk to me about it. It's small though. Not much more than a garden shed, really. I mean, there's a bedroom and ensuite bath and what passes for a tiny kitchen, but Pop—Dan's father—took his meals with us...well, except for breakfast. I'm not sure it would be suitable for your—"

"Okay. No worries." He held his hands palms out. "I had a feeling Rina kind of ramrodded this through. My apologies. I just thought if you *were* looking for a renter, it might help us both out and—"

She dipped her head. "I didn't mean to make it sound like I wouldn't...consider you. I just...I haven't really thought it through."

"The kitchen is no problem for me, if that's your concern. If I could bring a microwave and a coffeemaker in, I'd be good. I'm not much of a cook."

"Oh, those things are already there. There's a small electric stovetop and even a full-size fridge. It's counter space that's missing."

He went slowly backward down two steps. "Well... Once you decide, just let me know." He opened his wallet, brought out a rumpled business card, and handed it to her. "My number is on here."

She suddenly felt a little desperate. As if she might never see him again if she let him walk away. She quickly skimmed the card of what looked like a high-end firm. *Hartner & Hartner.* Grasping for something to keep him on her doorstep, yet not sure why she even wanted to, she studied him. "Kansas City? You're headed back there?"

"Just for a few days. I have some loose ends to tie up."

"I figured you must. With work and everything." She held the card up. "I just hope you can spend more time here—because of Wynn...and the baby, of course." She was stammering like a schoolgirl.

"Listen, I..." He held up a hand, but before speaking, he looked at the ground, clearing his throat. "I want to be upfront with you. I don't work at Hartner & Hartner anymore." He touched the business card in her hand, then held up his cell phone. "The number is for my private cell phone. That's why I gave it to you. But... I don't want you to think I'm trying to pull something over on you."

"Why would I think that?"

"I just mean… I can see why you wouldn't want to rent to someone who's currently unemployed." He took another step back. "Not saying that's why you turned me down. I only meant—"

"I didn't turn you down. I said I wasn't sure I even wanted to rent the place at all. Yet. There's still a lot to do before it's really ready to be on the market."

He cocked his head. "Maybe I could help. I'm pretty handy with a hammer and I know my way around a toolbox."

"I don't know. I'd probably need to have—"

"I'm not saying I'd work off my rent, if that's what you mean. I understand you'd need to have the income. I was just meaning if—"

"No, that's *not* what I meant. The money, I mean. I was trying—"

"You don't owe me an explanation. I—"

"I was *trying* to say I just need more time. To get everything ready."

He chuckled and held up a hand. "Okay. Maybe this conversation would go better if we each let the other finish a sentence. Or two. My fault."

She was liking this man better by the minute. And yet the memory of Char's long-ago diatribes against her ex niggled at Tess. Still, it wasn't like she was inviting him to move into her house. This was no different than if he were considering renting the house next door, right? And if it didn't work out—if he turned out to be the renter from you-know-where—she could always ask him to leave. "You first," she said. "You were saying…?"

"Just that I can put any fears you have about the payments to rest. I could give you a deposit and three or four months in advance. Just so you wouldn't worry about whether I'm good for it or not."

She shook her head. "I'm not worried about that. And it

actually would help me decide if I knew you'd be willing to help with some of the repairs. I'd pay you, of course. And it'd be nice if I didn't even have to advertise the place."

"I'm sure we could figure something out that would work for both of us. The thing is, my house in Kansas City sold the first week it was on the market, so I don't really have a place to go back to. At least not for long." He looked so hopeful she couldn't bear to tell him no now.

And yet, Char's voice was strong in her head. J.W.'s ex-wife would have had a fit that Tess was even considering such a thing. "Let me think about it...just for a couple of days. I'll get back to you before Monday. Would that be okay?"

"Sure. Another night or two in a hotel won't *totally* bankrupt me." His grin told her he was being facetious, but if he was unemployed, there was probably good reason for his caution when it came to spending money. He was too young to retire.

"You said you had loose ends to tie up?"

"I need to get moved out of the house before the closing. And say some goodbyes and—"

"Of course. I'm sure you're leaving a lot of friends behind. That can't be easy."

He shrugged. "This trip is mostly about wrapping up things with the house. I still have some furniture and stuff to get into storage."

He seemed eager to change the subject from "goodbyes," and for the first time, it struck her that he might be breaking off a romantic relationship in Kansas City.

He looked at her as if he was waiting for an answer to a question she hadn't heard. "I'm sorry. What was that?"

"I said, if you do decide to rent to me, I'll need to know what furniture I should bring back."

"Oh. The shed is fully furnished. If you wanted to trade out for some of your furniture, that would be okay, but I don't have room to store anything extra. Right now I can't even park my car in the garage."

"No problem. Apparently my buyers want some of the furniture to stay anyway, and I can rent a storage unit for the rest if I need to."

"I'm not sure you understand how small the shed is. I'm not good with square footage, but maybe...twenty by thirty? Twenty-four by thirty? Plus the bathroom and a tiny closet. It's very small...like I said. Why don't I show it to you? You may not even be interested after you see it." Her laughter fell flat.

"Well, I can't be too picky at this point, but if you're willing to show it...and maybe point out what you'd like me to work on"—he held up a hand—"*if* you decide to rent it, I'd be glad to take a look."

She studied him. Char had made him out to be uncaring and a jerk, but not a monster...not abusive or dangerous. There was no reason not to take him around back and show him the shed. Maybe once he saw Pop's tiny space, he'd come to his senses, and then she wouldn't have a decision to make.

CHAPTER FOURTEEN

Gravel crunched beneath their shoes as Tess led him around the side of the house to her backyard. J.W. felt odd about having her show him the place when she was so obviously ambivalent about renting it—well, at least renting to *him*. But maybe if he saw the shed, he could put the idea out of his mind. Heaven knew she'd done everything she could to make it sound like a dump.

"There's a parking pad on the other side of the building. Entrance from the back alley," Tess said as they rounded the corner to the back of the house. She pointed to the tree-lined yard with a lawn that could have passed for NFL turf. "And excuse the grass. It needs mowing, but I just haven't gotten around to it this week."

"It's a beautiful yard. Looks like you have a green thumb for more than just the city park."

"Well, I try. I enjoy it, even if things sometimes get away from me. The yard was always more Dan's domain. But I've grown to really enjoy it."

He pointed to the lean-to built on the side of the detached garage. "And this is the shed?" It was a rhetorical question, given that the wide covered porch of the lean-to was obviously the entrance to a dwelling. A rather charming one from what he could see. A little girlie, maybe, with the pastel painted rockers and dainty pink and white flowers spilling over hanging planters on the porch, but he could picture himself sitting out here in the cool of evening, listening to the crickets and frogs.

"Yes. We fixed it up so Dan's dad could live with us after his health started to decline. It hasn't gotten much use since the girls went off to college." She reached up and slid a key from above the doorframe. She gave him a sheepish grin. "Not the sneakiest place to keep a key, I suppose. But this is Winterset, after all."

"I remember that about this town. Guess I didn't expect it to still be that way. Everybody trustworthy and looking out for each other."

"Well, maybe I'm a little too trusting."

He wondered if that comment was directed toward him personally, but chose to pretend otherwise. "It's a good quality. But I might find a...more original hiding place for the key. If I *were* to rent from you, of course."

She ignored his comment and unlocked the door, opening it wide and motioning for him to precede her.

He stepped inside the shed, not sure if the flowery whiff that met his nostrils was the scent of the house or Tess's perfume. The apartment was larger than he'd expected, sunnier too, given that the entire back wall had no windows, butted against the garage as it was. But windows were plentiful on the other three walls and even this late in the evening, they offered plenty of light.

The windowless wall held a built-in bookcase that reached from floor to ceiling. It was mostly empty but his beloved collection of books would be right at home here—well, half of his collection anyway. That would go a long way toward making it feel like home. However, if he'd thought the porch was "girlie," the apartment was full-on fairy princess. He reached for a ruffled pastel purple curtain. "You say your father-in-law lived here?"

Tess laughed. "The girls put their touches on it after Pop passed away. This place has hosted more slumber parties than I care to remember. And don't worry, I still have the curtains and bedding that were here before. Pale beige stripes. Very masculine." She winked.

"Whew." He gave a comical swipe of his brow. "That's good to hear. I know a truly manly man should be able to sleep with purple curtains and not feel threatened, but these are pretty danged purple."

"Not to mention ruffled. And the color is *lavender*, actually, but I get your point. I don't think Dan could have handled living out here either. And he was as manly as they come." Her laughter faded, and she bit her lip, turning away. "Um... The bedroom and bath are through that door, and the kitchen is back here."

He couldn't tell if she was embarrassed or emotional, so he said nothing, and followed her to the kitchenette. "This is nice."

With the purple curtains behind him and out of sight, he could appreciate the simplicity of the all-white kitchen. The refrigerator hummed away in the corner, and an old-fashioned apron sink big enough to bathe a dog in took up the rest of the back wall. Late afternoon sunlight canted beneath the porch's awning, casting dappled splotches on the cream-colored walls.

Tess turned to face him, seeming perfectly composed again. "It's small, but it works. Like I said, Pop cooked a full bacon-and-eggs-and-pancakes breakfast out here most mornings."

"Well, now you're making me hungry. I sure don't see anything wrong with the place." He smirked. "Well, nothing some manly curtains wouldn't fix anyway. I'm definitely interested."

A look akin to panic came to her eyes. "It still needs some

work. The roof should really be re-shingled—or at least patched —before I put it up for rent."

"That's probably something I could do. If you trust me. Let's take a look." He ducked through the door and walked far enough out into the yard that he could get a better angle on the roof.

Tess follow him, turning back to look up at the gray shake shingles. "I'd hate to ask that of you."

He walked to where the porch's awning was low enough to reach and stretched to lift a loose shingle. It came off in his hand. "Definitely needs some work." He tucked the shingle back underneath its neighbor. "I'd be happy to do it for half of whatever you've been quoted. Or take it out of my rent if that works better for you."

"I… Let me think it over." Her smile was apologetic.

But this was getting ridiculous. He took a deep breath. "Look, you seem to want to rent the place. I need a place to rent. Is there a problem I'm not seeing here? If you don't want to rent to *me*, fine. Just please say that, so I don't have to waste any more of my…of *either* of our time."

Her eyes went wide and he felt bad for pushing her, but there was obviously something she wasn't telling him. He tried to soften his voice. "Listen, you've got my number. I'll wait to hear from you."

He felt her eyes on him as he strode across the lawn and exited through the side gate, but she didn't utter a word. So he kept walking.

~

THE CICADAS TOOK up their nightly chorus, and from her rocking chair perch on the back porch, Tess shivered as a breeze swirled through the yard from the north. The hanging planters on the shed's porch twirled and creaked. She ought to go in and get a jacket, but she knew if she went inside, she'd get distracted by all that needed doing in the house and never get back out here.

This back porch was her best thinking spot. And she had plenty she needed to think through.

She couldn't remember when she'd been so torn about what should have been a simple decision. It would have been a whole lot easier if Jaci had just come home. Tess felt a little guilty that she'd even left open the option for her daughter in the first place. She'd let her loneliness cloud her judgment. Thankfully Jaci hadn't taken the easy way out, and Tess was genuinely glad Jaci had decided to stay on and work through the issues at her job. Jaci was growing up, and she'd made a good choice.

But now Tess had no out where renting the shed was concerned. If she sat down and made a pros and cons list, she felt certain the cons would outweigh the pros. Yes, she could use the money, and she'd like to see Wynn work out a relationship with his dad. And there was no reason for the shed to sit empty if Jaci wasn't coming home. But was it worth the risks?

She'd heard horror stories about tenants who moved in and wreaked havoc with their landlord's life. Or murdered them in their sleep and assumed their identities––oh wait, maybe that was only a movie she'd seen recently. Her shoulders shook with silent laughter. She was being ridiculous now.

Still, so much could go wrong. For all she knew, J.W. was a complete slob who would leave cigarette butts on the lawn, dirty dishes on the porch, and completely trash the shed. She thought of the tidy interior of his Dodge Ram that night he'd slept in the park. She was pretty sure he wasn't a slob. Or a smoker. He smelled too good for that. She inhaled deeply and could almost remember the woodsy citrus scent he'd worn the first time she met him that day in the cemetery.

But what if he had less than honorable motives toward Wynn. What if he needed money and intended to weasel his way into his son's life in order to take advantage of him financially? Or her? She was a prime target of that kind of scam––a widow living alone in a small town...

She loved Wynn like a son, but did she really know his father at all? She only knew what J.W. had chosen to reveal to her. And so far, there was a night-and-day difference between the J.W. McRae she'd spent time with and the picture Wynn and Char had both painted of him.

Memories of that criticism had been returning in annoying force. Granted, an ex-wife was probably the worst critic a man would ever have. Still, she didn't think Char had been lying. And Wynn seemed to hold the same opinion of his father, though until this month, he claimed he hadn't seen the man since he graduated from high school.

That did it. She was crazy to even be contemplating such a thing. With a low growl, she unfolded herself from the rocker and gathered up her coffee mug and the novel she hadn't read one word of.

Her landline phone was ringing when she walked in the back door. "Hello?"

"Hi, Tess. It's Rina. I was about to give up on you."

"Sorry, I was outside. It's such a pretty evening."

"I won't keep you then, but I was just wondering if J.W. had gotten hold of you about renting the shed yet?"

"He did."

"Oh, good. I was afraid he might be too shy to call you."

J.W. did not strike her as shy. "He came by the house today actually. I gave him the tour of Pop's shed. Such as it is."

"You did? That's great! So, he's renting from you?"

Tess cleared her throat. "I haven't decided yet."

"Oh? I hope I didn't steer him wrong."

"No. I just... There's still quite a bit of work that needs doing."

Tess wondered if he'd put Rina up to this phone call. For all she knew, J.W. was standing beside her this very moment, coaching her on what to say. The rebel in Tess wanted to say no right now and be done with this whole vexing decision.

But something kept prompting her in the other direction. She could always toss him out on his ear if things didn't work out. But she wasn't going to tell Rina that. Just in case J.W. *was* behind this phone call.

"I told him I'd give him my decision in a couple of days."

"That's great, Tess. I just really want Wynn and his dad to be on good terms. For their own sakes, of course. But for Amelia's too."

Tess felt her attitude softening, especially as she realized Rina wouldn't be saying these things if J.W. or Wynn were there with her. "I understand that," she told Rina. "It's so sad when families can't put their differences aside."

"I don't think Wynn even realizes how much it affects him… this bitterness he holds toward his dad. I don't want Amelia to ever have to see that."

"I'm sure Wynn won't let it become an issue where that sweet baby is concerned. You can already see what a great daddy he's going to be."

"Oh, I didn't mean that. He's a wonderful father. I couldn't ask for better. But Wynn's…attitude toward J.W. is not a good example. And he can't seem to help himself."

Tess couldn't deny that she'd seen what Rina was referring to. "I think if you just give them time, they'll work things out. After all, Wynn agreed to see him again, and J.W. did come when you reached out to him."

"Yes, but that didn't end very well. And if J.W. doesn't stick around, they'll never get a chance to know each other. And then I'm afraid it would be too easy to just let things go back to the way they've always been."

"Yes, I see your point." She didn't want to let Rina pressure her. But already the guilt nudged at Tess's conscience. Rentals were next to impossible to come by in this little town. Especially at the price she'd be asking. If she decided not to rent the apartment to J.W. he may not have a choice but to go back to Kanas City.

Maybe it wasn't Rina's manipulation that was getting to her. Maybe God was trying to tell her something. After all, if she could play even a small part in bringing about reconciliation between Wynn and his father, why would she withhold her offering? Especially when it was such a small thing, really...and one that would actually help her at the same time. "I'll definitely let J.W. know the minute I decide. He's at the top of my list."

As she hung up, a wry smile lifted one corner of her mouth. *He's at the top of my list.* She was pretty sure it was a Freudian slip, but exploring that thought right now would only complicate things.

CHAPTER FIFTEEN

J.W. placed the Gideon Bible back in the drawer and eased his legs over the side of the hotel bed. The now familiar aroma of Super 8 coffee wafted under his door. The lobby down the hall from his room seemed especially noisy this morning. Didn't people sleep in on Sunday morning around here? If he never stayed in another hotel room it would be too soon. And to think he was paying good money for the privilege.

He showered and dressed, thinking all the while about what he'd been reading in that Bible about going to someone you knew had something against you, and reconciling with them. It was good to have his "intuition" about making things right with Wynn confirmed this way. It shouldn't have surprised him that such a concept was so clearly laid out in the Bible, but somehow it did. He wondered if there was anything in there about what to do if that person spit in your face and sent you packing. He had a Bible somewhere at his house--gathering dust. He made a mental note to find it when he went home to pack up the house.

He needed to call the Realtor tonight and find out if he could buy some more time to get moved out. She'd told him the couple was paying cash and they were pushing for a July 8 closing date. It was crazy—a little over two weeks away—and that meant he had to be moved out before then. Not that he had a ton of stuff, but what was he going to do with everything until he found some place to live? But he did need to get out of this hotel soon. Another week here and he'd have eaten up half a mortgage payment.

He'd given up on Tess Everett renting her shed to him. It had been obvious that she wasn't interested. The place was small, but then, he didn't need anything big. Maybe he should be thinking about Des Moines. It was only forty miles away, and the job market would be far more promising there.

But he knew himself well enough to realize that if he didn't stay here in Winterset it would be too easy to avoid Wynn.

Again, as they had too often these past few days, the faces of the boys back in Kansas City—the Creve brothers—plastered themselves on his brain.

He shook the images off. He'd have to deal with the boys later. He wouldn't just move away without telling them, of course. And he'd try to stay in touch, help out as much as he could from afar. They'd be hurt—or ticked off was more like it. Especially DeShawn, the youngest.

DeShawn had developed a good-sized chip on his shoulder over the past few months. J.W. suspected it had something to do with the fact that his mom claimed she didn't even know who his father was. And though DeShawn sometimes tried to pretend he shared a father with his older brothers, it was apparent by the kid's dusky complexion, dark eyes, and kinky hair that his father was not the same man who'd given Michael and Patrick their flaxen hair and blue eyes.

Lesa Creve had said some thing that made him think she did know DeShawn's father. That she'd named the boy after him, probably hoping to keep the man around. But none of the bros remembered ever having a man in their house—at least not one who stuck around for more than a one-night stand.

They'd desperately needed a male role model in their lives. Still did. But what good would it do to insert himself into the lives of someone else's kids if he lost a relationship with his own son?

No, if he was ever going to make amends with Wynn, he needed to get serious about finding a place here in Winterset. The lady at the Chamber of Commerce had said it was a buyer's market here right now. That, along with the words he'd "just happened" to turn to in the Gideon Bible this morning, gave him a little more confidence about uprooting and committing to something semi-permanent in Winterset. Of course, if it was a buyer's market, he might lose his shirt on a house if he decided to turn around and sell it this time next year. But look how quickly he'd sold his Kansas City residence.

Where was his faith? There'd been a day he would have embraced the idea that if God meant for him to buy a house, God would also help him sell it again when and if the time came. But it wasn't lost on him that his dusty Bible on the night-stand at home was a metaphor for what had happened to his faith. Faith needed feeding and watering, and he'd neglected his for too long.

He turned out the lights and went out to the lobby for breakfast, avoiding the table occupied by a family with six kids who ran amok through the tiny breakfast area, jelly donuts in hand.

He ate quickly then got up to pour himself a second cup of coffee to take back to his room. Mid-pour, he heard a familiar voice behind him.

"Hey. Can we talk?"

He turned to see Wynn staring at him, eyes narrowed.

"Wynn. What are you doing here? Do you want a cup of coffee?" He nodded toward the unruly gaggle of children.

"Maybe we could take it back to my room...talk where it's quieter?"

Wynn nodded and waited while J.W. poured a fresh cup of the weak brew. "How do you take it?"

"Just black, thanks."

J.W. fit a plastic lid on the foam cup and handed it to Wynn, then led the way back down the hallway to his room. At the door, he wordlessly handed Wynn his coffee while he fished his room key out of his wallet and opened the door.

The room was as rumpled as he'd left it, and he moved his duffle bag off the small desk chair in the corner and offered the seat to his son. Wynn took it, perching on the edge, his eyes darting from the window behind him to the door as if he was scoping out an escape route.

J.W. opened the heavy drapes to the prairie view outside before sitting on the edge of the bed. "How did you know I was still here?"

Wynn gave a mirthless laugh. "I do talk to my wife occasionally. Besides this is Winterset. Fifty people have told me they saw you in town."

He forced a smile. "Should've known."

"So, why *are* you sticking around Winterset?"

"Wynn..." He looked at the floor. He'd been thinking for three days––and even before that––what he could say to his son that might begin to heal the wounds that were obviously still festering after almost two decades. And now, complicated by Wynn's accidental discovery that J.W. had taken surrogate sons into his life in the form of the Creve brothers.

Now, like always, he drew a big blank for an answer. He supposed the truth was a good place to start. But what *was* the truth? He knew some of it. Some he simply couldn't tell Wynn. Not without throwing Char under the bus. "Son, I––"

Wynn visibly recoiled, and J.W. suspected it was because he'd called him "son." The endearment Wynn had overheard when

J.W. talked to DeShawn the other night. How ironic that all three of the Creve Brothers ate it up when J.W. used the term with them.

He pushed aside the rejection and continued. "I'm here because I want to make things right between us."

"Yeah, so you said."

"Let me start over." He held up a hand. "Please, hear me out. I know I failed miserably as a father. I know that. I ignored you too much when your mom and I were still together, and I ignored you for too long after we separated. And even when I *was* there, I was…distracted. I know that. Your mom and I had a lot of issues—"

He stopped himself. He was not going to blame this on Char. If he had to bite his tongue *off*, he wouldn't lay the blame on a dead woman, guilty or not. He regrouped his thoughts. "You said the other night that you were trying to learn how to be a dad. I'm so sorry I wasn't the example you needed––I was…the *opposite*. I'll regret that for the rest of my life, Wynn. But I want to do whatever I can to make up for––"

"And you think hanging out in Winterset is a good start?"

He huffed a humorless laugh. "I was trying to come up with a plan." He looked at the floor again. "Not having much luck, if you want to know the truth."

"So, you've been here all this time?"

"I actually went home that first night after you threw me out and—"

"I never threw you out."

He held up a hand. "Sorry. That's just how it felt."

Wynn's knee bounced up and down as if it had a life of its own. "It caught me off guard. Rina didn't tell me she'd invited you to stay."

"I know. I'm sorry about that."

"Forget it. It wasn't your fault." He put a hand on his knee as if to stop its nervous bouncing. "So, you came back? From Kansas City?"

"I never actually got as far as Kansas City. I should have said I went *partway* home. I came back. Listen, I don't know what you believe about God..."

Wynn shrugged, looking as if he didn't see what that had to do with anything.

J.W. tried again. "I felt like I was supposed to come back and stay until things are"--he grappled for a word--"*mended* between us."

"Yeah, well...you might want to start looking for a permanent residence then." There was obvious sarcasm in his tone.

J.W. heard it, but chose to take him literally. "You don't know of a place, do you? Wouldn't have to be a house. An apartment would be okay."

"What? You're serious? You're going to commute? To Kansas City?"

"No." He heaved a sigh. May as well put all his cards on the table. "I got laid off, Wynn. I don't have a job to go back to in KC."

"Whoa." Wynn's cheeks puffed up, and he blew out a slow breath. "I'm sorry. I didn't know."

"I haven't told anyone yet." That was the really sad thing. Work had been his life. There was no one to tell because his only friends--if he even could call them that--already knew about his layoff because they'd been there at Hartner and Hartner when it happened.

Wynn regarded him. "So, what are you going to do about a job?"

"I don't know yet. I got a decent severance package and I'll be okay...financially..."

"You're not retiring, are you?"

He shrugged. He didn't have an answer. He was adrift.

"Well, there's not much around here. Not in advertising anyway."

"I know. I may have to go to Des Moines. Or do something different."

"Like what?"

"I wish I knew."

Wynn studied the patterned carpet. "And what about the guy in Kansas City. Your…little brother?"

"I'm not sure. I've got a lot to figure out. But listen, Wynn…" He swallowed hard. "About DeShawn. I—"

"Hey, you don't owe me any explanations." Wynn held up a hand like a stop sign. "I get it."

"No, I don't think you do. And maybe I don't *owe* you an explanation, but if you're willing, I'd like to tell you about them."

"Them?"

"Yes. DeShawn has two older brothers. I actually started out with Patrick as my 'little,' and Michael and DeShawn just kind of fell into place. But Wynn… They are *not* my sons. Nothing like that. I just want you to know that. They were a work project that just kind of…kept going."

"Well, then I guess I wish *I* had been a 'work project.'" He drew air quotes as thick as the sarcasm in his voice.

J.W. bowed his head, struggling for the right words. Already he felt like a traitor to the Creve brothers for having relegated them as *projects*. It was all impossible to explain without bad-mouthing Char.

Finally, he looked up and waited for his son to look him in the eye. "I'm sorry, Wynn. I don't know how many ways I can say it. I screwed up and I want to make up for it if I possibly can."

Wynn waved him off like it was no big deal. "Forget about it." But his eyes said otherwise.

"I don't deserve it, but I'd like a chance to start over with you."

"I'm a little old for starting over."

"Okay, then...starting from where we are. I'm not looking for anything more than...friendship. And a chance to get to know my only granddaughter."

"Only. Your littles—the *brothers*—don't have any kids?"

"No. Not even married. But when they do, Wynn, those won't be my grandkids. It's not like that. Our relationship."

He seemed to ponder that, then gave another huff. "Well, as long as you're in town, you may as well have supper with us next week. Rina's making tacos. We do a Tuesday Tacos night. Or anyway, we did before the baby got here. That's why I came. To invite you."

J.W. looked up quickly, trying to gauge the enthusiasm in Wynn's invitation. Realization dawned and he chuckled. "Ah, so your wife made you come, huh?"

Wynn replied with a roll of his eyes.

"Regardless, I appreciate that. And I'd be happy to accept. Thank you, son."

Wynn's jaw immediately tensed, his eyes darkening. J.W. kicked himself for using the word again. It was a habit formed of his relationship with the Creve brothers, but also from how he thought of Wynn. *His son.* But J.W. didn't blame him for resenting it. He hadn't earned that right.

"What time shall I come?" he said, changing the subject. "And what can I bring?"

"You don't need to bring anything. As for what time we eat... with this baby, who knows? Did I mess up *your* schedule this bad? When I was a baby, I mean?"

J.W. started to laugh, but quickly sobered when he realized Wynn wasn't laughing. "Surely that sweet little girl isn't causing any trouble? Does she have her days and nights mixed up or something?"

Wynn shook his head. "Just when we think we have her on a schedule, she pulls an all-nighter. I'm about to pull my hair out.

Rina too. But at least she doesn't have to get up and be in to work by eight a.m."

"Well, I'm no expert, but the baby's only a couple weeks old. I think it takes a while before they get…acclimated." The truth was, he didn't remember whether a baby had messed up his schedule or not. If he had to guess about those days, he'd probably stayed late at the office, waiting until the baby was in bed to come home…maybe until Char was in bed, too. He decided candor was a good first step in winning back his son's trust. "I honestly don't remember much about when you were a baby. Knowing me back then, I probably let your mom handle most of it. She had certain ways she liked to do things and I pretty much tried to stay out of her way."

Wynn seemed to be listening, not withdrawing, so J.W. risked more. "Rina is lucky––blessed––to have you. I wish I'd helped your mom half as much as I see you helping Rina. Between the two of you, you'll get through these first months. It's tough. I wish…I wish I'd understood how hard it was. But I can tell you're a good father already, Wynn. I'm glad you *didn't* follow in my footsteps." Saying the words aloud hurt more than he'd thought they could. Right now he would give just about anything to be where Wynn was in life––to have a fresh start at being a father to his son.

He ran a hand over his face. Being a husband to Char had not been an easy thing, but that wasn't Wynn's fault, and he wished to God that somebody had opened his eyes to that truth before it was too late to go back and do something about it.

Wynn put muscled forearms on the narrow arms of the chair and levered himself out of it. "Okay, well… I'd better get back. Rina's going to think I murdered you or something."

J.W. laughed softly, but he was deeply curious about the conversation they'd had that resulted in Wynn coming here looking for him. "Glad you didn't feel the need. And I'll try to behave at supper. What time did you say?"

"Oh." Wynn pulled his phone from his jeans pocket and checked the time. "I guess I never said. Do you mind if we play it by ear? Probably around seven, but it'll depend on the baby. How about if I give you a call Monday or Tuesday? See if we have a schedule by then." He gave a crooked half-smile.

J.W.'s heart went out to him. "Sure. And I'll be glad to help Rina in the kitchen if that would help."

"Or maybe you can entertain Amelia while I help Rina?"

"Even better."

Wynn gave an awkward wave, clearly not wanting to shake his hand—or God forbid, hug him—and backed out of the room. J.W. followed him to the door, but he could only think of one thing as he watched his son trudge down the corridor: It was a start. Rocky and messy and uncertain. But it was a start. And God bless Rina.

CHAPTER SIXTEEN

Hey, it's Shawn. You know what to do.

Shawn? Where had that come from? J.W. huffed, punched End, and poked his phone into his back pocket as he pushed open the door and strode across the hotel parking lot. Calls to DeShawn's phone had been going straight to voicemail since Friday night. And the kid had a new recording. And now this "Shawn" business? He'd never gone by a nickname. If he hadn't recognized the distinctive husky voice, he would have wondered if he'd called the wrong number.

He hoped DeShawn was just working an extra shift and had his phone turned off, but he suspected the kid was ignoring his calls on purpose.

The parking lot was almost empty on a Sunday morning, and J.W. headed for the park with the newly purchased art supplies stacked in the passenger seat beside him. He wished he'd brought an easel and his good brushes with him from Kansas City. He'd have to get them out of storage whenever he next made the trip back.

Next weekend probably—maybe sooner if he couldn't get hold of DeShawn. He hadn't called the other Creve brothers yet.

He didn't want to alarm them if there was nothing wrong. Michael and Patrick had enough on their plates without having to raise their little brother.

The training courses J.W. had taken early on with the mentor program had been firm that he wasn't supposed to take on a guardian role except temporarily, during the actual time he spent with the boys. But that was easier said than done.

He parked in his usual spot, scouring the lot for a certain silver Mariner. Of course, it was Sunday morning. She was probably still in church.

Tess. Even her name was beautiful. Part of him felt guilty even showing up where she might be when he'd promised to be patient about her decision whether to rent her shed to him. But it wouldn't hurt for his presence to be a subtle reminder either.

He climbed down from the truck and went around to the passenger side to unload the watercolor pad and a cardboard box he'd scavenged from the trash in the hotel's breakfast nook to hold his paints and brushes. He looped a folding director's chair over one shoulder and carried everything over to the restrooms. At the sink in the men's room, he filled a water bottle. Once he got down to the bridge, he'd divide the water between two clean drinking glasses he'd borrowed from the hotel.

The tray of watercolors he'd bought was barely a notch above the quality of the kids' palettes they used in elementary schools, but it had thirty-six colors. It would do the trick for a few quick sketches.

He didn't even know if he could paint any more. Oh, he'd dabbled off and on through the years, but how long had it been since he'd put any serious effort into his painting? Probably since right after he and Char separated and he'd had time to explore his passion for the medium for the first time since college art courses. He'd been good back then though, at least according to his professors.

He tucked the sketch pad into the box with the other supplies, propped it on one shoulder, and strode down to the bank near the bridge, the empty glasses rattling in opposite corners of the cardboard box.

The Cutler-Donahoe Bridge, probably the most famous of Madison County's covered bridges, stood sentinel over the park. The bridge owed its hyphenated name to the fact that two families had claimed naming rights to it since they lived nearby so the county gave it both names. Now it didn't matter, since the bridge had been moved into town when J.W. was a kid. Of course, back then the bridges hadn't been the nationally known tourist attraction they were now. If the covered bridges had been immortalized on canvas ten thousand times, they'd been captured on film a hundred thousand. That was thanks to the apparently famous novel, *The Bridges of Madison County*, about a National Geographic photographer—or more likely thanks to the Clint Eastwood movie that followed the novel.

J.W. had watched the movie at the hotel a couple of nights ago. He was not impressed and hoped Tess hadn't been comparing him with the Clint Eastwood character when she teased him about it the other day. He'd made plenty of mistakes in his life, but taking another man's wife was never one of them.

He chose a spot in the shade of a maple tree at the corner of the structure's mouth near a historical marker that told the bridge's story. He set down the box and opened his canvas chair, unfolding its small arm table. He already felt like a cliché—one of the many attempting to capture the venerable structures with brush or pen. Yet the covered bridges were worthy subjects. Each of the six bridges had its own personality, its own architecture, its own history. Cutler-Donahoe just happened to be the most convenient today.

He folded back the cover of the art pad, then poured water from the bottle into each of the glasses perched precariously on the chair's narrow arm table.

"How'd you know I was thirsty?"

He heard the smile in Tess Everett's voice before he turned and saw her walking his way looking at the glass in his hand. "I'm not sure you'd want to drink this." He plopped a paintbrush into one glass and held it up as if toasting her. "Watercolor. Cheers."

"A man of many talents! May I look?" She nodded toward the art pad.

He held up the blank page.

"Don't tell me... Polar bear in a snow storm?"

"Nothing that ambitious. Cotton ball on a white sheet."

She tilted her head. "Of course! I see it now!" Her laughter had a strange—and rather wonderful—effect on him.

"I figured you'd be in church this morning."

"I go to the early service." She lowered her voice to a stage whisper. "Don't tell anyone, but I skipped out on Sunday school."

He imitated her furtive glance. "Don't tell anyone, but I skipped church and Sunday school altogether."

"Shame on you."

"I do want to find a church, but I didn't exactly bring the wardrobe for it."

She took in the cargo pants and faded Royals T-shirt he wore. "I don't know... Churches around here are pretty casual. You probably wouldn't get kicked out."

"Just as I am...without one plea, huh?"

"Ah, a good Baptist."

"Actually, non-denominational these days, but yes, First Baptist is where I rid my soul of one dark blot."

Her smile said she recognized the hymn lyrics he was quoting. "Good people there."

"Yes, but no doubt somebody's taken over my spot in the pew by now. Left side, fourth row, outside aisle."

When her lilting laughter faded, she turned serious. "I'm glad

I ran into you. I was going to call. If you'd like to rent my apartment, it's yours."

"Really? That was quick."

"Well, not really. I appreciate your patience. And I'm sorry you had to pay for the hotel."

"Eight nights. Eight hundred dollars…soon to be nine." He shrugged. "I'll survive. Did Wynn tell you he hunted me down at the hotel this morning?"

"No. But that's good. Not the money… About Wynn, I mean." It came out more like a question.

"I think his mission was more to ream me out for every bad thing I ever did"––he shrugged—"but at least we talked. That's a start, I guess. And he invited me to their house for supper. I think that part was Rina's doing."

"Still, that's a *good* start." She clapped her hands together. "That's wonderful, J.W.!"

"Well, I don't think it's anything to write home about. But yes, it's a start, for sure." He eyed her. "So, the shed…how soon could I move in?"

"Tonight if you want."

"Really? You just saved me a hundred bucks…well, minus whatever a night in your shed comes to."

A gleam came to her eyes. "I did take the lavender curtains down yesterday. Everything is tailored, buttoned-down beige and blue. Very manly. Not a ruffle in sight."

Laughing, he tipped an imaginary hat her way. "Much obliged. Seriously, though, this is good news. Do I need to sign a contract? Get a key from you?"

"We can just rent month to month if you're okay with that. I haven't come up with a contract yet, but I can probably find something online. I'll be home around two. You can come by and get a key any time after that. I'll show you where things are, and we can talk about what furniture you want me to put in storage."

"Sounds good. It'll probably be about one when I get there... whenever I check out of the hotel. I don't have much to move right now, not until I get some stuff out of storage in Kansas City in a week or two."

"I'm sure it will all work out. Now I'd better let you get back to painting. You've got a great start there." She winked in the direction of his blank art pad.

He shot her a wry smile. "To be honest, I haven't held a proper brush in my hands for a dozen years. Everything at work was digital."

"Is this painting for a new job?"

"Oh, no. I'm still quite unemployed. Well, except for doing some consulting work." Never mind that no one from Hartner & Hartner had reached out since the day he'd practically hung up on Matt's assistant. "Don't worry, I'm not broke." He'd actually been encouraged when he crunched the numbers. The millions he'd anticipated when he'd retired with Hartner & Hartner wouldn't happen now unless he got back in the rat race. He'd expected to work at least six more years, retire at sixty. That was his grand plan. Still, his 401K was in decent shape, and between the severance package and the sale of his house, he wouldn't have to withdraw from his retirement fund for many years. Ironic that finances had been such a huge issue between him and Char, and now, he could have kept her in the luxury to which she was accustomed.

"You don't owe me any explanations. As long as you pay your rent." But she looked skeptical.

And he didn't blame her. "Like I told you when we first discussed it, I'll be glad to pay you in advance, plus a deposit, of course. I don't blame you for being worried about how I'll pay my bills."

"I never said I was worried about that."

"No, you're right, you didn't. But I would understand if you were." He took a breath and plunged in. "And Tess, *something's* bothering you about this whole thing. Do you want to talk about it?"

"I just…didn't know if you were looking for work here in town or…"

He shook his head. "No, I'm not going to let you off that easy. I'm not a man who likes to play games. I'd just as soon get things out in the open." He waited, watching her eyes change like a stormy ocean.

Finally she met his gaze. "Okay, fine. I'll tell you what's bothering me. And I hope you've got a while because there seems to be an ever-growing list."

"Whoa. That—"

She held up a hand, her eyes ablaze. "Do you want to hear it or not?"

He nodded, concealing the grin that wanted to come, but he didn't dare argue.

"First of all, right or wrong, J.W., I had some preconceived ideas about you based on Char's…comments about you."

"Nice of you to soften that."

She ignored him. "You aren't at all who she described, and I'll be honest, I'm struggling to reconcile that. I'm not sure who to believe."

"Hey, I haven't said *anything* about me."

"I'm not talking about who you *say* you are. I'm talking about who I see you to be. And it's *not* the man Char talked about."

"Could you give me a little credit for having grown up slightly over the last decade or so?"

She nodded. "Okay. I'll try."

"So…next?"

"I'm a widow, J.W. I'm still trying to figure out how to navigate these waters. I sometimes feel…vulnerable." She held up a hand. "That's not your problem. I know that. But I just need to know you acknowledge that."

He gave a single nod. "So acknowledged."

"And okay, as long as you're forcing complete honesty…" A glimmer came to her eyes. "I like you. And I'm not the kind of woman who dates the man living in the shed in her backyard. So there. You happy?"

"No. I'm *not* happy. Not at all. Because I like you, too. And if I thought moving in to your rental meant that we couldn't be friends, well…"

"I'm sorry then…"

For a minute, he thought she was going to renege on her offer. But after a few seconds he realized she was fighting tears. He wondered what that was about, but decided against asking, since she seemed to be trying mighty hard to keep it together.

She bent to yank a couple of weeds from the grass at her feet. When she straightened, her steady voice belied the emotion her face had worn only moments ago. "Okay. As long as we got that out in the open. I'll see you this afternoon."

"Wait. So, let me get this straight. You're agreeing that we *can* be friends, right? Even if I rent your shed?"

She nodded. "Friends."

"But not more than that? Even if things…happen while I'm living there? Turn into more…?"

"Let's just leave it at friends for now, okay?"

He gave a reluctant nod. She hadn't really answered the question, but neither had she said a flat-out no. He could live with that.

WHAT HAD she gotten herself into? Tess dumped out a half-empty Coke can on the ground, stuffed it into her garbage bag, and looked back to where J.W. sat painting in the park.

How could she have been so insensitive? The poor guy had lost his job, was probably trying to keep his dignity while still being frugal, and she'd been fighting him all the way. Giving him grief about sleeping in the park and taking her sweet time to make a decision about renting the shed to him. Meanwhile he was spending money he probably didn't have on a hotel.

She blew out a sigh. Sometimes she could be so dense.

She moved to a flowerbed that afforded her a concealed view of J.W. and knelt to pull a few tiny weeds while she watched him in the distance. He looked so at ease, his shoulders relaxed, his brush dipping into the palette, then hovering over the sketchpad like a hummingbird.

Her phone dinged from her pocket, and she jumped, feeling as if she'd been caught spying. Laughing under her breath, she rose and tucked the trash bag under one arm before pulling the phone out to read a text from Jodi.

Is Jaci okay?

She tapped out a one-word reply, even as alarm streaked through her. *Why?*

Her daughters seemed to get a thrill out of scaring their mother to death with their cryptic messages. She was learning not to plan funerals until she had all the facts...or at least not to let the twins know they'd made her blood pressure spike.

Jodi's reply dinged back. *She hates her job. Freaking out a little.*

Tess sighed and typed back, *I'll call her. How are YOU?*

I'm good. On break at work. I like MY job. ☺ Talk to you soon. Just wanted you to know Jace is freaked.

They sent simultaneous *I love yous* and Tess switched to phone mode and dialed Jaci.

She picked up on the first ring. "Hi, Mom."

"Hey you. How's it going?"

"Jodi called you, didn't she?"

"She texted. Said you're freaking out. What's going on?"

"What do you think? My stupid job. I seriously don't know if I can take it."

"I thought things were better."

"The money's better. The boss is still a royal jerk."

"Well, at least he's royal."

"Ha ha. It's not funny, Mom."

"I'm not laughing, honey. I'm sorry this job has been so hard."

"Hard doesn't even begin to describe it. I'm serious. I might just come home."

Tess bit her lip. "Well, if you do, you'll be staying in your bedroom. Here in the house."

"Why? Why not Pop's shed?"

"I've rented it out."

"What? Already? Mom, why'd you do that?"

"I told you I was thinking about it. And you said you weren't coming home."

"Can't you tell them you changed your mind?"

"I'm not going to do that." She waved at two hikers headed up to Clark Tower and settled into the crook of a tree along the wooded trail, sensing this was not going to be a short conversation.

"So, did the renter already move in?"

If she didn't know better, Tess would have thought her daughter knew it was J.W. she'd rented to. But despite the hint of suspicion in Jaci's voice there was no way she could know.

Tess made her voice casual. "They haven't moved in yet, but maybe this afternoon. It wouldn't be right to back out now."

"Why not? Who is it? Anybody I know?"

"Why not? Because... what I just said. I've already made a commitment. I wouldn't do that to...anyone. But don't worry, I haven't rented *your* room out. Yet." She was dodging the question of *who*. She wasn't ready to have that conversation.

Jaci was quiet for a minute, then, sounding confused, she said, "You're not seriously thinking of renting *our* room out, are you? Where would Jodi and I stay when—"

"Hey...chill. I'm just kidding. And Jace, I won't tell you that you *can't* come home for the summer, but as much as I'll miss you, I really wish you'd stay there. Stick it out. Sometimes you just have to do hard things. Because it's the right thing to do."

Silence again, and then Jaci's whisper. "That's what Dad used to say... Sometimes you just have to do hard things."

Tears came unexpectedly. "Yeah, he did say that, didn't he?"

"A lot."

"He was right, you know."

"Okay, fine." Her daughter's sigh came across the miles. "I'll do stinkin' hard things."

Tess laughed. "I'm proud of you, honey. I know you'll do great. And I'll be praying every day."

"Well, you'd better pray hard. That guy is the most frustrating man I've ever met."

"Even more than your ol' mom?"

"It's a toss-up." The smile in her daughter's voice made Tess feel like a crisis had been averted.

They talked for another twenty minutes, and Tess was congratulating herself for managing to avoid a conversation about J.W. But after she'd said goodbye for the second time, Jaci said, "Wait a minute. Who *did* you rent Pop's shed to?"

"You don't know him, but it's—"

"*Him?* Mom, you didn't really rent it to a guy? Do you think that's wise? Who is it?"

"I was trying to tell you. It's Wynn's dad."

"Wynn? Wynn McRae?"

She laughed. "Do you know any other Wynn?"

"No, but... I thought his dad was like...a real loser."

"He's actually a very nice man." She shifted in her tree-trunk perch and kicked at a broken twig with the toe of her tennis shoe. "I think maybe Wynn's mom soured him against his dad. But J.W. is trying to rebuild his relationship with Wynn."

"J.W.? That's his name?"

"Uh-huh. He's been in Kansas City. But Rina asked him to come. Because of the baby."

"Why doesn't he stay with them? They have a guest room."

"He didn't want to impose...when they have a new baby and all."

"Yeah, right. They just probably know better than to let him get close."

"Why would you say that?"

"I don't know. But seriously, Mom, do you even know the guy? He could be an axe murderer for all you know."

Tess laughed nervously. "He's not an axe murderer. And I might not know him very well, but I knew Char and..."

"And they were divorced *because*...? Probably *because* he was an axe murderer."

"Oh, stop." But she knew Jaci was making more sense than she wanted to admit. Not about J.W. being an axe murderer, of course. But she was right about one thing: Tess didn't really know anything about J.W. McRae. At least not enough upon which to base a decision this important.

CHAPTER SEVENTEEN

"*I*t looks like a completely different place!" J.W. looked around the little apartment, genuinely in awe.

Tess had transformed the place from the lavender girls' club he'd toured a couple of days ago into a tidy, bright studio apartment. Even the gaudy floral painting had been replaced with a serviceable mirror. He could set up his easel in the corner opposite the bed and get great north light, and there'd be room for his leather chair and ottoman, maybe even the lamp table he'd inherited from his mother.

"Well, it's nothing fancy, but hopefully it'll work for you." Tess stood by the door, looking as if she'd already given up her rights to the space. "I took out everything but the basic furniture—I thought that'd make it easier for you to see what you had to work with—but if you need more chairs or a bookcase or anything before you have a chance to get your own furniture, just let me know and I'll be happy to bring some things back in."

"It looks great." He gave her an appreciative smile. "I'm already arranging furniture in my mind."

"The girls were always able to get online out here with the house's wifi, but let me know if you have any trouble." She motioned to the small dinette table where a small card lay with the password handwritten on it, along with the keychain that held the apartment keys and a key to the garage where her husband's workshop was.

"It'll be fine, I'm sure."

"Okay. Well, unless there's anything else you need, I'll let you get settled."

He stepped outside the door beside her, noticing for the first time the black Adirondack chairs that had replaced the rockers. "I hope you didn't get new chairs on my account."

She pointed over to the back porch of the house. "No. I just traded you. I'm kind of liking the girlie chairs for a change."

He followed her gesture and caught a glimpse of the pastel rockers that had been on "his" porch the day she first brought him back here. "Ah, I see. That was thoughtful of you. And they look nice up there."

In reply, she tossed a smile over her shoulder and crossed the yard.

He watched, enjoying the graceful sway of her form more than he should have. He knew full well he was wrong not to have made his intentions known—that he wanted to explore more than just being friends—before he accepted the offer of the rental. Not that he hadn't tried. But it was too soon to ask her out and too late to risk missing a chance to rent this apartment. And in the end, his finances won out.

He trudged back and forth to his pickup, hauling his suitcase and the few boxes of belongings he'd brought from Kansas City —mostly books. The Realtor still hadn't let him know for sure if they'd made the early closing date, but he would need to get the last of his stuff cleared out within the next week or ten days at the most. Fortunately, he'd become something of a minimalist. And if the buyers actually wanted to purchase some of his furniture, that would simplify things greatly. Maybe Wynn and Rina could use some of it. Or Michael or Patrick might want some of the household items. Or Lesa Creve. If he could ever get hold of DeShawn, he'd have him ask his mother.

He checked his phone. Still nothing from DeShawn, but he had a text from Wynn. Frowning, he opened it.

Hey, sorry, but Amelia isn't feeling well and we're going to have to cancel tonight. Rina will get back to you about another date.

He blew out a sigh. Sounded like a flimsy excuse. But probably just as well. He needed to get to the bottom of this thing with DeShawn. He tried calling. Straight to voicemail again.

Okay, now he was officially worried. He pulled up Patrick's number and tapped Call, hating to bother him, knowing the middle Creve brother was working like a dog to pull himself out of the circumstances life had dealt him and his brothers.

"Hey, J.W.! What's up, man?"

"Hi, Patrick. I'm up in Iowa. Visiting my new granddaughter."

"Hey, congrats, man. That's cool. I remember you said you were gonna be a grandpa."

"Yeah. It happened. She's pretty cute, if I do say so myself. Listen, uh… DeShawn called me Friday pretty upset. I've been trying to get back to him, but he's not answering his phone. You happen to know where he is?"

"No. I haven't seen him in a couple days. Do you know why he was upset?"

"He didn't mention anything to you about…school?"

"No…" Patrick's voice dropped. "It's actually been a few days since I talked to him—maybe a week," he admitted.

J.W. sighed. He did not want to be the one to break the news to the older brothers that DeShawn was in trouble in school. He especially didn't want to tell them that DeShawn suspected their mother was using again. Reluctantly, he gave Patrick an abbreviated version of what DeShawn had told him Friday.

"Has he told Mom yet? About cutting school."

"I don't think so. He said…she's not doing so good. I don't know exactly what that means, but—"

"Yeah, well, you can guess. I'll see if I can find him. We'll figure something out. You've got a grandkid to see. You said it's…a girl?"

"Yes. Amelia."

"Like the flier? Earhart?"

"Yep. I think the baby is named after a grandmother though. Not the aviatrix."

"The what?"

"Never mind. Sorry to dump this on you, Patrick."

"Hey, it's not your problem." There wasn't a trace of sarcasm in his tone.

"Well, it shouldn't be yours either."

"Hey, he's my brother."

J.W. almost couldn't speak over the lump in his throat. These boys had been there for each other through some pretty rough times. "Let me know, will you? When you hear from him? I can come back early if I need to." He just couldn't tell Patrick—or any of the bros—that he was moving to Iowa. Not yet. Not over the phone. He'd tell them in person when he went back to close on the house.

"Thanks for calling, man. Sorry if this messed up your trip. That's cool about the baby."

"Thanks, Patrick. And hey, seriously, if you wouldn't mind, send me a quick text when you hear from your brother. Tell him I did try to call him."

"Will do."

He hung up feeling the weight of the world on his shoulders. But at the same time, feeling so proud of Patrick Creve. The original "bro" had turned into a fine young man. The fact that Patrick had apologized for DeShawn, that he'd taken the burden on himself to find his brother…that was huge. J.W. hoped

DeShawn appreciated his older brother. And would emulate him someday not too far down the road.

And he prayed with all his heart that he wasn't abandoning DeShawn at a time the kid needed him most. Especially not if his efforts to reconcile with his flesh-and-blood son were in vain.

He took the last box inside, slipped off his shoes, and flopped onto the bed. It shouldn't be this exhausting to move from a hotel to a one-room apartment.

~

WHAT WAS THAT? Tess sat up on the edge of the sofa where she'd dozed off reading a slow-moving novel. She lifted her head, listening.

There is was again. *Bang-bang-bang.*

She went into the kitchen and looked out the window to the backyard where the noise seemed to be coming from.

Across the yard, the branch of the elm tree that hung over the roof of the shed rustled and swayed as if two squirrels were wrestling among the leaves. But the ladder leaning up against the shed told the story.

She opened the back door, and stepped out, then thought better of it and went to check her reflection in the mirror. She wiped a smudge of mascara from her cheek and smoothed a hand over her hair. Then, letting the door slam to announce her presence, she walked out to the shed.

"Hey!" She shaded her eyes and looked up to the roof of the garage. "What's going on up there?"

J.W. half-slid down the roof and peered over the edge at her. "Thought I'd see what we're dealing with up here."

She couldn't help but smile. "You've lived here for two whole hours and you're already fixing the roof?"

He looked sheepish. "I just climbed up to see how much

work it needed. Guess I kind of got started and…got carried away." He shrugged.

"Am I going to have to make a rule about working on Sundays?"

"Um, I think God beat you to that."

She laughed up at him. "I appreciate your work ethic, I really do, but I think you could take a day or two to get settled in before you go too handyman crazy. Besides"—she glanced back toward Kressie Bayman's yard—"my neighbor might not take too kindly to all the racket."

"Sorry if I made too much noise." He brushed off his hands and started down the ladder. He jumped off the bottom rung and stood in front of her, hands propped on his slender waist. He studied her, a glint in his eye. "Looks like I woke you from a hard nap."

Self-conscious, she rubbed under her eyes again. "That obvious?"

"Just a few creases from what looks to be a corduroy pillow." He lifted a hand as if to touch her cheek, but stopped short of actually doing so.

She laughed and rubbed hard at her cheeks, hoping they weren't as pink as they felt.

He seemed not to notice and pointed up at the roof. "It actually doesn't look too bad up there. The flashing needs to be replaced around the chimney, and there are a few loose shingles, but I found a couple of packs of those in the garage that should be plenty to replace any damaged ones." He gave a little wince. "I hope you don't mind that I rummaged around in there. You'd mentioned that's where the tools were…"

"Sure. That's why I left you the key. But I truly didn't mean for you to start *today*."

"I was bored. Figured I'd make myself useful."

"Well, thank you."

He gave her a knowing look. "Sorry about waking you up. A Sunday afternoon nap should be sacred."

"I was reading. I…must have drifted off."

"Hey, I like myself a Sunday afternoon nap, too. It won't happen again."

"It's okay." She motioned toward the garage. "Did you find everything you'll need for tools? I don't even know what all is out here."

He pointed to a black toolbox on the ground under the ladder. "I actually used my own. Had them in my truck. I wasn't sure if you'd want me using…the ones on the tool bench."

"You're welcome to use anything you can find on that side of the garage. By the way, I found a simple contract online. For the rental. I'm okay either way, but if you'd feel better signing that, I printed out a copy. It protects both of us…just outlines the month-by-month rental agreement. It's only a page."

"Sure. I'll sign it whenever it's convenient for you."

She curbed a smile. "Just one thing…"

"What's that?"

"I'll need your full name to complete the contract."

He didn't crack a grin. "I'll be packed and out of here in ten minutes."

She reached to put a hand on his arm. "Okay, okay… Maybe we can get by with first name and middle initial. For now."

She was starting to worry that he'd taken her seriously when he burst out laughing. "I'll sign, but you know how doctors—and artists—have a reputation for having illegible signatures…?"

She waited.

"Just saying." He winked, turned on his heel, and went to fold up the ladder.

CHAPTER EIGHTEEN

It was hard to remember the bitter-cold winters of his Iowa childhood when he could already feel July breathing down June's neck. J.W. poured himself a glass of iced tea and carried it out to the porch of his new digs.

Since Sunday, he'd finished repairing one side of the roof, and tonight he'd gotten a good start on the other. He'd forgotten how good it felt to do physical labor. These last two days made him hope he never had to go back to a desk job.

The "shed," as Tess called it, was small, but he already felt settled in and was looking forward to bringing some of his own things back from Kansas City. He wasn't sure the shed was a long-term solution to his housing situation, but he was comfortable here, and it accomplished the one thing he'd become determined to make happen—keeping him in place so he could work on a relationship with his son.

He'd been supposed to have dinner with Wynn and Rina tonight, but Wynn had called and said the baby wasn't feeling well and could they have a rain check. He thought his son sounded sincere, but it could have been an excuse too. At least Wynn had called himself. He'd give his son some space.

He'd kept plenty busy with repairs on the shed roof, final paperwork on the house sale, and trying to track down DeShawn.

The boy still hadn't called him, but Patrick had heard from him and thought he was stable for the time being. "Just let him stew for a while," Patrick had said when J.W. offered to come back and try to talk to DeShawn. "He doesn't need to think that his moping will always get people to come running. Michael's gonna talk to him, too."

The bros were working things out, taking care of each other. Good for them. Although if things escalated and it looked like DeShawn's situation was going to cause trouble for his brothers, J.W. might have to interfere. He hoped it didn't come to that, but he didn't have a good feeling about this.

The back porch light went on at the house and Tess came out. He didn't think she saw him in the twilight. He couldn't decide whether to say something and risk startling her or just be quiet. But after a few minutes, watching her water the potted plants and sweep off the porch steps, he started to feel a little like he was stalking her.

He cleared his throat. "Beautiful evening."

Her head popped up and she squinted into the darkness. "Oh…hi. I didn't see you there."

"Sorry. I didn't mean to scare you."

"No problem." She puttered with the plants for a few more minutes then disappeared inside. But a minute later, she was back again, this time with a little step stool. She proceeded to switch several hanging plants to different locations, then lugged the potted flowers from place to place on the porch. Trying to give them equal time in the sun, he guessed? But then she began scooting the table and chairs to the other side of the porch.

When she started rocking some kind of monstrous potted tree back and forth in an effort to move it, he jumped up and went to her aid. "Can I help? Where are you headed with that?"

She put a finger to her chin and surveyed the landscape. "Maybe put it..." She took a step back and eyeballed the tree, then *his* porch, then back to the tree.

"Ah, I get it. Trying to build a wall between our two porches?"

Even in the dim light, he could see the sheepish expression on her face. "I thought it would give you—well, both of us—a little more privacy."

Once the pot was in place, he started down the stairs, but turned back to her. "I'm sorry. I should have let you know I was out here. If this is going to be a problem, I'd be glad to move my chair to the back side of the shed. There's plenty of shade back there. You wouldn't even know I was there."

"No... I wouldn't ask you to do that." She shook her head, wrinkling her nose. "Your view back there would be the alley and your truck."

He huffed. "And what's wrong with my truck?"

"Well, it's a very nice truck, but it's not exactly what I'd call a view."

"It wouldn't compare to this, that's for sure." He waved a hand to encompass the beautiful lawn and the wooded area beyond. He was tempted to include her in the scope of his wave but decided against it.

She gave no response and instead went to heft one of the pastel colored rockers that had previously been on his porch.

"Here... Let me." He stepped forward and relieved her of the burden. "Where do you want it?"

"Maybe here in this corner."

Together, they moved the rocker to the spot she'd indicated.

She stood back and assessed the arrangement. "So sorry, but... I think it was better where it was before."

He promptly returned it to its original space. "Anything else?"

"That should work for now. Thank you. I didn't mean to put

you to work again...after all you've already accomplished this week." She looked up to the roof, appearing pleased.

"No problem." He started down the stairs again, but on a whim, turned back. "Can I interest you in a glass of iced tea? I just brewed a fresh pitcher..."

She looked like she was going to decline, but instead she smiled up at him. "That would be lovely, actually. Do you need ice?"

"Ice, I've got, but I only have paper cups."

"Oh? Weren't there dishes in the cupboards out there?" She'd checked the cupboards the day she changed out the curtains and bedding and had thought they were fully stocked.

"Plates and mugs. Maybe some cereal bowls, but I didn't find any glasses."

"I'm so sorry. I bet they came in to the dishwasher the last time the girls had friends over and never made it back out to Pop's pla—*your* place," she corrected. She put a hand on the knob of the back door. "You go get the tea, I'll meet you back here with glasses and ice. We'll see how this new arrangement works."

"It's a deal." He bounded down the steps, feeling half his age. And liking his new digs better by the minute.

TESS FOUND the glasses that were supposed to have been in the apartment and boxed up four of them, then rinsed two others. She filled them with ice and tucked them into the cardboard carton. She lifted the box, but just as quickly set it down again and hurried back to her vanity table, checking her appearance in the large round mirror.

She ran a brush through her hair, wishing she'd spent more time on it this morning. *Ah well...too late now.* Thankfully it was almost dark. Even so, she uncapped a pale pink lip gloss and smoothed it over her lips. Strictly in the interest of looking presentable. But *she* was the only one she had to convince, and she wasn't doing a very good job of it. Pushing the thought aside, she tossed the lip gloss into the vanity drawer and went to the kitchen.

She grabbed a few napkins and a bag of potato chips from the pantry and took them outside with the box of glasses.

J.W. was standing beside the table, where a sweating pitcher of tea sat at the center—along with an identical red-and-white bag of Fareway barbecue chips.

They laughed. "Great minds, huh?" He pulled out a chair for her, and once she'd been seated, he sat down across from her.

She put a glass of ice in front of each of them and he poured tea. "I didn't sweeten this. Do you take sugar?"

She took a swig. "Nope, just like this. Thank you. That hits the spot."

He reached for the bag of chips he'd contributed, opened it, and held it out to her.

She took a handful and deposited them on a napkin, spreading a second napkin over her lap. J.W. did likewise and they sat in companionable silence for several minutes, the cicadas' song drowning out the sound of their crunching.

"So, besides drinking glasses, do you have everything you need out there?"

"I'm good to go. And I certainly didn't expect you to supply me with a fully stocked kitchen."

She shrugged. "May as well. It was all there for my father-in-law. Of course, if you have your own dishes to bring, we can box things up out there. But until then, you're welcome to use what's there." She started to slide the box of glasses toward him but realized he might think she was hinting for him to leave. Which she did not want. Instead, she picked up the pitcher and refilled both of their glasses.

"Are you sleeping okay?"

"No complaints," he said over a mouthful of barbecue chips. "I've been sleeping with the windows open, and it's been very comfortable."

"I have a feeling you'll need to run the AC tonight."

"I haven't looked at a forecast for a few days. I suppose I should subscribe to a newspaper. Do they still deliver the *Register* here? Or do I need to get a TV?"

"I'm not sure. I just read the paper online. But"—she flashed him a teasing smile—"isn't that what phones are for? Weather? News?"

"I have an aversion to smart phones." He patted the breast pocket where his iPhone was tucked. "Necessary evil."

"Well, if you want a TV, I think we have the little one that Pop used when he lived here. Unless one of the girls took it. I'll look though—"

"Hey." He put a hand briefly on her wrist. "You aren't responsible for supplying me with all of life's necessities."

"I know, but..." She probably sounded like an overeager child. Or worse, a fawning secret admirer. "It's just that we still have those things from Pop's time here. Someone may as well be using them."

"I have everything I need. I'm a big boy. I've been on my own for a few years now. I can take care of myself."

She felt strangely chastened, but his comment opened the door to a question she'd wanted to ask. "So, how long were you and Char together before..."

"Apparently, about ten years too long."

She wondered if his neat diversion of the question was on purpose. She didn't have the courage to press. "How are things going with Wynn?"

"I was hoping you could tell me. I haven't seen him since Sunday. They invited me over for tacos, tonight but then they had to cancel at the last minute because the baby is sick."

"Oh? I didn't realize Amelia had been sick."

"It didn't sound too serious. To be honest, I'm halfway suspicious it was an excuse. But maybe that was better than getting kicked out later."

"Kicked out?"

He waved her off. "A story for another time. Never mind me. I'm just...wary. I'll touch base with them again later this week. Maybe see if I can go over and see the baby. I don't want to overwhelm them when they're trying to adjust to a new baby in the house. It's been a while, but I do still remember what that was like."

"That's thoughtful of you. Just don't be too much a stranger. I have a feeling Wynn might need a little push."

"That's putting it mildly. If it wasn't for Rina, I probably wouldn't even know I'm a grandfather."

She couldn't honestly argue with him. Wynn had a pretty bitter core when it came to his father. "I need to get over and see that baby again myself. They grow so fast."

"That's for sure. How are your girls?"

"They're good. I miss them."

"That's a good thing."

She looked askance at him.

"If you miss them, that means you have a good relationship with them."

She nodded, touched he would say that. It made her realize how hurtful it must be to J.W. when Wynn rejected him at every turn. And yet, he'd brought it on himself. She didn't know the whole story, but was there ever any excuse for a father to drop out of his kid's life? Especially when Wynn was his only son, his only child.

J.W. started to say something else, but was cut off by the muffled chime of his phone. "Sorry. I'd better check this."

"Of course."

He fished the phone out of his pocket and read a message,

then blew out a deep sigh. "Speaking of relationships with kids…"

"Wynn? Is everything okay?"

"No, not Wynn. I— It's kind of a long story, but I'm a mentor to three kids. It's a Big Brothers kind of program we sponsored at work. They're great kids, half-brothers—and not even kids anymore, really. But the youngest one is struggling. I think I may need to intervene."

"He's in Kansas City?"

J.W. nodded and scooted his chair back. "I hate to cut the evening short…" He held up his phone. "This was the reason I had to leave Wynn and Rina's the other night."

"Oh dear. That probably didn't go over very well."

His forehead furrowed. "What do you mean?"

"I was just thinking…it was probably hard for Wynn to see you invested in another 'son.'" She drew quotation marks in the air, but was hesitant to say more. She could imagine how it would feel to Wynn knowing J.W. had poured himself into three other young men while all but ignoring him.

"Hmm." J.W. scratched at his chin. "I guess I'm dumber than I thought. I've never considered these kids my sons. But I could see how Wynn might think differently."

"Did he seem upset?"

"As a matter of fact, he did. He's never once asked about my life, so it just never came up."

She didn't like the bitter tone that had crept into his voice, but she agreed that him telling his son about the brothers he'd mentored wouldn't earn him any points with Wynn right now. "I'm sure Wynn will come around. As you're more involved in Amelia's life, he'll open up to you."

"You're assuming he'll let me be involved in my granddaughter's life."

"Oh, I think he will, J.W. It might take time, but Wynn is a good man."

"I hope you're right. These boys—the Creve brothers—have been a big part of my life. I'm not trying to hurt Wynn, but I'm not going to tiptoe around about the fact that I mentor these boys. either"

"I wasn't suggesting you keep it a secret. Just…maybe tread a little lightly. If—" She stopped mid-sentence. Why was she sitting here acting as if she was the man's counselor? He hadn't asked for her opinion. "I'm sorry. I don't know why I said that. It's really none of my business."

She wouldn't blame him if he told her where she could put her holier-than-thou advice.

But instead, a soft smile came to his face. "It's okay. I know you said it because you care about Wynn. I understand that. And…thank you. For taking him in after Char's death. I wish it had been me. But Wynn wasn't open to that. I don't blame him. He was practically a grown man by then. And I hadn't earned the right. Still haven't, I guess."

"Give it some time," she said again.

He started to reply, but his phone dinged again. He turned it over on the table and glanced at the screen. "I really need to take this." He scraped back his chair and rose, then pushed the chair under the table. "Thanks for the snack."

"Thank *you*. You contributed more than I did."

He gave a shrug. "No problem." While he answered his phone, he packed everything into the box with the extra drinking glasses, tucked it under one arm, and headed down the stairs and across the yard.

CHAPTER NINETEEN

ess washed the few breakfast dishes, keeping one eye on the shed in the backyard. She hadn't seen any sign of J.W. this morning, which wasn't like him. Not that she knew his schedule intimately. He'd only been here three nights now, but with the days growing hot by mid-morning, he'd been getting an early start working on the roof each morning. Now, the silence—on a weekday morning—almost worried her. Especially since he'd left her porch abruptly last night after getting a phone call. She hoped everything was okay.

She finished the dishes and went to her room to get her shoes. She planned to put in a couple of hours at the park and grab a few groceries on the way home, maybe pick up ingredients for chocolate chip cookies. She hadn't baked in ages and—

She checked the thought even as it came. She didn't have to play games with herself about why she was suddenly in the mood to bake cookies. *Just admit it, you're baking for* him... Well, it *was* nice to have someone to bake for again. Was that so wrong? Maybe she'd even take a plate of cookies over to Kressie.

Yeah, right. She ignored the chiding voice and went out to the car.

She worked at the park until the sun grew unbearably warm around three o'clock. She did a quick trip through the Fareway for groceries, and when she approached her street on the way home, she went around the block instead, driving through the alley to see if J.W.'s truck was there. It wasn't.

After putting the groceries away, she checked her reflection in the mirror and gave her lips a quick swipe of lip gloss. Out on the back porch, she filled a watering can and went to check the flowerpots hanging from the shed's eaves. She lifted the watering can and gave the flowers a drink they didn't really need since the wind had blown last night's rain into the pots. Once she saw there were no lights on inside the shed, she set the watering can down.

Straightening, she noticed something fluttering from the screen door. She inched closer and saw a folded note stuck in the door. Her name was written on the outside in tidy block letters.

I had to run to K.C. to deal with a couple of things. Be back tomorrow afternoon or Friday noon at the latest. (Just didn't want you to think I was skipping out on finishing the roof.)

The note was signed with a flourish—a mostly illegible J and W. She could almost see the spark in the man's eyes as he scrawled his "name," but the smile his note brought quickly faded, replaced by disappointment that he was gone, even if only for a while.

Tess folded the note in half and tucked it in her jeans pocket. With her excuse for checking out the shed gone, she emptied the watering can into the bushes and turned to go back to the house. At the far end of the shed's porch she spied J.W.'s toolbox. It reminded her of the way Pop always had his rusty old toolbox at the ready in case a shingle came loose in a storm or a lightbulb needed changing in one of the outdoor sconces.

J.W.'s toolbox was larger and sturdier than Pop's, but it fit the man. Noticing a tarnished monogram on the front of the black case, she bent to inspect it. *JWM.* She gave a little snort. No clue there. Eventually, she'd get J.W.'s full name out of him. She smiled, remembering his adamance that she would not. Showed how well he knew her.

She ran her palm across her mouth as if she could physically wipe the smile from her face. She had to quit acting like a teenager every time she thought of the man. He was going to misinterpret her friendliness as some kind of romantic overture.

But wasn't that exactly what it was? She didn't put on pink lip gloss for the UPS man. Oh, what had she gotten herself into?

It was after ten o'clock when J.W. pulled up in front of the run-down apartment building where Lesa Creve lived. Hyper-aware of his surroundings, he climbed out of the truck, scanning the parking lot for the beater DeShawn drove. Not seeing it, he locked the truck and said a quick prayer over his vehicle before starting up the sidewalk. He hated that DeShawn had to live in this sketchy part of the city where drugs ruled and your hubcaps may or may not still be attached to the vehicle when you came back to your car.

He nodded at a couple of men smoking on the steps and went to the second floor to knock on Lesa's door. The sun beat down on the concrete walkway, and he rolled up his shirtsleeves while he waited. After he knocked a second time, the curtains swayed slightly and then the door opened a crack.

"It's J.W., Lesa. May I come in?"

Without a word, she opened the door, shielding herself with it, and waited for him to step inside. Closing the door behind her, she motioned to a chair.

He waited for his eyes to adjust to the dim light filtering through the curtains while she cleared a pile of laundry—dirty, judging by the locker-room stench—from the stained recliner. He didn't miss the empty whiskey bottle she quickly slid beneath the pile of clothes.

Her straggly blond hair looked like it might house a litter of rats and her pupils were dilated. It took everything he had not to lay into her. But then, she was at least present in the home where her son was growing up. More than Wynn could have said about him. "Is DeShawn here?"

She pulled a cigarette from a crushed pack on the cluttered coffee table and motioned toward the door to DeShawn's bedroom. "Haven't seen him but he might still be sleeping, but you can look if you want." She lit the smoke and took a long drag. "Is there a problem?"

"Did he tell you about...school?" J.W. was pretty sure DeShawn wasn't here, but he rose and went to knock on the bedroom door. When there was no answer, he pushed open the door and glanced around the room. It was empty, but from the wads of rumpled clothes and bedding scattered about, it was hard to say whether the kid had been here recently.

"What about school?" Lesa exhaled the words on a stream of smoke.

"He cut classes."

She rolled her eyes. "That's news? And yeah, I think he did say something about it."

"He won't be able to graduate with his class next spring if he doesn't figure out a way to make up the work."

"So, he'll figure out a way."

"Has he arranged anything yet?"

She shrugged and took another drag.

"Lesa, this is serious. If he doesn't get his diploma he won't be able to get a job."

"Well, if you can't make 'im do it, *I* sure can't." She cursed under her breath.

"When's the last time you saw him?"

That apathetic shrug again. It made him want to shake her. "Yesterday maybe? Or Tuesday? Wait…what day is this?"

"It's Wednesday. Lesa? Think! This is important! Patrick and I have both been trying to call him and he's not answering his phone."

"Well, what am *I* supposed to do about that?"

"You're his mother. You're at least supposed to know if he came home last night or not. Good grief." He blew out a tremulous breath.

She flicked a long cylinder of ash into a coffee cup. "I *think* he came home. I'm pretty sure. Last night. Must've left again."

"Well, I need to talk to him. Could you try to call him? Maybe he'll pick up for you."

She shrugged. "I've got no service."

"What do you mean?"

"I was late paying. They shut me off."

Maybe if you'd lay off the whiskey you could afford to pay your phone bill. But he didn't say it aloud. "Well, when you see him, could you ask him to call me please?"

"Sure, I can ask him."

"It's important." He started to rise, afraid he'd say something he'd regret if he stayed another minute.

"Hey, J.W., um…DeShawn could really use some new clothes. Could you maybe help with that? I'm late on the rent and I'm about broke trying to keep all these kids in clothes."

He knew for a fact that she hadn't paid for the two older boys' clothes since they left home. He also knew her angle all too well.

She tilted her head and looked up at him. "I could get the money to him, if you want to leave it. You know, so you don't have to wait around for him."

And there it was. He straightened and started for the door, but with his hand on the doorknob, he couldn't leave without one last plea. "Get yourself together, Lesa. One more year... eleven months. I don't care what you do after that, but right now, you have a son to raise. Please don't screw up *his* life too."

He didn't wait for a response. Breathing hard, he slammed the door and strode down the walkway to the stairs. When he reached the first-floor landing, he was nearly bowled over by a lanky kid flying up the steps two at a time.

"Hey, easy there, bud—"

"J.W.? What're you doing here?" DeShawn took two backward steps down the walkway, looking guilty as sin.

"DeShawn! Where have you been? Patrick and I have been calling you for three days!"

"Oh that... Sorry. Uh—lost my phone."

J.W. strode toward the kid and put a firm hand on his shoulder. "Don't you stand there and look me in the eye and lie to me." He couldn't be sure, but he thought he smelled cigarette smoke on the kid. Maybe it was just from Lesa's apartment. But DeShawn's hair was wild and wooly and his clothes looked like they'd been slept in.

DeShawn averted his gaze and shrugged out from under J.W.'s grip. "Don't you tell me what to do."

"DeShawn." He waited until the boy finally looked up. He forced his tone to soften. "Hey, bud, it's me. Come on... What's going on?"

"You talk to my mom?"

"I did."

"Then you know what's going on." His big, brown eyes flitted toward the stairs leading to the apartment, then back to J.W.

"No. I guess I don't. Tell me."

"She got evicted. We have to be out by tomorrow morning. I just came home to get some clothes and then I'm outta here."

"To go where?"

"I don't know, but not here. Anywhere but here."

"Could you stay with Michael? Or Patrick? Just for a couple of nights?"

He shook his head adamantly, his mop of tight curls bouncing. "No. They got away from all this. I'm not dragging 'em back in on my account. Besides, we're kicked out."

J.W. cast about for a way to keep DeShawn from running. "Listen, how about you come home with me for a few days?" A few times he'd had the three of them over to his house to barbecue and watch a game, though not since the older two were on their own.

DeShawn cocked his head, clearly entertaining the thought.

Which made J.W. bold. "There's just one thing..."

The boy eyed him suspiciously.

"I'm not living in Kansas City right now."

"Huh? Why not?"

"Well, bud, the truth is, I lost my job."

"What?" He had the kid's attention now.

And for a desperate minute, J.W. wondered how he was supposed to inspire the kid to stay in school, when his own almighty education and determination hadn't even guaranteed him a job. "Yeah, so I needed to sell my house. But I've got an apartment. For now."

"Where?"

"Iowa." The absurdity of it brought a wry grin.

"*Iowa?* You mean Iowa Street?"

J.W. couldn't help but laugh. "Nope. The state of Iowa. Winterset. You ever hear of it?"

"That's where you're from."

He looked askance at him. "How do you know that?"

"You told us. Remember? About the tree house you built and those covered bridges. Right?"

J.W. chortled. "Oh, yeah... I guess I did. Surprised you remember."

"Oh you'd *be* surprised what I remember."

He ignored the remark. "You up for a little drive? I need to go get some things out of storage. I could use some help loading furniture. And then Winterset is three hours from there."

"Three hours? In a car with you? I don't know..." But J.W. heard the teasing in his voice. That was the DeShawn he knew. It was a good sound.

He smiled back at him. "You game?"

"I might be."

"Okay, but listen. I need to call and make sure it's okay with my...landlady."

"Landlady? What's that?"

"Super. Landlord. Except mine's a lady."

"Oh, okay. You think she'll let me stay?"

"For a few days maybe. It'll give us time to figure something out." He risked gripping DeShawn's shoulder again, and this time the boy didn't flinch. "What about work? When's your next shift?" Shawn had a part-time job at a local diner where he bussed tables.

"Not till Sunday night."

"You sure?"

"I think I know my own schedule."

He chose to ignore the sass. "Okay. You go up and take a quick shower, pack some—"

"I don't need a shower!"

"Trust me, you do. Shower, then pack some clean clothes, and grab a sleeping bag. I need to make that phone call, then I'll talk to your mom. I don't want to get arrested for kidnapping you across state lines." He forced a laugh, but he was only partly kidding. "I'll let her know you're going home with me for a few days. And you need to call your brothers and let them know where you are. Oh, wait." He smirked. "You lost your phone."

"Hey, I really did, man."

"Okay, fine. You can use mine once we get on the road."

"What if she says no?"

"Your mom?" J.W. studied him. "You think she'll say no?"

DeShawn shook his head, his full lips crimping into a tight line. And the sorrow in his eyes about broke J.W.'s heart.

CHAPTER TWENTY

*H*er cell phone was ringing when Tess came in from watering. J.W.'s name lit up her screen. "Hello?"

"Hey, it's J.W."

"Hi. I found your note. How's it going in Kansas City?"

"Good." He hesitated. "Well, mostly good. But I have a question for you—and be honest, Tess. If you need to say no...or just need some time to think about it, I understand."

"Okay..." Curiosity made her take a seat at the kitchen table and listen closely.

"I told you about the three kids I'm mentoring?"

"Yes, sure."

"Well, the youngest, DeShawn, is with me here in Kansas City. His mom is using again—drugs—and she got evicted, so he needs a place to go for a few days...just until she gets her act together."

Tess doubted a relapsed drug addict would have her act together in "a few days" but she kept silent on her end.

J.W. cleared his throat. "I wondered if you'd mind if I brought him back to the apartment with me. Nothing permanent, I promise. He just needs a couch to flop on for a few days until we can work out a place for him. I can pay extra. I'd expect to."

That sounded like he had a more realistic picture of the situation and she let the tension go from her jaw. "Of course not. There's nothing in our contract that says you can't have company." That was true, but if she were honest, she felt a bit pressured. She had no way of knowing what baggage this kid might carry and how he'd been affected by a mother who was an addict. But how could she say no without sounding heartless?

"Well, I wanted to be sure. I appreciate it. He's a good kid. He won't be any trouble, I promise."

Tess wasn't sure how he could make a promise like that for someone else, let alone a teenage boy. "That old sofa bed isn't very comfortable but I don't have a cot or extra sleeping bags or anything—"

"No, of course not. DeShawn's got a sleeping bag. He'll be fine on the couch for a few nights. I'm going to bring some furniture—just a few things—back with me."

The tension in her jaw ebbed further. It didn't sound like he was talking about more than a few days. "Okay. If you're sure he'll be comfortable."

"Trust me, your back porch in the rain would be a step up from what he's used to."

"Really? That sounds awful, J.W. I'm so sorry."

"Yeah, well, I'd better run. I've got a couple more calls to make before we hit the road. We should be back before dark."

"J.W...." She hesitated. "You don't have to give me a play-by-play. I trust you."

"I appreciate that. See you tonight."

Tess put her phone back on the charger and surveyed the kitchen. "See?" she said to the ceiling, "I knew there was a reason I baked those cookies." And she *would* take a plate of them to Kressie Bayman too.

∽

IT WAS after eight before she heard voices out back. She turned off the TV show she'd been watching and went to the kitchen to gather the bag of cookies and a carton of milk. It'd felt strange offering food to J.W., but a hungry teenager was a different story—even if he did have a connection to J.W. McRae. Besides, couldn't a person be nice to their renters if they felt like it? Of course they could.

She watched through the kitchen window until she saw J.W. come around the back of the shed from where he parked, then went out to greet them. "Hi there."

"Hey there." He looked behind him and waited until a tall black kid with curly brown hair appeared around the corner. "DeShawn, this is Tess, my landlady." He turned to her. "Tess, DeShawn Creve, a…good friend from Kansas City."

The boy gave J.W. a sidewise look, but extended a hand to Tess and shook firmly. "Nice to meet you. And…it's Shawn. Just Shawn."

She liked the way he looked her in the eye. "Nice to meet you, Shawn." She held up the cookies and milk in her left hand. "You hungry?"

"Yeah, man! Thanks." He took the snack eagerly and started opening the bag.

Tess laughed and motioned at J.W. "You might need to share just a few with this guy."

"That's right." J.W. punched the boy's shoulder affectionately. "And don't even *think* about drinking straight from that milk carton."

Tess laughed. "That's a battle I never won with my girls. Or Wynn, for that matter."

"Wynn?" Shawn asked over a cookie.

Tess shot J.W. a look of apology.

"You remember. My son," he said, wresting the bag of cookies from Shawn's hand. "I told you about him."

Shawn shrugged. "Guess you never said his name."

So, J.W. *had* mentioned Wynn to the brothers. She'd have to apologize later, in case she'd spoken out of turn. "Well, I'll let you get settled in. Do you need anything, Shawn? A pillow? Or maybe an extra fan?" She looked past him to J.W.

"I've got an extra pillow," he said. "And I've been sleeping with the windows open. DeShawn can have the fan if he needs it."

"Nah, I'm good." He shot J.W. a look and lowered his voice. "It's Shawn."

"Ah, you go by a nickname, too, huh? Just like J.W." She gave the man a sideways glance.

"J.W. is a nickname?" Shawn looked surprised. "I never really thought about it."

"Nope, just initials." He glowered at her.

"So, what's it stand for?" Shawn's countenance held intense curiosity.

Tess couldn't curb the smile that came. "Yeah, J.W. What's it stand for?"

Shawn waited, but J.W. just smiled and turned away. "I'll go get your stuff." He strode toward the back of the shed.

Shawn looked at her, head cocked, as if she could answer the question.

She shrugged. "I've been trying to get that information out of the man since I met him."

"Not happenin'," J.W. shouted over his shoulder. "Come on, son, let's get that furniture unloaded."

"Seriously, you don't know his real name?" Shawn shot Tess a grin. "I'll see what I can do."

"Oh, that would be worth another batch of cookies."

"I'm on it then." He held up a half eaten cookie—his third. "These are awesome."

"Thank you. They're my girls' favorite. But they're both away at college so those are all yours. Just leave a few for J.W."

"Cool. Thanks for making them."

"You're very welcome. Let me know if you need anything."

"I will... Thanks."

She was impressed with the boy's manners. It wasn't fair to judge, but he was not at all what she'd expected from J.W.'s description of the fatherless son of a drug addict. She wondered if the manners were J.W.'s influence on the boy. Of course, he could be totally pulling the wool over her eyes and might steal her blind by the time he headed back to Kansas City.

She rebuked the thoughts. She knew almost nothing about Shawn and it wasn't fair to judge him on what little she did know. Besides, J.W. wouldn't have brought him here if he'd thought it would put her at risk in any way.

DESPITE HER SELF-ADMONISHMENT, Tess slept fitfully that night, and got up several times to go look out into the backyard—watching for what, she didn't know. But she was glad when the dim light of morning shone in her bedroom window, making her qualms seem foolish.

She'd just finished a late breakfast when she heard a knock at the back kitchen door. She found J.W. standing there, hat in hand. "We're headed to the park. I'm going to do some sketches and thought I'd show DeShawn—*Shawn*—Clark Tower."

She laughed at the snide tone he used when he spoke the boy's nickname. "What? You have a problem with the name Shawn?"

"The name is fine, but the kid's gone by DeShawn since the day I met him. Not sure why he suddenly knocked off the 'De.'"

She narrowed her eyes at him. "I *sure* hope you're not pooh-poohing his choice to go by a nickname."

"What?"

"How old were you when you started going by J.W."

The sheepish look he gave her said she'd hit her mark. "Well, it was long before I turned seventeen, I can tell you that."

She smirked. "What, sixteen and a half?"

His expression said she wasn't far off.

"And what did your mom think about you not using the perfectly good name she gave you?"

J.W. looked down, shuffling his feet on the step. When he looked up, a determined grin tipped one corner of his mouth. "Don't think I don't know where you're trying to lead this conversation. Give it up, woman. Do you want to hike up to the tower with us or not?"

"Let me change my shoes." Laughing, she closed the door on him.

"Don't get too far ahead of us, buddy!" J.W. hollered at DeShawn, who was jogging toward a bend in the winding, wooded road that led up to Clark Tower. "And don't get too close to the edge. There are some pretty steep drop-offs."

Tess smiled up at him. "Aww, J.W., you're such a spoilsport."

"You don't know this kid. He's a bit of a daredevil."

Her expression turned apologetic. "I was only teasing. I didn't mean to interfere."

"No. You're fine. I knew you were just giving me a hard time." He hitched his backpack up on one shoulder and slowed to match her stride. He'd brought his sketchbooks and pencils with him, but realized now that it would be too awkward trying to work with an audience.

"He seems like a great kid. So polite…"

"Well, he could still use a spit and a polish, but he's getting there. I'd like to throttle his mother though." He lengthened his stride.

She did the same, nodding in solidarity. "Hard to see how someone could mess up their kid's life that way. Drugs. I hate them."

"You and me both."

"Do you think he'll be able to go back home?"

He studied her, accessing. "Don't worry, Tess. I'll figure something out. I promise you, he's only here for a few days."

"No, that's not what I meant. I wasn't hinting." He heard the hurt in her voice. "I was truly just asking."

"Of course you were. I'm sorry. That wasn't fair. You've been more than generous. And the answer to your question is that I think it's more likely he'll end up living with one of his brothers."

"Would that be a good thing?" She clapped a hand over her mouth. "I'm being too nosy. Sorry... I have that tendency."

"You're just fine." She was more than just fine. "It would be okay for DeShawn. *Shawn*," he corrected. Tess's comment about his own nickname had softened him a bit on the topic. "That's going to be hard to get used to."

"Hey, you're doing great. That's the second time I've heard you correct yourself today." That smile again. A man could drown in that smile.

"Anyway, it'd be fine for Shawn, but I hate to put that off on his brothers just when they've finally gotten out on their own. And they're both doing great. School, jobs, responsibility... They're great guys."

"That must make you proud."

He shrugged and shook his head. "Oh, I sure don't take any credit."

"Well, you should."

"I didn't do anything except help them believe in themselves."

"If that isn't something to take credit for, I don't know what is. No doubt they—"

Shawn came jogging toward them and Tess cut her words short.

"You're going to hike twice as far as we do if you keep circling back."

"This place is pretty cool. I think I saw a coyote back there." His eyes were big, and J.W. suspected he'd come back out of fear.

"Really? A coyote?" J.W. looked to Tess, thinking she might know whether that was possible. He didn't remember ever seeing the animals in the park when he'd lived here, but that was a long time ago.

"I've never seen one up here," Tess said, "but I'm sure it's possible. There's a good population of them in Iowa. And they've probably lost some of their fear of people here at the park."

"Do they bite?"

J.W. rumpled the kid's curls and they sprang perfectly back into place. "Not if you don't bite first."

Tess laughed and Shawn narrowed his eyes as if trying to figure out whether he was serious or not.

Tess shot him a look before answering the kid. "They won't hurt you unless you corner them or something. And I doubt you could even get close to one before it ran off."

"Patrick said there are coyotes in Kansas City. In *town*."

Tess nodded. "I've heard the same about Chicago and other big cities. That'd scare you to death, wouldn't it? To be walking on the Plaza minding your own business and all of a sudden a coyote strolls by."

Shawn laughed at that. It was obvious he and Tess had hit it off, and J.W. shot up a prayer of thanks, glad he'd risked bringing the kid here. He should have known Tess would welcome him with open arms. Just like she'd welcomed Wynn after Char passed away.

"I'm going on ahead, okay?" Shawn jogged backward in front of them.

"Sure. Just make sure you're in sight every so often, hear?"

He nodded, spun, and took off running.

"I like him," Tess said when Shawn was out of earshot.

"Yeah, well, it's pretty obvious the feeling is mutual." He hoped she couldn't read his unspoken thoughts: how could anyone *not* like Tess Everett? In fact, why on earth was she still single after three years?

CHAPTER TWENTY-ONE

Tess watched Shawn Creve jog up the hill and despite the warmth she felt toward J.W., seeing his winsome way with the teen, she couldn't help but wonder how Wynn felt about J.W.'s relationship with Shawn and his brothers. Still, she wished Char could have seen this side of him. More importantly, that *Wynn* could have. How different things might have been if Wynn had grown up with this version of J.W. But that wasn't how it worked. *Thank you, Lord, for being a God of redemption.*

But for Wynn's sake, she felt compelled to mention what J.W. seemed clueless about. "Has Wynn met Shawn and his brothers?"

"No. He didn't know they existed until the other night."

"Will you introduce Wynn while Shawn's here?" She knew she was trespassing, but she did not want to see Wynn get hurt any more than he already had been.

"I hadn't really planned on it." His tone was gruff. "Why?"

"Not that it's any of my business, but I just wonder how Wynn will feel, knowing you have another...*son.*"

"DeShawn isn't my son." He looked genuinely confused.

"No, I know that. But I think that's how it will feel to Wynn."

"Well, he'd be wrong."

"I'm just saying that I think it might be hurtful to him to learn that you've had these three brothers in your life all these years...when you *didn't* have any relationship at all with Wynn."

J.W. slowed his steps. "That wasn't all my doing, just so you know."

"Of course not. I know that." She hated that this had created tension between them. "I do know, J.W. And I'm sorry to stick my nose where it doesn't belong. I guess I just feel a little defensive for Wynn's sake."

"Well, while we're on the topic of feeling defensive, I'll just put this out there." He blew out a sigh. "It's not easy knowing that it was your husband that Wynn looked up to and is modeling his own fatherhood after. Not only was your husband there when *I* should have been, but he died a hero. Meanwhile, I'm still just the deadbeat dad. Maybe always will be."

"J.W. That's not true." Maybe she shouldn't have been shocked to learn he felt that way toward Dan—a man he hadn't even known. But she'd never stopped to think about it from his perspective.

"Well, true or not, I feel like I'm in competition with him. And there's no way I can measure up."

"J.W....nobody is making this a competition except you."

He frowned. "That might be, but I don't think it should count against me that I've tried to make up for my failures as a father by helping out some kids who needed a male role model."

She felt rightly chastised. "I didn't mean it to come out that way. That it should count against you. Of course, it shouldn't."

"I know. You were just thinking of how Wynn might see it. That's understandable. But it's not like I didn't want to be involved in Wynn's life. I did. Maybe I should have fought harder, but at some point it just felt like the conflict with Char was more damaging to Wynn than not having me in his life at all."

"I'm sorry. What I said…wasn't fair." She swallowed back tears, wishing she'd never brought it up.

J.W. stopped in the lane and gently turned her to face him. "Hey… I didn't mean to make you cry."

His sweet tone *did* make her cry and now the tears fell unchecked. She tried to speak, but could only shake her head—and hated that her tears had made it all about her.

He grasped awkwardly for her hand and held it between both of his. "Come on now. Please don't cry. I know you were just trying to spare Wynn's feelings. I can't blame you for that."

"It's really none of my business, J.W.," she said again, struggling to regain her composure. "I'm so sorry I even said anything."

"Just cut that out. You had every right to say what you thought. I shouldn't have snapped at you."

"You didn't snap." She attempted a smile, but knew it fell short.

The sound of gravel crunching made them both look up.

Shawn raced back down the lane toward them and Tess hurriedly swiped at her eyes. But too late.

Shawn's brow furrowed. "What's wrong?"

J.W. waved him off. "Nothing for you to worry about."

Shawn looked between them. "Did something happen?"

Tess gave a shaky laugh. "Everything is fine. I'm just being an emotional woman."

J.W.'s knowing smile almost brought tears again, but he clapped Shawn on the shoulder and took off at a jog. "Race you to the castle!" he called over his shoulder.

The boy took the bait and sprinted past J.W. in a flash. When Shawn was half a football field ahead of him, J.W. jogged back down to Tess, breathing hard. "Man, I'm too old for this!"

She laughed. "Thank you, though."

"For what?"

"For the diversionary tactic."

He acknowledged it with a little swagger, but quickly sobered. "Are you okay?"

"I'm fine." She fanned her face with her hands. "I'm totally fine." And she meant it. He'd somehow managed to make her feel completely at ease. And far less guilty than she probably should have felt for meddling where she had no business.

They rounded a curve and the castle came into view.

"Whoa! This is totally awesome!"

They looked up toward the voice to see Shawn peeking between two turrets, arms stretched to the sky.

"You be careful up there. It's a long ways to the ground." J.W. made his voice stern, but Tess heard the smile behind it.

He gave her a sidewise glance. "Race you to the top?" He ran across the grassy hill toward the steps, looking back over his shoulder.

Something possessed her to take him up on the offer. She beat him to the base of the stairwell and they jockeyed for position on the narrow curved stairway. She clambered ahead of him, but when she looked back, he pushed past her, laughing like a kid. By the time she'd climbed the slanted ladder to the top, he stood there, leaning against the limestone wall, arms folded over his chest, as if he'd been waiting for an eternity.

"No fair! You took the shortcut!"

He shrugged. "What can I say? Hometown advantage."

"You should have seen him!" Shawn crowed. "He was hanging from that ladder like a monkey in a tree!"

"You didn't know I had moves like that, did you, buddy?" J.W. laughed, but then rubbed his lower back. "Sadly, I have a feeling I'm going to pay for it later."

Tess grinned. "That would only be fair."

"Did somebody used to live here?" Shawn strode to the opposite side of the open castle and leaned over the low wall.

The wind blew his hair into his eyes and he swiped the curtain of tight curls back to no avail.

"No, it was built as a memorial." J.W. pointed. "You can read about it on the plaque down there."

"Man, I'm gonna build me a house like this someday."

"Oh?" Tess tilted her head. "Are you interested in architecture?"

Shawn shrugged. "Maybe. Except for the math."

"Oh, I hear you on that," she said. "I stink at math."

"Seriously?" J.W. inserted himself into the conversation. "How'd you get a nursing degree without the math?"

"Oh, I'm not a nurse."

"But I thought—"

"Hospice, you mean?"

He nodded.

"No, I was just a volunteer."

"I see. I misunderstood."

She wondered if he thought less of her at the discovery. And then she wondered why she cared so much.

Hanging out of a turret, Shawn stretched his arm into a rifle and made shooting sounds with his mouth. "*Pitchew! Pitchew!*"

Tess smiled at J.W. behind the boy's back. "What is it with boys and guns?" she whispered.

"I'm not allowed to have a gun," Shawn said over his shoulder.

Tess cringed at J.W. and made a mental note that the kid had sonar hearing.

After a few minutes Shawn started toward the ladder. "I'm going back down to the park, okay?"

"Sure. We'll be right behind you."

Tess caught J.W.'s eye. "And no, I do *not* want to race you to the bottom."

J.W. chuckled. "You ready to head back though?"

"Sure, but I thought you wanted to do some painting? Or sketching?"

"Changed my mind."

"Well, that's disappointing." She affected a pout. "I was looking forward to seeing the master at work."

"Which is exactly why I changed my mind. No offense, but I don't think I can sketch with an audience. Too much pressure."

"I won't watch then." Little did he know that she'd already watched covertly that day he'd painted the Cutler-Donahoe bridge. "I have a few volunteer things I can do down at the park while you paint."

"Maybe." He pointed to the opening in the floor where the ladder accessed the second floor of the tower. "Ladies first."

She turned around and started down, choosing her footholds carefully. She waited for him at the bottom, grateful he'd let her go first. They descended the stairs single file, then crossed the parking lot to the lane that led back down to the park. Shawn had disappeared. Probably halfway down by now, mountain goat that he was.

They walked the first few minutes in silence, then J.W. turned to her. "Thanks for coming with us."

"Oh, my pleasure. Thanks for inviting me. It was fun to get to know Shawn a little better. Do you have everything you need in the shed—*apartment?*" It probably didn't sound the best calling it a shed when she was charging him rent for it.

He started to say something, then quickly clammed up, shaking his head.

"What?"

He gave a wry laugh. "It's probably best I keep my mouth shut."

"No, J.W. If there's something you need, please let me know. I want you guys to be comfortable out there."

"We're perfectly comfortable. It's not that."

"What then?"

"The truth is, I'm having serious regrets about renting your shed."

"Why? Is something wrong?" She tipped her head, waiting, curious.

"What's wrong is—" He stopped in the lane and kicked at a stone before looking up at her, his eyes earnest. "I think it could get really awkward."

"Awkward? Because of Wynn, you mean?"

"No, Tess. Because of you."

She blinked, confused.

"I'm just going to come out with it: I'd really like to ask you out—on a date...or whatever they call it when old people...keep company." His impish grin reminded her of a little boy. "But rumor has it you're the kind of woman who wouldn't be comfortable dating the guy who lives in her backyard."

CHAPTER TWENTY-TWO

He couldn't help but laugh at her deer-in-the-headlights expression. "You can't be totally shocked. I made no secret that I...have feelings for you."

Tess swallowed and stared down at the gravel beneath their feet. When she looked up, a glimmer of a smile touched her lips. "What happened to *friends*? I sure wish you'd *said* something..."

"Hey, I did! I asked you to clarify and you said let's just leave it at friends for now."

"So you think, what?...five days later it's time to march forward?" She rolled her eyes. "Why didn't you *say* something?"

Hope inflated his lungs.

"...before it was too late," she continued.

And just as quickly, his breath left him. "Does that mean I was right?"

She gave a little huff. "You were right about me not being the type of woman who'd be comfortable dating the guy who's living in my backyard."

He snapped his fingers and gave an exaggerated wag of his head.

Her laughter gave him hope again.

They started back down the lane but it was a full minute before Tess spoke. "J.W. I don't know what to say."

"So, does that mean you *do* feel the same?"

"Let's just say I probably would have said yes to a first date if you'd asked."

"*Would* have?" He pouted.

"You know this town. The rumors would be halfway to Springfield before we got out of the driveway."

He lifted his brows. "We could thwart them and stay home. Have a picnic in said backyard."

She appeared to entertain the idea, but then a frown creased her pretty forehead. "What about Wynn, J.W.? Your relationship with him is tenuous as it is. I don't want to interfere with that. He's the whole reason you're here, after all."

He was starting to wonder if maybe *she* was the whole reason he was here. But now was not the time to voice that.

"And what about Shawn?"

He eyed her. "You're just full of excuses."

"Sorry, but you've got to admit the whole idea is rather fraught with roadblocks. Or at least speed bumps."

"Of your own making."

She shook her head adamantly. "Not true."

"I'm just kidding. Licking a wounded ego."

"Awww. Poor baby." She reached up and patted his cheek.

He captured her hand briefly. "You're not doing anything to discourage me, I hope you know."

"Sorry. Not fair." She stepped to the right, putting a bit of distance between them.

They walked another hundred feet before he tried again. "Let's go back to that backyard picnic idea. What would it hurt? No one would know except us. If it's too uncomfortable for you, or if we just decide it's not going to work, no one is the wiser."

"So, you're suggesting we…get to know each other…but we keep it a secret?"

He could have sworn she was warming to the idea. "That would solve pretty much every excuse you gave me, no?"

She shrugged. "I guess it would. But...how much more awkward will it be if things *don't* work out? Then I have an *ex*-boyfriend living in my backyard. *Ugh.*"

"How about I promise to move out if we decide to call it quits?"

"Wait a sec"—she held up both hands, palms out—"how can we call it quits if we haven't called it starts yet?"

"Assuming we do, I meant."

"Assuming." Her flirtatious grin was a drug he couldn't get enough of. She gave a bob of her chin. "There's just one thing."

He waited, feeling as giddy as a kid with a new BB gun.

She raised one eyebrow. "I have a policy never to date someone until I know their full name."

He laughed. "We'll see about that." Before he could think about what he was doing, he pulled her into a playful side hug. She fit so wonderfully into the crook of his shoulder, it was all he could do to let her go.

And maybe she was feeling it too because she circled his forearm with her long fingers, her touch searing his senses.

"No, I'm serious, J.W. McRae." But the lights dancing in her eyes said she was anything but.

~

"WHERE'D YOU GUYS GO?" From his perch on top of the picnic table, feet on the bench, Shawn narrowed his eyes at them as they approached the park.

Tess could have sworn he was suspicious. But maybe that was just her own guilt talking.

"Hey, give us old folks a break, will ya?" J.W. teased. "We don't move as fast as you young bucks."

Tess was grateful for his diversion, even if she wasn't

convinced Shawn bought it. She felt conflicted about the emotions this man evoked in her. Not for the first time, she was having trouble reconciling the J.W. that Char had ranted about with this altogether decent—and decidedly easy-on-the-eyes—man standing beside her. She wished she could discuss the man with Char, but just as quickly realized the absurdity of that wish.

Maybe she should feel guilty that she was even here with Char's ex, enjoying his company immensely, and entertaining the idea of *dating* the man. It was bad enough he was Char's ex, but what would her girls think? And Wynn?

Considering Wynn's reaction gave her almost more pause than anticipating her own daughters' reactions. After all, the whole reason J.W. was here was to attempt to reconcile with his son. If their relationship interfered with that in any way, she would never forgive—

"Isn't that right, Tess?"

She blinked. J.W. studied her, apparently waiting for an answer to a question she hadn't heard. "Sorry, what'd you say?"

He and Shawn burst out laughing. "Told you!" J.W. said.

"Sorry, what did I miss?"

"He said you were daydreaming." Shawn's curls swayed en masse in the wind.

She gave a nervous laugh. "I guess I was. Sorry. So, what was the question?"

"We're hungry—"

"Starving!" Shawn corrected.

"And we wondered if you have time to go grab a bite to eat with us?"

She hesitated. It was almost two o'clock and on a Thursday, restaurants wouldn't be too crowded, but she wasn't ready to face the small-town gossip machine. And how would she introduce J.W. and Shawn if they ran into some of her friends? Or Wynn and Rina? That could be disastrous if her hunch was right and Wynn was jealous about Shawn and his brothers. "I have a better—cheaper—idea." That ought to win him over. "How about we go back to the house and grill some burgers. I have ground beef in the fridge, and I think I have buns and chips. Maybe even a can of baked beans I could open."

J.W. looked at Shawn for approval.

He shrugged. "Sounds good to me."

"Burgers it is, then." J.W. fished his keys out of his pocket and aimed the remote fob at the door. The truck's lights flashed and the horn sounded a truncated blast. "I'll man the grill, if you'll make up the patties."

"I can do that," Shawn volunteered. "That's always my job when I cook with my brothers."

"Ooh, I'm liking this plan better all the time." Tess grinned, hiding her relief.

She and Shawn walked around J.W.'s pickup and he opened the passenger door and motioned for her to climb in first. Shawn had ridden in the middle between them on the front bench seat on the way to the park, but now she was forced to scoot beside J.W. to make room for Shawn. It was tight quarters between the two big men and she might have enjoyed the unaccustomed closeness if she weren't so conflicted about her feelings for J.W. McRae.

Correction: there was no doubt where her *feelings* were concerned. She was falling for the man in a big way. The conflict was whether it was a good idea to let herself give in to those feelings. There were so many hurdles, so many facets to consider. And things were moving faster than she could control.

J.W. turned the key and the truck's engine revved to life. "Need anything from the store before we head home?"

"No, I think I have everything." She might have to improvise with a few items, but traipsing through the Fareway with these two in tow would start more rumors than appearing at any local restaurant.

CHAPTER TWENTY-THREE

"Ahh... Now that's what I call a real meal." J.W. leaned back in the metal lawn chair they'd pulled out onto the lush grass in the backyard. He patted his belly, then rubbed his hand in circles.

"It *was* good," Tess agreed. "Everything tasted extra delicious."

"That's because we didn't eat lunch until almost four!" Shawn clutched his heart. "A piece of cardboard would have tasted good by then. I thought I was gonna keel over from starvation."

Tess and J.W. laughed at Shawn's comical exaggeration. She was pleased with how easy things had gone. They'd worked together like a well-oiled machine, with J.W. manning the grill and Shawn helping her doctor the baked beans and put a salad together.

The three of them sat talking for almost two hours after dinner, and this kid was charming her socks off. She could see why J.W. had such a heart for him. It was hard to imagine how a mother could throw away her life when she had a son who needed her.

Without warning, Shawn let out a thunderous belch, then looked surprised by its volume. "Oops. Sorry."

"I would hope so." J.W. slugged the boy's bicep, not angrily, but with purpose. "What do you say?"

Tess hid a grin.

"I *said* sorry."

J.W. glared at him, waiting.

"Excuse me." Shawn gave Tess an apologetic glance. "Sorry about that."

Tess smiled and leaned back in her chair. "I shouldn't tell you that my Jaci could give you a run for your money in a burping contest."

"What? A girl?"

Tess laughed. "Her dad taught her and her twin sister a few skills I'd rather they hadn't learned."

J.W. grinned. "Hey, it's all about equal opportunity, right?"

"You have twins?" Shawn seemed surprised. "Any boys?"

"No. Just the twins. They're nineteen now and away at college. But when they were little, they were enough work that we decided two was plenty."

"Yeah, that's what my mom said about my older brothers. But then I came along and changed her mind." His grin held pride, but just as quickly, a hint of uncertainty moved into his eyes.

"I can't imagine raising three boys." She shook her head. "Especially since girls are all I know."

"Yeah," Shawn said, fiddling with his knife. "It was wild. Sometimes." He glanced at J.W. "Can I be excused?"

J.W. deferred to Tess with a nod.

"Of course," she said. "We can have ice cream later if you're still hungry."

J.W. shook his head. "This kid is never not hungry."

"I don't know... I'm pretty full right now. Thanks. It was

really good." Shawn patted his belly and rubbed circles on it, exactly the way J.W. had moments before.

"You're very welcome, Shawn." Did J.W. understand how much this kid looked up to him and imitated everything he did?

"I'm gonna go watch some TV—if that's okay?"

"Sure," J.W. said. "Just be sure it's appropriate. And keep the volume down."

Shawn rolled his eyes, but he didn't argue.

"Oh, and call your mom first. I told her you'd keep her posted."

"What am I supposed to tell her?"

"Just tell her you're doing fine. And that you love her. You can surely figure out the rest."

"Whatever."

J.W. chose to let the snarky remark slide and Shawn disappeared into the shed, leaving the yard quiet except for night sounds of frogs and crickets and the distant hum of cars on the through street two blocks over.

A long minute passed in silence before Tess looked at J.W. "I hope I didn't hurt his feelings."

J.W.'s brow furrowed. "How would you do that?"

"What I said about raising boys. I...wasn't thinking."

"Good grief, no. There was nothing wrong with what you said. Besides, I don't think *you* could hurt that kid's feelings if you tried."

"Well, I'm glad he's a good sport."

"He is, but that's not what I meant."

"Oh?"

"He likes you a lot, Tess." He grinned at her. "I've never seen him warm up to anyone that quickly. He's usually pretty suspicious of people in general."

"He probably has good reason." She frowned. "I'm glad he feels comfortable with me."

Grinning, J.W. touched her wrist briefly. "Maybe I should be jealous. I think he has a little bit of a crush on you."

She laughed. "I'm practically old enough to be his grandma."

"Don't be ridiculous."

"Okay. Slight exaggeration. But I seriously doubt Shawn has a 'crush' on me." She chalked quotation marks in the air.

"That's good, because I've got a little crush going myself."

She didn't know how to respond. His words warmed her and embarrassed her a little at the same time.

He reached for her hand. "It's been a fun day. Thank you."

"It *was* fun. And thank *you.*" His hand felt heavenly wrapped around hers, yet at the same time, it made her a bit uncomfortable. She wondered if he'd let go if Shawn came back outside. Would she have let go of his hand if one of the girls appeared in the yard? She had no cause to feel guilty. She was a grown woman. She had a right to enjoy a man's company again, didn't she? "Are you ready for some ice cream?"

"No thanks. I'm good." He rubbed her thumb gently with his and she felt his eyes on her.

"J.W....?"

"Yes?"

"Yoo-hoo! Anybody home?"

Kressie Bayman appeared around the fence and Tess pulled her hand out of J.W.'s and tucked it safely in her lap. "Kressie. Hello."

"Oh." Tess's neighbor stopped short on the sidewalk. "You have company. I'm sorry."

Tess would have bet her life that Kressie knew perfectly well that she had company.

She rose and went to fetch a wrapped burger and bun from the cooler beside the grill. "I do have company, but let me send you home with a hamburger. We couldn't eat them all and they'll just go to waste here."

"Oh. Are you sure?" The foil packet was tucked into the pocket of her thin sweater before she finished her question.

"Of course. Enjoy." She put a hand on the woman's humped back and steered her toward her house next door. She felt a little rude not introducing her to J.W., but she had no idea how she would explain him. She just hoped to goodness Kressie hadn't seen them holding hands! "You'll have to come for coffee some morning. Maybe next week?"

"Oh, I'd like that. You just let me know when. Can I bring anything?"

"Just your appetite."

Kressie turned for one last look over Tess's shoulder. "Enjoy your company."

"Thank you, Kressie. Have a lovely evening."

Tess closed the gate behind her and watched over the fence to be sure the woman kept moving toward her own house.

When she was sure they were alone, she returned to her chair beside J.W. "I'm sorry. That was my neighbor. I probably should have introduced you, but I'm afraid she would have stayed all night." Tess shook her head and gave a little laugh. "She has a tendency to appear whenever there's something on the grill."

He chuckled. "Smart lady. I noticed that burger got squirreled away in a hurry."

Tess frowned. "To be honest, I think she might have a little trouble making ends meet."

"Well, you're sweet to share with her."

"I should do it more often. She has a good heart, but she can be a bit of a pest, too." She winced. "I hope that didn't sound unkind."

"Not at all. Now—" Smiling, he captured her hand in his again. "Where were we?"

She glanced toward Kressie's house and reluctantly escaped

from his grasp. "I-I'm not sure about this, J.W. It's happening too fast."

"Forgive me." He clasped his hands in his lap as if that would make her feel safe. "I didn't mean to rush you. I thought...after what we talked about up at the tower..."

"I know. I feel bad about that."

His brow furrowed. "Explain, please. Which part do you feel bad about?"

"I guess...I kind of gave you permission for something I'm not sure I'm ready for."

"I won't rush you, Tess, but...it's been three years. He's not coming back." His voice dropped to a whisper and his tone couldn't have been more tender or careful.

She shook her head. "It's not that. It's not Dan. Really, it's not. I...I thought I was ready."

"What's holding you back then?"

"A lot of things. When we talked at the tower, I wasn't thinking with my brain."

"Sometimes, about some things, it's better to think with your heart." The sun had started to slip behind the tall oaks at the edge of the yard, leaving them in the shadows, but his smile shone bright.

"No." She wished he wouldn't use that smile with her. It was too hard to resist. "No, the heart is deceitful above all things." Was she really quoting Bible verses at him now?

"And beyond cure. Who can understand it?"

It somehow comforted her to have him quote the rest of the verse from Jeremiah back at her. But that didn't change the misgivings she was beginning to have about a relationship with J.W. McRae. "I sure don't. Understand it, I mean. The feelings I have don't make any sense."

"Do they have to make sense? Is it so terrible to just...fall for someone for no good reason?"

"Yes. It is. I mean...if it was just...*because* and there weren't any roadblocks, that'd be one thing. But there are *so* many road-blocks, J.W. So many."

"Like?"

"Like Shawn." She nodded toward the shed where the light from the small TV flickered through the window. "You've started something great with him and his brothers. But they're in Kansas City."

"That's not even relevant, Tess."

"Why ever not?"

"For one thing, the Creve brothers are grown, all but Shawn. And I came here because of my son. I want to redeem the time I've lost with him. I can't do that if I'm in Kansas City."

"Are you saying you intend to move here…permanently?" Why did that thought give her such joy? Such hope?

He shrugged. "I guess that depends on Wynn. If it's going to cause trouble for me to be here, then no. I won't do that to him. But I'd like to at least have a shot. Get to know that grand-daughter of mine."

"See, that's another reason it's just not a good time for this." She motioned between them. "You need to be concentrating on Wynn's family. And on that baby. I'm a…distraction."

He gave a little harrumph. "I'll give you that. But I know for sure the way to win over Wynn McRae is *not* to spend every waking moment at his house. I *liked* my old man and I wouldn't have wanted that."

"Still… Not knowing what Wynn—or Rina—would think about…*us*… It just would complicate things. Why risk it?"

"Tess, I want a relationship with my son and his family. But I'm not going to put my life on hold while I wait around to see if he's interested. Right now, it's not looking all that promising."

"Exactly, so why make it more complicated?" She inhaled deeply, wanting so badly to just let him convince her, win her over. But there were other reasons she was hesitant. And diffi-cult as it would be to talk about these things, if she wasn't honest with him now, neither of them were making their decisions with eyes wide open. "Those aren't the only reasons I'm hesitant."

His brow wrinkled. "What else?"

"I don't mean for this to sound judgmental because I don't know the whole story, but..." She closed her eyes and dropped her voice to a whisper. "I promised myself, after Dan died, that if I did ever start dating, I wouldn't date a divorced man. I'm so sorry if that sounds like I'm judging you, but it's just something that was—*is* important to me."

He looked askance at her and his voice turned gruff. "What does that have to do with *me*?"

"What do you mean?"

"I've never been divorced, Tess." He raked a hand through his hair. "Maybe that's just semantics in your eyes, because, yes, we were separated. And I don't know what Char told you, but I *kept* my marriage vows, Tess. As far as it depended on me, I kept them. Till death do us part."

"But..." Confusion made her stutter. "How can you say that when you were divorced?"

He cocked his head. "She told you we were divorced?"

"Well... Char called you her 'ex' and—I feel sure she said you were divorced. I *know* she called you her ex. Do you mean... you're *not*? She talked about her marriage ending and—"

He shrugged. "I suppose that's how she saw it. We were separated, obviously. So, yeah, she wasn't wrong to say the marriage ended. But we were never legally divorced. I wouldn't agree to it. Don't believe in it. And she never pressed me."

Memories of her conversations with Char swirled in her mind. J.W. had never given her reason to think he was a liar—although that was surely one of the many labels Char had glued on him. She wracked her brain. Maybe she'd just assumed. But Char *had* used the term "my ex." Of that, Tess was sure. She met his eyes and saw what looked like disappointment there. It gutted her. But was that just her falling for a charmer?

It seemed like a stretch…a strange technicality, but after Dan died, she had prayed that if she ever met someone else, that he would also be widowed. Maybe God had answered her prayer. Just not in the way…or for the reasons she'd thought.

"What happened with your marriage? Char told me a little bit, but I'd like to hear it from you."

He narrowed his eyes. "I was hoping you could tell me."

CHAPTER TWENTY-FOUR

J.W. shifted in the lawn chair, wishing this conversation didn't have to happen. Even though— if he wanted to have a relationship with Tess—he knew it did.

It was apparent his reply to her straightforward question wasn't what she'd expected, but she was playing hardball and he could play with the best of them. "I'm not messing with you. I'd tell you if I knew where things went wrong with Char. Not saying I was a saint in the marriage, that's for sure. But I don't think anything I did was divorce-worthy."

Tess shook her head. "Do you realize you said the same thing when I asked you how things were going with Wynn the other night?"

"What's that?"

"That you were hoping I could tell you...how things were. You're surely not so dense where your own relationships are concerned, J.W." She grimaced, as if she regretted the words already.

He gave a humorless laugh. "Oh, I probably am that dense. I

do think I know where things are with *this* relationship." He motioned between them the way she had a few minutes ago.

"Oh, you do? And just where is that?"

He rolled his eyes. "In the toilet, it's starting to sound like."

She gave a disgusted growl. "You really *are* clueless."

"*Not* in the toilet?" What kind of game was this woman playing with him?

"No. Not in the toilet. I hate that expression, by the way."

"Duly noted."

"J.W." She closed her eyes and blew out a long breath. "I'm crazy about you."

He smirked to hide the genuine smile that wanted to come. "You have a funny way of showing it."

"That's because I'm not sure it's right."

"Hey, a woman can't help it if she falls head over heels. Just saying." He felt like he was swaggering even though he sat perfectly still on the lawn chair, one ankle crossed over his knee. "And why *wouldn't* it be right? Feels mighty right to me."

Her smile said she saw the swagger and forgave it. But her expression quickly turned serious. "Char said you neglected her and Wynn. That you were a workaholic, but that you never made enough money…" She hesitated. "That's all I could swear to, I guess. It was more of an attitude she had."

He released a slow breath. "I don't want to speak ill of my dead wife, and I rarely have—for sure never to Wynn—but I am going to defend myself here, just this once, because the stakes are high."

"I'm listening."

"Yes, I worked hard, and long hours, so maybe you would say I was a workaholic. But whether it was sixty or seventy hours a week, it was never enough for Char. My paycheck, I mean. Never enough to keep her in the lifestyle to which she was accustomed. I grew up poor in Winterset, and she was a privileged girl from Des Moines. A lawyer's daughter. It was not a match made in heaven."

"Yes, she did like nice things. I remember that." A smile touched the corner of Tess's mouth. "We almost got in a fight one time because she asked me to order her a certain bed jacket for the hospital before her last surgery."

He frowned. "What's a bed jacket?"

"You know…a little short robe that you wear in the hospital."

He shrugged.

"I still remember that it was a hundred and twenty-nine dollars! I found one for a third that price at Target and suggested she order it instead. She freaked out." A faraway look came to her eyes. "Of course, I guess *I* freaked out a little over the expensive one. Still…a hundred and twenty-nine dollars? We had kids in private school at the time, and that was my clothing budget for an entire year. It made me furious!"

J.W. laughed. "Welcome to my world. Well, my world with Char. And as you've probably guessed, my solution to Char's spending was to become a miser."

The light that dawned in her eyes said she had not yet connected those dots. "Still," she said, "it was petty of me. After all, it was her money and she was dying, for heaven's sake. If she wanted a pretty bed jacket, I should have just kept my mouth shut and ordered it, no matter the price. And in the end, I did. I'm only telling you this to say that I do understand that she had expensive taste and she didn't have a problem spending money."

"Well, in her defense, she was born into it, so what do you expect?" He ran a hand through his hair. "So, you believe me?"

She tilted her head, studying him. "I've never known you to lie to me, J.W. Yes, I believe you. Char was…rough around the edges. I don't mean that as an insult. I loved her dearly as a friend, but even Dan said—more than once—that he wouldn't have wanted to be married to her. I'm sure being married to her was…a challenge.

And please don't think I blame you alone for whatever went wrong in your marriage. I'm still trying to wrap my head around the fact that you never divorced. But what about the house? Char said she got the house. I assumed she meant in the divorce settlement."

"No. I gave her the house. She wouldn't take any child support. Said she didn't want to be beholden to me. There was an unwritten—but not unspoken—understanding that I would not be part of Wynn's life." He looked down, his countenance shadowed with regret. "I'm pretty sure her parents had something to do with that. They used their money to control Char. And me. I'm not proud of that fact."

Tess nodded. "I knew she got an inheritance when her dad died. She never worried too much about money."

"Not if she was buying hundred-dollar bed jackets." He didn't like the tension that mounted at the thought. He needed to let it go.

"Hundred *twenty-nine*!" Tess clapped a hand over her mouth. "Sorry. I guess I need to let that go."

He laughed and wanted to hug her for siding with him, at least on that point. But he resisted the temptation and sobered, wanting to get this whole conversation out of the way. "I'm not proud of the fact I didn't fight harder to be part of Wynn's life. But by the time it reached that point, I was just ready to be done. Done with it all."

Tess nodded, but didn't speak.

"Neither of us was perfect. And we were young, Tess. Char and I went into marriage ill-prepared. I deeply regret that I didn't try harder, for Wynn's sake. But it's important to me that you know I did not divorce my wife. There was never anyone else...not until after she died."

"Oh? So, tell me about *that*."

He waved her off. "Nothing to tell. A few ill-fated dates that never amounted to anything. To my shame, I went on one of those stupid dating sites, looking for someone compatible."

She cringed. "Not that I could ever do that myself, but I don't think it's anything to be *ashamed* of."

"Maybe that's too strong a word. But it was a waste of time, for sure. That's the thing though, Tess. *This* hasn't been." Again, he motioned between them in a gesture that was starting to become their signature. "This just...happened. Slow and natural. The way it should be in my mind."

Her reluctant nod told him she agreed, but a hint of a smile crept over her face. "I wouldn't exactly call it 'slow.' We've known each other for, what? Two weeks now?"

He grinned. "Okay. Relatively speaking."

She turned serious again. "So, what are you saying?"

"Just that, well, you have to do whatever you feel right about. I don't want you to ever be able to say I pressed you into something you didn't want. But"—he shot her a grin—"I also totally disagree with every reason you gave for the time not being right. Lame excuses. Every one. I am capable of multi-tasking. I don't need to be with you every minute and I sure don't need to be with Wynn or DeShawn or anyone else in my life constantly. There's plenty of me to go around."

He couldn't read her expression, but she seemed to be contemplating his words. After a minute, she rose from her chair and leaned over him. Taking his face in her soft, graceful hands, she planted a kiss on his left temple. "Let me sleep on it, okay? Let me think about everything you've said. And let me pray about things."

"That sounds hopeful." Almost as hopeful as that kiss he could still feel burning his skin. "I can't very well argue against that."

"Good." She gathered their empty glasses and a crumpled napkin. "Do you mind if we hold off on ice cream until another night?"

"Not at all. Although..." One side of his mouth tipped up. "Shawn might be a little disappointed."

"Oh! I didn't even think about that."

He waved her off. "Don't worry about it. We'll go get some if he's still hungry. You go think and pray. And sleep. We'll talk when you're ready."

"Thank you, J.W."

He rose, but it was all he could do to resist the overwhelming temptation to take her in his arms. "Sweet dreams."

"You too."

J.W.'s truck was already gone at seven the next morning when Tess went to water the tomato plants in the backyard. All was quiet at the shed, and she wondered if maybe he'd taken Shawn back to Kansas City, though he hadn't said anything about it last night.

If that were the case, she'd be disappointed. She really liked Shawn Creve, and it had been good to have him around. Not only because he added a spark of youth and fun but because he served as a buffer—a chaperone—for her and J.W. She was tempted to tell J.W. that Shawn was welcome to stay indefinitely, but that wasn't her business. And besides, Shawn had a job in Kansas City that he'd have to get back to. She'd already gotten too involved in the whole situation with Wynn and Rina. She needed to keep her nose out of J.W.'s life. She was his landlord and that was all.

Except, after last night, she couldn't really say that was *all*.

She couldn't help the smile that came. Despite the abrupt end to the evening last night, she'd slept like a veritable log. She watered the flowerpots on her back porch and was just going in to fix a cup of coffee when she heard his truck pull in behind the shed. The engine cut and a car door slammed.

She stepped back into the shadows of the porch and waited

for him to come around to the shed, but instead, his head bobbed behind the fence. What was he up to?

She kept watching, feeling guilty for spying on the man. When he came to a gap in the fence, she saw that he was carrying bulging grocery bags. But where was he going with them? He answered that question by slipping through the gate to Kressie's yard. She could just see the top of his head as he stopped at her neighbor's back door. Seconds later, he retreated, retracing his path back toward the shed.

This time, when he came to the gap, she could see that the grocery bags were gone. The man had left groceries on Kressie's stoop! Bless his sweet heart! And it meant all the more knowing how frugal he was. Kressie would probably suspect that Tess had left them—not that she'd ever been that thoughtful or generous before, but who else would her neighbor suspect? Certainly not Tess's "company."

What other surprises did this man have up his sleeve? She wanted to run across the yard and hug him. Instead, she slipped into a chair, lest he see her surveilling him.

He moved quietly into the yard and reached for the door to the apartment, then stopped and looked toward her house. "Good morning."

Her breath caught. He'd seen her! She inhaled. May as well come out of hiding. "Good morning, J.W. Did you just do what I thought you did?"

"I don't know. That depends on what you thought I did."

"Did you just take groceries over to Kressie's?"

"Maybe. Did you just get caught spying on me?" He approached her porch.

She giggled. "Maybe."

"Nobody needs to know where those groceries came from. Understood?"

"That was very sweet of you." She wrapped an arm around the column that held the porch roof, lest she not be able to resist the intense urge to pat his stubbled cheek. "Have you had coffee?"

"I have not."

"Would you care to join me? It's still cool enough here on the porch. Is Shawn sleeping?"

"He was when I left."

"That was so sweet of you, J.W. The groceries. I'm serious."

"Were you serious about coffee?"

"I was. Sit down. I'll be back in a jiffy. Cream and sugar?"

"No, just black, please." He climbed the steps slowly, his eyes never leaving her face.

She offered a smile, then hurried inside to start the coffeepot.

She could get used to this.

CHAPTER TWENTY-FIVE

"This is literally like burning money." J.W. eyed the armful of fireworks Shawn was schlepping to the checkout at the fireworks stand on the edge of town. "You don't need to blow your entire month's salary, bud."

"Not even close."

"What? Only *half* a month's salary."

The kid had the decency to look sheepish, and J.W. gave up. Shawn was young. He could always make more money. And the Lord knew he'd had too few carefree holidays in his short lifetime.

Shawn had convinced a friend to fill in for him at the diner through the weekend, leaving him free to stay in Winterset for the town's big Independence Day celebration. J.W. balked at the news at first, but only a little. Shawn needed something to take his mind off of his mom's situation. They'd taken in some of the city's festivities downtown, including a car show that had the kid dreaming about saving his money for a tricked-out 2002 T-bird. He hadn't been quite so vocal about that now that he'd spent almost a hundred dollars on fireworks.

Now they were headed back to Tess's to grill brats and burgers until it got dark enough to set off their fireworks.

Pulling in from the alley to the gravel drive behind the shed, J.W. almost couldn't let himself think too hard about the life he'd lived these past few days. Leisurely morning coffees on Tess's porch, evenings working together in the yard—J.W. finishing repairs on the shed while Tess watered and pruned the flowers. And during the day, he drove to the covered bridges, setting up his plein aire easel and sketching and painting the bridges.

He was rusty, but still pleased with the results. The shed's small kitchen had begun to look like a darkroom with dozens of watercolored pages hung along a crude clothesline to dry. Some of them would eventually be relegated to the trash, but others he'd deemed keepers. Tess had raved about them, even suggested he open an Etsy shop and try to sell them. While he appreciated her enthusiasm, he had no illusions that his paintings were as good as she seemed to think.

It wasn't a life he'd ever imagined for himself, and yet he didn't want it ever to end.

Even Shawn's presence, which was definitely cramping his style where Tess was concerned, was a pleasant distraction and admittedly a much-needed hedge around J.W.'s growing desire for the woman. Her laughter, the sparkle in her eyes, that smile that seemed reserved for him alone—she stirred him like no woman had in ages. Maybe ever.

Shawn helped him carry in groceries and he sent the kid to Tess's back door with a few items she'd asked him to pick up. "Hurry back though. We need to get the beans on the stove."

"And don't forget we're gonna try that chip dip you told me about."

"I haven't forgotten."

Shawn was becoming a pro in the little kitchenette, making them bacon and eggs each morning and trying his hand at cookies and other snacks. He patted his belly at the thought. The kid was going to be the death of him, weight-wise.

With Tess's permission, he'd invited Kressie Bayman to join their backyard picnic. The older woman seemed delighted and promised to contribute her famous angel food cake to the festivities. More damage to his waistline.

His cellphone jangled in his pocket and he dug it out to answer. Tess. Just seeing her name on the screen made him smile. "Hey, there."

"Hi. Listen, I just had a thought."

"Okay...shoot."

"What if we invited Wynn and Rina to come tonight?"

Instantly, his stomach turned over. "I don't know, Tess..."

"Won't they be hurt if we *don't?*"

"It's just...Wynn hasn't met Shawn yet and I'm not sure this is the place for that."

"Well, I don't want to interfere, but I was thinking this was exactly the place for that. Low-key, no pressure. It wouldn't be nearly as awkward as if you call a special gathering for them to meet each other."

He'd talked to his son on the phone once since their dinner, and it had gone okay, he guessed, but Wynn and Rina had never reissued the dinner invitation they'd backed out on when Amelia got sick. So maybe that just meant it was going to be up to him to get the ball rolling. He just wasn't sure what to expect with Shawn in the mix. "I guess it'd be okay. Let me call and see if that'll work for them. What time are we saying?"

"Anytime after six is fine, but we won't eat until seven and it won't be dark enough for fireworks until almost ten."

"Okay. I'll call them."

"Let me know how many to expect, okay? And tell Rina she doesn't need to bring a thing."

"Okay, I will." He hung up and sucked in a breath...and his courage.

Wynn answered on the first ring.

"Hey, Wynn. Kind of short notice, but we're having a little cookout in Tess's backyard tonight and wondered if you guys want to come?"

"Oh…sorry, man. We've um…already got plans."

"Sorry to hear that. I should have called sooner."

"Yeah well…maybe another time. Tell Tess thank you though."

"I will. Everything going okay there? Amelia doing okay?"

"Yeah, she's fine. Still has her days and nights mixed up, I think, but she's okay."

"Okay, good. Well, I'll let you go. Sorry it didn't work out."

"Yeah. Okay. Thanks." The line went dead.

J.W. was partly relieved that he hadn't had to tell Wynn that Shawn would be there. Maybe he knew and that was why he'd turned down the invitation.

Or maybe he and Rina really did have other plans. But it had seemed more like he was making excuses. He wished Tess had never made the suggestion. Because the awkward phone call had put a damper on what had started out to be a great day. And it made him wonder why he was trying so hard with Wynn when his efforts with Shawn had gone so far. In fact, he was dreading having to take Shawn back to Kansas City tomorrow.

Lesa had moved in with another single mom and they would stop by her apartment and see if things were any better there, but he'd made arrangements for Shawn to stay with Patrick for the rest of the week. He'd promised Tess that Shawn would only be here for a few days, but seeing how Shawn had thrived these few days in the small town, J.W. was starting to regret that he couldn't just keep the kid here until he graduated high school. Yet, if Lesa gave permission for that, it would be its own kind of rejection for Shawn.

~

TESS WAS ultra aware of her shoulder touching J.W.'s as they sat on a blanket, reclining enough to see the fireworks show that was lighting up the night sky—but not so much that they were actually lying side by side. Still, the darkness had made them both bold, and J.W.'s hand had brushed hers several times, and he rested his arm lightly around her shoulder when no one was looking.

"Oooh! Aaahh!" The admiring cries mingled with the snap-crackle-pop of the fireworks going off overhead and the three teens wielding lit punks laughed like maniacs as they bent to light another wick, then ran for their lives.

Shawn had made friends with the two teenage brothers who lived across the alley, and the minute it got dark, the three boys put on a fireworks show in Tess's backyard that rivaled the one the city threw. The boys' powerful fireworks quickly drew an audience, and by the end of the evening, Jim and Patty Taylor and several other families in the neighborhood had gathered in Tess's backyard. And J.W. had befriended most of them.

Tess wished she'd thought to invite Wynn and Rina sooner. J.W. had been a little terse about the whole thing, so she hadn't pressed him about why they weren't able to come. And maybe it was best they weren't here, since J.W. hadn't introduced Shawn to Wynn or vice versa, and Shawn was pretty wound up hanging out with the neighbor kids.

She had to admit, it was good to have people—especially the teens—in the yard again. It made her miss her daughters and all their friends who used to hang out here.

From the corner of her eye, Tess saw Kressie Bayman folding up her lawn chair and heading toward the fence with it. She whispered to J.W. beside her. "I think Kressie's leaving. I'm going to go tell her goodbye."

She started to get up, but J.W. stopped her. "You stay here. I'll walk her home."

"Oh, that would be so sweet. Thank you." She stood and

dusted off her jeans. "I'll just come and say goodbye real quickly."

She followed him to the gate and they caught the older woman just before she slipped out.

"I'm so glad you could come, Kressie."

"The angel food cake was delicious."

"Oh! Were there any leftovers? You should take them home." Tess looked back to the table where the desserts were still sitting.

"Oh, no, it was gone before it even got dark."

"I'm not surprised," J.W. said.

"Don't tell anybody, but I used a mix this time."

"Well, you apparently mixed it just right," J.W. teased.

Kressie rewarded him with a smile, then turned to Tess. "You should hang on to this one." She stabbed her index finger into J.W.'s chest. "You two are cute together."

J.W. put an arm around Tess. "Now, you listen to this lady, Tess, you hear?"

"I'll take that under advisement." But she couldn't help the broad smile that came.

"Let me walk you home, Mrs. Bayman."

"Oh, now stop that. You call me Kressie."

Tess's jaw dropped. It had taken the woman fifteen years to make that offer to *her*. Grabbing some leftover potato salad from a cooler under the table, she thrust it into Kressie's hands. "Take this, would you? I don't want it to go to waste."

"Well now, I wouldn't turn it down. Thank you."

J.W. made a V of his elbow and offered it to her. "Shall we?"

Kressie giggled and took his arm. "Good manners, this one," she tossed over her shoulder to Tess as they disappeared through the gate in a new volley of fireworks and *oohs* and *aahs*.

It was after midnight when the fireworks finally ran out and everyone drifted back home.

Tess wiped down the folding tables, and Shawn helped J.W.

fold them up and lug them back to the garage.

"I'm invited to go to the lake with the Taylors tomorrow," Shawn told J.W. in what sounded like a well-rehearsed spiel. "They're going up to Lake Red Rock and taking the boat. It'll be a blast!"

"I'd feel better if you wait till sometime when I can go with you. See how you handle swimming, and all that."

"I know how to swim!"

"It's different swimming in a lake though. I'd want to be sure—"

"Grayson's parents aren't stupid. They'll make sure I'm safe. Please? Come on, J.W."

He held Shawn's gaze. "I can tell you right now that your attitude is going to play a big part in my decision."

"What attitude?"

"That comment about"—he mimicked Shawn—"'his parents aren't *stupid*' was uncalled for. You understand?"

"Yes, sir. Sorry."

"Forgiven." J.W. put a hand on his shoulder. "Listen, bud, I don't think it's going to work out this time. I need to get you back to Kansas City in the morning, remember?"

"Yeah, but I don't have to be to work until six."

"You forget it's a three-hour drive. Besides, I have some things I need to get done tomorrow when I get back, so I don't want to be gone all day."

"So? I could call and get somebody to work for me and then you wouldn't even have to make the trip."

"It's pretty late notice for that. And besides, you're not going to like the tiny number on your paycheck very much with all the hours you've missed."

"I don't need anything. I'm good."

J.W. put a hand on the boy's shoulder. "It's just not a good habit to get into, DeShawn. You want your boss—"

"It's Shawn."

"Sorry. *Shawn*. As I was saying, You want your boss to know you're dependable."

"I am. And he doesn't care. As long as I get somebody to fill in for me."

"Sorry. Maybe another time."

"Come on, man!" Shawn stomped a foot. "There might not be another time. I've never been to Lake Red Rock."

J.W. chortled. "You've never been to a lot of lakes. But there'll be time for that."

"Yeah, right." Shawn's voice took on a surly tone Tess had never heard from him before. "You just don't want me to have any fun."

J.W. laughed and Shawn's jaw tightened more.

Tess caught J.W.'s eye. "Hey, goodnight, you two. I'm wiped out. It was good to have you here, Shawn. Have a safe trip back."

Shawn harrumphed and looked at the ground. J.W. opened his mouth to say something, but Tess shook her head almost imperceptibly.

J.W. must have caught it though, for he let his breath go. "Goodnight, Tess. Thanks for a fun evening."

He leveled a look at Shawn obviously meant to prompt a thank-you, but the teen pretended not to see and stomped back to the shed.

J.W. gave her an apologetic shrug before turning to follow Shawn into the shed.

Tess smiled, remembering similar tension when the girls were Shawn's age. But even from inside the shed, their voices grew loud enough that Tess hoped it didn't wake Kressie.

She hated that the evening had ended on such a harsh note—and she was disappointed not to have some time alone with J.W. But it was probably for the best.

Besides, he'd be back tomorrow evening and then they could get back to the early morning coffee "dates" that she'd come to love with him.

CHAPTER TWENTY-SIX

*T*he next morning, Tess carried her steaming mug out to the porch, trying to be quiet since it was still early and she'd be drinking her coffee alone.

She'd seen Shawn head for the back drive with a suitcase a few minutes ago. By the set of his shoulders, he was still put out with J.W. about making him go back to work his shift, so she kept quiet and watched him disappear around the corner of the shed.

Twenty minutes later, she went inside to pour herself a second cup of coffee and carried it out to the porch. Smiling, she looked out over a yard littered with fragments of firecracker wrappers and spent Roman candles. A couple of times mowing the lawn would take care of most of the mess.

Maybe Shawn could do the mowing. Though she wasn't sure when—or if—he would be back. For now, J.W. told her Shawn planned to stay with one of his brothers until they could work out other arrangements. Looking across at the empty chair where J.W. usually sat, she was surprised how much she missed him. Coffee together had quickly become the highlight of her day. J.W. would appear in the misty shadows of early morning, and they'd sit together sipping and talking quietly while the birds serenaded them and the rest of the world slept. She'd found his companionship to be the most sublime mix of calm and thrill. The man centered her, somehow.

She checked her phone. It was almost eight o'clock. She hadn't seen J.W. or heard his truck leave, but maybe they'd gone while she was inside getting coffee.

This would be a good time to give the twins a call. If they weren't up yet, they should be. She dialed them on FaceTime then laughed when they each answered from their beds in different states, groaning and threatening to hang up on her. "Get up, you lazy bones. You've already wasted half the morning!"

"Mom! Stop it. This is *so* lame." But there was a smile in Jaci's voice.

Jodi yawned and took her phone under the covers. "Just because you went to bed at nine-thirty doesn't mean we did!"

"I'll have you know I was up past midnight."

"What?" Jodi threw off the covers and sat up in bed, her phone's camera struggling to keep up with the chaotic movements.

"Why, Mom? Were you sick? You *never* stay up that late."

"Oh, we had a little Fourth of July party here last night. A cookout, actually."

"We?" Suspicion displaced Jaci's sleepy-eyed expression.

"A bunch of people from the neighborhood. And Wynn's dad and Shawn, a kid that's staying with him."

"Hey, how's it working out with your handsome renter? I've been meaning to ask."

Tess held the phone away, making a quizzical face. "How do you know he's handsome?"

"Mom." Jodi glared at her through the screen. "You don't

think for a minute that we'd let some stranger rent Pop's shed without googling the heck out of him first, do you?"

"Yeah, Mom. What kind of daughters do you think we are?"

"Girls! That is terrible." But she couldn't hide the smile that came thinking of the twins vetting her and checking up on J.W. "So, what'd you find out?"

"He worked for a big PR firm in Kansas City."

"Won a bunch of advertising awards," Jaci added. "Pretty impressive."

"He's kinda cute, Mom. Maybe you should ask him out."

Tess laughed, but she couldn't tell if Jodi was serious or not. She decided to test the waters. "Maybe he's already asked *me* out."

"What??" the twins crowed in unison. "Mom?"

"Are you serious?" Jaci cocked her head, waiting.

"No, we're definitely not serious yet"—she grinned at her own play on words—"but I do like him."

"That's not what she meant," Jodi said. "She meant 'are you serious that he asked you out?'"

"So, he *has* asked you out?" Now her daughter's voice held a trace of trepidation.

Tess gulped. "He kind of has, actually." If they only knew.

"Kind of?" Jaci grilled her. "What's that supposed to mean?"

"We've talked about going out."

"And you said yes?"

"We haven't actually had a date, but…I think we will." That much was totally true. She tried to "correct" the smile she saw plastered across her own face in the tiny image in the corner of her screen.

"Mom! Do you like him?" Jaci sat up straight in her bed.

"Well, duh. Would I even be considering it if I didn't?"

"Oh. My. Gosh. I can't even believe this."

Jaci sounded more excited than upset and Tess laughed again, elation welling up inside her.

"Well, believe it. I can't wait for you guys to meet him. But hey, pray for him and Wynn."

"Why?" they asked in unison.

"The whole reason J.W. came to Winterset is to try to reconcile with Wynn. But Wynn's being kind of a stinker." She confided in them about how Rina was pushing for the reconciliation. "Wynn's been…polite, I guess, but not too open to having his dad back in his life."

"But that's his baby's grandpa!"

"I know. And J.W. is so good with her."

"I can't believe we haven't even met Amelia yet." Jodi frowned. "She'll be in kindergarten before we finally get to see her."

"Why is Wynn being such a butt about it?"

"Jaci," her twin chided. "You'd have been pretty hacked if Dad left us when we were little and never made an effort until we had our first kid."

"Don't rush to conclusions." Tess felt her defenses rise. "It wasn't all J.W.'s fault."

"The divorce, you mean?"

"Actually they were never divorced."

"What?"

"He doesn't believe in divorce and I guess Char never pushed for it. They were only separated. The whole time."

"Don't you think that's kind of weird?" Jodi wrinkled her nose.

"Yeah," Jaci agreed. "And that's a long time to be essentially single."

"Well, they were both pretty soured on marriage. And then Char got sick and…well, you know the rest. Just pray that Wynn and J.W. can work things out. That Wynn will forgive him."

"Don't worry…"

"…We will."

She laughed. Her adorable daughters were still speaking that uncanny twin language and finishing each other's sentences. But they hadn't flipped out about the fact that she had a man friend.

Maybe this wouldn't be as hard as she'd feared. Now, if she could just win Wynn over. She was disappointed that he and Rina hadn't come for the cookout last night.

She talked with the girls for another twenty minutes, mostly Jaci venting about her job and the boss from "you-know-where." But Tess was heartened that Jaci seemed to be able to joke about her situation. That was progress.

"Tess?" The side gate unlatched and Wynn appeared around the corner. "You back here?"

"On the porch, Wynn. And speak of the devil!" She turned her phone so the girls could see Wynn coming up the steps to the porch. "We were just talking about you!"

"Hey, Wynn!" Jodi squealed.

"It's our big brother!" Jaci said with the same inflection.

"Hey, you guys!" Wynn warmed to the adoration in their voices. "You need to get your butts back to Winterset and come meet Amelia!"

"That's what we were just telling mom!"

"She's pretty stinkin' cute, if I do say so myself. And growing like a little weed, so don't wait too long."

Tess held the phone for Wynn and let the girls talk to him for a few minutes, trying to think how she'd handle it if they dared mention their earlier conversation about J.W. to him.

But they talked about Rina and the baby and other innocuous topics. She loved the relationship they still had with Wynn and couldn't help but feel that would make things easier if she and J.W. ended up...together. She swallowed hard. She still dared not think too far into the future.

The girls said their goodbyes and Tess hung up and turned to Wynn. "How are things in your neck of the woods?"

"Pretty good. Amelia is *finally* sleeping a little longer between feedings."

"Oh, good. Poor Rina. The newborn stage is challenging, that's for sure."

"Yeah. I don't even know how you survived twins."

She laughed. "Well, I *am* glad they grew up."

Wynn shuffled his feet and looked toward the shed. "Is Dad here?"

"He's on his way to Kansas City, but I think he'll be back yet today."

"Oh." He shuffled again and hung his head.

"Is everything okay, Wynn?" She scooted her chair back. "Can I get you some coffee?"

"No, but…can I ask you something?"

"Sure. Sit down." She didn't like the lines that creased his forehead.

He pulled out a chair and sat. But from the acrobatics his Adam's apple was doing in his neck, he was having trouble spitting out whatever was bothering him. "I heard you and Dad had a party here last night."

"Well, party might be stretching it, but we had fun. We were sorry you guys couldn't make it. Your dad said you had other plans?"

He ignored her question. "So, who was here? What'd we miss?"

"Shawn and some of the neighbor kids—you remember the Taylor boys? They bought fireworks and everybody just kind of congregated here."

"Shawn?"

Oh, brother. She'd stepped into that one. "You know…your dad's…Little Brother."

"I thought his name was *De*Shawn."

"Oh. It is. I guess he wants to go by Shawn now though."

"So..." His adam's apple worked harder. "What's the deal with this Shawn, anyway?"

She knew her sigh said more than she should have already. "That's really a question you should ask your dad."

"Seems like he's pretty close to the kid."

"He's been a mentor for sure..." She chose her words carefully. "But it's nothing to be jealous about, Wynn. He—"

"I'm *not* jealous." He said it with a little too much force.

"I'm sorry. I didn't mean— The brothers—the mentoring program—was something your dad's company set up. Years ago, as I understand it. I don't think he sought out the relationship." She shouldn't be making light of what the Creve brothers meant in J.W.'s life, but the sadness in Wynn's eyes compelled her to do just that.

"Well, he sure kept it going, didn't he? The relationship."

"That's to his credit, Wynn. Give your dad the benefit of the doubt. He's changed."

Wynn huffed. "So, what's the kid doing here? In Winterset? Shawn? Is that a...*permanent* thing?"

"No..." Tess chose her words carefully. "In fact, that's where your dad is right now. Taking Shawn back to Kansas City. He's got a job there."

"But Dad's still staying here? In your shed? And Shawn was too?"

She nodded. "He was. Shawn's going to stay with a brother now, I think. His mom is messed up on drugs and...he just needed someplace safe to be for a while. But your dad took him back today. You should probably talk to *him* about all this. I really don't know all the details."

"You apparently know a whole lot more than I do."

"Well, no offense, Wynn, but whose fault is that?"

"Well, it sure isn't mine, if that's what you're implying."

"Wynn, I'm not implying—" She stopped short. "No, that's

not true. I *am* implying that. Yes, your dad made mistakes... maybe a lot of mistakes when you were growing up, but he's trying to make up for that. Can't you see that? He wants to make things right and have a relationship with you."

"Relationship? He says he came here on my account, but he can't even stay an hour before he gets a phone call and blows."

"What do you mean?"

"The other night when he was over for dinner...we were barely through eating when he gets some phone call that was apparently more important than me...than us. Amelia. He doesn't even know me. And he never will if he can't take the time."

"And you don't know him either, Wynn."

"I know he can be a jerk."

"Wait—" She tilted her head and studied him. "I thought you canceled a dinner invitation with him the other night."

He looked caught. "Amelia was sick."

"And have you given him a raincheck?"

Wynn rubbed his thumb on the arm of the chair. "We're working on it."

"Well, given that you canceled one invitation and declined another, I'd say the ball's in your court." She narrowed her eyes at him. "What has your dad done—recently, in these last few weeks—that makes him a jerk? It seems to me he's trying pretty hard."

"Forget the last few weeks. I'm talking about most of my life. He's been a jerk most of my life."

"That's not fair. You only think of him that way because your mother told you he was a jerk. And I don't know...maybe he *was* back then."

"Oh, trust me, he was."

"Well, people change, Wynn. *He's* changed. He's a different person now. Would you want people judging *you* for who you were even four or five years ago?"

"Why are you so defensive of him all of a sudden? Do you think you can—" Wynn stopped and his eyes narrowed. "Wait a minute… Are you and my dad—" He shook his head, realization plain on his face. He slumped in his chair, burying his forehead in the palm of his hand. "Oh, my gosh. Why didn't I see this?"

CHAPTER TWENTY-SEVEN

*T*ess swallowed hard and met Wynn's gaze. "Wynn, that has nothing to do with why I want you to reconcile with your dad. It has far more to do with Amelia, first of all. And you. Your dad is doing his best to make—"

"So, it's true then? You and my dad...are a *thing*?" His tone was pure disgust and he refused to meet her eyes.

"Your dad and I are...becoming...good friends. We have you in common, Wynn. We both love you very much. And like I was starting to say, your dad is doing his best to make up for things he can't possibly go back and change."

"Then it's a little hard to make up for them, isn't it?"

It was difficult to keep the anger from her voice. "So you're just going to write him off then? Not even give him a chance?" She balled her fingers into tight fists. "I'm sorry, but that makes me furious, Wynn McRae. You are a better man than that."

"Apparently not," he muttered.

"Wynn." She took a breath, forcing her voice to steady. "Think about it. If you mess up with Amelia someday and she refuses to let you into her life, how will that make you feel? If she doesn't even give you a ghost of a chance to make things right."

Wynn closed his eyes, and she knew she'd struck a chord. But she also knew that she'd made the same judgments of J.W. that Wynn had. She'd filtered her opinion of him, her lack of trust in him, through Char's words. As she'd told Wynn, maybe Char's estimation of J.W. had been true back then, but that didn't make it fair for him to forever be judged for the person he'd been back then.

To rid my soul of one dark blot. He *had* "rid his soul." She'd learned so much about him over their coffee "dates" on her porch. And J.W. McRae was one of the best men she knew. Kind, funny, caring. Just look at all he'd done for Shawn and his brothers. But she couldn't exactly say that to Wynn right now. She blew out a little sigh. "Please, Wynn. Just give him a chance."

"Yeah, well… It seems like he has plenty of other 'kids' to deal with." He formed angry quotation marks with his fingers.

"Wynn, come on…you are better than that. I love you and…" She paused to swallow the emotions that came. "I'm not your mother, but I think *she* would tell you to *grow up.*" She was treading on thin ice, invoking Char's memory, but there was so much at stake. And Wynn *was* being childish. And selfish.

"You weren't there."

"No. You're right. I wasn't. But your mom and I had a lot of long talks. I think I knew her pretty well. And I loved her, Wynn. She was a dear friend. But she was very bitter when it came to your dad. There are probably things you don't know. And it's not my place—"

"Things? Like what?"

She paused long enough to whisper a prayer that God would give her the words. That she would tread carefully on Char's memory. But Char was gone, and J.W. was still here and hopefully, would be for a long time. He deserved for Wynn to know the truth. "For one thing… Well, you know how opinionated your mom was. She could be a formidable opponent in an argument. Not that that's a bad quality, but maybe not so great in a marriage."

"Yeah, I remember." Thankfully, the memory brought a wistful smile.

"Also, Wynn... Your mom grew up wealthy. When your parents were first married, your mom...struggled to live on your dad's income. It was a source of pretty strong conflict between them. Your dad felt like he could never make enough to satisfy her. And it caused problems in their marriage. And in their finances."

"Well, I don't see how leaving helped that any."

"Wynn, I'm not sure what your mom told you, and...forgive me if this isn't my place, but I think it's time you knew. According to your dad, your mom *asked* him to leave. And refused the child support he offered. She took the house he offered and essentially asked him to leave. And to leave the two of you alone. Not only that, but *her* parents used their influence against your dad."

"Their influence?"

"Financially."

"But they weren't rich." A look of confusion shadowed his face. "Mom said Grandma and Grandpa Welton lost everything in the stock market."

"Yes, she told me that too. But that didn't happen until your parents were long separated. They had money and they used it to drive a wedge between your parents."

Wynn blew out a breath and narrowed his eyes at her. "Are you just telling me this stuff because you have a thing for my dad?"

His question angered her, but she forced her voice to remain steady. "No, I'm telling you this because your dad has a thing for *you,* and it's breaking his heart that you don't seem open to letting him into your life." She rose and started to gather her mug and a crumpled napkin. "And I've probably said way too much already. But would you please just think about what I've said. And again, I'm sorry if I've meddled where I shouldn't have, but I can't just stand by and watch you destroy your relationship with the only father—"

"Tess?" J.W.'s deep voice rent the air.

Tess looked up to see him striding across the yard from the shed.

"Wynn?" His brows knit.

"J.W.? I thought you left a long time ago." Had he heard them arguing? The deepening furrows in his forehead said he likely had.

"Have you seen Shawn?" J.W. looked between her and Wynn, his expression now holding curiosity—or confusion?—about Wynn's presence here.

Tess shook her head and walked to the edge of the porch. "Not since he carried his stuff out to the truck. But that was"— she checked her phone—"almost two hours ago."

"What? He packed the truck?"

"Well, I assumed that's what he was doing. He hauled a big bag out there. And maybe a sleeping bag?"

J.W. gave a low growl. "I have a sneaking suspicion he went to the lake with those kids after all."

"Uh-oh." Tess shook her head.

"He didn't say anything to you?"

"No. But now that I think about it, he definitely looked like he was trying not to wake anyone up. I just figured you'd told him to be quiet."

"So help me..." J.W.'s jaw tensed. "He is in so much trouble." He mumbled under his breath.

"I'd better get going." Wynn scooted his chair back, apparently seeing his opening. "I'm going to be late for work." He went down the porch stairs and with a brief wave, backed toward the side gate he'd entered by.

"Yeah...tell Rina hi." J.W.'s words were gruff and distracted, and Tess could see the effect they had on Wynn. She knew J.W. was worried and angry about Shawn, but his attitude was only confirming every single fear and insecurity Wynn had just expressed.

Turning his back to Wynn, J.W. barked at her. "Do you have the Taylors' phone number?"

"Yes, hang on... I'll get it."

∾

J.W. TAPPED End on his phone with a weighty sigh. "Sure enough. He's at the lake."

"Oh boy..." Tess shook her head. "Is it just the boys or are Jim and Patty there too?"

"It's Jim and the boys. I got hold of Patty at home. But I sure didn't want to ask them to bring Shawn home. No reason to ruin everybody's day."

"Well, at least you know he's safe. The Taylors are a good family."

"Yeah, he's safe until I get my hands on him. That kid is in so much trouble..." J.W. spoke through a clenched jaw, his forehead a field of furrows. "I'd go get the stinker myself if I didn't think it would make them have to change their plans and wait around for me to find them."

Lake Red Rock was over an hour away and was the largest reservoir in the state with dozens of inlets and tributaries.

"So, will they be back in time for Shawn to get to work?"

"No. Jim said it'd be after dark. He offered to bring Shawn home, but I wasn't going to do that to them." He kicked at a stone at the edge of the sidewalk. "Shawn claims he found somebody to fill in for him at work. As if that makes it all okay."

Tess wasn't sure whether he was looking for advice or

confirmation that he'd made the right call. "At least he won't be in trouble at work," she offered.

"No, but he spent a small fortune on fireworks. He'll be short on money before the month is up."

"Well, that will be a good lesson learned."

J.W. raked a hand through his hair. "I am not good at stuff like this."

"No parent is, J.W."

"I've never really had to be the disciplinarian with the boys. DeShawn's brothers pretty much took over with him after Lesa checked out. Did a darn good job, too. But they've both got good jobs now, and it's not fair for them to get stuck being the parent to a wayward little rebel, and it's a sure bet Lesa isn't going to do it."

"So *you* feel responsible?" She tried unsuccessfully to push down the thoughts that came with her question. It was selfish to wish for J.W. to stay in Winterset when Shawn obviously needed him. And Wynn apparently didn't.

"I *do* feel responsible. I abdicated with Wynn. I'm not going to make that mistake again. Especially not when Shawn has the potential to screw up his brothers' lives along with his." A strange look came over his face. "So...this is what I missed out on with Wynn, huh?"

She smiled softly. "I think Wynn was a pretty good kid overall. I'm sure he had his moments, but I don't think he was ever really a rebel. By the time I knew him well, he was in college and a fine young man. But so is Shawn. I'm not defending what he did today, but he's got a lot on his plate right now with his mom, and you moving to Iowa. It's not really surprising that he'd test the waters a little. And I think the Taylor boys are pretty good kids. I doubt Shawn is going to get in too much trouble at the lake. Especially with Jim there."

J.W. blew out a heavy breath. "I sure hope not."

They sat with their own thoughts for a few minutes before

J.W. looked up at her. "May I ask what Wynn was doing here? Earlier?"

"Actually, I'm not sure. We kind of got sidetracked. I was on the phone with the girls and they had a good visit with him. They think the world of Wynn."

"Yes, you said that."

"He did ask about Shawn. That might have been why he came."

"He did? What did he say?"

"He wanted to know exactly what Shawn is to you. I hope I didn't say too much. But it seems like Wynn has a right to know. If he's going to have a relationship with you after all these years." It was a below-the-belt hit, she knew. But J.W. was faced with a choice between two "sons" and it seemed only right that his flesh-and-blood son—and his new granddaughter—should have the best of him, of his time.

She amended the thought immediately. Wynn was a big boy, and he had Rina in his corner. Shawn needed a "father" more than Wynn did at this point. Again, her opinion was being colored by her own desire to have J.W. stay in Winterset.

"Well, he's making it pretty hard to have any kind of relationship."

"I think you're going to have to make the first moves, J.W. Wynn doesn't know how to start with you. And Shawn isn't making things any easier for Wynn."

"Wynn doesn't even know—"

"That's not what I mean. I'm not blaming Shawn. But can't you see how Wynn might feel like he's in competition for your affection."

"Well, that's just stupid. He's my son."

Tess put up her hands. "I think I need to stay out of this. But…" She bit her lip. "I should probably…confess that I told Wynn some things about Char that maybe weren't my place to tell." She gave him a quick rehash of the conversation with

Wynn, feeling sick to her stomach at how deep in the middle of this she'd let herself get.

But when she finished, a crooked smile touched the corners of his mouth. "I was always determined I would not bad-mouth Char, but"—his smile grew—"I guess I don't mind if somebody else does it for me. If that's what it takes." He reached across the table and put his hand over hers, letting it linger there. "Thank you, Tess."

CHAPTER TWENTY-EIGHT

Tess offered to make breakfast, but J.W. waved her off. He wasn't hungry anyway. "I've already wasted enough of this morning. Present company excluded, of course. But this day is going to drag if I don't find something to kill some time until Shawn gets back. I thought I'd drive out to Holliwell Bridge and do a little painting. Maybe go over to the Roseman Bridge too. Would you want to come with me?"

"Only if I can watch." she teased.

He winked. "As long as you keep very quiet."

"Fine, but don't think I'm going to play Francesca to your Robert Kincaid"

"What?" The names sounded vaguely familiar, but he didn't remember who they were.

"You know...the novel. *The Bridges of Madison County.* You grew up in Winterset and you seriously haven't read that book?"

So that was where he knew the names from. "Haven't read it and don't plan to. Watched the movie the other night though. Hated it. So you can quit quoting the characters. And I'm insulted you would compare me to the sleazy Clint Eastwood character." And Tess was no Francesca either.

"Actually, I hated it too. Novel *and* movie." She eyed him, head tilted to one side. "So, you really watched the movie?"

"I did. Figured if you were going to keep bringing it up, I'd better get up to speed. But I've got to say, I do not like the comparison. I have a lot of faults, Tess, but I would never try to move in on another man's wife like that."

She placed her palm on his cheek. "Oh, J.W. I know that. I wasn't comparing *that* aspect of Robert Kincaid."

"Okay. Good." He didn't dare ask which aspects she *was* comparing him with. "Now that we got that settled... Shall we go find some bridges to paint?"

"THAT LOOKS BEAUTIFUL! I've never seen any of the covered bridges painted from that perspective before." Tess peered over his shoulder, careful to stand far enough away that he didn't feel crowded. The sun was warm on her shoulders, but the breeze that shushed through the bridge was still cool.

She'd watched J.W. get set up just inside the entrance to Holliwell Bridge and then had gone for a walk in the surrounding countryside. She was back now, knowing he'd be eager to get back to the house to wait for Shawn's return from the lake.

J.W. swished his brush in muddy-looking water and daubed on a few spots of blue paint, creating shadows in the rafters of the bridge's interior. All the covered bridges were painted red on the outside, so she'd expected to see that reflected in his painting. Instead, the heavy paper showed the crisscross pattern of the rafters overhead in shades of soft yellow and pale blue. It was a unique perspective and it drew her in.

He looked up at the rafters, as if comparing his painting to the real thing, then turned and looked over his shoulder at her.

"Gotta admit I'm pretty happy with the way it's turning out. You must be my muse."

She laughed, but she was flattered. "I wasn't even here while you painted most of it, silly."

"Yes, but I could see you walking yonder." He pointed through the bridge to the lane beyond. "It inspired me."

She needed to turn away from the longing look he cast her way. But she didn't want to. "*You* inspire *me*. This is really fascinating. I don't even know how you do it."

"Honestly, sometimes I don't know how I do it."

"It's a gift."

"Yes, it is. I give credit where credit's due." He pointed heavenward.

"But you had to develop it. Use it."

He chuckled. "I'm just getting started at that. But I've got to say, I'm having a blast."

"That's what Dan always said. About his woodworking." Why had she brought him up? She laughed nervously. "I never did think all that sanding and gluing looked like that much fun. But Dan had a talent for it, and I guess that's what made it fun."

J.W. gave a little snort but said nothing.

"I'll go walk some more if you're not finished," she said after an awkward minute.

He unclipped the watercolor paper from his easel. "I'm done." He held the heavy paper to the breeze to dry, then held it out to her. "You mind holding this while I pack up?"

"Sure." She took the piece gingerly by the edges, surprised by his talent. He'd always made it sound like he merely dabbled. "This is really gorgeous, J.W."

"I'm not sure it's finished, but I'll sleep on it and see what I think in the morning. I do like the perspective. It reminds me of a covered bridge between here and Kansas City. Maybe I'll take you to see that one sometime."

"I'd like that." She liked that he'd begun to speak as if they had a future ahead of them. Together.

He folded the easel into its carrying case and they walked back to his truck in silence. As soon as he got behind the wheel, he checked his phone, then quickly slipped it back in his pocket.

"Have you heard from Shawn," she risked.

"No. Don't expect to either. But he'll be hearing from me, I can tell you that."

She winced. "I sure wouldn't want to be in his shoes."

He turned the key in the ignition but looked at her before putting the truck in gear. "You think I'm going to be too hard on him?"

"No. No, I never said that. I'd say he deserves whatever he has coming."

"Murder?" He gave her a lopsided grin.

"That might be a little extreme. Although... Dan used to always say we never used the D word, but sometimes the M word came up." Why did she keep bringing him up?

"Is that true? You two never used the word D-I-V-O-R-C-E?"

"Never." She shook her head solemnly. "And if we did use M-U-R-D-E-R we were joking. Just wanted to make that clear."

He steered the truck onto Holliwell Bridge Road and headed west into town. After driving in silence for a few minutes, he turned to look at her briefly. "I've got to tell you, I'm struggling with that a little bit."

"With what?"

"The way you talk about Dan. About your husband."

She met his gaze. "What do you mean 'the way'?"

"With so much... The fact that you've already known true love."

"You haven't? You *never* loved Char?"

He frowned. "I think I was too dumb and too selfish to even recognize what love looked like. But what I see it in your eyes when you talk about Dan...I wish it was for me." He reached across the console and stroked her cheek with the back of his hand.

She placed her hand over his, cherishing the warmth of his fingers against her skin. But dodging his intent, she pressed him. "It scares me a little bit, thinking about falling in love again. I've seen too many second times around fail. Epically."

"We're even then. It scares me more than a little that your marriage ended while you were still in love with Dan. I don't want to feel like I'm always being compared to...the better man."

"No. It's not like that at all, J.W. And I'll be honest, I worried that it would be. I was afraid I'd never find anyone who could measure up to Dan—and that was before I ever met *you*. But it's not a contest. And I honestly don't find myself making comparisons. I mean, I am aware of the ways you're different from Dan. But it's not a comparison between good and bad. Not at all. You're just different. And I find that"—she shrugged, searching for a word—"fascinating. And exciting and terrifying all at once."

He sought her hand again and entwined their fingers. "It's all that, isn't it? Fascinating, exciting, terrifying. And...centering. I feel like I've found something I've been looking for my whole life without even knowing I was lost. Not unlike the beginning of my relationship with God."

She laughed. "Now there's a comparison that *should* terrify me." But she knew what he meant, even though she didn't want to tell him that this was exactly how it had been for her when she fell in love with Dan.

Yet that was exactly the reason she knew that what she felt for J.W. *was* true love. Or the beginnings of it anyway. Maybe genuine love was a better way to put it. Because as different as J.W. was from Dan, he filled that empty space, that need for a beloved companion that had created such a chasm inside her when she'd lost Dan.

J.W. made her heart thrill. And he made her better. That was the key. The man made her want to do what was right by everyone in her life. His generosity had made her more generous with Kressie. His patience with Wynn made her more patient with her own daughters. His compassion for Shawn and his brothers made her want to be more giving.

But she hadn't even known this man beside her for a full month yet. And she knew what Merrie—and probably just about anybody else—would say about that.

But frankly, right now, with her hand wrapped in his, she didn't care what people said. They passed the city park and when they hit a red light at John Wayne Drive, he turned to her. "You need anything before we go home?"

"No, I'm good."

He let loose of her hand for the first time since they'd left the bridge and fished in his pocket for his phone. In reply to her curious expression, he shook his head. "Shawn. Nothing."

"He'll be home soon. It'll be okay."

"Promise?"

She frowned and gave a little shake of her head.

"Thought so."

He drove through the alley behind Tess's house and pulled his truck under the shade of the massive oak tree behind Pop's shed. *J.W.'s apartment,* Tess corrected in her mind.

She reached for the passenger door handle, but when J.W. didn't turn off the engine, she looked to him for an explanation.

He reached for her hand again, his voice husky. "I want to kiss you so bad I can hardly stand it. Would that be...too soon?"

In reply, she leaned across the console and took his face in her hands, meeting his smoldering gaze. He looked deep into her eyes, searching again for permission that she willingly gave.

And though his kiss was tender and sweet, she felt the desire behind it.

With one last brush of her lips to his, she made herself pull away. Long before she wanted to.

"I feel better now." He shot her an impish grin.

She returned it over a ragged breath. "I'm not sure *I* do."

He looked startled and gave her a questioning look.

She quickly reassured him. "It just…wasn't enough."

"Then you'd better get out of this car."

She laughed.

"I'm serious, woman."

With a soft smile, she nodded and reached for the door again, but he pulled her to himself, not seeking her lips this time, but simply cradling her head against his chest.

She wished she could stay there forever.

CHAPTER TWENTY-NINE

"Do you understand what I'm saying, Shawn?" J.W. dropped his voice, but it was an effort to keep from yelling. And it didn't help that the kid in the passenger seat beside him sat with arms crossed over his chest, staring straight ahead, refusing to look J.W.'s way.

He'd already given this lecture once when Shawn got home from the lake, but the kid had been too exhausted and too angry to listen then.

The din of the highway beneath his wheels filled the silence. J.W. gripped the steering wheel and waited a long minute before pressing for an answer. "Shawn?"

Shawn shuffled his feet on the floor of the truck. "I understand that you're forcing me to go back to a job I hate in a town where I don't know anybody to live with a brother who doesn't want me there."

J.W. could tell the line had been well-rehearsed.

"None of that is true, Shawn." He cleared his throat. "Well, maybe the part about hating your job. But Patrick is happy to have you and you know people there."

"Not in Mission, I don't."

"You're not that far from your old neighborhood. You can get wherever you need to be. You've got wheels." Patrick had assured Shawn that the beater was parked at his new apartment in the Kansas City suburb of Mission, Kansas. Which probably meant Lesa was unemployed again.

Shawn grunted. "That's debatable."

J.W. ignored the comment, even though he agreed. The old car was not long for this world. And if Lesa got her act together and got a job, she'd need it back. That was, if she hadn't lost her license. "One day at a time, bud. And we'll figure something out before school starts so you don't have to change schools."

"I don't see why I can't finish school in Winterset. I could find a job there."

"What?" This was the first he'd heard anything about that.

"Well… Why not? I have more friends in Winterset than I do back in K.C. Zach and Grayson like it there."

Shawn had become thick with the Taylor brothers in the short time he'd been in Winterset, and J.W. assumed that was what was driving this. "Your family is in Kansas City, Shawn. I don't think your mom would be very happy about you—"

"My mom doesn't care what I do." He straightened in his seat and angled toward J.W. "And don't say that's not true, 'cause you *know* it is!"

J.W. couldn't argue. Talking to Lesa was on his list of things to do once he dropped Shawn off at Patrick's. But there were far bigger issues dictating Shawn's future. Lesa might not care where he lived, but Michael and Patrick would.

Still, the more J.W. thought about the idea of Shawn moving to Winterset, attending school there in the small-town environment, the more he liked the idea. Shawn would be eighteen by the time school started. Old enough to make his own decisions. But J.W. didn't want Michael and Patrick to feel like he'd "stolen" their brother from them.

And even if they all agreed for Shawn to move to Winterset,

where would he live? The shed had been fine for a long weekend visit, but there was not room for two man-sized bodies in that space. Especially once winter set in, Shawn would need a place besides the kitchen table to spread out and do his homework, and J.W. would need the sofa where Shawn had been sleeping to watch TV and read in the evenings. Not to mention, if he did any consulting work, the kitchen table would be *his* desk. He supposed he could buy a small house in Winterset where there'd be room for both of them. But what kind of message would that send to Wynn? Would his own son feel like J.W. had come back to flaunt what a good "father" he was to DeShawn Creve, when he'd been almost completely absent from Wynn's life?

The fact that he was even thinking through the possibility of Shawn staying in Iowa gave him pause. He wasn't Shawn's legal guardian. He had no say over the boy's life. And it wouldn't be right to take him hours away from his mother and brothers. But if he didn't get involved, it was possible Shawn would go into "the system" he so feared.

Oh, God, what have I gotten myself into?

When they stopped for gas, he plugged Patrick's address into his GPS and headed west. Shawn had gone sullen and silent.

"You need anything before we get to Patrick's? You have enough clothes to get by for a week or so?"

"I'm good." He leaned his head on the passenger-side window and closed his eyes.

"I'll call Patrick's phone if I need to get hold of you, okay?" Shawn was still saving up to replace the phone he'd lost.

No answer. But when Shawn opened his eyes a few minutes later, J.W. broached a topic he'd been wanting to discuss for a while. "Have you told your brothers that you're going by Shawn now?"

"Yeah...kind of." He shot J.W. a sidewise glance. "Why?"

"Just making sure about your reasons for doing so. This isn't about dissing your dad, is it?" Lesa had hinted that DeShawn was named after his dad, but Shawn claimed he'd never even met his dad.

"If by *dis* you mean d*istance*, then yeah, maybe. You were the one who was all about I should stay away from trouble and anybody who wasn't a good influence."

"But you've never met your dad, right?"

"Exactly. So how good of an influence could he be?"

Shawn couldn't know how hard that hit its unintended mark, since Wynn might have said the same thing.

Not to mention, as Tess had reminded him, he couldn't really say much, given that he'd shed his own full name and started going by his initials when he was even younger than Shawn. "Okay then. That's…a good answer." He ruffled the kid's mop of fuzzy curls. "Shawn."

The boy gave him an odd look, then dipped his head. "Probably the main thing…" He swallowed hard. "Kids were saying it wrong. My name."

"What do you mean?"

"They said it like 'DUH, Shawn.' Like I'm dumb or something."

"Well, that just shows how dumb *they* are." J.W.'s heart clutched and he reached over to put a hand briefly on the boy's shoulder, surprised at how muscular he'd gotten. "And hey, you want to know something?"

Shawn looked up at him, curiosity swimming in his eyes.

"It was dumb kids like that who made me start going by J.W."

"Seriously? What'd they say? About your real name, I mean?"

He cocked his head and studied the kid. "Did Tess put you up to that?"

The grin that came was his answer.

"Did you tell her about *your* name? Why you started going by Shawn?"

He shook his head. "You're the only one."

"Got it. Your secret is safe with me."

"Yours too. I promise I won't tell anyone." He looked so expectant, as if J.W. would divulge his secret any minute. When he didn't, Shawn added, "Not even Tess."

"That's right, you won't tell anyone. Because you won't have anything to tell."

"Oh, man!" Shawn gave an exaggerated snap of his fingers.

But then he rewarded J.W. with that grin that had the power to win over the biggest skeptic.

Still, he *wasn't* telling.

PATRICK WAS WAITING outside the apartment and greeted them both with high fives and bear hugs. Shawn seemed genuinely glad to see his brother, but five minutes after they'd carried Shawn's stuff into the apartment, he turned to J.W. "You're picking me up here next Monday, right? What time?"

"I don't know, bud. It'll depend on what time I get out of Winterset. But I'll let you know as soon as I know."

Patrick had warned J.W. that he'd be traveling for his job next week, and he was nervous about having Shawn at the apartment alone. Patrick had offered for J.W. to stay with Shawn at the apartment while he was traveling, but Shawn begged to come back to Winterset since the Taylors had invited him to go to the lake with them again.

J.W. wondered if he should just tell Shawn no to the lake outing. It would be a fitting punishment for him sneaking off without telling anyone on the Fourth. But the lake would be a better alternative than Shawn being alone in Patrick's apartment all week. And *he* sure didn't want to stay in the city.

He hated to impose on Tess about Shawn staying with him in the shed again, especially after he'd promised her it was only for a few days, but his only other option was back to the hotel with Shawn. And that made no sense, since a hotel room was smaller than the shed and minus a kitchen.

"Just don't forget, okay?" Shawn drummed his fingers on the Formica countertop, waiting for an answer.

"Good grief, son! You won't *let* me forget," J.W. teased. He really couldn't change his mind now.

"Come on, bro!" Patrick playfully whopped his little brother upside the head. "You just got here. You that anxious to get away from me already?"

"Not you," Shawn said, his expression serious. "This town."

"What do you mean, this town? You've never even been to Mission before."

"You know what I mean. K.C."

"Hey, it's not that bad. We'll find stuff to do. After I get off work."

"I thought you had classes."

"Well, after that then."

"Yeah, unless *I* have to work."

"Hey, bro, we'll figure it out. Maybe I'll skip class." Patrick threw an impish look J.W.'s way. "Just kidding, man. I'm pulling straight A's right now."

"Good for you. Keep it up."

Patrick turned back to Shawn. "We'll figure it out, bro, okay?" He hooked Shawn's head in the crook of his elbow and rubbed his nappy hair.

"Knock it off, man!" Shawn fought to get out of his brother's chokehold.

"Knock it off? You mean your head?" Patrick tightened his hold. "That can be arranged."

Shawn hollered and struggled but they were both laughing.

It warmed J.W.'s heart. And made it easier to drive away a few minutes later. Shawn was in good hands. He was with his brother, where he belonged.

The more miles he put between him and Kansas City, the

more eager he felt to see Tess. He'd been looking forward to some time alone with her, but a better part of him knew that it would not be a bad thing to have a "chaperone" there when they were together. Things were feeling pretty intense with Tess, and he was starting to think it wasn't such a wise idea for him to be living in her backyard.

CHAPTER THIRTY

J.W. finished the drive-through burger he'd stopped for on the way out of town and wadded the wrapper into a ball. The closing had gone off without a hitch and just like that, with a few signatures on a ream of paper, his house and most of his furniture belonged to someone else, and his ties to Kansas City were broken.

But were they? The Creve brothers were there. He'd stopped by the address Patrick had given him for the friend Lesa was staying with, and what he'd witnessed let him know that Lesa was not going to be able to give Shawn what he needed here. At first, no one had answered his persistent knocks, but when a thin, shirtless man finally opened the door, the smell of marijuana smoke wafted thick from the living room. He'd asked for Lesa and was told she wasn't here, but the man's furtive glances didn't give J.W. confidence he was telling the truth. He'd left a message for Lesa that Shawn was at Patrick's, but he doubted the guy was even sober enough to remember to pass it along.

The more he thought about Shawn's future, the more he believed this break from Lesa's influence might be a good thing. If he moved back to the city, he could offer Shawn a home, some stability. Just for a year until he graduated and was out on his own.

But the thought depressed him. He wanted to wash his hands of Kansas City. In these past few short weeks, Winterset had begun to feel like home again. And J.W. desperately wanted a relationship with Wynn and his little family. Hadn't that been the thing God had called him to that day he'd gotten halfway to Kansas City before turning around to come back to Winterset?

He'd never felt such an agonizing tug-of-war rage within him. Had he heard God right? Between Wynn and Shawn, Shawn seemed to be the more urgent need right now. *And the more receptive one.*

His thoughts went a thousand different directions. Maybe this was about trusting Michael and Patrick to take care of their brother. Until today, he'd felt like the two older brothers were fragile, that it wouldn't take much to push them to the brink of the same downhill slide their mother had made. But leaving Shawn at Patrick's apartment today, J.W. felt good about the young man. Patrick had a good job with possibilities for promotion. He had a little money saved up and was taking some online classes toward a bachelor's degree. He'd talked about a girlfriend, which may or may not be a good thing. He hoped Patrick would get his degree before he got distracted by a woman.

He huffed out a breath. He sure knew all about that. He'd relived Tess's kisses a thousand times in his mind, and he wished she was with him on this trip. Here to see a little of what his life had been like. To see the house he'd owned...so she would know he'd made something of himself. That he wasn't just an aimless drifter, a wannabe painter living in some woman's shed. Most of all, he wished he had her beside him to talk out the dilemma he faced.

Except she was a huge part of that dilemma. Tess weighted his thoughts decidedly in favor of Winterset. Wynn was the priority, of course—the only reason he'd been back to Winterset and met Tess in the first place. But every thought about what he should do—and certainly every thought about anything that might take him away from Winterset—was colored by her presence in his life. Her beautiful grace in his life.

He pressed the accelerator, eager to get back to her. It *would* help to talk things over with her. She had a level-headed way of looking at life. He trusted her insight. He thought about how she'd helped her daughter with the decision about whether to quit her job and come home for the summer. Tess hadn't forced an opinion on Jaci, but simply guided her to see what was no doubt best for her in the long run. Even when that decision disappointed Tess. He could trust her to show the same level-headed wisdom with him. Even though he was pretty sure she cared for him. That kiss wasn't something she'd accepted lightly.

The terrain rolled by in a blur, but when he'd been on the road for about an hour, the landscape began to look familiar. A church steeple poked through the treetops in the distance, and he remembered it as a landmark on the way to the old covered bridge he'd told Tess about, where his parents had often stopped to picnic on the way to visit his aunt in Nashville.

He couldn't remember the last time he'd been out there. Not since he was a teenager maybe. But he thought he could still find the place. If they hadn't torn down the big barn at the crossroads.

On a whim, he aimed the truck in the direction of the church. Studying the canted sunlight that played on the west side of the steeple. He wished he'd thought to bring his camera. It would be interesting to compare the old bridge to Madison County's covered bridges. He could get some decent shots with his phone and maybe come back later with his good camera.

The barn was there just like he remembered, its red paint showing the wear of weather and years, but it let him know he was on the right track. He couldn't remember whether there'd been signs pointing the way to the bridge before, but if there had, they were gone now. He slowed the truck on the washboard country road. The ditches hadn't been mowed and he passed the entry to an overgrown lane and had to backup. But there was barbed wire stretched across the lane and a No Trespassing sign. This couldn't be it.

He drove a little farther and came to another overgrown lane, but this one was open and seemed to fit the route in his memories, even though the trees lining the lane were taller and closer to the road than he recalled. Of course they'd had decades to grow. And he'd been shorter.

The road didn't look like it got much traffic. Hunched over the steering wheel and peering through the windshield, he scanned the woods for a glimpse of the bridge. Back then, the sides of the structure had been left to weather a dark gray, but that could have changed. As it was, all he saw was green. Trees and vines and old utility poles strangled by kudzu.

The lane narrowed and he slowed to a crawl. He'd almost given up when he made out sharp, angled lines amid the crooked tree branches—a metal strut. And the bridge hidden amongst the vines. Still the same weathered gray he remembered. And it definitely wasn't open to vehicles or even foot traffic. He'd have to walk a ways if he wanted to get a better look.

He parked on the shoulder and climbed out of the pickup. The air was hot and humid, but at least the overhanging trees provided shade from the afternoon sun. He tramped through a mash of old leaves and pine needles, and climbed over a tangle of downed branches. His heart sank a little when he got close enough to see the bridge. The structure still had a rustic beauty about it, but it was obvious it hadn't been cared for in decades.

When he'd researched the covered bridges of Iowa, he'd read somewhere that Missouri had dozens of such bridges and only a handful of them were still in use and maintained. The creek bed under the bridge appeared to be dry, but it was hard to tell with all the grasses and wildflowers that grew beneath it.

He snapped some photos with his phone before stepping cautiously onto the floor beneath the bridge's cover, testing for loose or rotted boards. The roof might collapse on him, but the floor seemed solid. Of course, it had been protected from the elements by that roof, exactly as intended.

He looked through to the other opening, trying to remember where the lane had led. They'd driven across and eaten their picnic lunches on the other side when he was a kid, but they'd always come back through the bridge to return to the main road.

He picked his way across the bridge, more confident in its condition with each step. It didn't seem nearly as far to the other side as he remembered. As a boy, it had seemed like miles and miles. And even though you could easily see the light at the other end of the tunnel, when you were in the middle of the bridge, it was surprisingly dim. Dad had always turned on the headlights and honked the horn at that point, and he and mom would roll down the windows and whoop and holler to hear their voices echo back at them.

He smiled at the memory, and for a crazy moment, he wondered what it would take to restore a bridge like this. He started walking, stopping every little bit to test the floor of the structure and to take photos of the arch of light at the end, and his favorite view of any covered bridge—the rafters overhead. These, from beneath anyway, looked to be in surprisingly good shape. Structurally sound. Aesthetically a wreck. It struck him that this bridge was teaming with metaphors: *Don't judge a book by its cover. The only way out is through. Don't burn any bridges.*

That one stopped him in his tracks. If he left Winterset now, he would burn every bridge to a relationship with his son, with his precious granddaughter. He couldn't turn his back on what he'd felt sure God was leading him to do that day on the road to

Kansas City. His road to Damascus, in a sense. He'd felt the tugging at his spirit so strongly since that day. Longing for a closer relationship with the God he'd always believed in, but too often relegated to the heavens. He'd read his Bible more since coming to Winterset than he had in a lifetime before.

He still didn't have all the answers, but he'd found help there. And hope.

Through the words of the psalmist, the book of Proverbs, the Gospels, God had built a bridge back to Himself. Now, this ancient bridge and the stories it hid made him believe it might not be too late for God to build a bridge back to Wynn, too, back to a relationship with his son.

He wouldn't—couldn't—abandon the Creve brothers. Especially not Shawn. He wasn't sure how, but he'd do what was right by those boys. For one thing, he could help them financially. Now that a fancy lake house, a newer truck, a golf club membership, and everything else that went with his old dreams of retirement were no longer on his bucket list, his budget looked a whole lot healthier. No, Tess's shed wasn't an investment or a tax shelter, but he could live for three solid months in Winterset on what he'd paid in property taxes alone on his Kansas City house each year.

He walked the length of the bridge, strangely delighted to find that the picnic benches from his youth were still here, though almost completely overgrown with weeds.

An idea began to form and after shooting a few more photos with his phone, he crossed the bridge and returned to where his truck was parked.

The journey back to Winterset flew by quickly as the items on J.W.'s mental to-do list clicked into place.

CHAPTER THIRTY-ONE

"*I* was afraid you were going to cancel." Jaci looked so vulnerable, it pulled at Tess's heartstrings.

"I knew she wouldn't." Her twin sister's smug expression held an equal dose of confidence. Jodi sported a new shorter haircut, and Tess had been startled to realize that her daughters were each finding their own style, developing individual preferences, and separating from the twinship that had made so many wonder over the years if the girls were identical.

"I honestly wasn't sure if we could work around both of your job schedules, but I'm so glad it all worked out. Even if it is just for two nights." Tess felt like a teenager again, flanked by her beautiful daughters on the sofa at a cozy Airbnb in Kansas City. They'd had to jettison the original plan for a full week in the city, but they'd spent today shopping and dining on the Plaza, and now they were snugged in for a movie night with popcorn and a two-liter of Coke.

Since Dan's death, times like these were precious, even as they made Tess think of him and wish she could tell him how well his daughters were doing. What a good job he'd done raising them.

"Okay, everybody ready?" Jodi spread a wooly throw over her bare legs and looked from Tess to Jaci, remote poised in the air. They nodded and the music crescendoed.

But ten minutes in, a plot point in the drama made them hit Pause and start a discussion that turned into a two-hour gabfest. It delighted Tess to hear her daughters thoughts and to realize how deeply held were their ideas about life. And love— the topic of the scene from the movie that had started this whole rabbit trail.

"I still think he should have told her about the letter." Jaci frowned.

"But he tried!" Jodi argued. "The stupid woman wouldn't let him get a word in edgewise."

"Hmm, sounds like somebody I know." Jaci reached across Tess and smacked her sister's knee.

"Cut it out you two." But Tess was laughing.

"Speaking of letters...and love..." Jodi raised her eyebrows mysteriously.

"What?" Jaci acted surprised that she didn't know what her sister was referring to.

Jodi dipped her head, looking reluctant.

"You have to tell us now!" Jaci punched her twin again.

"I agree. Not fair," Tess teased. But a frisson of apprehension raised the hair on her arms. Something in Jodi's demeanor told her it wasn't just a fleeting thought that had precipitated her comment.

"Well... Since you're forcing me. I have some news." She looked from Tess to Jaci and back again and burst out laughing. "I wish you two could see your faces."

"Get on with the news already!"

Tess grabbed Jaci's arm before she could punch Jodi again.

"There's a man that I might kind of be falling for—"

"A *man*?" Tess stared at her daughter.

"Boy. *Boy*, Mom. Calm down. He's nineteen, just like me."

Tess's pulse resumed its normal pace, and she wished she hadn't "freaked out" lest Jodi edit whatever it was she was about to tell them.

"And we are just now finding out about him *because*...?" Jaci drew the word out. "After all we've been hanging out all day long. Quit holding out on us, sister. You would have thought you could mention it while we sat in Houston's for two hours over lunch!"

"Because...I knew Mom would freak out. Like she just did, I might add."

Jaci threw off the blanket and rose to her knees on the sofa to face her twin. "Just quit with the excuses and spill."

"Yeah," Tess chimed, "Spill."

Her daughters gave the cackling laugh they always did when she tried to sound "cool."

But Jodi quickly turned serious. "There really is a man in my life—or *boy*, Mom, if that makes you feel better—and I think... he might be the one."

"Get out of here!" Jaci squealed. "What's his name? How'd you meet him?"

Tess waited, watching Jodi closely. This girl had a solid head on her shoulders. She wouldn't walk into anything as serious as a boyfriend lightly. In fact, she'd only had a few dates throughout high school, and none that Tess knew of since the girls had left for college. Although since she hadn't known about this guy, maybe she was wrong about that.

"His name is Finn Laughlin."

"Finn? I love that name." Jaci sat enrapt.

"Yep. Finn Laughlin." She clasped her hands in front of her. "Jodi Laughlin. That has a nice ring to it, don't you think."

"Good grief, are you already talking about marriage?"

Tess thought she detected the slightest twinge of jealousy in her firstborn's voice.

"It's come up once or twice." Jodi smiled. "Don't worry,

Mom, we both want to finish school before we do anything crazy."

"What's he studying?"

"Chemistry. Yeah, he's an egghead." She shrugged. "He's specializing in analytical chemistry."

"And what does one do with a degree in analytical chemistry?"

"Mom, don't worry about it. He'll be able to support me."

"No, that's not what I meant." Tess felt unjustly accused. "I seriously am curious what he wants to do that requires that degree."

"Oh. Sorry. Well, there's actually a lot he can do with his degree, but he'd like to work in the healthcare industry. Kind of has his eye on a couple of companies in Nashville."

"Nashville?" Jaci shook her head vehemently. "Too far away."

"I agree." Tess frowned, but she was genuinely happy for Jodi. She just wished her daughter hadn't met this guy until she had a couple more years of college under her belt. But she wouldn't say that tonight. "Is he a year ahead of you in school?"

"No. He'll be a junior too. Why?"

"Just surprised he's already got companies picked out."

"I told you he was a man, Mom," Jodi teased.

"Well, I'm impressed."

"How about you, Mom? Anything new with your boyfriend?"

"Eww." Jaci gave her twin a shove. "Don't call him that."

"Fine." Jodi returned the shove, then turned to Tess. "Anything new with J.W. McRae?"

Tess couldn't help but laugh at the identical unrestrained curiosity on her twins' faces. "Actually..." She drew out the word, laughing harder as they leaned forward simultaneously.

But in truth, she was scrambling to think how to explain to her daughters. She'd wanted to wait until there was something definitive to tell. No sense upsetting the girls if nothing came of her and J.W.'s relationship. But maybe it would be good to prepare them, in case she and J.W. could figure out a path forward.

She realized in that instant that *she* would be crushed if things *didn't* work out between them. These weeks with J.W. in her life had been the happiest she'd known since she'd lost Dan. She breathed deeply, then released her breath along with a prayer that God would give her the words to make her daughters understand. "You girls know how much I loved your dad. And I will always love him, no matter what."

Two sets of beautiful blue eyes grew wide, waiting.

"But I...I've really enjoyed J.W.'s friendship. It's made me realize how lonely I've been since your dad died."

"But it's not like you don't have friends, Mom. Rina and Merrie and..."

"I know. I do have good friends. But it's not the same." She opened her mouth to say more, but it didn't feel right talking to her daughters about how J.W. had made her feel feminine and desirable and witty again. How wonderful it felt to have strong arms around her, and warm lips upon hers.

When her daughters didn't respond, she went on. "But things are complicated with J.W." She hesitated, deciding how much to say. "He feels responsible for Shawn and his brothers. And their lives are in Kansas City. So I'm not sure where we... where he'll end up."

"But what about Wynn? I thought that was the whole reason his dad came back." Jaci's voice held defensiveness.

Tess smiled, grateful that the girls hadn't freaked out when she mentioned her growing feelings for J.W. "It was. Though I think Rina kind of forced things. It's been a rough go with Wynn. He's more bitter than I realized."

Jaci frowned. "Can you blame him?"

Tess couldn't help herself. She leapt to J.W.'s defense. "It's not J.W. Wynn should be blaming."

The girls both leaned toward her, their eyes questioning.

"Don't you dare say anything to Wynn, but his mom was not honest with him about the situation. I already told you that J.W. and Char never divorced."

They nodded.

"Well, J.W. offered to pay child support, to be part of Wynn's life, but Char refused. It seems like her parents had a lot of money and used it to control her. J.W. signed over the house where Rina and Wynn live now to Char and that's all she would accept. In exchange, he agreed to leave them be."

"Sorry," Jodi said, "but who would agree to that?"

"I don't know all the details, girls. But I do know that J.W. is a different person now. And he's trying his hardest to make it up to Wynn."

"You're sure you aren't just being swayed by a smooth-talking man?" Jaci's expression was enigmatic.

Tess couldn't tell if she was teasing or serious.

"Yeah, Mom. You haven't known him very long."

"I think I'm a pretty good judge of character. And even though we haven't known each other long, we've talked a lot. About deep things."

Jodi tilted her head and studied Tess in a way that made her squirm. "How deep?"

"Are you in love?" No mistaking the seriousness in Jaci's tone now. "Have you *kissed* him?"

Tess's skin warmed, and she knew her daughters saw the pink that crept into her cheeks.

"You have!" The twins' eyes widened. "Mom!"

"Have you...done *more*?" Jodi wore a look of horror.

"No. Of course not." It saddened her that Jodi would think that of her. Not that she was a saint, but the fact that J.W. hadn't pressured her was part of why she trusted and respected him so. She told her daughters as much now. "Have *you*, Jodi? Done more? You and this new boyfriend?"

It wasn't her best moment, deflecting the question. But she waited anxiously for a reply.

"We've kissed, yes. But don't worry, Mom. I'm taking it slow."

Tess wasn't sure she wanted to know what her daughter meant by that. And she decided not to pursue it. She and Dan had worked hard over the years to instill their faith and morals in their daughters. Now those decisions were between them and God.

But Jaci did pursue it. "Good for you, sis. And I knew you weren't like that, Mom." Jaci gave her twin a disgusted look.

"So..." She looked between her girls, testing the waters. "If things got serious with me and J.W., you two would be okay with that?"

Tears sprang to Jaci's eyes.

"Oh, honey..." Tess reached for her and pulled her into a hug, including Jodi with her other arm. "I know how I would have felt if it was my mom."

"It's just that...things aren't the same anymore. Without Dad."

"I know. And they never will be, honey. Your dad was the glue that held this family together."

"No, Mom. That's you." Jodi's voice was muffled against Tess's shoulder. "Even Dad said you were the glue."

"Well, then, I guess we three will just have to stick together." She grinned. "Get it? *Stick?*"

The twins groaned in unison at her corny joke and pulled out of her embrace.

"Just don't rush into anything, okay, Mom?" Jodi looked so serious it tugged at Tess's emotions.

"I promise. I'll take it slow and I'll be absolutely sure I'm hearing from the Lord before I do anything crazy. Will you promise me the same about your Finn?"

"It's not the same thing, Mom. At all."

"Oh, yes it is." Jaci rarely sided with Tess against her twin. But she was grateful for her daughter's support now.

"Okay, fine." Jodi smiled and put her hand over her heart. "I promise I'll make sure I'm following God before I do anything crazy."

"I'll believe it when I see it," Jaci muttered under her breath.

They all laughed. It was a good way to close a conversation that was surely to-be-continued, but it had recessed on a good note, and Tess took comfort in that.

CHAPTER THIRTY-TWO

*D*renched in sweat and stippled with grit after opening a new package of shingles, J.W. straightened and took in the view of the neighborhood from his perch atop the shed. Just then Tess's Mariner pulled into the driveway. He gave a wave of the nail gun in his right hand and she tooted the horn at him.

She climbed out of her car and looked up at him, holding up some kind of shopping bag. She looked rested and refreshed and years younger with her hair pulled up in a sleek ponytail.

He'd only spoken to her briefly when he got back from Kansas City Monday night. He'd forgotten she was meeting her daughters in Kansas City for a little mother-daughter getaway. He and Tess shared a brief kiss before she'd left early Tuesday morning, but other than letting her know how the closing had gone, he hadn't really talked to her since then. Gone three days, and he'd missed her more than he could say.

And yet, having her away had given him time to think and pray about what to do about Shawn. He hadn't wanted to bother her before she left to meet her daughters, but he needed to talk to her about Shawn coming back next week and staying in the shed with him.

But first, a shower. He sniffed his T-shirt and wiped the perspiration from his face with his shirttail before starting down the ladder. "Hey, pretty lady. How was your trip?"

Her smile said she'd missed him too. "It was fun. We had a great time." She looked up to the rooftop where he'd been working. "Looks like you've been busy."

"Almost done. I should finish it tomorrow."

"It looks good. Thank you. But I hope you're done for the day. It's hot!"

"Yeah, it was getting a little warm up there."

She flashed the bag again. "I come bearing a doggie bag. Houston's. We only ate there three times."

He laughed.

"You want to share leftovers with me for supper? Rotisserie chicken?"

"I sure wouldn't turn it down."

"You hungry now?"

"Whenever. But let me shower real quick first. I smell like a musk ox."

"I hadn't noticed. You look good to me."

"Likewise. I missed you." It was all he could do not to lean in for a kiss. But he spared her the offense, folded the ladder and laid it on its side in front of the garage before heading inside to shower.

TESS POURED two glasses of iced tea and carried them out to the back porch. It was still warm, but in the shade the ceiling fan would keep it bearable and fend off the bugs too. The leftover roasted chicken that she'd brought back from Houston's was reheating in the oven.

A sense of excitement and anticipation rose in her. Given her daughters' response to her and J.W.'s growing friendship, she felt a new freedom about going forward with him. She was eager to hear how things had gone with Shawn. And about the closing on his house. She was thankful that tie to Kansas City was behind him. Knowing how responsible he felt for Shawn and his brothers, she'd secretly feared that he might back out of the sale of his house and stay in Kansas City. Especially since Wynn had been mostly unreceptive to J.W.'s overtures. Of course, just because the sale of his house went through didn't mean J.W. would stay here. He could always buy another house in Kansas City.

She took a sip of iced tea and let the cool beverage trickle down her throat. She couldn't let herself think about that possibility. As much as she admired J.W.'s dedication to the Creve brothers, it would be a cruel "trick" if God allowed him to move away from Winterset.

The sound of the shed door closing caused her to shake off the troubling thoughts. And J.W.'s boyish jog up her porch steps made her smile.

His hair still wet from the shower, he leaned to give her a gentle kiss. "Hope I didn't keep you waiting too long." He eyed the empty table. "Wait. You didn't eat all the chicken without me, did you?"

She laughed. "It's in the oven. Hang tight and I'll be right back."

She scooted her chair back and started for the back door, but he waylaid her, pulling her into his arms.

"Mmm…" She breathed in the scent of him, nuzzling his neck. "You smell incredible."

"Amazing what a little soap can do, huh?"

He kissed her again, but she pulled away playfully. "Do you want that chicken or not?"

He let her go, but his reluctance to do so made her heart swell.

A few minutes later, they were seated adjacent to each other at the porch table, enjoying the leftovers along with a fruit salad she'd put together from the sparse selection in her refrigerator.

He took a bite of the apricot-glazed rotisserie chicken and closed his eyes appreciatively. "To think I never discovered this in all those years I lived just a few blocks from Houston's."

Tess laughed. "The girls and I ate there three times this week! I wish you could have tasted the salad that came with this. It was so good the girls and I ordered it twice. But I ended up bringing home half a chicken."

"Well, I'm not sorry."

They ate in comfortable silence for a few minutes before she broached the subject of Shawn. "Did everything go okay with him? About his lake escapade, I mean?"

J.W. swallowed and wiped his mouth on a paper napkin. "I probably wasn't nearly hard enough on him, but I didn't want that hanging over him all week—*and* me."

"I understand. He's a good kid."

"He is. And that brings me to a question. And please know that I completely understand if you say no."

"Oh? What's that?"

"I wasn't able to talk to Lesa—Shawn's mom—but she's been evicted and is staying at a friend's apartment. I can guarantee it would not be a good thing for Shawn to be there. He stayed with Patrick this week, but Patrick is traveling for work next week, so Shawn would be alone there." He looked at her with apology in his expression. "I told him I'd pick him up Monday and bring him back here. We can stay at the hotel...or I could just stay there in Kansas City at Pat—"

"Don't be ridiculous, J.W. Shawn is welcome to stay here."

"I know I promised it would just be for a few days before. I don't want you to regret agreeing to that. But if you're sure, I know that will make Shawn happy."

"I'm very sure. He's no trouble. I want you to feel like the shed is yours, J.W. You're not my guest. You're a paying renter."

"Well, thank you. The Taylors invited him to the lake next weekend so he'd be here a full week. You sure you're sure?"

"Of course."

"The lake invite is for overnight. Basically the same invitation he got in trouble for sneaking off to without permission." He gave her a sheepish look. "I suppose this would be the perfect opportunity to ground his butt, huh?"

She laughed. "Not necessarily. It's not my place to say, but if he was apologetic about sneaking out last time—at least if it was my girls who'd done that—I'd probably reward them for asking permission this time."

He let out a sigh of obvious relief. "I was hoping you'd say that."

"I'm no expert, J.W. No parent is."

"Yes, but you raised two great young women. I value your opinion."

"That's all it is."

Ignoring that, he sighed again. "Shawn told me he wants to stay in Winterset."

"You mean for good?" She hadn't thought about that possibility, but it offered some relief. It would mean J.W. would stay here too. "That would be awesome. It sure seems like he fits in here. At least with the Taylor boys."

"Maybe, but I don't like the thought of taking him so far away from his brothers."

Her high spirits sagged. "I guess that's true. And what about his mom?"

"Lesa would be the one reason I'd want him to come here for good. She's gone down a road that I don't see her coming back from any time soon...certainly not before Shawn graduates high school."

An idea struck and she sent up a quick prayer that she wasn't reacting rashly. "What would you think of Shawn staying in the house when he comes next week?"

"Your house?"

She nodded. "He could take the girls' room in the basement. It might be a little frilly for Shawn but—"

"Lavender?"

She laughed. "Pink, actually. And lime green, but at least there's a bathroom down there so he'd have more privacy. And you would too."

J.W. got a funny look on his face. "Are you just putting a chaperone in place?"

"What?" But she knew exactly what he meant. She flashed a coy smile. "It never crossed my mind, but now that you mention it, it might not be a bad idea."

He nodded knowingly. "And honestly, that might be better... for Shawn to have his own space, but I don't want you to feel like you have to cook and clean and do laundry for him. I'll take care of all that."

"I was thinking he could do his own laundry and cleaning. And maybe even help me cook. We could grill together outside. The three of us."

"You are an amazing woman, do you know that?"

She laughed nervously. "J.W., I'm just thankful you're not going back to Kansas City. It will be fun to have a kid in the house again, but the truth is, I'm willing to do whatever it takes to keep you here in Winterset."

He studied her for a long minute. "I don't want to get the cart before the horse or jump the gun or whatever the cliché is, but...someday, down the road, if it seems like it's best for Shawn to be back in Kansas City, would you even entertain the idea of moving to Kansas City?"

His question hit her like a thunderbolt. Her voice came out in a squeak. "Move away from Winterset? Sell this house?" She rose from the table and started stacking their empty plates.

He held up a hand, palm out. "Okay. Too soon to even ask. I'm sorry." He reached for her hand and pulled her close. "Pretend it never came up."

"But it *did*." She frowned. "You're thinking you need to go back to Kansas City, aren't you? For Shawn's sake?" She could barely choke out the words.

"I don't know. Maybe."

"Permanently?"

"No. I'd visit. As often as I could. I'd still want to try to mend things with Wynn. And watch Amelia grow up."

She pulled her hand away, as if doing so might prevent the deep disappointment his revelation brought. But it was too late. She'd given him her heart—whether he knew that or not—and it was going to hurt mightily to take it back. "J.W., my life is here in Winterset. It's the only home the girls have ever had. It just wouldn't be right to take that from them when they've already lost so much. And what about Wynn and Rina and the baby? Isn't that what you came here for in the first place.

"Maybe I came for you, Tess." He pushed back his chair and stood.

She stared up at him. "What do you mean? You didn't even know me before you came here."

"No, but maybe God brought me here so I could meet you."

"And drag me back to Kansas City with you?" She was only halfway kidding.

"By your hair." He tugged at her ponytail.

"Not funny. And way too convenient." She yanked the ponytail holder and let her hair fall around her shoulders. Still, she couldn't curb the smile that came.

"Okay, so I could just commute."

"J.W. Be reasonable. It's a three-hour drive."

"Two hours and forty-nine minutes, actually. It really isn't that bad. Not when it'd be *you* waiting for me on the other end."

She patted his cheek. "That's a very sweet thought, but I'm not sure I buy it. Besides, if you got a job there, you can't work forty hours and have a six-hour commute every week too."

"I was thinking I'd just come back every other weekend. If I even get a job. I might just paint." His scowl turned to an ornery grin. "Think about it, Tess. We'd never get tired of each other. And twice a month we'd have a hot date."

She smirked and rolled her eyes. "A hot date in Winterset?"

"Well, sometimes you could come to Kansas City instead and––"

"Clean your apartment? Do your laundry? I don't think so."

"Hey! Did I say that?"

"No, but you were thinking it."

"I was not." He pulled her to him. "We're going to figure out a way to make this work if it kills me, Tess." His voice went husky. "I'm not letting you go."

Everything within her wanted to lean into him and never let him go. But they were thinking with hormones––aging hormones, at that––and she saw a thousand things wrong with his plan. And even though she hated the thought of him going back to Kansas City, she loved that he was doing it out of dedication to Shawn. But there didn't seem to be any other options open to them.

She pushed away from him and took a step back, meeting his gaze. "I have loved everything about these past few weeks, J.W. McRae. But I just don't see how our lives can intersect if you're not here. I––" Her voice broke. *Don't cry, Everett. Do not cry.* "You'll come to Winterset every so often––to see Wynn's family. I'd love to see you...whenever I can. Whenever you have time. Maybe we can play it by ear...see what happens."

He glared at her. "What? And I'm supposed to believe that

you'll just be waiting? That someone else won't snatch you up while I'm away?"

"You flatter me. Or maybe insult me. If we are meant to be, then I will wait. And I will be faithful."

"What, so maybe when I retire, we can see if there's anything left? I don't want what's left over of your time, of our lives... I want you now, Tess. While we still have some life left in us. While we still have a nice long future to share."

His anger—no, *passion*—scared her a little. And at the same time, it thrilled her to see him fight for her. The way he'd fought for Wynn. *And oh, Lord, I pray he wins that fight.*

And this one.

CHAPTER THIRTY-THREE

J.W. paced the length of the shed's porch, wiping his palms on his jeans, rehearsing what he would say. Or more importantly, what he should *not* say. He hadn't been this nervous since his first encounter with Wynn.

Part of him wanted to "call in sick"—to just crawl into bed, tell Tess to put the food away, and call Wynn and Rina and tell them not to come. But he had to do this. It was why he was here in Winterset. It had now been more than a month since that day he'd arrived in town. He chuckled to himself, thinking of how Tess had caught him sleeping in his truck that first night, and now, here he was living in her shed.

But Tess was right. It was time for him to be proactive where Wynn was concerned. He'd only seen Wynn once in the past ten days when he delivered a coffee cake Tess had made. Rina was her usual warm self, but his son had been polite but standoffish.

So, at Tess's suggestion, he'd invited Wynn and Rina over for a cookout. To meet Shawn. It was time to test those waters. Wynn needed to know that Shawn and his brothers were part of J.W.'s life, and Tess thought it might be less intimidating if they gathered at her house. He harrumphed. *Less intimidating for who?*

But maybe they'd underestimated how traumatic this might be for Wynn. Not only would he and Shawn meet, but hosting the dinner with Tess would almost surely confirm for Wynn that he and Tess were a couple.

At least he thought they still were. Tess had been decidedly cooler toward him since their conversation last weekend when she'd gotten home from her outing with the twins. She had welcomed Shawn into her home warmly, but J.W. suspected that was partly because Shawn served as a buffer between them.

He looked toward the back door of Tess's house where she and Shawn were cooking. They were supposed to be bringing the steaks out any minute. The door was open and he could hear them laughing and joking around inside.

Guilt pinched his conscience. Shawn had immediately bonded with Tess. J.W. hadn't thought about that when he agreed to letting Shawn stay in her basement. But the kid was hungry for a mother's love, and Tess had taken him under her wing with a vengeance. If J.W. didn't know better, he would have thought she was transferring her affection for *him* to Shawn. And Shawn was eating it up.

J.W. went to start the grill. At least it would give him something to do besides pace while he waited for Wynn and Rina to arrive.

TESS AND SHAWN were still in the kitchen and J.W. was flipping steaks on the grill, when Wynn and Rina came through the side gate. Wynn had the baby in a carrier in one hand, a large covered salad bowl in the other, and a diaper bag slung over one shoulder.

J.W. hung up the tongs, wiped his hands on his jeans, and went to hug Rina and take the bowl from Wynn. But there was no question of them shaking hands or embracing—a little too convenient, J.W. thought. Instead, he bent and gave the baby's cheek a gentle pinch. "She's gotten so big already."

Too late he realized that Wynn might take that as an accusation for not following through on the invitation he'd canceled. Why did every word have to be so wrought with undertones of guilt?

"Where do you want these?" Rina held up a bag of potato chips.

"Tess is in the kitchen. Go on in and she'll tell you."

Before he finished speaking, the back door opened and Tess emerged, with Shawn in her shadow.

"Hey, Tess." Rina climbed the porch stairs with her hand outstretched. "And you must be Shawn. I'm Rina."

"Hi." Shawn was subdued, but polite.

J.W. quickly turned down the flame on the grill and went to put a hand on the boy's shoulder. "This is Shawn Creve. Shawn this is my son, Wynn."

Wynn gave a single nod, but when Shawn put out his hand, Wynn shook it, but didn't meet the teen's gaze.

"You met Rina, Wynn's wife," J.W. told Shawn. "And *this* little pilgrim is Amelia, my granddaughter."

"She's cute." Shawn knelt in the grass in front of the carrier that Wynn held. He looked from the baby up to Wynn. "How old is she?"

Rina didn't give her husband a chance to reply. "She'll be six weeks old on Saturday. And she's already ten pounds!"

"Wow. That seems small." Shawn squeezed the baby's cheek the way J.W. had done.

"Oh, you should have seen her when she was first born," she chirped. "Wynn could carry her like a football."

Shawn looked up at Wynn as if for confirmation, but he seemed not to hear and took a step forward, forcing Shawn to move.

J.W. gritted his teeth. The teenager was acting more mature than the grown man.

Thankfully, Tess came out just then and put everyone at ease. By the way she fawned over Wynn, J.W. wondered if she'd heard the exchange. She lifted the baby's carrier and Wynn and Rina followed her into the kitchen.

Shawn lagged behind.

"You want to help me with the steaks, buddy?"

He nodded and went to sniff the fragrant air above the grill. "Man, I can't wait to get one of these in. mah. belly."

Laughing, J.W. handed over the tongs and mimicked the kid's goofy tone. "First you need to get them all on. mah. plate. And if you drop one, that's yours."

Shawn rolled his eyes. "What if I drop 'em all? Are they all mine?"

"You wish." J.W. held the platter over the grill while Shawn transferred the meat.

"Wait a minute..." Shawn counted the steaks. "How's come there's an extra?"

"Tess wants to take a plate over to her neighbor. Maybe you could offer to do that."

"Just so my steak is still here when I get back."

"You can eat your steak first, don't you worry." J.W. carried the platter to Tess's back porch and put it in the center of the table she and Shawn had set earlier. With brightly colored table-cloth and dinnerware, it looked like they were having a party. He hoped it still felt that way when this evening was over.

Tess refilled the water glasses and carried the pitcher back to the kitchen to refill it. Listening to the sagging dinner party conversation through the open window overlooking the porch, she mentally kicked herself for not making place cards. Wynn had purposely positioned himself as far away from J.W. as possible and had avoided eye contact with his dad the entire night.

Shawn, bless his heart, had tried to converse with Wynn, but the man wasn't having it and had eaten his steak in sullen silence. And the few times it looked like he might answer one of Shawn's questions with more than a curt yes or no, Rina jumped in and answered for him. She wanted to smack the whole lot of them—Shawn excluded. And baby Amelia, of course. Although the infant might have had the courtesy to entertain them instead of sleeping in her carseat the whole evening.

Taking a deep breath to steel herself, Tess went back to the porch and started refilling water glasses. "Who's ready for dessert?"

Shawn's hand shot up, but J.W. put an arm around his shoulder and leaned close. "Why don't you take that plate over to Mrs. Bayman first, okay?"

Shawn opened his mouth—to protest, judging by his bearing—but J.W. beat him to it. "Don't worry, buddy, we'll save you a slice of pie."

"And ice cream," Tess added. "Follow me and I'll finish making up a plate. Mrs. Bayman lives next door," she explained to Wynn and Rina.

"I can do that, Tess. You haven't even finished eating." J.W. started to scoot his chair back.

But she stopped him. "It's okay. I'm done. Saving room for dessert."

"If you're sure."

Tess waved him off and motioned for Shawn.

Tess added salad and bread to the paper plate they'd reserved a small steak on. While she covered the meal with foil, Shawn watched.

"How's come you didn't just invite Mrs. Bayman to eat with us."

"Well, honey…" Tess scrambled for words. "This was kind of a…family dinner. A chance for Wynn and Rina to meet you, and you to meet them. We just wanted it to be more…private. So you could visit."

He made a face. "I don't think Wynn got the memo. He doesn't talk much, does he?"

She gave him an apologetic smile. "He was pretty quiet tonight. I think it's kind of hard for him—being around his dad. They didn't have a very good relationship when he was growing up."

"Yeah. J.W. said."

She was curious what J.W. had told the Creve boys. She finished sealing the edges of the foil around the plate and handed it to Shawn. "We'll wait till you get back for dessert. Tell Mrs. Bayman I said hello. You remember which house it is?"

"Blue door. I remember." He balanced the plate on his left palm and headed out the door.

"Careful!" Tess called after him.

He gave her a thumbs-up with his right hand—and promptly tripped on the bottom step. The foil covered plate sailed across the lawn. Shawn dove to save it, but ended up on his face in the grass.

J.W. leapt from his chair and ran to Shawn, who was now on his knees, his face buried in his hands.

"Are you okay, buddy?"

"I'm sorry," he moaned. "I didn't mean to."

J.W. put an arm around him. "Of course you didn't. And hey, look at that…" He pointed in front of them, waiting for Shawn to follow his finger. "Right side up."

The plate lay on the lawn in front of them, still tightly covered. J.W. went to get it, lifted a corner of the foil and checked the contents. He looked back at Tess with a shrug.

"Do I need to fix a new plate?" She came down the steps.

"I think it's fine. But you might take a look."

"I'm really sorry, Tess." Shawn sounded near tears.

"It was an accident, honey. I'm just glad you're okay." She checked the plate.

"Is it okay?" He winced.

"Looks fine to me. No harm done." She put the plate back in his hands. "Hurry back for pie."

He granted her a smile and carried the plate across the yard toward the back gate.

J.W. and Tess climbed the steps to the porch together but found Wynn and Rina gathering up their things getting ready to leave.

"Aren't you going to stay for dessert? I made cherry pie. A la mode," she finished weakly.

"Don't run off!" J.W. seemed shocked that they were leaving.

But Tess wasn't surprised. She'd watched Wynn closely while J.W. comforted Shawn on the grass. And she could see he was struggling.

Rina gave them a look that said, *Don't push it.*

Wynn mumbled a thank-you to Tess but ignored his dad.

"Thanks for everything, Tess, J.W. We...we need to get Amelia to bed. And hey..." She turned to Tess. "Don't worry about my salad bowl. I'll get it from you next time."

Tess nodded. But she wondered if there would ever be a next time.

CHAPTER THIRTY-FOUR

Sleepy-eyed and still in the gym shorts and T-shirt he'd slept in, Shawn looked up from the sandwiches he was making at Tess's kitchen counter. He gave her a look she couldn't quite read.

"Do you have everything you need, bud? You want bacon on those?"

His eyes lit up. "You have bacon?"

"It's the pre-cooked kind, but it's good on a sandwich."

"I love bacon." He flashed that look again. "Thank you for everything, Mrs. Everett. It was…really nice staying here."

"Tess. Please."

"Tess," he parroted.

She'd been reminding him all week to call her Tess, but she appreciated the respect he'd shown her too, and suspected it was J.W.'s influence she had to thank for that. "I've loved having you here, Shawn. You're welcome any time."

He dipped his head. "Not sure J.W. would agree."

"I don't know why not. You haven't been any trouble at all. And don't tell J.W."—she leaned in and affected a stage whisper

—"he never would have gotten that garage painted if it wasn't for you."

That earned her a wide grin.

"I didn't mind. Mostly I'm just glad I got to sleep in here so I don't have to listen to him snore."

She laughed and went to the refrigerator for the bacon. "You sure two sandwiches is enough?" The cooler she'd loaned him for his outing to the lake with the Taylors was barely half full.

"You must be thinking of feeding twins."

"No, I've just seen you eat."

He shrugged. "Don't worry. Mrs. Taylor said they'd bring enough food for everyone. This is just for the ride over to their house."

The boy cracked her up, and she could tell Shawn was proud of himself for making her laugh. She'd loved having him here, and somehow, Shawn's presence had been good for her and J.W. too. The situation with Shawn—and the one with Wynn too—had instigated some deep conversations that made Tess feel she knew J.W. even better. And—she couldn't seem to help herself—she fell deeper in love with the man the more she learned about him.

His compassion and care for Shawn was the most attractive thing about him, and she had determined that, hard as it would be, she would not stand in the way of whatever decision J.W. made concerning Shawn. The way things had gone at their cookout last night, she wouldn't blame him if he gave up on Wynn. She was determined that if he thought it best to move back to Kansas City for Shawn's sake, she would not make the decision any harder than it already was.

But she also knew—and she'd told J.W. so—that *she* couldn't leave Winterset. Her life was here. And her daughters had already lost enough. She wouldn't take their home away from them too.

Could she really do it? Move away from this house that had

sheltered her for more than two decades? So much of those twenty years had been lived within these walls.

Before she'd gone to bed last night, she'd turned off all the lights and stood for a long time in the doorway between this kitchen and the living room. These walls had sheltered her and her family for so many years. She wasn't sure she knew how to live life anywhere else. *With* anyone else besides Dan and their girls.

A long distance relationship wasn't something she could get excited about, but Shawn would graduate less than a year from now. If what she and J.W. had couldn't survive that, then it wasn't what she believed it to be. A lump came to her throat. She'd had one great love with Dan. She wouldn't be greedy, thinking she deserved another.

Still, her resolve crumbled every time J.W. touched her. Kissed her.

She thought back to a conversation they'd had Tuesday night while Shawn was over at the Taylors helping them plan the boys' trip to the lake. They'd shared most of their evenings with Shawn this week, but J.W. had seemed glad for a chance to talk to her alone.

He'd brought up the subject of Char—an uncomfortable topic for Tess, but it was a conversation she knew they'd needed to have sooner or later. They'd been sitting in the Adirondack chairs on his patio, enjoying the evening breeze that wafted through the shed's porch.

He'd turned to her, looking more serious than she'd ever seen him. "Do you think I misjudged Char?"

"I'm not sure what you mean."

"I've always seen her—remembered her—as harsh. Self-centered. Manipulative. Not that I was a saint, mind you. But... you knew her. Was I blinded by my own faults, Tess? Was I *that* wrong about her?" He shifted in his chair. "I don't want to lay all the blame for our problems on her if I've had it all wrong. And if I owe even more of an apology to Wynn, then I don't want to ignore that."

Tess thought for a moment, choosing her words carefully. "I suppose you can never apologize too much. And I've said before that I do think Char had changed. Softened. But she still...had some rough edges. Wynn was respectful of her, and he stepped up when he found out she was sick. But he told Dan some things that made him think Wynn had some grudges against his mom."

"Like what? Would you feel comfortable telling me?"

"I honestly don't know." She shook her head. "Dan thought it would be best if I didn't know. Since Char and I were friends. He went to his grave with those conversations. I don't think it was anything horrible, but I wouldn't say that Wynn and his mom were especially close. And yes, Char was self-centered. I wrote it off to the cancer. Being sick and in pain tends to make you turn inward. I guess I never really considered that just might have been Char's personality—even before she got sick."

"Okay. Then I'm not remembering wrong?"

"I don't think so. And like you said, she could be harsh too. So many of my clients when I was with hospice would lash out at the volunteer. It kind of shocked me at first. It hurt. I was there to help, after all. But I came to realize that it was better for me to be the punching bag so the patient's family didn't have to be. I got used to it, but quite honestly, it's one of the reasons I didn't stay with hospice very long."

"Thank you for being there for Char. At the end."

"It was a privilege, J.W. And I hope it doesn't sound like I'm bad-mouthing her. But you asked. And I want to be honest."

He took her hand, massaging it between both of his. "I just want to be sure that...if we're going to be serious about each other...that I don't make the same mistakes with you."

"J.W." She angled her body toward him, placed a hand on his cheek, and captured his gaze. "I don't hold anything you were in your youth against you. I learned very quickly that you are nothing like Char described you."

A soft smile painted his countenance. "That's good to hear."

"And I just hope Wynn will give you a chance to show him that you have changed."

"Yeah. Me too."

Tess daubed grease from the bacon strips and arranged them on Shawn's sandwiches. Thinking back on her and J.W.'s conversation now, Tess almost wished it hadn't happened, because it had put to rest the last qualms she had about J.W. McRae. He wasn't the same man Char had known. He'd become a man of integrity. A man who loved God. And now after everything with Wynn last night, she was afraid none of that mattered now. At least as far as she was concerned.

She pushed the worrisome thoughts away and added some peanut butter cookies to Shawn's cooler. "You'd better go get dressed. Didn't you say the Taylor boys are picking you up at six.

"Yeah, but they're always late." He put a lid on the cooler. "J.W. said to wake him up before I leave."

"You'd better hustle then." She gave him a little push, loving the easy way they'd come to have with each other over these days Shawn had stayed at her house.

J.W. WAVED as the Taylor boy's car backed out of the driveway. Zach Taylor was eighteen—plenty old enough to be driving, but still J.W. heaved a worried sigh and shot up a prayer that the boys would stay safe. He remembered all too well what kind of driver he'd been at that age: confident and completely clueless to the dangers of the road.

There was a lot of responsibility when you were making decisions for someone else's kid. But knowing that Jim and

Patty felt comfortable with their sons driving to the lake alone made him feel a little more at ease.

Tess appeared on the porch with two steaming cups of coffee in hand. He gave a little wave. "I sure hope one of those is for me."

"Only if you'll sit with me for a minute to drink it. Do you have time?"

"I want to go down to the Cedar Bridge and do some painting later this morning, but I'll make time for coffee with you." Before he stepped under the porch roof, he looked up and scanned the sky. He hadn't checked the weather forecast this morning, but these clouds were looking a little iffy.

"You didn't happen to check the weather, did you?"

"When I went to bed last night the news was saying chance of thunderstorms."

"Those boys may be back before lunch then." He motioned to the driveway as if their car might pull in any minute.

"Well, that was the forecast for Madison County. Lake Red Rock is an hour away so could be a different story there."

"True. I may not be doing any painting either." He took the mug from her and took an appreciative sip.

"I'm just glad you got the important painting done." She looked past him to the garage he and Shawn had given a fresh coat of white paint over the course of two mornings this week. "It looks so much better. Thank you."

"Just earning my keep. And Shawn's."

"I think you've done that and then some. And I enjoyed every minute of having him here, J.W. He's a great kid."

"He is. Speaking of kids..." He took another sip, gathering his courage. "Did I miss something last night?"

"Miss something?"

"Wynn. I don't think it was the baby that had them leaving early. Did I say something I shouldn't have?"

Tess became preoccupied with the rim of her coffee cup,

running her finger in circles around it. "I don't think you did anything wrong, J.W. But I agree. It wasn't the baby."

"What then? He just can't stand to be in the same room with me?"

"I can't speak for Wynn, but I was watching him when Shawn dropped Kressie's plate of food." She reached across the table and put a hand over his. "I can't possibly know for sure what Wynn was thinking, but if I had to guess, seeing you be so tender with Shawn had to make Wynn wish that he'd known... that kind of love from you."

J.W. closed his eyes and dropped his head. When he finally looked up again, his expression was downcast. "I would give anything if I could do things differently. I don't know why I didn't fight for my son, fight for the right to be part of his life after I left. It just..." He raked a hand through his hair. "It seemed like the anger between Char and me would do Wynn more harm than not having a father in his life at all. I'm still not convinced that wasn't true."

"Then tell him that, J.W. He needs to hear those things. Even if you were wrong or he disagrees. I know you've apologized to him for what you missed, but let him know you didn't make the decisions you made without thought. Because otherwise, it feels to him as if he didn't matter to you. And I know better. You wouldn't be here otherwise."

"That's true. But why can't he see that?"

"Because emotions blind us to the truth."

He started to answer but was interrupted by his phone jangling from his pocket. He checked his phone. "I'm sorry, Tess, but I need to take this. It's Patrick."

"Of course."

"Thanks for the coffee." He punched Accept on his phone and slid his chair back.

"You're welcome." Tess rose and carried their mugs into the kitchen. She could hear the low drone of J.W.'s end of the conversation outside her window, but she couldn't make out the words.

She went to start a load of laundry but a few minutes later she heard J.W.'s distinctive knock on her back door. She answered with an expectant smile.

"Do you have a minute?"

"Sure." She stepped out onto the porch and motioned for him to take the same chair he'd sat in when they had coffee.

She didn't like the look he gave her and sat down across from him.

"I wanted to let you know...that was Patrick calling. Lesa—the boys' mom—was arrested last night. They're offering to get her into a rehab program in lieu of jail time."

"Oh, wow... I'm so sorry. Is he pretty upset?" It was a stupid question. What young man wouldn't be upset to learn that his mother had been arrested.

"He's doing okay. Handling it pretty well, actually. But then this isn't the first time."

"Was it for drugs? I mean...I assume. What does this mean for Shawn?"

"Yes, drugs. Possession, but this isn't her first offense. The program they're trying to get Lesa into is a minimum of three months. Patrick is insisting that Shawn come and live with him. He's afraid Shawn will go into the system otherwise."

"I'm so sorry, J.W. Is Shawn going to be crushed? About his mom?"

J.W. shrugged. "I'm not sure about crushed. I don't think he'll be surprised. He won't be very happy about moving in with Patrick, I can tell you that."

"Could he come here, J.W.? To Winterset? Finish school here?" She hoped he couldn't hear the desperation in her voice.

He chewed the corner of his lip, shaking his head. "I don't think so. I'm not crazy about the idea of Patrick taking Shawn in. Even if Michael would help, that's a big responsibility. But I can't take Shawn away from his brothers. They're close. And they're good for each other. I don't want to be responsible for splintering their family any more than it already is."

"So, what will you do?" Even as she spoke the words, she knew what he would say.

"I'm sorry, Tess, but I think it's becoming clear that I need to be there for Shawn. For all three of them. I'm not their dad, but I'm at least a stable influence in their lives."

"So...you'll go back to Kansas City? Move back?"

"It doesn't seem like I have a reason to be here."

That cut deeply and her face must have shown it.

"Oh, no..." He rose quickly and came around the table to pull her into his arms. "No, I didn't mean *you*, Tess. I just meant because Wynn doesn't seem open to me at all."

"I know what you meant. And I'm sorry." She *was* sorry. About Wynn, yes. And Shawn. And so much else. Why did the world have to be so broken? She leaned her cheek against his chest, feeling the thrum of his heartbeat and wishing this moment would never end.

CHAPTER THIRTY-FIVE

J.W. released Tess, kissed her forehead, realizing that in a very real way, they were both saying good-bye. The glorious promise that had imbued every kiss they'd shared was dissolving like sugar in the rain now. "I'm sorry. We'll talk about things later, okay? I need to call Michael, and then if it doesn't rain, I'm going out to the bridge to paint.

He wanted to invite her to come along, but that would only prolong the inevitable. If she wouldn't come to Kansas City with him—and who could blame her?—then they were over. Finished. A sweet but fleeting summer romance. He should have known it was too good to be true.

She offered him a forced smile. "Don't get wet."

"I'll try not to. Talk to you later," he said again.

"I know." The sadness in her eyes about broke him.

He walked across the yard, dialing Michael as he went. But when it went straight to Voicemail, he hung up. Hopefully Patrick had gotten hold of him, but in case not, this wasn't the kind of news you delivered in an automated message.

He loaded his backpack with painting supplies and his

camera gear. A few clouds made for nice light and shadows, and besides, the sky matched his mood.

It took him about five minutes to reach Cedar Bridge northeast of town. There were no other vehicles in sight and he parked as close as he could to the bridge's entrance deck—just in case the forecasted rain materialized.

He got set up with a view of the bridges trusses and had just started painting when the wind picked up and changed direction, riffling the pages of his watercolor pad and knocking over a tin can of brushes from his easel. As he went scrambling for them, a weather alert blared from his cell phone. He looked up to see dark clouds roiling to the northeast. So much for painting today.

He quickly gathered things up and tossed them in the truck without bothering to fold up the easel properly. Fat raindrops pelted his truck and he could hear the faint wail of what sounded like tornado sirens coming from town.

He glanced at his phone and saw that Madison County was in a tornado warning. He didn't see any funnel clouds, but he didn't like the looks of the sky to the east, especially since that was the direction of Lake Red Rock where Shawn was.

Shawn had left Grayson Taylor's phone number with J.W. since he hadn't saved up enough to replace his lost phone yet. J.W. dialed that number now but it rang half a dozen times and then went silent. *Great.*

He thought of Tess and wondered if she'd taken cover. Maybe Shawn had called her. Dialing her number, he backed the pickup around and headed for Winterset. Maybe he should go to the lake, but chances were they were fine. Tess was in more immediate danger.

She answered on the first ring. "Hey, we're in a tornado warning!"

"I know. I'm on my way back. It's looking pretty dark out here."

"Be careful!"

"You too. Get to the basement."

"I'm going. But I'll leave the door unlocked. Just come on down when you get here."

"Whoa!" The rain that had been falling turned to hail and marshmallow-sized hunks of ice clattered against the windshield.

"J.W.? What's wrong?"

"There's hail coming down now. I'll be there soon."

"Please hurry!"

Tess's heart raced as she went through the house closing windows. The sirens continued to sound, and Tess ran to check the back door to be sure she'd left it unlocked for J.W. She looked out the door when she heard the hanging plants swaying in the wind, banging against the porch columns.

She stepped onto the porch and lifted the plants from their hooks, tucking them underneath the table. One of the chairs on J.W.'s porch had blown into the yard and she ran down the steps to retrieve it.

But before she reached the chair, something stopped her. She turned 360 degrees, looking all around the yard and realized the wind had stopped completely. The sky bore an odd green cast. In fact, the very air looked as if it was bathed in a fine gray-green mist. *The calm before the storm.* She'd experienced the phenomenon one time before, when she was a little girl. What had followed was major destruction. She had to get the basement!

Frantic, she raced back toward her porch. The wind howled as if it was chasing her, and its roar turned into the rush of a train. Praying out loud she scrambled for the steps, but the sky opened before she reached them, and in seconds, she was drenched. Climbing the steps on all fours, the slippery bottoms of her flip-flops sent her flying. She landed on the edge of the top step, cracking her kneecap and scraping an elbow. Wincing in pain, she dragged herself inside and slid down the basement stairs, limping into the corner where Dan had always made them go whenever they were under a storm advisory.

A thunderous noise overhead—a crash and breaking glass— made her cower and cover her head. It sounded like her house was being blow away. The lights flickered and then the electricity went out. The tiny window high on the opposite wall barely let in enough light that she could see her own hand in front of her face.

She huddled there, crying in pain and fear—and praying desperately. Where was J.W.? Breathing hard, she patted her pockets and then the floor all around her. She must have dropped her phone outside. Her imagination created a dozen tragic scenarios. She prayed the Taylor boys and Shawn weren't trying to drive home in this. And she prayed for J.W. He should have been back by now.

When the tumult finally died down and she dared to venture upstairs, she sagged with relief to see that her house was standing. But the kitchen window was broken and the sink was full of glass shards. That must have been the racket she'd heard.

She leaned to peer out the jagged window and her heart froze. The roof of the shed had caved in, and the porch overhang was detached from the shed hanging by a precarious thread of shingles. The entrance to J.W.'s front door was blocked.

"J.W.!" She screamed his name at the top of her lungs, then waited for a reply. Nothing. She called again, to no avail. Pulse pounding, she limped back inside to her bedroom, kicked off the flip-flops that had nearly killed her and stepped into a pair of tennis shoes.

"Tess! Tess!" *Wynn.* "You in there, Tess?"

She hobbled to the back door. "Wynn! Are you okay? Did you guys have any damage?"

"We're fine, just a few missing shingles. But where's Dad?" His eyes were wide, accessing the damage to the shed.

"I don't know. He went to Cedar Bridge to paint, but he was on his way home. Is his truck in back?"

Wynn started to run around to the alley, but a shout from J.W. turned him around.

"Oh, thank God," Tess whispered.

"Are you okay?"

"I'm fine. Just cracked my stupid knee. I was worried sick about you."

He ignored her and jangled his truck keys in one hand. "The radio said the storm hit the lake. I'm going to find Shawn."

Wynn jogged over to where they stood. "I'll go with you."

"Thanks, Wynn." J.W. put a hand on his son's shoulder. "Are you sure your family is okay?"

"We're fine. It just brought down some branches on our side of town."

"Do you want me to come too?" Tess couldn't keep her voice from trembling.

Wynn answered before J.W. could. "Somebody should probably stay here in case the boys show up."

J.W. put an arm around her. "You have the Taylors' phone number, don't you? See if Jim or Patty know which beach they were going to."

"Yes. I'll try to reach them. And I'll check on Kressie next door. You guys go! I'll let you know if I get hold of anyone."

Tess waited until J.W.'s truck was out of sight. Then she sank to her knees and wept.

CHAPTER THIRTY-SIX

*T*he pickup bounced over roads strewn with downed limbs and wilted leaves. J.W. kept sneaking glances of his son sitting beside him in the passenger seat. He was curious —and confused—about why Wynn had showed up at Tess's. Maybe it was his habit to check up on her in situations like this, but she'd never said so.

"So, you knew the other side of town got hit harder than where you and Rina live?"

"Yeah, it was on the radio."

"It was nice of you to check on Tess. She could have been hurt real bad." He was tiptoeing around the real question, but he didn't want to say the wrong thing.

Wynn was silent for a second, then cleared his throat. "I wasn't checking on Tess."

"You weren't?" He looked over at Wynn, more curious by the minute.

"If…if anything had happened to you, I could never forgive myself."

"Forgive? For what?" He was fishing, but he needed to know.

"You've been trying to make things right between us. And I've been a butt."

"Well..." A slow smile came. "I don't know if I'd go that far."

"No, I've been a total butt. Rina even said so. And she would know."

J.W. laughed, elation rising in his chest even as his concern for Shawn threatened to overcome it. Remembering what Tess had observed last night, he knew he'd need to be careful how he responded when they found the boys. For Wynn's sake. "So... This is an apology?"

"It is...Dad. I've held things against you that you already apologized for. Things you can't exactly go back and do over. I've been a stubborn...brat."

"Well, you come by that honestly, son." He winced inwardly, remembering how that word had triggered Wynn.

But he didn't react and simply said, "I'm sorry."

"Not as sorry as I am."

"Can we...shake on it then. Call it even?"

J.W. pounded the fist Wynn offered, but he wanted to pull him into a bear hug. It was probably a good thing he was driving.

"I'd like to see you more...Dad. And I promise I'll try to act like a halfway decent human being."

J.W. swallowed hard. "I'd like that."

Wynn grinned. "The decent human being part?"

He chuckled. "That, and the 'see you more' part too." He could not bring himself to tell his son that it was too late. That he'd already made his decision, and Shawn had won. He was moving back to Kansas City. He might pay later for leaving out that information now, but he swallowed again and said, "I'd like that a lot, Wynn." That much was true.

They rode in silence for a while, following the highway signs to Lake Red Rock.

As they drew closer, Wynn turned to him, his forehead

furrowed. "You think they had enough sense to get off the water?"

"The Taylor boys?"

"And Shawn."

"I hope so. Unless they got caught in the middle of the lake. That storm came up awfully fast out at the bridge."

"Yeah, it did at our house too. Have you heard any more news about what it's doing at the lake?"

J.W. flipped on the radio, scanning for a station that was broadcasting the weather. His phone signaled a text coming in from Tess. He lifted the phone and read.

Jim and Patty still haven't heard from the boys. They're on their way to the lake...about twenty minutes behind you guys. I'm praying!

Tess SURVEYED the storm's damage, afraid to go too close to the shed, lest the porch overhang fall on her. She checked her phone for the dozenth time in as many minutes. Why weren't the boys answering their phones?

Her imagination carried her places she did not want to go, so she tried to pray instead. She went back to the kitchen and cleaned the remaining glass out of the window, then cleaned out the sink.

She locked the back door, laughing to herself when she realized that anyone who wanted to could get in through the kitchen window. She picked up branches on her way to check on Kressie again. Her neighbor was pretty shaken up, but the only damage to her place was a few fallen branches. One of them was too big for Tess to move by herself, but she could pile the others up by the street.

Kressie was sitting on her back stoop, surveying the damage. Watching her before she'd spotted Tess, she realized how alone she would have felt if not for J.W. and Wynn. And judging by

Kressie's downcast countenance, she must be feeling the weight of her loneliness right now.

"You doing okay?" Tess called, not wanting to startle the woman.

Kressie straightened and gave her a strained smile. "It could have been worse. Everything still okay over at your house?"

She'd told Kressie about the broken window and J.W.'s roof. She wasn't sure if her neighbor had forgotten already, or if she was asking about Shawn and the Taylor boys. She'd given Kressie an abbreviated version of that story. "J.W. is on his way to the lake, but we'll get things fixed up when he gets back."

Kressie sighed. "I don't know how I'm going to get this mess cleaned up." Her voice wavered as she stared out over the yard.

"That's why I'm here." She stooped and picked up a few small branches from the grass around her. "I'll start piling them by the trash can if that's okay."

"You don't have to do that, Tess. You have work to do at your own house."

"I've already dealt with the broken glass and picked up the branches and twigs I can. The rest of them are too heavy, so I can't do a thing over there until the guys get back." She added more debris to her pile.

Kressie grabbed the railing beside the stoop and pulled herself to standing. "Let me go get my rake and I'll help you with the smaller stuff."

"That'd be great."

"My daddy always said, 'many hands make light work.'"

Seeing the weight lift from her neighbor's shoulders, Tess's heart swelled. "Dan used to say the same thing. Let's get this mess cleaned up."

~

J.W.'s phone rang—a number he didn't recognize—but he wasn't about to ignore it under the circumstances. He slowed the truck before answering. "This is J.W."

"Hey, it's Jim Taylor."

"Hi Jim. Any news?"

"No, we're still about fifteen minutes from the lake. Are you there yet?"

"Yeah. We're there now. There are some branches down, but it doesn't look like they got hit as hard as we did in Winterset. We just passed Elk Rock—my son's with me helping me search —but we didn't see anything there." He crawled along the road that went around the lake. Wynn watched out the passenger side window while J.W. looked out his side, keeping their eyes peeled for the older blue-gray Taurus the Taylor boys drove. "We're headed over to the bridge to Cordova. Tess said you thought the boys might have gone there?"

"Who knows where they went. I don't know *why* they aren't answering their phones." Jim sounded more mad than scared.

"Did Tess tell you Shawn doesn't have a phone."

"Shawn told us, actually. Said he lost it?"

"That's right." He decided then and there that he would take Shawn to buy a phone tomorrow and let him make payments to him. He should've done that weeks ago. But he'd been too determined to teach Shawn a lesson about responsibility. He knew, too late, that safety was more important. And he would never forgive himself if something had happened to the boys. It didn't help that they saw emergency vehicles dotting the roads.

He hung up and they crossed the mile-long bridge to the other side of the lake. On an ordinary day in July, the lake would be teeming with boats, but only a few were out on the water now. As they neared the other side, they could see campers and trucks lined up on the roads below the bridge near the boat ramps. They seemed to be watching the sky. Probably deciding whether to stay or not.

They came off the bridge and turned onto an access road to the park. The skies were clearing now and the sun broke through, but gusts of wind buffeted the truck. Here and there an overturned tent or small camper showed the power of the earlier storm.

The boys had taken kayaks, but J.W. took comfort in knowing they would have been following the shoreline, close to the beaches. They would have at least had a chance to get out of the water before the storm hit. *Please, God.*

As they drove into the park, Wynn cried out and rolled down his window. "Hey, Dad! Stop. I think I see the car."

J.W. slowed to a crawl and pulled over to the side of the road. He followed Wynn's line of vision and his heart sank. A blue-gray car was on a grassy area of the park, but it was hard to tell if it was a Taurus since the vehicle was flipped over on its bashed in roof.

He drove as close as he could, his heart sinking when he saw that, without a doubt, it was the Taurus. Wynn jumped out before he put the truck in Park. J.W. grabbed the keys and ran to catch up.

People were milling around nearby, but he didn't see any of the boys. He took small comfort in the fact that there were no emergency vehicles nearby and the people nearby didn't seem to be paying attention to the car. When they got close, he and Wynn squatted down to look inside. The interior was empty. All the windows were open—rolled down, not broken—but there were no keys in the ignition. His eyes landed on what could have been blood on the back passenger-side door. But he couldn't be sure.

Wynn jogged over to speak with a small group of people gathered on the beach. "Anyone know what happened to the kids that were driving this car?"

J.W. followed him, heart pounding.

An older man in swim trunks shrugged. "We've been here for at least thirty minutes and the car was already here."

The woman beside him added, "We called 9-1-1 but they said it had already been called in."

"So you don't know if anyone was injured? Did they wreck it, or did the wind flip it?"

The man shrugged again. "All the dispatcher said was that they already got the report. There's so much other damage they're working overtime."

"So it was kids in the car?" The woman gave a motherly *tsk tsk*. "I'm so sorry. Were they yours? Are they?" she corrected quickly.

"Close friends," J.W. told her. "They had kayaks." He didn't know whether to be encouraged that the kayaks were nowhere to be seen, or whether that knowledge should terrify him.

Wynn seemed to read his mind. "They probably had the kayaks out on the water. If the wind did this"—he pointed at the overturned car—"they may not even know it's wrecked yet."

J.W. blew out a stream of air. "I need to let Jim know what's going on. Then maybe we should drive the shore and see if we can see—"

"J.W.!"

"Mr. McRae!"

J.W. and Wynn whirled at the voices behind them. Relief flooded over him as the three teens trudged down an embankment, kayaks on Shawn's and Grayson's shoulders. J.W. wondered where the third one was.

As they got closer, J.W. could see that Shawn's face was bloody. The younger Taylor boy's shirt was torn and hanging off one shoulder.

He jogged toward them. "What happened?"

"Hey, you're bleeding, man." Wynn took the kayak Shawn was carrying and put it on the ground, then reached up and carefully pushed back his hair to reveal a two-inch cut over one eye. He winced. "That's pretty deep. You might need stitches."

"Really? Cool!"

For a brief moment, J.W. wondered if Shawn had been drinking. He'd never seen the kid so wound up. But he didn't smell alcohol on any of them and they were walking straight, speaking clearly. Apparently adrenaline was doing the talking.

"What happened?" He looked each of them up and down. "You guys are okay? You sure?"

The brothers nodded.

Shawn launched into a dramatic monologue. "It was *awesome*, man!" He stretched out the word and motioned toward the lake. "You shoulda seen it! One minute we were on the water in the kayaks just minding our own business and the next, we look up and there's this monster of a cloud *right* on top of us. Grayson starts paddling like a crazy fool, and Zach's like, 'you're never gonna make it, man!'"

Grayson shoved Shawn good-naturedly. "Yeah, well at least I *did* something. You just sat there looking up at the sky with your mouth hanging open."

They all laughed.

But Grayson suddenly turned sober. "Did you see the car?"

"Yes. What happened?"

"I don't know, man, but my dad's gonna kill me."

"Your dad is going to be grateful you're alive," J.W. said sternly.

Grayson nodded. "It was crazy! Stuff was flying everywhere, so we left the kayaks on the beach and ran for the car, but when we got here it was just like that! Upside down!"

"You're lucky you weren't in it," Wynn said.

"No kidding," Shawn said. "And when we went back for the kayaks, mine was missing. And then we saw it halfway across the lake."

J.W. shook his head. "I'm glad you weren't in that either."

Zach started to say something, then held up a hand to silence them.

A faint ringtone came from the direction of the overturned car.

J.W. gave Zach a shove. "Go answer that. Your parents are worried sick!"

"I've got it." Grayson took off and a few seconds later they could hear him telling the same story as Shawn's with equal enthusiasm. Zach waved and ran over to add his two bits to the account.

J.W. pulled Shawn into a one-armed hug. "I'm glad you're okay. Wait till your brothers hear."

"Oh, man! Can I call 'em?"

"On the way home maybe. Let's get that cut taken care of first. I've got a first aid kit in the truck."

"I'll get it." Wynn ran to the truck and came back with the kit. He opened it and started cleaning the wound.

J.W. watched over Wynn's shoulder as he bandaged the wound. "What do you think? Do we need to take him to the ER?"

Wynn moved the gauze to show J.W. the injury. The cut was deep, but it had mostly quit bleeding, and it was clean.

Shawn looked between them, waiting.

Wynn eyed the kid with a smirk. "I'd say that depends on whether you want a killer scar to show your friends or not."

Shawn shot J.W. a wicked grin. "No ER."

J.W. SWITCHED off the light on the nightstand and stared up at the unfamiliar ceiling. After returning from the lake and telling Tess three versions of their adventures, he and Wynn had fixed Tess's kitchen window and managed to get his porch roof safely detached, but they'd discovered a broken window behind it so Tess had invited him to stay in her guest room.

Shawn had gone to bed at nine o'clock in the twin's room in the basement.

J.W. had kissed Tess goodnight half an hour later. He was wiped out from the events of this crazy day, but now he couldn't sleep.

Part of it was knowing that Tess was two doors down the hall. Mostly, he was wrestling with the decision he'd made. Six hours with his son had changed everything. And now the one thing that had made him decide to go back to Kansas City was the one thing that made him feel like he needed to stay here in Winterset.

Still, Shawn was his main concern. He was the one who needed stability—and his brothers—more than anything.

He closed his eyes and put his arms behind his head, staring into the darkness. "God, show me what to do. I've never been so torn, Lord. I know what I *want* to do. But help me to want the right thing. *Your* thing."

His phone buzzed on silent on the nightstand. He chuckled. Wouldn't it be nice if God answered prayers with an instant phone call?

But it was only Patrick. He clicked Accept. "Hey, buddy. How's it going?"

"It's been kind of a wild day, if you want to know the truth."

"Oh? Did you have storms too?"

"Storms? No, why, did you?"

"Oh, man. We were in a tornado, that's all. Shawn didn't call you?"

"No! Seriously, man?"

He gave Patrick the short version of their day. "Shawn tried to call you on the way home. He talked to Michael. I figured he'd gotten hold of you by now."

"I was going to call him later."

J.W. smiled into the phone. "He's already sawing logs. He was pretty wiped out."

"That's okay. I'll call him tomorrow. But...I wanted to run something by you first. You have a minute?"

"Sure. What's up?"

"I know I might have to turn this down...because of Shawn. And Mom and everything. But I got a job offer today. And man, I wish I could say yes."

"Well, why not? What's the job?"

"Managing a health club. They're offering me almost twice what I'm making now. They had, like, a ton of applicants. I still can't believe they offered it to me."

"So, why can't you take the job? Sounds like a great fit to me."

Patrick sighed into the phone. "I can't leave Shawn in the lurch like that."

"Oh, so it's not in Kansas City?"

"No, It's in Omaha."

"Wait... Omaha, Nebraska?" J.W. started laughing. "Have you looked at a map yet?"

"What do you mean? I know where Omaha is."

"Yeah, but do you know where *I* am? Where Shawn is right now? Winterset, Iowa?"

"I know it's in Iowa. Hang on... Pulling up a map now. How do you spell that? Winter, like the season?"

J.W. spelled it for him.

"Got it." J.W. heard tapping, then an incredulous, "Holy cow, man. That's not even two hours. That's closer than we are now."

"It sure is. Okay, so let me run something by *you*. How would you feel about Shawn finishing high school here in Winterset?"

"Uh... Would he *want* to?"

"I think he would. In fact, I know he would. Especially after he hears your news. Have you talked to Michael?"

"About the job? Yeah, he's good with it. He's so busy with

work that we hardly get to see each other anyway. And he's doing some traveling with his job. Said he could ask for the Omaha route maybe."

"Well, if you took the job, we'd do everything possible to get Shawn to Omaha whenever he can."

"Wow. That's not how I thought this call would go down." Patrick gave a gruff laugh. "I think I'm gonna take it then. You sure you think that's okay?"

"I think that's better than okay, son. I think you just answered three people's prayers."

"Three?"

He chuckled. "I'll tell you all about it next time I see you."

CHAPTER THIRTY-SEVEN

J.W. patted his belly and pushed away from the table. "You ladies are going to be the death of me."

Tess and Rina laughed, and Tess went to clear his dishes away and put them in the sink. Wynn and Rina's house felt homey with the days quickly growing shorter and the canted evening light casting a glow on the cozy eat-in kitchen.

Wynn went to the refrigerator and pulled out a cream pie heaped with meringue. "You did save room for dessert, I hope."

Tess couldn't help but remember a night, barely a month ago, when Wynn had got up in a huff and left her dinner table without eating dessert. She smiled to herself. She could never have dreamed that night that things would turn out the way they had.

"Is that lemon?" J.W. leaned to look around his son.

Wynn nodded. "Made from scratch. Rina said lemon meringue is your favorite."

J.W. moaned. "I'll *make* room."

"You'd better take a slice home to Shawn too," Wynn said.

Rina repeated Wynn's offer. "I'm sorry he couldn't come tonight."

"He won't turn it down, I'm sure. The kid eats like a horse."

"I can testify to that." Tess laughed. "But I'm not complaining. It's great having a teenager in the house again. Not that I ever see him. He's at a football game tonight."

"So he's liking it here?" Rina asked.

"I'd say he's getting along well." J.W. looked to Tess as if he needed confirmation.

"I'd say he's *thriving*." Tess suspected the three of them had become the talk of the town. A man she was not married to living in her backyard shed, his "little brother" living in her basement. Even she saw the oddity of it all. But she couldn't care less what people thought. She had no doubt God had put them in each other's lives, and she was loving every minute of it.

THEY'D JUST FINISHED their pie when Amelia started fussing. J.W. hadn't gotten his hands on the baby all evening and he saw his chance now. "I'll do baby duty if somebody else will do dishes."

Rina laughed. "You've got yourself a deal."

But Tess waved her off. "You go sit down. You cooked. I'll do the dishes."

"Hey, I helped cook." Wynn pouted. "You remember...that made-from-scratch lemon meringue pie..."

Tess gave him a playful shove. "You go sit down too."

"No, I'll help you." Throwing her a teasing grin, he rose and gathered the dessert plates.

J.W. fiddled with the safety latch on the baby carrier. "You'll have to help me get her out of this contraption." He still hadn't gotten the hang of all the new-fangled baby equipment.

Rina released the latch in a nanosecond, picked Amelia up, and put her in his arms. He edged his way to the swivel rocker, clutching the baby as if she were one of Char's three-hundred dollar Limoges teacups.

In the background, he heard Tess and Wynn laughing and talking as they cleaned up the kitchen. Sometimes he thought he was dreaming when he realized that God had given him back his son. And a whole new, cobbled together family.

And Tess Everett, to boot.

He settled back in the rocker and cradled the baby on his lap. Amelia squirmed and her eyelids fluttered. She gazed up at him like he was the most fascinating creature she'd ever laid eyes on.

He was smitten. "Well, hey there, little pilgrim."

Rina laughed. "Wynn said you used to call him that."

"He remembers that? Little pilgrim?"

"Fondly." She looked back toward the kitchen and lowered her voice. "He has a lot of memories of you, J.W. That's why it hurt so bad when he…lost you?"

He couldn't speak over the lump in his throat. Rina seemed to sense his emotions and excused herself to the kitchen.

The baby couldn't seem to take her eyes off of him. He started singing softly, and off-key. It was a song he'd sung to Wynn when he was a baby. And just like riding a bike, it all came back to him—the tune, the words…well, most of them anyway. He improvised where he couldn't remember. And his granddaughter watched in rapt attention.

And then, wonder of wonders, she smiled! Actually smiled right at him. He suddenly understood what one of his co-workers had meant when he said their little girl "has me wrapped around her finger."

Amelia smiled harder, kicking her little bootied feet.

J.W. had to wait a minute before he trusted his voice. But then he started a little conversation with his granddaughter. "What's so funny, huh? Are you laughing at me? Does ol' J.W. have a silly voice?"

Rina appeared from the kitchen and gave a wry snort. "You can't have her call you J.W.! What do you want your grandpa name to be?"

"What do you mean grandpa name?"

"What do you want Amelia to call you? Once she starts talking?"

"Oh." Until that moment, it hadn't occurred to him that this baby would grow up and someday be able to have an actual conversation with him. "Hadn't really thought about it," he grunted.

"Wynn suggested 'Duke.' What do you think?"

"Duke?" He didn't take his eyes off the baby, who was about to turn her toothless self inside out smiling at him. "That's what they called me in high school."

"Yeah, that's what Wynn said."

"Hmm... Surprised he remembered."

"He thought you'd like it. I think it's an adorable grandpa name. And unique."

He thought about it for a minute, tried to picture a diminutive version of Rina looking up at him and cooing, *Hey, Duke, wanna have a tea party with me?* He let his own smile widen and bobbed his chin at Rina. "Yeah. Duke. I like it."

Tess finished the dishes and came to steal the baby from him. He let her go reluctantly, especially after he found out it was time for a diaper change. Tess and Rina went back to the nursery and Wynn came to join him in the living room.

"So you really made that pie?"

"From scratch." Wynn laughed, since he'd only mentioned that fact half a dozen times so far tonight.

"It was good. Thanks for having us over. It means a lot."

"I know." Wynn said it with a swagger.

J.W. laughed. "Rina said maybe you were warming to the idea of having me here in town?"

Wynn rolled his eyes good-naturedly. "It doesn't look like I really have a choice. When the two best women in my life are in cahoots—and in *your* corner—I'd be stupid to fight it." One corner of his mouth curved into a half-grin. "I swear even Amelia is on Team Duke."

J.W. laughed softly. "Smart girls. All three of them."

Wynn gave him a sideways glance. "I hear Rina bestowed your grandpa name on you tonight."

"She did. I like it."

"Speaking of names, has Tess managed to drag the secret out of you yet?"

"What secret is that?"

"Don't pretend you don't know."

J.W. chuckled. "*Nobody* knows. And I intend to keep it that way."

"Even if you end up marrying her?"

J.W. looked up, surprised. He had every intention of marrying Tess Everett, but he hadn't told *her* that yet. "Even then."

"Wow. That name must be *really* awful."

He laughed. "Oh, no you don't. But do you know the story behind *your* name?"

Wynn's brow furrowed. "There's a story?"

"There is. I admit I'd completely forgotten about it. But Tess trying to pry my name out of me reminded me. I told her, and figured you knew, but she said I ought to tell you if you didn't."

Wynn shook his head, curiosity in his eyes.

"We were on our way to the hospital, your mom in labor, and we still hadn't agreed on a name. Your mom had a whole list written out—boys and girls. We didn't know which we were having, but she'd approved everything on the list. I was just supposed to pick one in each column. I knew as soon as I saw *Wynn* that was it." His throat tightened with unexpected emotion.

"Why?"

He swallowed hard and recovered with a joke. "Because the other choices were so terrible! Horatio? Rupert?"

"Seriously?"

He laughed at Wynn's expression, but forced himself to turn serious. He'd prayed for a chance to tell Wynn this, and it had been handed to him on a platter. He was learning not to let such opportunities get away. "I honestly don't remember the other choices. I just knew *Wynn* was it. Because I felt like a winner that God gave me a son." He looked at Wynn. "Get it? Winner?"

"I get it." The words came out gruff, but he was smiling in a way that made J.W. think the story meant a lot to him.

"Not that I was all that well-acquainted with God back then, but even then, I knew you came straight from Him, son. I sure didn't deserve you."

"Cool."

"Yeah, well, I wanted to spell it W-I-N. You can thank your mom you haven't had to spend your life explaining that one."

Wynn laughed, but quickly turned serious. "It's funny, Mom never told me that. Never told me a lot of things, apparently."

"I'm sorry."

"Tess said that Mom…wasn't exactly fair to you. In what she told me about you. Said Mom tried to turn me against you. That she wasn't exactly the nicest person back then. Why didn't you ever say anything?"

"She was your mother, Wynn. I wasn't going to badmouth her."

"Tess said you tried to be part of my life, but…Mom wouldn't let you."

He stayed silent.

"Is that true?"

"Wynn, there's nothing to be gained by pinning this on your mom. I made plenty of mistakes, with or without her help."

Head down, Wynn rubbed his palms on his jeans. "I guess I always thought Mom was cranky all the time because you left us, but…maybe it was the other way around."

"What do you mean?"

"Maybe you left us because she was cranky all the time."

"It's... Marriage is hard. I'm sure you've figured that out by now. It takes two—" He chewed his bottom lip. He would keep his mouth shut. There was nothing to be gained by throwing Char under the bus now.

"It can be hard sometimes," Wynn admitted. "I got blessed... to find Rina."

"I'm just starting to know her, but I can see that already."

"Did I hear my name?" Rina appeared from the hallway.

"Just saying what a great wife you are," Wynn teased.

"Yeah, I bet."

"Actually, we were." J.W. smiled.

"Whatever."

Tess came down the hall behind Rina. "Shawn will be home in a few minutes. We should probably go."

He rose, and Rina went to the closet for their coats. She handed J.W. his. "Come again soon, will you...Duke?"

"You bet I will."

Duke. He liked it a lot. Especially since it meant Wynn saw him having a relationship with Amelia as she grew. Maybe they were building some bridges after all.

EPILOGUE

Tess brushed off her garden gloves and looked up at J.W. "I'm always a little sad to put the garden to bed for the year."

"I thought fall was your favorite season."

"There is that. Thanks for the reminder." She smiled up at him.

He didn't think he would ever get tired of that smile. Especially not when it was aimed at him. "Don't you want to empty those flowerpots off my porch?"

She shook her head. "I think we've done enough for one night. I checked out a movie at the library for us to watch. Are you game?"

"Sure. Let me shower and I'll meet you back here in fifteen minutes."

She shook her head. "No woman can shower in fifteen minutes. Make it thirty and I'll have popcorn when you get there."

"Deal." He laughed. "You do realize, don't you, that you tried to lure me with popcorn the very first week I knew you."

"You do know," she said coyly, "that it worked."

"It worked quite nicely." He admitted, trying to pull her into a hug.

But she demurred. "I'm all sweaty. You can hug me while we watch the movie."

"Deal."

Half an hour later, hair still wet, he hollered through the back door screen. "You ready for me?"

"Come on in." Her voice wafted through the screen along with the heavenly scent of fresh popcorn.

"You go get the movie started. I'll pour drinks and bring the popcorn. Should we wait for Shawn?"

"No. He won't be home till late." He opened the DVD player and looked around for the movie.

Tess brought popcorn and went back to the kitchen for drinks.

A well-used copy of *The Searchers* lay on the coffee table in front of the TV. "Is this the movie you're talking about?"

"It's on the coffee table," she hollered from the kitchen. "John Wayne."

J.W. froze hearing that name. But seeing the DVD case, he realized what she was referring to. A John Wayne *movie*. Seriously? He turned the case over and skimmed the back.

She came in and set two tall glasses of Coke on coasters. "Ready?"

He gave her a suspicious look. "This is what you picked out? *The Searchers?*"

"Hey, you watched *The Bridges of Madison County* on *my* recommendation, so I figured it wouldn't kill me to watch one Western on yours."

"Sounds fair." But he shot her a look meant to say he still thought she was up to something. He was pretty sure he'd mentioned that he liked westerns, but he'd gone out of his way *not* to mention Winterset's most famous native son.

"What's wrong? Is this not a good one?"

He inserted the disc and pressed Play. He stared at the title screen that came up on the TV. "No. This is a good one. One of his best, probably."

She tilted her head and held his gaze. "You sure? You're acting funny."

It took everything in him not to squirm. "Hey, I'm just a funny guy."

"Haha," she deadpanned, grabbing a throw to cover her legs. "But okay. I'm ready when you are."

He aimed the remote at the television and turned up the volume. Tinny theme music filled the room.

He settled on the sofa beside her, loving the feel of her head on his shoulder. But all through the movie, he kept giving her sidewise glances. Had she guessed? Was she just playing a game with him? Setting him up?

He laughed to himself that he'd made such a big deal of his name with her. It was true that no one else on earth knew his real name. Even to the IRS, he was legally J.W. McRae. His mom, God bless her, would have considered that a waste of a perfectly befitting name. But he'd gotten tired of kids making fun of him. Okay, maybe making fun was too strong. But it got old in a hurry when every introduction led to the same conversation. Kind of like the six-foot-two kid who always gets asked if he plays basketball.

Besides, he liked J.W. Never mind that he still got asked what the initials stood for almost as often as he'd had jokes made about his full name. He'd been happy when his friends started calling him Duke in high school. And he was especially happy that Duke had turned into his "grandpa name."

He glanced over at Tess again. She was intent on the movie, her cupid's-bow lips parted, eyes wide, as a gunfight played out. A few minutes later, the movie credits rolled.

Tess's eyes narrowed as John Wayne's name appeared on the screen. She turned to study him, an enigmatic look on her face.

She turned back to the screen where the actor's name had faded, then looked back to J.W. again.

Except this time, there was a wicked gleam in her eyes. "J.W.! Jay Double-U. John Wayne!" She drew out the syllables triumphantly, then squealed like a little girl. "John Wayne! That's it, isn't it? That's your name!"

He wanted to play it cool, lead her down another track. But the glee in her bearing was too delightful, and he could only laugh. "How did you figure it out?" he asked when she finally quit rubbing it in.

"So I *am* right!" She punched his chest playfully. "It's been right under my nose the whole time. When those movie titles came up the first initials were bigger than the rest of the names"—she pointed to the now black screen—"and I noticed he had your initials—JW—but it wasn't until the final credits rolled that I put two and two together. And then I was like, *duh!*"

He laughed harder.

"So I'm right?" Her eyes danced.

"You're right, but listen, nobody else needs to know this. You hear me, woman?" He captured her hands between his palms.

She giggled and snuggled into him, pulling her feet up under her on the sofa. "Actually, I'm surprised you're the only John Wayne in this town."

"Oh, I'm probably not, but nobody needs to know that. Did you hear me?"

"I don't see what's so terrible about that name. John Wayne? It's a perfectly nice name."

"Yeah, well, you haven't walked a mile in my shoes."

"I mean, your mom could have named you Marion...that's the Duke's real name, you know?"

"Oh, believe me, I'm aware." He gave her hands a squeeze. "You still haven't answered me. This will be *our* little secret, right?" He found it delicious to have a secret with this woman.

"I'll try." Her voice held mischief...and a challenge. "But gosh,

I sure hope I don't slip up and accidentally call you that in public."

He gripped her hands tighter and pulled her even closer. "That sounds like blackmail to me. What do I have to do to keep you silent."

She looked up at him coyly. "I don't know. I suppose you could—"

He lowered his head and silenced her with a kiss. One that meant business.

When he pulled away, she huffed out a little breath and wrapped her arms around his head, pulling it down to hers again and kissing him good.

"Well, thank you, ma'am," he drawled, doing his best John Wayne imitation.

She laughed and he kissed her again, hungrily, then pulled away, alarmed by where his desires were taking him. "If you don't stop that right now," he whispered huskily, "I'm going to need to leave."

She gave a clipped nod that said she was feeling the same emotions. She stretched her legs and scooted over a few inches on the cushion.

"Maybe we should go for a walk." He rose from the sofa and pulled her up with him. But then she was in his arms and they were kissing again.

"Oh, woman," he breathed against her cheek. "What are we going to do?"

"I don't know." She shook her head against his chest, sounding distressed. "All I know is that I love you, John Wayne McRae."

With a low chuckle, he wrapped her in a warm embrace. "Well now, when you attach it to words like that, I guess it's not such a bad name after all." He pulled away and met her gaze. "I love you too. And I seem to remember you telling me that you couldn't marry me until you knew my full name."

"Actually, what I said was I couldn't *date* you until I knew it."

"Wow, you sure caved on that one, didn't you?"

She laughed. "Just so you know, I would have caved on the marriage part too."

"Well, now you won't have to, will you?"

"No, sir, I won't."

And then they were kissing again.

"WHERE ARE YOU TAKING ME?" Despite the unseasonably warm October afternoon, Tess wrapped her coat around her and peered out the windshield of J.W.'s truck.

"You don't like surprises, do you?"

She laughed. "I guess they make me a little nervous."

He took her hand. "I think you'll like this one. And I promise, we're almost there."

"That's good because I was starting to think I should have packed a suitcase."

"I'll have you home in time for supper." He looked at her as if seeing her for the first time. "You look good in red."

She glanced down at her wool coat. "I've had this thing for at least ten years, but I still like it."

"I like that about you. That you don't get tired of things too soon."

"That includes you."

He rewarded her with a grin.

They'd attended the early worship service this morning, and leaving the parking lot afterward, J.W. had asked if she wanted to grab lunch and go for a drive.

"Oh, so *that's* why you told me I needed to wear semi-comfortable shoes."

She'd laughed when he told her that before they left for church this morning. "J.W., what is that supposed to mean? Semi-comfortable heels? Semi-comfortable trainers, semi-comfortable flats, semi-comfortable wedges, semi-comfortable clogs?" She paused to take a breath—and think up some other kinds of shoes. "Semi-comfortable ballerina slippers, semi-comfortable house slip—"

"Now you're just being ridiculous!" J.W. had grabbed her and shut her up with a kiss. So much kissing these days. And J.W. was taking full advantage of the fact that Shawn was visiting his brother in Omaha this weekend.

They picked up tenderloin sandwiches and onion rings at Frostee's, and J.W. headed south. They'd been driving for almost an hour now and Tess's curiosity was getting the best of her. "Are we going to Kansas City?" That was the direction they were headed.

"Now, I just got through saying I'd have you home in time for supper. You do the math." He gave her a smug smile and turned back to the road.

"Okay. So not Kansas City."

He chuckled. "You need to learn to just enjoy the journey and not worry so much about the destination."

"Ouch."

"Well? Am I right?"

She rolled her eyes. "You're always right. And I *am* enjoying the journey. The countryside is absolutely gorgeous." The trees were at that autumn stage she loved most, where there were still plenty of green leaves, but the orange and gold and russet was starting to take over.

They drove on. She was beginning to get a little suspicious that he was going to propose today. She wanted to be married to the man—oh, did she ever—but she really hoped he didn't get down on one knee and try to make a big production of it.

Still, the clues were adding up. Shawn was "conveniently" in Omaha, and she noticed J.W. had his camera with him. Not that he didn't usually carry it with him, but he'd brought the tripod too. It seemed like one more piece of evidence.

After ten minutes, J.W. slowed the car and turned off on a side road.

"Oh, look!" She pointed, as a steeple spire came into view through the autumn-clad trees. "You need to paint that someday."

"I just might."

"Do you want to stop and take a picture?" J.W. had been painting almost every day since school started for Shawn. Tess was biased, but she thought his work was stunning. And at least one gallery agreed with her and had asked for four original watercolors. None of them had sold yet, but Tess had no doubt they would.

"We're almost there, but maybe we'll stop and shoot some photos on the way back. The light will be better then anyway."

They drove in comfortable silence until J.W. turned again at a crossroads. Tess grabbed the handle grip over her door as they bounced down a country road that resembled a washboard. The deeper they drove into the landscape, the more overdressed she felt.

But she forgot all about what she was wearing a few minutes later when he drove off the lane and stopped the truck in front of an old covered bridge. Nestled among the brilliant autumn colors, the scene would have made a perfect jigsaw puzzle. Unlike the bridges of Madison County, this one was bare of paint, its boards weathered to a deep gray, a rustic beauty. In fact, she thought she might prefer it.

J.W. reached into the back seat for his camera and tripod, then climbed out.

Uh-oh. Here it came. She jumped down from the truck's cab and traipsed behind him to the bridge's entrance, *oohing* and *aahing* all the way. "How in the world did you find this place?"

"My parents used to bring me here. We'd stop for picnics on

the way to visit my aunt." An ornery look came to his eyes and he pointed. "I used to climb on the outside of the bridge out over the water. On that ledge."

"What? That's a long way down."

"And a long way across. I never did make it all the way, but got almost halfway across once."

Tess grinned. "I can just hear your mother: 'John Wayne, you get down from there this minute.'"

J.W. laughed. "You're never going to let me live this down, are you?"

"Probably not."

He shook his head. "It is going to be a sad, sad day when you slip up and let somebody else in on our secret."

"Your secret is safe with me."

She motioned toward the camera now hanging around his neck. "You're going to shoot some pictures?"

"I thought I would. Some of the bridge, but what I really want is a picture of you. Of us."

"J.W.! Why didn't you say something?" She patted her hair, wishing she'd at least checked the mirror before they got out of the truck. "I would have done my makeup better. And my hair. Look at me!"

"I'm looking. You could not look more beautiful than you look right now."

"Yeah, right. Spoken like a man who forgot to tell the woman he was shooting portraits." But all she saw in his eyes was love.

He laughed and leaned to kiss her. "At least you have semi-comfortable shoes on."

"You're taking pictures of my shoes?"

"Hey." He tipped her chin upward. "Listen to me. I'm not teasing right now. You look beautiful."

She blew out a sigh and blurted, "You...you're not going to propose are you?"

He drew back. "Is that what you thought?"

"I was worried—"

"You don't *want* me to propose?"

"No, I do. I do!" He looked so stricken that she sought to reassure him. "I just...I'm not really a formal down-on-your-knees-make-a-big-production-of-it kind of gal."

He wiped his brow dramatically. "Whew. That's a relief."

She smiled. "Okay, now that we got that out of the way... You want pictures?"

"I do. But first, will you marry me?"

Her smile grew wider. "Right now?"

"Well, maybe in a few weeks."

Her heart swelled with the purest joy. It was a perfect proposal. Absolutely perfect. "I would be honored to marry you, John Wayne."

"Cut it out, Tess. I'm being serious."

"Oh, I am too, Mr. McRae. I am too."

And then they were kissing *again*.

DISCUSSION GUIDE:

SPOILER ALERT: These discussion questions contain spoilers that may give away certain elements of the plot.

1. In *Bridges*, J.W. McRae comes back to his hometown of Winterset, Iowa, which holds a lot of difficult memories for him. People sometimes find it difficult to return to a location where less than happy events occurred. What specific events colored J.W.'s attitudes toward Winterset, and could you relate to them? Have you ever had to make a trip (or permanent move) to a place that reminded you of unhappy times?

2. True to small-town familiarity, J.W. runs into Tess Everett and quickly discovers that they have very close connections among the people they know, even though Tess didn't grow up in Winterset. When you discovered the ties between J.W. and Tess, what did you think about their chances for eventually having a romance?

3. J.W. feels deep regret for not being a part of his son's life, even though Wynn's mother made it difficult for him to do so. Wynn

resents his father, but he doesn't know about the role his mother played in the strained relationship with his dad. How do you feel about J.W. not revealing Wynn's mother's role? What do you think motivated him for keeping such a secret from Wynn? How would you have handled that situation?

4. Once Tess and J.W.'s friendship gets serious, she "interferes" and reveals some things to Wynn without discussing it with J.W. first. What were her motivations? Were they selfish or generous. Or both? How do you feel about that?

5. Wynn's wife, Rina, also gets involved in trying to reconcile Wynn and his dad. When is it right for family members to push for reconciliation, and when is it best for them to step back and get out of the way? Discuss the attitudes and roles of J.W., Tess, and Rina in urging reconciliation. Do you think any of them rushed ahead of God's leading? Why or why not?

6. Rina's reasons for wanting reconciliation have a lot to do with her and Wynn's infant daughter. How important is it for children to know their grandparents and for grandparents to have a relationship with their grandchildren? And why?

7. How did you feel about Tess's decision to rent the shed in her backyard to J.W., knowing that she was attracted to him? Do you think she set herself up for temptation? What might have been other reasons for Tess's actions?

8. J.W. tried to fill the empty space left by not having a relationship with his son. He first filled that space with work and the goal of a comfortable early retirement. But later, he filled it by mentoring three young brothers. Discuss how each of those pursuits influenced J.W. Could he have done the second without

the first? What are areas in your own life where God might be instructing you to better follow his lead?

9. Wynn feels jealous of the youngest brother J.W. is mentoring. Was Wynn justified in his feelings? How could he have handled his emotions better? Did J.W. understand Wynn's feelings? Why do you think Tess was more sensitive to Wynn's pain than his own father was?

10. Were you surprised by the reaction of Tess's twin daughters when they learned that Tess had a special man in her life? Discuss how adult children might feel and react when their widowed or divorced parent begins a new relationship. Has this ever happened to you either as the adult child or as the parent? How did you work through the emotions?

11. How did you feel about the responsibility J.W. ultimately took on for DeShawn, the youngest brother he mentored. Did you see his actions as selfless, foolish, ignorant, or something else? How much did his decision complicate things with his own son?

12. Were you surprised when J.W. revealed the truth about his marriage to Wynn's mother, Char? Was Tess justified in being relieved by the way God answered her prayers regarding a future husband?

13. How did you feel about the novel's conclusion? Where do you picture each of the characters one year after the epilogue takes place?

AUTHOR'S NOTE

Dear Reader,

This novel was almost ten years in the making! Of course, I wasn't actively working on the manuscript the entire time, but these characters first found their way into my heart on a trip to visit our son in college near Des Moines. (He's now married with four children, so that tells you how long ago it was!) We took a little side trip to the charming historic town of Winterset, Iowa to see the famous bridges of Madison County and the castle-like Clark Tower.

I began writing J.W. and Tess's story shortly after, and we visited Winterset several times before our son graduated. But other contract obligations took precedence and my story languished. Still, I thought of J.W. and Tess often over the years, and when I finally sat down to finish their story this past year, I felt I was revisiting old and dear friends.

As with every novel I've ever written, I could not have accomplished this without the help of the many wonderful people God has placed in my life. My family and extended family could not be more supportive and I am forever grateful to each of them.

In editing this novel, I had the pleasure of working again with author Lisa Bergren, who was one of my favorite editors early in my career. Your amazing ideas and suggestions brought this book to life, Lisa!

Thank you, as always, to my brilliant writing critique partner of nearly twenty years, author Tamera Alexander; to my literary agent, Steve Laube of the Steve Laube Agency; and to the sharp-eyed people who proofread the manuscript, including Tavia Smith, Vicky Miller, and Terry Stucky.

Bridges is the first original novel from Raney Day Press. This means that my publisher, my art director, my graphic designer, my public relations person, and my accountability partner are all one and the same—my husband, Ken Raney. He can be a tough taskmaster at times, and he's a stickler for making me hit my deadlines, but I couldn't be more proud of the work he's done getting this novel to press. He designed the beautiful cover and promo pieces, and he's the one who keeps me sane through the sometimes intense process of finishing a novel. Thanks, babe. You're truly the best boss I've ever had.

Dear reader, *you* are the reason I write. I hope Tess and J.W.'s story will find a special place in your heart and that their experiences might inspire you to build your own bridges—to mend a rift with a friend, heal a broken family relationship, or find a brand new friendship or even true love.

But more than anything, I hope this story might be a reminder of my Lord and Savior, Jesus Christ, the one and only Bridge to God.

Deborah Raney
January 2021

ABOUT THE AUTHOR

DEBORAH RANEY dreamed of writing a book since the summer she read Laura Ingalls Wilder's Little House books and discovered that a Kansas farm girl could, indeed, grow up to be a writer. Her forty-plus books have garnered multiple industry awards including the RITA® Award, HOLT Medallion, National Readers' Choice Award, ACFW Carol Award, and have three times been Christy Award finalists. Her first novel, *A Vow to Cherish*, shed light on the ravages of Alzheimer's disease and inspired the highly acclaimed World Wide Pictures film of the same title. *A Vow to Cherish* continues to be a tool for Alzheimer's families and caregivers. Deborah is on faculty for several national writers' conferences and serves on the executive board of the 2500-member American Christian Fiction Writers organization. She is a recent transplant to Missouri with her husband, Ken Raney, having moved from their native Kansas to be closer to kids and grandkids. They love road trips, Friday garage sale dates, and breakfast on the screened porch overlooking their wooded backyard. Visit Deb on the Web at www.deborahraney.com.

YOU MIGHT ALSO LIKE

Here's a sneak peek at Deborah's RITA® Award-winning novel, *Beneath a Southern Sky* in the Camfield Legacy series. If you enjoy this novel, be sure to check out its sequel, *After the Rains*, and watch for the final book in the series, *Breath of Heaven*, coming soon.

BOOK 1 OF THE CAMFIELD LEGACY

Beneath a Southern Sky

DEBORAH
RANEY

PROLOGUE

A chill spring rain washed the Kansas Turnpike, and the angry grey skies overhead offered no hope for an end to the downpour. It seemed to Daria that hers was the only car on this lonely stretch of highway. The deserted road seemed a fitting metaphor for what her life had become. She passed the Emporia exit and shifted in her seat, settling in for the long haul. She'd been on the road for well over an hour, and her destination was still more than two hours away. Was two hours long enough to decide what she would do when she got there?

Was a lifetime long enough?

She took her hands off the wheel and rubbed away the beginnings of a headache. As she turned her head from side to side, trying to ease the taut muscles in her neck, her eyes fell on the yellow piece of paper that lay on the passenger seat beside her. In this world of fax machines and e-mail, she hadn't realized that people still sent telegrams. And yet it seemed appropriate somehow. She couldn't imagine news such as this 8 1/2 by 11-inch sheet of paper held coming any other way. Daria turned her eyes back to the road. She didn't need to read the telegram again. She had it memorized. But committing the tersely worded message to memory didn't answer the heartrending question it begged.

Barely forty-eight hours ago she had thought she was the happiest woman alive. But nineteen words on one thin yellow sheet of paper had changed everything, and now the reality of her dilemma nearly took her breath away. How did a woman choose between two men she had always loved with all her heart?

The relentless drumming of the rain on her windshield and the incessant rhythm of the wipers carried her back to another time, to another rain, and bid her to walk the paths of memory one more time. And like the silver ribbon of highway that curled ahead, the past three years of Daria's life spooled out before her.

Columba:
The Dove

CHAPTER 1

The fingers of the jungle breeze swept across the village, playing the palm fronds like so many harps. Under the conductorship of the wind, the symphony of the rain forest rose to a crescendo. Over the *plip, plip, plip* of the raindrops' chorus, thunder struck its clashing cymbals before the clouds moved in, lowering a curtain on the sun.

Daria Camfield looked up from the skirt she was mending, and her eyes scanned the village for her husband's tall frame. Though the rains weren't usually severe this time of year, she always breathed easier when Nathan was nearby.

As though her thoughts had summoned him, she spotted Nate loping down the pathway, holding a large banana leaf over his head. She knew his makeshift umbrella was not meant to protect him as much as to shield the book he was carrying close to his chest.

"Hey," she hollered in greeting as he jumped the narrow stream that separated their hut from the village proper. The wind had begun to blow the rain underneath the thatched roof of the stoop where she sat, so she wove her needle safely into the thin cotton fabric of the skirt and rose to greet him.

Nathan leapt gracefully onto the stoop of their stilted hut, flashing Daria a wide smile. "Hey, babe. What are you up to?"

"Oh, I'm trying to fix this stupid skirt I tore yesterday," she huffed. "What I wouldn't give for a sewing machine."

He gave her a long-suffering look. Nate had never been sympathetic to her complaints about the lack of modern amenities in this remote South American village. She let it go and tilted her head to receive the kiss he offered.

He tossed the soggy banana leaf over the side of the stoop and took his precious book inside the hut. Daria followed him in, leaving the door open behind them.

"I'm hungry." He glanced around the small room as though food might materialize at his declaration.

She threw him a smirk. "What else is new?"

"Hey, I'm a growing boy!" he said with mock indignation.

She reached up and tousled his damp hair affectionately as if he were a little boy, but when he reached for her, it was a man who took her in his arms.

"I love you, Dr. Camfield," she whispered huskily. They had been married for three blissful years when they arrived in Timoné, but during their two years as missionaries here, she and Nathan had found new meaning to a scripture they'd only thought they understood: *And the two shall become one.* What had grown between them made their earlier romance seem like an adolescent crush. Nathan Camfield was her life, and she loved him with a love so fierce it sometimes frightened her.

Extricating herself from his arms, she went to the narrow shelf that served as their pantry. She sliced a banana in half, then reached for the thermos. Without electricity or an indoor stove, she'd gotten in the habit of making extra coffee over the fire each morning so they could share a hot drink during the afternoon rains. She poured a mug for Nate and one for herself, then took them to the table where Nate had opened his book. It seemed her husband always had his nose in one science text or another. She wondered what he'd do when he'd finished reading everything they'd brought with them.

The rain on this day proved unrelenting, reminding her of the rainy season they'd recently endured. She finally took up her mending again and they sat together, listening to the drops on the roof, enjoying this excuse for a rare respite from the hard work that life in Timoné demanded.

She put her needle and thread aside and watched her husband now. His head was bowed over the book, and his forehead was furrowed in concentration. But any minute, she knew, he would look up with the light of discovery in his eyes, and read a passage aloud to her.

As though he'd read her mind, his voice broke into her thoughts. "Listen to this, Daria."

She started laughing.

"What?"

"You are just so predictable, Dr. Camfield," she chuckled.

He rolled his eyes, then, ignoring her laughter, he began to read to her from his book, his voice deep and authoritative. He hadn't finished one paragraph when a shout rose from below their hut. "Dr. Nate! Dr. Nate!"

Nathan and Daria jumped from their chairs and ran out onto the stoop. Quimico, one of the young men from the village, was hurrying toward them. Next to him was a native man Daria had never seen before.

Nate ran out into the rain to speak with the two men. Daria stood watching from the shelter of the doorway. The stranger gestured widely and spoke in a dialect that Daria didn't understand. The man waited then, while Quimico translated. She could make out a few of his words through the rain, and when Nate replied through Quimico, her heart began to pound. It sounded as though Nate was agreeing to go to another village with the man. Since their arrival, news had traveled that Timoné had a "medicine doctor," and Nate had been summoned to outlying villages on several occasions. Daria hated it when he left, abandoning the safe sanctuary of Timoné and her.

The men finished their conversation, and while Quimico and the stranger headed back into the village, Nathan came to the hut, his head bowed against the rain.

"What was that all about?"

He refused to look her in the eye and instead went to his side of their sleeping mat, lifted a corner and pulled an empty knapsack from underneath it.

"Nathan, what's going on?"

He answered with his back to her, stuffing provisions into the bag as he knelt on the floor. "There's an outbreak of fev—of illness in a village upriver."

He had stopped himself mid-syllable, and Daria knew exactly why.

"Is it dengue, Nate?" she asked, her voice tight.

"I'm not sure," he hedged. "I couldn't get much of what he said, but whatever it is it's devastated the village. They've lost twenty lives already—mostly children."

Anger rose in her. She knew his words were calculated for her sake, that she'd feel guilty if she selfishly asked him to remain when little children were dying upriver.

"Nathan, where is this village?"

"Upstream a ways," he said, still busily arranging items in his knapsack.

"How far?"

"It's a distance, Daria. Quimico thinks it's a couple of days up the Guaviare."

"Two days! Nathan, it takes one whole day just to *get* to the river!"

"You're exaggerating."

"You'll be gone a week."

"I might be, Daria." He yanked on a zipper and began adjusting the straps.

His steady, measured answers made her furious.

"When are you leaving?"

"First thing in the morning."

She started pacing the short distance of the room, desperate to come up with the words that would keep him home. "Nathan, what if it is dengue?"

Still kneeling on the floor, he turned to look up at her. "I honestly don't think it's dengue, Daria. It sounds more like some sort of influenza."

"But you don't know that."

"No, I don't."

"Nathan, you almost died the first time." She was pleading with him now, her hand on his shoulder, forcing him to look at her. "You're a doctor. You know dengue is worse if you get it again."

"It can be, Daria. But I don't think this is dengue." He looked down, ostensibly to check his watch.

"How could you possibly know?" she growled. "You're just telling me that because you've already made up your mind to go."

He stood now and put his hands on her shoulders. "Daria, stop it. You know I have to go. It's why we came here. You know that, Daria. God did not bring us this far to refuse help to those who need it."

She bit her tongue to keep from asking him what this "we" business was, and yet felt as guilty as if she'd let the words fly.

"Don't worry, babe." He softened a bit. "I'll be fine."

"Then let me go with you," she begged.

"Absolutely not. You'd just slow us down...and what would you do when you got there?"

"I could help, Nate. I could—"

"No. You're staying here."

She reached out and gripped his arm. "Nate, please...just listen to me."

"There's nothing to discuss, Daria." He set his lips in a tight line.

Why was he being so pigheaded? Couldn't he see that she was just worried about him? She hated him just a little at that moment. But she knew her husband well enough to know that nothing she could say now would change his mind, so she stood there watching him, silent.

The rains had stopped. Nate put the knapsack beside the door and stepped onto the stoop. "I'm going to go help get the boat ready."

Trembling inside, she followed him.

Nathan descended the steps, but when he got to the bottom he turned to look back up at her. "If it makes you feel any better, I'm going to ask Quimico and Tados to go with me."

She turned on her heel and slammed the door.

When Nathan returned to the hut that evening they ate together in chilled silence, the only sound that of spoons *thunking* against pottery bowls.

Daria refused to make eye contact.

"Is there any more of that great salsa you made?" Nate asked.

Daria rose and retrieved a Mason jar from the shelf, setting it in front of him a bit too forcefully.

"Thanks." Nate cleared his throat.

When they finished, he motioned to her with his finger. "Come here."

Daria put her hands on her hips, studying him.

"Hey, come here," he repeated, his voice coaxing and gentle.

She hated when he did that, because she knew he would melt her defenses. But she walked over to him, and he pulled her onto his lap.

"You know that I love you." He traced her cheek with a slender finger.

The tears came then, and he held her close, stroking her hair.

Finally he told her, "Daria, I'm sorry. I know you don't want me to go, but I think you understand why I must."

She nodded, resigned, now desperate to make things right between them before he left.

He put a hand on her cheek. "We need to talk before I leave, okay?"

She sniffed and nodded.

"You heard me speaking to Bob earlier?"

She nodded again. Bob Warrington was their radio contact at the mission in Bogotá.

"He's going to check in with you almost every day while I'm gone. But you know he can't always get through, so don't worry if a couple of days go by and you don't hear from him. And don't be afraid to try to contact him. I told him where I'm going, and he felt things were stable enough that it would be safe."

Nate didn't say the words, but Daria knew he was referring to the drug runners and the paramilitary who often posed a threat to outsiders. She tried not to think about it.

"I could be gone awhile," he said gently. "It'll probably take us three days or so to get there, and I have no idea what we'll be facing when we arrive. I promise I won't stay a minute longer than I need to. It'll seem like a long time. I just don't want you to panic if it takes longer than you expect."

She nodded.

"If anything happens and you need to...to get out...of Timoné, you go to Anazu. His nephews know the river well, and they can get you to the airstrip in San José. But you be sure Bob knows you're coming so he can meet you. I don't want you there alone."

She nodded solemnly, hating to have to listen. Why was he talking this way? Fear crept up her spine.

He tipped her chin, forcing her to look at him. "You okay?"

"I'll be okay, Nate. I'm sorry I acted like such a baby. I know that just makes it harder for you."

"Hey, I can understand how you feel. I *am* a pretty fun guy to have around."

She giggled in spite of herself, loving the way he could always make her laugh. But he turned serious and drew her into the tight circle of his arms. "I'll miss you like crazy, babe. Every single minute."

"Oh, Nate, I'll miss you so much."

As soon as it was dark, Daria dressed for bed and plopped down on their mat. Nathan sat on the bench at the table, reading, his white-blond hair catching glints of lantern light. Watching him, a heavy melancholy draped itself over her. Sleep eluded her, and she tossed and turned fitfully, wishing Nathan would come to bed.

He read until late, then he blew out the lantern and came to her side. Lifting the mosquito net, he crawled underneath, kneeling beside her. "Hey," he whispered, "are you still awake?"

"I'm awake."

He took her by the hand, lifted the net, and pulled her up beside him.

"Come on," he whispered, leading her outside.

"Nate! I'm not even dressed," she protested, stretching the oversize T-shirt she slept in over her knees, and trying not to lose the flip-flop sandals she'd slipped on just outside their door.

He pulled her down the steps and toward the crude path that ran parallel to the river behind their hut. The moon was full so they didn't have need of a light, though Nate lit a small torch and carried it in front of them to ward off the jungle's wild nocturnal creatures.

"*Shh!* Come on!" He had that gleam in his eye—the one he always got when he'd planned something special just for her.

She followed him in silence up a rise to a small clearing. The jungle's wild denizens made it dangerous to venture too far from the village at this time of night, and yet she felt perfectly safe with Nathan at her side.

When they came to the center of the clearing, he planted the torch in the soft earth. He came to stand behind Daria and wrapped his arms around her, cradling her head on his shoulder. He cupped her chin in one strong, rough hand and tilted it toward the heavens.

The sight above her left her breathless. "Oh, Nate! It's so beautiful."

In the village, their view of the sky was filtered through a meshwork of vines and palm leaves, but here the vista was unobstructed. The sky above them was a flawless canopy of navy-colored velvet sewn with a million glittering sequins. Daria felt as though she floated in a realm that was both sea and sky, fathomless and eternal.

But she wasn't frightened because Nathan was her anchor. They stood together in silent awe, matching the rhythm of their breaths each to the other. Nate had been studying the constellations of the Southern Hemisphere, and he began to point them out to her. His voice was soft in her ear, the bristle of his day-old beard sweetly familiar against her cheek.

"Look there, Dar," he whispered hoarsely, pointing, his arm brushing her cheek as he sighted a star pattern for her. "That's Virgo." He tipped her chin slightly to the left. "And see that star right there…the brightest one? That's Spica."

She nodded, standing on tiptoe to nuzzle her cheek against his. The star seemed to wink at her, as though it were in on Nate's little surprise.

He tightened his arms around her. "When you look at the sky every night I'm gone, find that star. I'll be looking at it, too, and thinking how much I love you."

Her throat was too full to reply. She wanted only to stand there forever, safe in his arms.

Morning came too quickly, and Nathan Camfield rolled out of bed with far more trepidation about the journey ahead than he had allowed his wife to see. He was hesitant to leave her here alone. He had asked Anazu and his wife, Paita, the only Christian converts in the village, to keep an eye on Daria. He knew they would take the charge seriously. The Timoné were a peaceable people, and he and Daria had always felt safe within the village. But still he worried.

He worried for himself as well. He wasn't sure what he would find when he arrived in the village to which he'd been called. *Chicoro*, the runner who'd come for him had called it. He only hoped the man had been right in judging the distance. For Daria's sake, Nate wanted to return as quickly as possible. She seemed so fearful.

Daria was already outside making coffee over the fire when Nate came down the steps of their hut.

"Good morning," she said, as if it were any other day.

"Mornin', babe."

"I fixed some fruit." She held up a bowl of sliced bananas, guava fruit, pitaya, and a variety of the succulent berries that grew wild all over the rain forest.

He started to tell her he'd just have coffee, but then saw the pleading look in her eye. "Sure." He forced a cheerfulness he didn't feel into his voice.

They sat companionably on the stoop as they did every morning, swinging their legs over the side, sipping hot coffee from their treasured University of Kansas mugs. Nate ate Daria's fruit salad with his fingers, touched by her offering.

He turned to say something to her and saw that there were tears streaming down her face.

"Hey, hey," he whispered. "It's only a few days."

She tried to smile but failed miserably, her face crumpling as she wept.

He jumped down off the stoop and stood in front of her. Taking her chin in his hands, he planted kisses on her tear-stained cheeks, memorizing the feel of her lips on his.

Then he wrapped his arms protectively around her. "Father," he prayed, "Please be with this woman I love. Keep her safe while I'm gone and help the time to pass quickly for both of us. Father, give me wisdom to know how to help the people you've sent me to minister to—both in body and in spirit."

Through tears, but with a voice that seemed stronger, Daria prayed for him too, in her simple, straightforward way. "God, go with Nate. Keep him safe. Guide him in everything he does. And, Lord, please bring him back to me because—well, I've grown kind of fond of him and I think I'd like to keep him for a while."

Nate laughed and held her at arm's length, appreciating the way her dimpled smile reached her blue eyes. A strand of wavy blond hair had escaped her braid and, returning her smile, he brushed it from her high forehead. He was so proud of her for giving him this gift of laughter before he went. "Amen," he said, his heart full.

Together they washed the few breakfast dishes and then he went into the hut for his things.

They walked arm in arm through the village, and beyond to the place where the worn forest trail led to the navigable waters of the Rio Guaviare. Quimico and Tados and their families were already waiting when they got there, chattering excitedly among themselves. Nate loaded his things into the boat, and the two young natives lofted the craft onto their shoulders.

Nate pulled Daria into his arms and kissed her one last time. "Goodbye, sweetheart," he whispered, aware the natives were watching and shaking their heads at this bold American display of affection. He released her and went to take his share of the boat's burden.

They started up the trail. The boat on his shoulders prevented him from turning and keeping Daria in his sight. But he didn't have to see her to know that her beautiful face was wet with tears and that her tender heart was praying for his safe return even now.

Made in the USA
Columbia, SC
02 February 2021